# DARK SHADOWS AND CATASTROPHE

### BY JAMES KEENAN

# Table of Contents

# 1.

# In the Beginning

My earliest memory is when I was around two years old and I drowned in my great uncle's pool. My mother and father tell me they believe it had to be the summer of 1973 or 1974. Whatever year it was, I was young, and for argument's sake, let us just say I was two years old at the time. This also happens to be the time when I began remembering everything in my life. I know it is a young age, but I think that my remembering is due to how traumatic it was to experience drowning. This tragedy was the beginning of many difficult and often strange events that would come to define my life.

We were at my great uncle's house in the Los Angeles area, and yes, I am from Los Angeles. In those days, I think, I was the anomaly as few people in Los Angeles were born there. Anyway, we lived in the Hollywood area. There was a family get-together, and I was later told that neighbors also joined the family that day. I have a vague memory of being with my mom in some room of the house, and I was on her lap as she was talking with family and neighbors. There were a lot of kids in the house, and I got off my mom's lap to see what the other children were doing. I went to the kitchen as its doors led to the backyard and pool. I guess I was fascinated with the water. I had this cousin who apparently was jealous that I was the new kid on the block and getting all the attention in the house at the time. Well, I think I remember my wonderful cousin unlocking the door and telling me to go get a ball that happened to be on the far end of the pool, and of course, the far end of the pool meant the deep end.

This was the 1970s. There was no care for safety, and people in the United States were not yet filing lawsuits for what seemed like every little thing that bothered them. Because of this, there was no fence around the pool. No one was watching me when I went to get the ball. Sure enough, I fell into the pool. I have a clouded memory of thrashing about. I remember trying to fight to get to the top of the water as I continued to sink. I remember being frantic. I sure as hell did not know what to do. I know I was kicking my feet as best I could, but it did not help, and I continued to go under the water. I remember starting to swallow more and more water. I have these clouded memories of trying to get to the surface and get to where I saw the sun shining, but it did not help. I believe that everything began to get dark.

By this point, I was fighting less and less to stay afloat, and I remember what looked to be sudden popping lights all around me in the water. Next, I saw streams of lights shooting around in the water, and finally, everything went dark. I no longer found myself scared, and I no longer found myself frantic or fighting to stay afloat. I gave in to the calm of the darkness and went to sleep. I know I was around two years old, but I have excellent recollection about my life from this moment on, almost at the level of how an adult would recall his past.

By this time, I was floating on top of the pool water, face down. I was in darkness, yet it did not seem to impede me in any way. I no longer felt that sight was that important as I could somehow feel everything without the need of the five senses that assist humans with surviving from one day to the next. I could also effortlessly move and be everywhere I thought about in an instant.

When I talk about moving everywhere, it is hard to explain what I felt was happening as I no longer needed to move my body to go places. I could just travel to anywhere I wanted at tremendous speed, so fast that I felt I reached my destination instantly. I did not see white light like others who have died say they saw or heavens opening and angels singing. I also did not remember meeting family members who have passed away.

It felt like I was everywhere in a void of space, and this type of darkness was not scary but felt comforting. I was traveling through countless stars and doing this without a body to hold me back. I was conscious without a physical form and I truly felt free. I also had little concept of age as it seemed like time had stopped and was no longer necessary. I also remember being aware of others around me, especially another being who felt very close – almost too close. I knew that I was not alone and that all this darkness and void space was filled with sentient beings such as what I felt I had become. I can sum it all up by saying I felt as if I had become an omnipotent being. I was not scared, hungry, upset or sad. I was a part of everything all at once.

Well, obviously, I am writing this story and could not do so unless I was alive. And I am telling my story because my mom got some type of sick feeling to her stomach and sensed something was wrong. When we talk about that day, she tells me it was only a few moments before she felt something was not right and went looking for me. She said she got up and was going to go upstairs to where the rest of the kids were playing to see if I was with them. Instead, she suddenly had this urge to go to the kitchen of her uncle's home.

In the kitchen, she ran into my shithead cousin, who had told me to go get the ball after he unlocked the sliding glass door for me. In my cousin's defense, he was probably four years old at the time.

"Timmy," my mother said, "have you seen Patrick?"

My cousin Timmy shook his head. That ass, he knew I was in the pool. I guess I was lucky my mom went to the sliding glass door and looked out. Later in life, my mother told me she saw my body floating on top of the water and that I was motionless due to being dead. My mom told me she started screaming for help as she ran out the doors and jumped into the water. She swam to my lifeless body and grabbed me. She pulled me out of the water and onto the side of the pool, where she was screaming and crying as only a mother could when finding her only child dead from drowning.

When I got older, I asked my parents how long they estimate that I was dead. My mother says only a few minutes, and my father told me it may have been as long as ten minutes. Needless to say, it was enough time for a toddler to drown. Well, by this time, my mom was screaming for someone to help me. Aunts were running outside to her, and they, too, started screaming when they saw me in her arms. There were uncles coming out who also did not know what to do. But obviously, someone knew what to do; someone was cool and collective under pressure and had been trained as far back as the 1960s in CPR and other first-responder techniques. Lucky for me, that person was my amazing father.

My old man was born during World War II in a poor area of the Bronx, N.Y. He had little opportunity growing up, and because of this, he joined the U.S. military right out of high school. He was a member of the 101st Airborne Division of the Army. Because of this, because of Uncle

Sam, my pops knew CPR. As I was later told, my dad immediately took me from my mom. He turned me on my side and hit my back several times to clear anything that may still have been inside of me. He then turned me onto my back and began providing his only son the lifesaving breaths and chest compressions needed to jumpstart me back to life. As my mom tells it, my father had to perform CPR for a good couple of minutes before I started breathing again and water emptied from my mouth. My pops is my hero, and I would not be able to tell you about me – about this life I have lived without him.

So, things were a bit fuzzy in my memory right when I was brought back to life, but I could almost swear that when I opened my eyes, I was staring right at myself, and even as a toddler, I knew this did not seem right. Then again, who knows what is possible after having suffered a full-on death experience? I then remember being in the back of an ambulance and having had something over my nose and mouth that I did not like as it made me uncomfortable. I kept trying to take it off, and the paramedic kept putting it on and then holding it so I could not remove it again.

From this point in my memory, I lose a bit of recollection and only later did I remember being in the hospital. I was being held by my mom as I cried. This took place in a hospital room, and I believe there was a doctor talking to my parents and telling them something about me. I later found out that the doctor was telling them I had suffered brain damage due to a lack of oxygen for a considerable amount of time and that I would be more vegetable than human. But here I am, writing this story, and I sure as hell can tell you that I do not feel mentally slow. I do not believe I suffered brain damage that could be linked to my drowning. That being said, I still like to think that if I did suffer from some sort of brain damage, that I most likely started out as smart as Albert Einstein or Nikola Tesla and was then reduced to a mere mortal like the rest of the population.

Life was anything but normal after what I know to have been an out-of-body experience. I played just like other children. I watched Saturday morning cartoons just like other kids. But what was not normal was that I began to experience things that scared the living hell out of me. I saw what could only be described as an Evil Pan. Yes, like Peter Pan but spliced with some crazy, evil, demon-looking attributes. This Evil Pan ended up playing a big part in the way this lifetime would turn out for me. This creature would become the beginning of supernatural experiences in my life that even my parents would end up experiencing with me.

When I was four years old I began having issues with this apparition – and yes, this creature was not a figment of my imagination as many people might think. It all began when we moved from Hollywood to La Habra, California.

My parents had purchased a new home that was just built in the hills of La Habra. The street we lived on was Calle Don Juan. The new home was massive compared to the apartment we had been living in during the first few years of my life. As you walked into the new home, to the left was a large living room, and straight ahead was the family room, with the dining area and kitchen off to the left of the back area. Before reaching the family room, one would turn slightly to the right and reach the first of four bedrooms. Farther down the hall was the next bedroom before the hall turned left. On the right side after turning left was a bathroom, and on the left, across from the bathroom, was another bedroom. This one would initially become mine. Then, farther up the hall was the master bedroom. The hall ended at the entry door of the master bedroom.

The house was also furnished with crap right out of *The Brady Bunch*. Can you now picture the interior? It was 1970s-style, nothing matched, and there was crazy wallpaper all over, mirrors on the walls and wood panels. I loved this home during the day. I had tons of space to play and a backyard that went on forever. The yard even had huge hillsides on which I could slide. But this is where the fun stops. As soon as the sun set and it got dark out, this home was like an old abandoned mansion in the middle of empty fields after an apocalypse. It was creepy, and I was a typical four-year-old who was scared, and soon enough, I would find out it was for good reason.

I just want to make clear that I saw some weird stuff after my drowning accident. I would see people around me who were not really there. I would turn and see them clear as day, then turn away for a second and they'd be gone. It creeped me out at first, but I eventually got used to it. I also heard voices all the time. It was never bad voices or ones where someone sounded like they wanted to kill me. It was just regular voices, but coming from nowhere and from no one. So I chalked this up to being a kid and just seeing or hearing things. But when we moved into this house, a lot changed. So initially, I was not sure if the house had anything to do with Evil Pan or if it was just a matter of timing and that the timing happened to coincide with moving into the new house.

I believe we had been living in the La Habra house for approximately one month when I had my first contact with this being, this creature, this demon. I was not sure what to call it. The time was 8 at night when I had to go to bed. My mother took me to my room. She turned on a nightlight that was always conveniently next to my bed as I was afraid of the dark. I remember her telling me to make sure I stayed in bed unless it was to use the bathroom. I also remember her telling me there is nothing to be afraid of at night and that everything I thought I saw or heard was my imagination.

My mom would always say, "Millions of kids go to bed each night and wake up every morning with no monsters getting them."

That was a comforting statement that I would soon find out was complete bullshit. She then left the room, and soon afterward, I fell asleep.

I am not sure how long I was sleeping before something caused me to get up. A motorcycle toy I had on my dresser fell over and landed on the floor. It scared the crap out of me as that had never happened before. I had not even played with that toy for days. I got scared and pulled the covers over my head but left a small opening where I could watch the dresser. I remember being unable to call out to my parents as I was stricken with fear. It was that fear a kid experiences when he thinks there are monsters in the room. Not a lot of time had passed when I suddenly saw several marbles I had on the dresser start to move. I watched as the first marble moved around and then fell to the ground. Then the second, third and fourth marble did the same thing. Each of the marbles first spun around on the top of the dresser before rolling off. OK, now I was terrified. I thought my mother had said there were no monsters and nothing to be afraid of in the dark of night. What then was this that was taking place? My nightlight started to flicker. I was panicking and did not know what to do. I could feel my heart thumping faster and faster but I could not move. I could not scream, and I started sweating. Suddenly, the nightlight went out, and I was alone in the dark. At this point, I held my breath. Then, my dad opened my bedroom door and noticed the nightlight was out. I started to cry, and he asked what was wrong. I told him, and he dismissed it as coincidence. He said the house was new and moving as it settled. I had asked him, then why did just the motorcycle and marbles fall off?

He replied, "Because they were probably on the nearest corner of the dresser. Now go to bed."

Needless to say, I did not go to my bed. I spent the night in bed with my parents, which was in the comfort and safety of their bedroom.

I slept the remainder of that night with no issues as I had my mom on one side and my dad on the other. The next morning, I woke up and could not help but immediately think about what had happened. I got out of my parents' bed and slowly walked out of their room. It was still pretty early, and the hallway was filled with pockets of darkness. I turned on the light in the hall and then went to my room. I looked in, and light was coming into the room from the single window just to the right of where my bed was positioned. The night stand was directly below this window. I turned on the light in my room and made sure the door was wide open.

I called out to my parents, "I love you guys. Are you both up yet?"

I got a response from my dad, and this made me feel safe as I entered my room and then continued all the way inside.

I immediately looked at the dresser and noticed the toy motorcycle and marbles were back up there. I do not remember my dad putting them back as he and I went to his room together the night before. I also remember my mom already having been in bed when my dad and I came in for the night. Maybe one of them put the toy and marbles back on the dresser while I slept. Whatever it was, it still did not sit well with me that the toys were not on the floor. I then went over and examined the nightlight as it still was not working. I turned the switch back and forth, but no light shined out of its bulb. I looked closely on the inside of the case that covers the bulb and noticed what looked to be black smudges all over the bulb itself. I turned it slightly, put the device back into the wall and turned the switch. It immediately turned on. I was four years old and did not take the time to think about how strange it was that the bulb had been slightly turned counterclockwise so that it would not light up. I just knew now that it worked, and it would be there for me if I was forced to sleep alone again in my own room that night.

The rest of the day went by and was filled with what a four-year-old normally does, meaning, I played, did chores, watched television and played some more. I felt safe during this time because it was still light out and I thought I was protected by it. Unfortunately, that soon changed as it got later and the sun began to set, which then allowed the darkness to overthrow the daylight. I knew this meant that my bedtime was quickly approaching, and I began to worry about having to spend the night in my own room, alone and afraid.

# 2.

# A Constant Fear

I still do not remember what day it was, but I remember watching my favorite television show that night, *The Six Million Dollar Man*. I loved that show and would constantly act as if I were bionic while it was on.

I always remember my mom telling me, "Do the bionic eye and jump with your bionic legs."

Sure enough, I would act as if I could see like the Bionic Man and jump as high as he did in the show. It was an entertaining hour. I even forgot about sleeping in my room alone for the night. But as all good things must come to an end, so did the show, and it was time for me to go to bed. As soon as my mom yelled out, "bedtime," I was immediately in a complete panic. I put up a fight and told her I wanted to stay up and that I would be good and quiet if I could just keep watching television. Of course, this did not work, and I was being marched off to brush my teeth, wash my face and go to bed. My mom let me know that I was too old to sleep with them and that I had to get over being afraid of the dark. She made her case that she and my dad were just next door to me and that I had a nightlight in my room. I brought up the scary closet in my room, and she let me know that she would close the closet door after inspecting the interior to make sure there were no ghosts or monsters inside of it. I was unable to challenge her, and before I knew it, I was tucked into bed; she closed the door to my room behind her, and I was instantly alone.

To this day, when I think about how I felt at that moment, my heart races a bit as I envision my room and me in my bed. I remember I had the covers over my head, except for a small space from which I could peep out and breathe. I truly was scared. How could I be forced to go through what I had experienced the night before? Would it happen again? Would things move by themselves and fall to the floor? Was the nightlight going to stay on or go out like it did the previous night? What was I going to do? I guess I worried for nothing as I must have quickly fallen asleep and no longer had to think about the horrible things that lurked in my room. Unfortunately, this peace of mind did not last long, and I quickly woke up to something telling me, "Get up!" and it sure as hell was not my mom or dad, and only the three of us lived in the house at that time. Needless to say, I was up, under the covers and scared like I had never been before. Lucky for me, nothing else happened that night. I made sure that I did not fall back asleep, and I kept my eyes open and looking out the small space in the sheets that I had made while the sheets covered my head. I saw nothing, and nothing weird or strange ended up happening.

The remainder of the night, I had continued to think about what happened earlier. What had I heard? Was it truly someone telling me to get up or was it part of a dream I was having? It just sounded so real. My parents must not have heard it because neither of them came in to check on me. I still could not move as I was too scared, and I could not yell out or call out as fear had totally gripped me. I lay there all night wondering what had happened that night and the one before. I thought about how I could get out of my room and over to my parents' room. But I could not move, and I just stayed in my bed looking out from under the covers until morning came, and it could not have come soon enough.

Soon, it was light out, and I slowly was able to feel my legs. I slowly was able to move and then eventually pull down the covers. I was then able to jump out of my bed and make a run for my door. I opened it and ran right into my parents' room. I saw my mom in bed by herself and I jumped in. It was still early, and I had awoken her, but she did not say anything, so I got under the sheets with her and soon fell asleep. I am not sure how long I had slept, but it must have been long enough for her to tell me to get up and get dressed so we could go eat breakfast. Just as most days begin, so did mine, with very little change from any of the other days in the new house. But again, all I could think about was that the night would eventually come and I would again end up in the same position I had been in the previous two nights. With this on my mind, the day flew by far too quickly. The next thing I knew, my father came home, we had dinner, watched television, it got dark outside, and it was again time for me to go to bed.

I had been tired all day as I had gotten very little sleep the night before. I was scared to go into my room and to bed, but at the same time, I was also so tired that I listened to my parents and did as I was told with little fuss. Before I knew it, my mom was closing the door to my room. There was plenty of light from my nightlight, and I fell asleep with very little effort. I am not sure how long I had been sleeping when suddenly I was up because my bed had moved. I am not sure if it was hit by something or was physically moved. I just know it moved enough to bring me out of my slumber and into a living nightmare.

The bed moved again, and the marbles on the dresser rolled off and fell to the floor. The closet door opened and closed, opened and closed. The nightlight flickered and then went out. Suddenly, around my closet, I saw a figure fly through the air. I could not even pull the blankets over my head as I was completely horrified. What became known to me as Evil Pan was in my room, and I could do nothing but watch this figure as it continued to sail through the air. It sailed around the room and then shot right under my bed. Then there was nothing but dead silence. Where had the figure gone? What was the figure? Was it real or purely my imagination? At this point, it did not matter as I was stricken with fear and I could not move. I could not look under the bed. As a matter of fact, I could barely breathe.

Then my covers were lifted off the bed and thrown over me. The sheets latched around my body, and I was quickly enveloped by them. I could not move as they were so tight that it felt as if people were holding them over me on each side of the bed and pulling the sheets down to the floor. I could not breathe. I could do nothing, not even cry as I was mortified. I felt it getting harder and harder to breathe as the sheets were pulling down on me, almost into my mouth and nostrils. During this entire time, I could hear what sounded to be laughter but at such a low level as if something were doing it directly into my ears, where no one but me could hear it.

I believe at this point I started getting lightheaded. I am not sure if it was from a lack of oxygen due to how tight the sheets were or if it was due to how gripped with horror I was. Just before I passed out, the sheets were lifted and thrown across the room, and I found myself lying on my back, looking up toward the ceiling and the dark figure directly above me looking down into my face. This dark figure was just inches from my body, almost mimicking how I lay in bed but facing toward me and the bed. I was inches from this thing and could not make out its face. I realized I could not as it did not seem to have a face. It continued to come toward me until it was just above my entire body and only an inch or so apart. At this very moment, somehow, someway, I let out a huge scream. I screamed so loud that the figure darted into the closet, and the closet door shut behind it. The nightlight immediately flickered back on and my mom and dad opened the bedroom door.

My dad came running in and asked, "What the hell is going on?"

I yelled out to him, "A monster, a monster is in my room."

"There is no monster. You were just having a bad dream."

"No! The monster flew into the closet and shut the door. The light just came on."

My mom went to the closet and opened the door and turned on the light.

"See, Patrick, no monster is in the closet," she said. "It was only your imagination or you were dreaming."

I tried to tell them it was not a dream. I let them know that this thing was in my room and squeezed me under the covers. Then it tossed the covers across the room and hovered above me. But my parents did not believe me. I was just a four-year-old with an active imagination, and they knew I was afraid of the dark. I knew I was not going to get them to believe me. I was crying and crying and let them know that there was no way I was sleeping alone the rest of the night. Sure enough, I ended up between my parents in their bed. I slept very little that night, and when I was awake, I could think only about what was back in my room, waiting for me to be alone with it in the dark. I guess after this, I fell asleep for the remainder of the night because when I again awoke, it was morning, and both my parents were not in the bed with me.

I was all the way in the back of the house and alone in their room. It was light outside, but still, I was scared. I knew I would have to get out of the bed and run as fast as I could past my room, down the hall and into the kitchen, where I believed both of my parents were. So, I mustered as much courage as I could, leaped off the bed, looked out the door and down the hall, closely scanning the area next to the door passage leading into my room, and then ran as fast as I could. I went flying down the hall and around the corner, through the family room and into the kitchen. There I found my parents at the kitchen table eating. I jumped up onto a chair and joined them. At this time, while with them and in the light, I again tried to plead my case about what had happened the night before. I tried telling them about the figure that had come into my room, but they did not want to hear it. They again continued to tell me I was only a kid and that I just imagined everything or that I had a bad dream. I know what I saw and what happened, and I know it sure as hell was no dream. It really happened.

During most of the morning, I continued to stay in the kitchen or in the family room and watch television. The cartoons I watched helped me think less and less about my room and that at some point, I had to go back into it. As a matter of fact, when I had to go to the bathroom, I had my mom take me and wait for me until I was done. I also had her go into my room with me and look around to make sure nothing was in the closet, nothing was under the bed and that the window curtain was pulled all the way open so the light of the sun shined into the room. I even had her leave the lights on in the room and the closet. Before she left, I placed a lot of blocks up against my closet door and under it so it could not shut while I was in there. I also got my six-shooter cap gun and had that at the ready. I made sure the door to the room was wide open and that blocks were also placed under this door to act as a makeshift door stop.

With all this in play, I began to look around to see if I could find anything related to what happened to me last night, but there was nothing. I noticed the marbles were still on the floor. The sheets were still across the room and in the corner. The cover to my bed was on the floor near the foot of the bed. But there was nothing – nothing I could find to back up my story and prove that what happened to me was not my imagination but in fact reality. The rest of the day passed and was uneventful. The morning turned into afternoon, and before I knew it, the afternoon turned into evening. Soon the sun set and the day turned into the night.

The night flew by as I realized the television show I was watching with my parents was over, and yes, you guessed it, it was again time for me to go to bed. I put up a tremendous struggle to stay up and not go to bed. I guess it somewhat worked because my dad took me to my bed and stayed with me until I went to sleep. The next thing I knew I woke up and it was daylight outside. I had slept completely through the night and nothing bad happened. I even realized that my dad left the bedroom door open, which he never did. I got up, opened the window curtain and let the light shine into my bedroom. I went about the rest of that day as if it had been any other day prior to my experience with the flying figure and absolutely nothing happened. As a matter of fact, it must have been a Saturday because my father made breakfast, and then the three of us went out for the rest of the day and we did not return until later in the afternoon.

I remember being pretty excited as I scored a couple of new Star Wars action figures while we were out shopping. I played and played with them well into the evening and night. I later went to bed with my mom, and she stayed with me until I fell asleep. Again, nothing happened, and I woke up to the sun shining in the room as no one had closed the curtain to my window. Nothing eventful took place, and this included nothing happening to horrify or scare me. As a matter of fact, several days and nights went by and nothing happened. I even began to forget about how scared I had been and how horrified I was about sleeping in my room and something coming for me. Maybe I got too confident, because several days later, when my dad took me to bed and said he would stay with me until I fell asleep, I told him this would not be necessary and that I was a big boy and could go to sleep by myself. I would soon come to regret this error in reasoning as sure enough, this night would be one of horror that felt to last an eternity.

I had been in bed for a short while when I began to think about the flying figure that had been in my room. I got scared and pulled the sheets tight over my head, with just a small opening for me to see out with one eye and breathe. I looked out the opening I had made in the sheets, and everything seemed to be OK. The nightlight was on, and it illuminated the entire room. I lifted my head up off my pillow as I slightly pulled down on the sheets with my right hand from inside and under the sheets and cover. The sheet slowly went down past the middle of my head, and I looked at the closet area that was again just to the right of the entry door to my bedroom and down past the foot of my bed. The distance was about six feet from the bed. Immediately I realized that neither I nor my dad had remembered to close the closet door completely when we came in the room and had gotten me ready for bed.

This immediately sent my heart racing. I felt panic envelop my entire body, and I could feel my heart pounding on the side of my neck. I laid there frozen, still with my neck slightly propped up and twisted, continuing to look at the closet door but being unable to do much else. I began to think to myself that I have to jump out of the bed, make a run for the closet door, close it as quickly as I could, run back and jump into the bed while covering myself back up in my protected cocoon of sheets. I was going to do it. I knew I could do it. I just had to picture it a few times in my head. Then, I jumped out of the bed with the sheets and covers hurling down to the bed side corner, I raced to the closet door as quickly as I could, shut the door, turned around and started running back. I could see the bed and was ready to jump into it and pull the covers over myself when the nightlight turned off. Darkness instantly filled the room, and no light entered through the window from the outside. Before I could make the leap into the bed, the flying figure came bursting out from underneath my bed and had cut off my passageway to safety. I stopped dead in my tracks, and I was frozen to the ground. I don't even remember breathing. Some of the most terrifying supernatural events of my young life were about to fully take place.

I could now see the entire creature from end to end. It was about four feet in length, with what looked to be an upper torso, upper and lower legs but no feet. It also had arms and hands. It flew closer to me and then all around me. It kept flying around and around me in circles. I moved my eyes only from side to side as it flew around, faster and faster until it did not look to have a body any longer but just became a blur. I realized that I could not feel it moving around me as I felt no wind force being created and neither my hair nor my clothes moved. I wondered how this could be possible with the creature moving with such tremendous speed all around my small body. Then he or it stopped right in front of my face.

We were now upright, both of us, and face to face. I was looking right into the face of my worst nightmare. I immediately realized that the creature's face was hard to focus on, and it was enshrouded in a vapor. It looked to have eyes, a nose, a mouth and other facial features, but it was hard to tell as it was wavy, almost fuzzy, in the facial region. No true eyes could be seen or focused on, just pure darkness where eyes should have been. And it had no mouth, yet it seemed like it was going to speak or make some type of sound. Whatever I thought was going to happen I was wrong. Before I knew it, I was being lifted off the ground by the creature. I was lifted off my feet and thrown upwards toward the ceiling.

I felt my back pushed up against what had to be the ceiling, and I was facing straight down toward the floor. The creature was again right in my face, horizontal with me but facing me and the ceiling. It almost seemed to grin or smirk in what I can only explain as a gesture of communication. It was holding me against the ceiling but without physically touching me, and I was unable to figure out how it could do this to me without putting its hands on me. In this terrible position I found myself in, I noticed that the creature was not fully there. I could somehow see through it, even though it was difficult due to how dark it still was. I believe this is why I best described it as a shadow figure of a young Peter Pan. Only this was no boy but a figure of darkness that seemed to want only to terrorize and torment me. It also felt to want to inflict pain on me as my back began to hurt by being pushed so hard up against the ceiling. What did it want, and what was it going to do? I think that at this moment, I began to cry slightly, and tears fell from my eyes. This only made it want to hurt me more. The Evil Pan looked to enjoy what it was doing to me.

As I continued to be pressed up against the ceiling by the creature, the head of the child demon began to twist and convulse. Its head moved side-to-side with tremendous speed, and it caused its neck and head to become completely blurred out due to such intense and fast convulsive movement. The dark shadow let me go, and I was falling toward the floor. Right when I was about to hit the floor I stopped, only inches from the lower surface of the room and in what would have been a horrific impact that would have done some serious damage to me. I was spun around and now facing upward toward the ceiling. The demon child hurled itself right at me from ceiling to floor.

Again it stopped in front of me with little distance between it and myself, and I then felt like I was being strangled. I could not breathe. I felt cold, followed by a heat around my neck and throat. I started to struggle for air; the grip around my throat was getting tighter and tighter. I was getting less and less air. I felt dizzy, and I saw popping lights all around me and then nothing. I must have become unconscious at that point. I am not sure how long I had been out and how long this entire ordeal took, but when I finally came to my senses, took in a deep breath and opened my eyes, I realized I was still on the floor and that it was already morning out as light was filtering in from around the sides of the curtain over my window. I continued to lie on the floor for several minutes, trying to take in everything that happened and make sense of it all. I was only four years old at the time and had little idea of what to do. No one would believe me; no one would help me. Worse yet, was this going to happen again? Was I going to go through this ordeal every single night? I felt lost, sad and alone, not knowing what to do. What would I do now? What would I do later, especially when night was to come and I would have to enter this room again?

I continued to remain on the floor for some time as I was still attempting to process everything that had taken place, including my apparent loss of several hours due to blacking out. As some time passed, I began to feel my entire body again since up to this point, I think I had been mostly numb. With great effort, I gathered as much strength as I could and rolled over to my side. Then I tucked my legs under me and pushed upwards until I was finally standing and looking around in my room. I noticed nothing out of the ordinary. There was no evidence of the events that took place the past night.

I slowly began to walk toward my closed bedroom door, and as I did, I could feel my body aching. My back and neck hurt, and I was pretty sure that when I would check in a mirror that I would find bruising. I slowly turned the door knob to my bedroom door and walked across the hall to the bathroom. I looked at my neck in the mirror but there was nothing – no bruising, not even any redness. I lifted my shirt up and looked at my back and also found nothing that would have been evidence of what took place the prior night. Now for sure no one would believe me. Heck, at this point, I even began questioning if it all took place and if I had not just had one terrible nightmare. But I know it happened and I know it took place and was not a dream. I may have been only four, but I knew reality from imaginary happenings.

After I had finished in the bathroom, I went to the kitchen and had breakfast. For the remainder of the day, I would not leave the family room unless I had to go to the bathroom, and even then, I went only to the guest bathroom that was closest to the family room. There was no way in hell I was going to use my bathroom down the hallway and across from my room. As the day passed, I thought about what happened to me the night before while I watched cartoons and other kid shows. What was that thing that attacked me? Why could I see a head but not a face? How was it that the shadow creature looked to have human facial features but I was unable to make them out, even when it was only an inch or so from my face? What did it want, and why did it hurt me?

I was searching for answers that not even an adult would have been able to come up with. One thing I was sure of was that the day was passing quickly as I could tell by what show was playing on the television. With my continual thoughts about the night approaching, I could feel my heart begin to beat like a drum. I could feel the pounding on the side of my neck as anxiety built up inside me. I started to panic and then cry. My mom came out of the kitchen and wanted to know what was going on. With one last-ditch effort, I tried telling her what happened the night before and about the monster boy that had attacked me. Just as she had done in the past, she dismissed the ordeal with the notion of it having been a bad dream or an active imagination of a four-year-old who was afraid of the dark and wanted to stay in his parents' bed instead of his own. But this was not the case, and I got angry with her for dismissing what I had been telling her as a tale or dream from a child's active imagination.

Instantly, my mom's demeanor changed and she said, "Don't you dare take that tone with me, Patrick. I will send you to bed right now and by yourself if you keep that up."

With that threat, I began to cry and then yelled out, "I am sorry mommy. Please, please don't make me go to bed. I love you and won't do it again."

That seemed to work as she turned and went back to the kitchen and made no other mention of punishing me by sending me back to the place I feared most. I then returned to watching television and trying to figure out some type of game plan for the night that was fast approaching.

Time passed quickly, and before I knew it, my mom blurted out, "Bedtime for you, young man."

I began to cry and scream out that I did not want to go to bed and that I would be extra good and quiet if I could stay up and continue to watch television with her and dad. But it did not work, and I was quickly marched off to get ready for bed by my mother. She must have had some small amount of pity for me as I seemed to have at least talked her into staying with me in my room. I quickly brushed my teeth, and then my mom and I walked into what felt like a large and vast dark cavern instead of my room. She turned on the nightlight for me, got me into bed and tucked me in. She then sat at the edge of my bed and began to explain how everyone has bad dreams.

"Only babies are afraid of the dark, and you are not a baby, right? You are a big boy."

At this moment in my head, I remember thinking I would not mind being called a baby for the rest of my life if it were to get me out of this bed and room and safely into the vicinity of either of my parents for the rest of the night. But I nodded in agreement with her and then closed my eyes and tried to sleep. I would occasionally open my eyes just to make sure my mom was still in the room, and she was. I am not sure how much time went by, but I must have finally fallen asleep.

I later woke up in my room to find the nightlight was still on but my mom was gone, and I realized it must have been late in the night as the television could no longer be heard, thus causing me to conclude that my parents had also gone to bed. I got up because I had an urge to use the bathroom. I realized that this would require me to get out of the bed, walk toward the closed closet door, turn left, open my bedroom door and then walk across a dark hallway to a dark bathroom. This thought caused me to freeze in my bed with my head partially lifted off the pillow as I looked toward the closed closet door and closed bedroom door. I realized I could not put my head back down as I could not get myself to quit looking at the doors.

I began to think about the nightlight again going out, me being in the dark and then the figure appearing in my room, floating or flying towards me. Chills went up and down my body, followed by that pins-and-needles feeling. Then I was struck by the need to urinate again, and I really had to go. I knew it was either get up and go to the bathroom or wet the bed, and I had never wet my bed before. I thought about both options for some time but as I did so, I really felt the urge to urinate. I had to go use the bathroom. With that final thought, I built up the last amount of courage I needed in order to get my body to move. I jumped up out of the bed, ran toward the closed closet door, turned left, placed my hand on the bedroom door knob and began to turn it. That was as far as I got.

Without any warning, I felt myself being lifted off the ground and thrown backward with a tremendous amount of force. The force was so great that I flew across the bedroom and into the opposite wall. I hit the wall and made a huge banging sound as my body impacted up against it. This knocked the wind out of me. I looked around and could see nothing in the room. The nightlight was still on and functioning, but there was no visual sign of the flying creature. I tried moving but realized I was still being pinned to the wall by some unknown force. It hurt as I felt every inch of my body that was touching the wall being crushed up into it. I noticed that my feet were not touching the floor and that I was approximately eight inches off the ground and completely pinned to the rear wall of my room.

I let out a huge scream and started crying. You could hear two loud thumps as my mom and dad both jumped out of their bed and ran to my bedroom door. As soon as one of my parents began opening the door, I was released from the grasp of whatever was holding me and I fell to the floor with a mild thump.

My dad ran in screaming, "What's wrong? What are you doing?"

Both of them looked worried from the massive scream I must have released. I tried telling them that I was trying to go to the bathroom when something picked me up and tossed me against my back wall. I told them that it was the boy monster and that he was trying to hurt me. My parents told me to stop making up stories and to never play like that again as it scared the hell out of them.

"How do you think I feel?" I replied.

This only got them to yell louder at me for messing around in the middle of the night. I knew there was no way they were going to believe me.

Needless to say, I begged and pleaded for them to wait outside in the hallway while I used the bathroom. When I was done using the bathroom, I got my mom to stay with me for the rest of the night. She ended up falling asleep right up against me in my small twin-sized bed. Nothing happened to either of us while she was in the room. In the morning, I felt her get up, so I did the same as there was no way in hell I was staying in the room by myself. Whatever attacked me the previous night did so in the light. I had realized this while I was in the bathroom the prior night. This only complicated things and added to my fear as now I had to worry about things happening in the light and knew that the light was no protector of little boys from terrifying flying shadow creatures.

The next day and night came and went. I spent the night with my mom and dad in their room, and they let me sleep in between them. I guess I had put up such a fuss at bedtime that it was easier for them to just let it happen than to get me to go to sleep in my own bedroom. If they only knew and understood, they would never have me go to that room again. They would close up the entry with bricks so no one would have to enter. But was this creature confined just to my room or was this Evil Pan able to go and do as it pleased? This question would soon be answered.

Another day came and went, followed by the evening. Most of the good television shows I watched with my parents were about to begin. The three of us were sitting on the couch that faced the television when my father realized he forgot some work documents in his car. It was parked in the garage, and he asked that I go get them from the front seat. Not thinking twice as I realized the garage entry door was close to the outside guest bathroom and that the garage had two windows that were not covered, I jumped up and headed out the door. I flipped the light on so I had greater illumination than just the poor lighting coming through the two windows of the garage due to the quickly fading sun.

My dad's car was farthest on the left as the garage door was in the rear right corner. I began to head around to the far side and open the passenger door. I had to slightly jump up to get the documents that sat in the middle of the two front seats. My legs lifted slightly off the ground as my stomach hugged the corner of the passenger seat. I grabbed the documents with one hand and then tilted back and up, which allowed for my feet to again make contact with the garage floor. All of a sudden, something grabbed my feet and pulled them out from under me. The same force tugged at me, and this sent the rest of my body backward. As I began to fall back, I saw all the documents go flying out of my hand, and they then rained down to the floor.

I felt a sharp object come in contact with the back of my head, and I began to feel something warm and wet in my hair. The next thing I knew, I was being pulled under the car. I was stiff and could not move from the sudden fear that had gripped every part of my body, and I was numb. I then found myself completely under the car. I was frozen in fear yet I still felt my body being turned around for me. I initially was facing outward and toward the garage wall but was being rotated so that I was now facing the other direction.

With the utmost fear, I was staring at the dark, shadowed face of the Evil Pan. This time, it almost seemed like its facial expression was screaming at me. I could hear the shrilling in my head but could not really detect audible sounds. My head felt heavy and weighed down. I could hear something that sounded like the creature was speaking to me, but again, I could not see any type of mouth, and no actual sound or audible voice was coming from the shadow creature. It just seemed like the sounds were immediately being placed into my head, and I could not understand how this was possible. The next thing I knew, I had passed out.

I later gained consciousness and noticed there were two men standing over me and doing something to me. I was groggy and could hear my mom telling me not to move but to let the firemen take care of my head. As I continued to regain my senses, I felt this huge pain in the back of my head. Apparently, when the creature grabbed me and I fell backward, I hit my head on one of those metal peg holders my dad had put up on the garage wall to hold some of his tools. The metal peg pierced through my head and then tore a gash down the back as I was pulled under the car. I looked around and saw blood all over the garage floor. After that, I again lost consciousness. When I awoke, I was in an emergency room, and I had a huge bandage on the back of my head.

The doctor in the ER came over when he saw me awaken.

"You are one lucky boy, Mr. Patrick. If you had fallen back any harder, you would not be here with us anymore but would have most likely been dead."

The doctor then told my parents and I that I also suffered a concussion that was most likely due to me hitting my head on the garage floor and that this was also the most likely answer for the large lump on my head. The hair on the back of my head had also been shaven so the medical staff could clean the gash and staple my head closed. It took the doctor four staples to close the wound correctly. Because of all this, I would require parental supervision through one or two nights and being awoken every hour if I fell asleep. That part was the only good news from the entire ordeal as I knew my mom and dad would be watching me like a hawk and this would allow no opportunity for the creature to get me again. We later left the hospital, and my dad drove us back home.

When we got home, my dad carried me inside.

"Patrick," he said. "What happened? I asked you to go get me some papers out of the car and the next thing I know I found you bleeding and knocked out in the garage."

I wanted to tell him the truth, but I knew he would not believe me. I figured that if I told him the truth, he would most likely get angry with me and say I was lying and making up this great story about a monster pulling me under the car so that I would not later get in trouble for all these shenanigans. Instead, I told my mom and dad I must have lost my balance or footing when I got back out from the car and then fallen on my own. They asked why I went under the car when I was hurt, and I just told them I did not remember how that happened. With that, I was safe from my Evil Pan as I was closely watched the next two nights by my parents.

After the attack in the garage, nothing happened for at least a week. My head hurt, and I constantly felt nauseated, like I needed to always vomit. I also was very interested in the back of my head and the missing hair. I was constantly touching the staples and the wound and would get the same response from my mom, "Quit touching your head, you are going to get the cut infected."

But I would continue to touch it when she was not around. As for the nights, I slept with my parents for the entire week. One other thing began happening during this time. My mom and dad asked me what I was dreaming about each night. I could not remember and let them know this. They then told me that I had been talking in my sleep and that I was having complete conversations. The only problem was that they were not in English but sounded more like a made-up language or gibberish and that I went on and on for long periods of time. My dad even said he had considered getting a tape recorder so that he could tape me at night and then play it back for others to hear, but he never did that.

After one week, my parents decided it was time for me to go back to sleeping in my own room and my own bed. I knew the inevitable would happen at some point. I knew this was going to be when I felt better and the staples were removed. Well, my follow-up appointment with the doctor was that same day, and sure enough, he removed the staples and said I looked to be doing well. So that night, I was again being carted off to bed by my father. He made sure the nightlight was on, the closet door was closed and that I was tucked in and had everything I needed. Once this was all done, he walked out of my room and closed the bedroom door behind him. I was again all alone in my room with no parents to protect me from the evil that was in this house.

Needless to say, I did not sleep. I had pulled the sheets over my head and was looking out from a small slit. I continued to scan the room from top to bottom. I could not see the closet door or bedroom door without lifting my head and pulling the sheet in a different direction, so I just continued to watch the part of the room I could see. I stared for a long time at the wooden dresser and the toys that were lying on top of it. I thought to myself that I would much rather be in my parents' bed and between the two of them as they slept, but this was no option for me tonight. I was definitely on my own and in for the long haul. As I continued to scan the room, I began to feel my eyes get heavier and heavier. I felt myself getting sleepy. I wanted to fight the urge to sleep and instead continue to watch for signs of the flying figure but I could no longer do so. Before I knew it, I had fallen asleep.

I am not sure how long I had been sleeping when I woke up and something was on top of me. I had been sleeping on my stomach with the covers over me so now I was being pushed into the pillow. I could not scream or cry because I was being suffocated. I was being pushed into my bed and pillow with such force that I could hear parts of my body cracking as I was bent inward toward the bed. Slowly, things began to get dark, and this was followed by me losing consciousness.

Whatever was suffocating me must have stopped as soon as I had passed out because I came to my senses slowly and realized I was not dead. It sure felt like I was being killed with the life force being crushed out of me and no opportunity to take in oxygen. As I gained more of my senses, I pulled the covers off and turned over in the bed. As I opened my eyes, there on the edge, sitting down and looking directly at me was the faceless spirit or demon that had continued to rain terror down on me. The creature bent over and came within inches of my face. It stopped, turned and flew into the closet as the closet door had been open. As it entered, the door quickly slammed closed behind it. I had somehow, someway survived another night with this creature – this demon that stalked me.

This creature continued to attack me during the nights. Weeks went by and it did not stop. There were nights when I was physically assaulted and nights when it just flew through my room for hours. There were nights when I did not see it at all but things would get tossed through the room. It also learned that slamming my closet door brought my mom or dad over to the room. I would get yelled at and blamed for this in the middle of the night, and this brought great joy to the creature. Whatever this creature was, whatever it wanted, it was not through with me.

# 3.

# Religion

Months had gone by and I continued to be terrorized by the creature, although not as often as earlier on. So much time had passed that we were even getting ready for a new addition to the family. My mother was about to give birth to a new baby brother or sister. Because of this, I was being moved to the larger room at the end of the hall. My new sibling would have my old room as it was much closer to my parents' room. I thought about this change and came up with positives and negatives. One big positive was I would not have to be in the bedroom where I was constantly being attacked. Up until then, I had only been attacked by the creature twice outside of my room. The one time was in the garage and another time was when I went to the bathroom. The negative was that it was a big room with a large closet and located farther from my parents. Would the creature stay out of the new room or come more often now that there was greater distance between my parents and I? Another big positive was that the new room had two windows instead of one, and this meant more sunlight. Another negative was that there being light did not always stop the creature from coming. I had already been attacked before it was dark, and the creature did not seem to mind flying through my room when the nightlight was still on. Yet another negative aspect was, what would the creature do to the new baby? This I did not like to think about. Could you imagine this thing having its way with an infant?

There was another interesting thing going on at this time in my life. My parents had never been too religious up until then. I think my father mentioned once to me that we were Catholic but we never went to church, and the last time I was at church was apparently when I was an infant for my baptism and christening. Well that was all changing. These two young guys in suits were coming to our house a lot. They would ride their bikes over and share their message all the time. They constantly wanted us to get down on our knees and pray with them. I was told by my parents that they were elders from The Church of Jesus Christ of Latter-day Saints and that soon we would also be members. These two elders asked me if I had any questions, and I did. I asked them if God can protect people from monsters. They laughed and told me that was definitely one of the things God can do for little boys. With this answer, these two guys began to speak my language. I thought to myself, "Was there really a way to be protected from the creature?" I guess I would find out since I was apparently becoming a Mormon.

To this day, I am not sure if missionaries being in the house or God being discussed so often were the causes of the next big encounter with the flying figure. One night I was in my new room sleeping when the figure came darting out of my closet and went right through my bed. It did this a few times and then attempted speaking with me. It again placed its thoughts directly into my head without making any type of verbal effort to communicate.

I remember it telling me, "Emon nactune adama."

I had no idea what this meant, but it continued to come across my thoughts and seemed to be originating from the flying creature.

The figure then stopped and looked at my bedroom door. The door opened with tremendous force, and I watched as the Evil Pan flew out of my room and turned to the right. I lost sight of it and was not sure what was going to happen next. Then I heard my mother screaming and my father saying something. I got so scared that I jumped out of bed and ran out my door, down the hall to the right and into my parents' room, where all the commotion was taking place. I saw my parents' bed violently bouncing up and down with them in it. It was being shaken so hard that the bed and my parents looked as if they were going to get crushed up against the ceiling.

"What's going on? What is happening? Make it stop," my mother yelled.

I could see and so could they, my flying figure at the bed, and it was practically on top of my parents as they were attempting to get up, even as they continued to be tossed around like rag dolls. I looked at my mom as she finally was able to exit the bed and so did my dad. They looked at the creature, this flying apparition, and were truly horrified. It continued to look at them and follow them as they moved around the bed and toward each other. The bed continued to be lifted and dropped, lifted and dropped, frame and all. The creature then turned to me.

As it did so, I heard myself say out loud and directed toward my parents, "Emon nactune adama." I said it over and over again. "Emon, nactune adama, emon nactune adama." I apparently did not stop saying this; I could not stop saying this.

Then I heard my father say, "In the name of Jesus Christ, I command you to leave!"

The bed stopped shaking, and I stopped repeating whatever it was that I was saying. The flying figure stopped staring at me and instead turned back toward my father and began looking at him with what almost seemed like curiosity. I, to this day, do not believe that what my father said had power over the creature. I felt that it interested the creature as to why my father would say such a thing in such a commanding voice when this was all taking place. Or did what my father said really affect the creature? My father again repeated himself and advanced on the cloudy, almost transparent, flying figure. As he did so, it backed away and vanished through the wall of my parents' bedroom.

I turned back to both of my parents, looked them in the eyes and said, "I told you there was a monster this whole time, but you didn't believe me. Now you know I am not lying."

Nothing else was said. I think my parents did not know how to respond. I do know one thing: I sure as hell did not have to go back to my room that night, and my parents made sure all three of us slept together in their room. This was, of course, after a thorough inspection of the bed by my father.

The following morning, my parents woke me up and took me to the kitchen with them. They did not want anyone to be alone. They asked me questions the entire morning about the creature. I found out that what I saw as being the figure of a flying boy looked to them to be a large dark cloud, almost comparable to a medium-sized bear. They said it had no real shape and no physical body. They wanted to know everything – everything that had happened to me and about the encounters with the creature. My mom kept calling it a demon or the devil, but I was not too sure it was. I said it was a flying Evil Pan. She asked why I thought this, and I told her because it looks just like the Pan in the children's book she would read to me – just dark, scary and violent. My parents also wanted to know what I was saying and repeated in the bedroom, but I told them I don't know and that I do not remember why I was saying it and that it was coming out of my mouth but that I had no control over it. I assured them I had just heard the same thing in my room before the monster attacked them. I just did not know, and I did not have answers for them.

After this took place, I spent several weeks sleeping in my parents' room or one of my parents slept with me in my room. I was not left alone. Soon after, my mother also gave birth to a girl, my new baby sister, who they named Ann. They watched my baby sister all the time, as well, and would not let her out of their sight. As a matter of fact, I do not believe she ever slept in her room alone. My dad even moved her crib right next to their bed. After a couple of weeks, things turned back to being more on the normal side, and the creature had not been seen or heard this entire time. I remember wondering if that night in my parents' room was the end of this living nightmare I had been put through for long enough. I still had terrible dreams about the flying monster, but at least I could wake up from these dreams and not find metal objects lodged into the back of my head. Things were looking brighter, and times felt to be changing.

Before I knew it, my family and I became Mormon. With this happening, we began to go to church every Sunday, and there were also lots of other church members who came to our house all the time. I am not sure if becoming Mormon had anything to do with the creature's absence for such a long period, but whatever it was, I was hoping that this lack of evil in my life would be permanent.

My family did a lot of church stuff that included constantly going to sacrament meetings and gatherings, and not just on Sundays. They became very busy, not just with work and the house but especially with church functions and callings that were given to them. Before I knew it, eight months had passed, and there was no sign of the evil figure that had relentlessly tortured me, night after night for so long, only to now be nowhere in this physical realm. I still had nightmares of it daily, and some nights, they were so bad that the creature might as well have been in my room, inflicting the mental and physical pain that it knew how to do so well.

For a little kid, time now seemed to fly, and before I knew it, my birthday was fast approaching. I had been without the monster for so long that I began to forget what it looked like up close and what it felt like when it was in a room with me. It was at this time that I let my guard down and at this time that the creature returned.

I remember it well: I had just turned six years old that week and had a wonderful birthday. We had friends and family over, and that meant I got a lot of gifts at the party. The cake had been on the dining room table, and while it was being served, one of my cousins pushed another cousin into the dining room wall, damaging the glass that had been placed on the entire length of the back wall. The cake was knocked to the ground and made inedible. Because of this, my parents had to get the glass repaired and had then decided to put glass tiles on all walls in the dining room. At the time, my dad had a very good friend named Ralph Tortelli. Not only was Ralph my dad's good friend, but he was also my dad's business partner. I had no idea what they did, only that they owned a small business. Ralph had been a carpenter before going into business with my dad. He was going to do the work for free in the dining room, and all my parents had to do was purchase the supplies.

About a week after my birthday party and the fiasco that ensued, my parents had acquired all the glass tiles, glue and other materials needed to do the work. It was a Saturday morning, and Ralph had come over to start on the project. By early afternoon, Ralph had hung the tiles on the first two walls and was about a third of the way done with the final wall when my mom had almost finished with preparing lunch in the kitchen. I had remembered constantly going in to the dining room area and asking Uncle Ralph what he was doing and how he was doing it. He was not really my uncle, but that is what my parents always had me call him. He was not too patient of a person and would be short with me in his answers and then stop talking to me altogether and go back to work. Even at the age of six, I could take a hint, and I left him alone. Well, my mom and I were in the kitchen, and she put a sandwich down and soda for me on the table to begin eating lunch.

Right at that moment, I heard Uncle Ralph say, "Patrick, don't get near that. You are going to make it fall!"

There was a large bang and crash, and glass was heard breaking.

"Oh my God, Jesus Christ; I am bleeding," Uncle Ralph yelled.

My mom and I ran out of the kitchen, through the family room and quickly turned into the formal living room that led to the dining area. I looked at Uncle Ralph and he was holding his nose, and blood was gushing everywhere from its upper bridge. My mom started screaming, and this caused my father to come running in from the garage and into the room where the three of us had been. My dad saw Ralph and ran into the kitchen to grab towels. He came back and began to apply the towels to Ralph's face. My dad had to make another trip to the kitchen for more paper towels. Ralph continued to bleed, and it did not look like it was going to stop any time soon.

While my dad and Ralph worked on stopping the bleeding, Ralph blurted out, "Patrick, why did you do that?"

"Do what Uncle Ralph?"

Ralph said that I had come around the corner running toward him so quickly that it looked like I was flying. Ralph had been on the floor preparing the glue on the back of the next glass tile when I supposedly went over him and yanked the tile off the wall, causing it to fall. It hit Ralph in the nose, almost slicing it off, and then shattered all over the floor.

"I didn't do that Uncle Ralph, I promise,"

My mom then told Ralph and dad that when this all happened, I was in the kitchen with her, and it could not have been me.

"But I saw him do it," Ralph replied.

My mom got angry and began yelling at Ralph. My dad told her to stop as they were still trying to stop the bleeding. Ralph then looked forward and into the glass tiles hanging on the wall that he had already completed; he saw the flying figure. The dark shadow creature was in every single tile, looking out of each one as if it were imprisoned behind each tile, and there were a hundred of my Evil Pans.

"Jesus Christ, what is it?" Uncle Ralph asked.

The creature came out of the glass and began flying through the dining room. It got faster and faster, and none of us knew what to do. It flew toward my father and knocked him off his feet, causing him to fall on top of Uncle Ralph. Then it stopped, turned toward my mother and I and flew toward us. I screamed as it flew right into my body and was then gone.

It was nowhere to be seen after it entered into me. I started to panic and scream. I did not know what to do. This thing flew inside me and most likely was still there. My mom did not move; she did not breathe; she did not scream. My dad ran over to me and began to shake me fiercely back and forth, but there was nothing. Then Uncle Ralph passed out, and I don't think it was due to what just happened but the loss of blood. Nothing else was seen of the creature. Nothing!

My dad had to put Ralph into the car. They drove to the hospital as Uncle Ralph was still losing large amounts of blood from where the tile struck the bridge of his nose. My mom and I were left inside alone, and she had still said nothing. She just continued to stare at me and even seemed to back away. Another minute passed, and finally I saw life come back into her eyes, and she broke her stare. She grabbed me and started crying. I got scared and also started crying. She told me everything would be OK and that I should not worry. She told me that she and dad would figure everything out and get me help.

As soon as she had said this, I looked over toward the dining room table, where was a plate with a piece of my birthday cake from the prior week – the one that had been knocked over and ruined. But this piece of cake was perfect. Not a bit of frosting out of place. My mom and I approached it and realized there was writing on the frosting. This was a good-sized piece of cake. As we slowly approached, my mom was able to read the writing. It looked to have been drawn into the frosting by a finger. My mom grew quiet.

I asked her, "Mommy, what does it say?"

She did not say anything.

"Mommy, what does it say?"

She grabbed the cake, walked it over to the kitchen and tossed it into the trash. She then tied the bag up, pulled it out of the can and took it to the large trash can in the garage. She never told me what was written on the cake.

Several hours had passed, and it was already dark. My mom and I were sitting in the family room with Ann in my mom's arms. We were watching television when we heard the garage door open and my dad's car pull in. My dad and Ralph came in and they were having some type of heated argument.

"Fuck this place and fuck whatever happened here today. I am getting my tools and tool belt and getting the fuck out," Ralph said.

"Get the fuck out," my dad replied.

"You have got to do something about your kid. He has some fucking devil inside him."

My father responded, "Shut your fucking mouth, and get out of my house."

Ralph grabbed his tools and slammed the front door behind him. That was the last I ever saw of him. I later learned that my dad and Ralph dissolved their business and went their separate ways. What a way to end a friendship and a business partnership. Without being able to talk to Uncle Ralph, I never really got a chance to ask him about why he continued to yell and use my name while he was in the dining room hanging the glass tiles. I later came to the conclusion that because of the size of the flying figure, he must have mistaken it for a little boy, and I would have been the only one who fit that description in the house that day. I guess I will really never know.

# 4.

# An Unknown Anxiety

What had happened to my parents and Ralph really scared them or at least creeped them out enough to where they no longer wanted to live at the home on the hill in La Habra. Because of this, they put it up for sale, and it was almost immediately purchased by a young doctor and his wife. So, my parents hired a moving company, packed our belongings up and moved the four of us to Tustin, Calif., where they rented a beautiful, small three-bedroom home in a new neighborhood that was built on former strawberry fields. As a matter of fact, the neighborhood was the only thing around in the entire area that was still not some type of agricultural field. Another neighborhood feature was the community pool across the street from our house. It fascinated me as I knew just how much fun it was to swim and play in the water. That is, as long as you know how to swim and don't drown. Yes, I was both excited and scared as I had not been in a pool since I drowned several years back, and that meant I still did not know how to swim.

The house was nothing extravagant in any way, shape or form. It was a one-story home with all three bedrooms along the same main hall. The remainder of the home consisted of a living room, a guest bathroom, and a large open kitchen with a dining area. It was definitely smaller than the La Habra home, and it also was a lot brighter. I remember there being so much natural light coming in that some mornings it was difficult to sleep in past 7.

It was now summer and the days were warm in the Tustin area. My mom really wanted me to learn how to swim. She took me to the pool every day. I learned to swim within one or two days, but I did not like going underwater. This caused my swimming style to look more like a dog trying to stay afloat rather than a graceful Olympian. It was not that I could not hold my breath underwater but instead the fact that I refused to open my eyes. I am not sure what the reason was but I would not open them for any reason. This went on for several weeks until my mom had enough of me splashing everyone all the time and her having to incur the evil looks of all the other moms in the neighborhood.

"Patrick," she said, "I am ordering you to go under the water and open your eyes. Nothing will happen; you just wait and see."

"But what if I don't want to go underwater?"

I know I was testing her patience at this point, but I really was afraid to open my eyes, and I was not quite sure why.

"You will open your eyes under the water now or you will never swim again. Do I make myself clear?"

She made herself very clear, and with that, I dove underwater, still with my eyes closed. I went as deep as I could, paused to collect my courage and then opened my eyes. As I did so, I realized I was surrounded by darkness, even though it was midday with not a cloud in the sky.

I started swishing around under the water like an injured fish, panicking more and more. I turned to my right, and to my utter shock, saw my Evil Pan swimming toward me in the darkness. It moved with amazing speed from the opposite end of the pool up into my face in what felt like a split second. He was staring into my eyes and was less than several inches away. Again, as I stared back; I looked to be staring into nothingness. The creature's face looked cloaked. You could make out facial features but you could not see anything distinctive. I could not move, and I again must have stopped breathing. I began to lose consciousness. As I was about to enter what seemed would be permanent sleep, I was quickly brought back to the living. My mom had reached down and grabbed me out of the water. I quickly took in a deep breath and felt my life returning to this mortal body of mine.

"Don't be playing around like that under the water," my mom yelled.

And that was that. I never made mention to her about what happened, and I sure as hell did not open my eyes underwater again for a very long time.

The summer came and went with no incident in the new home. The flying apparition had not made its presence known or felt inside the house. The only time it had appeared while we were in Tustin was that single sunny afternoon while I was swimming in the pool. With the end of summer came autumn, and that meant it was finally time for me to be off to school. My parents had enrolled me in the local public elementary school. I remember having been excited for classes to start. I had been practicing my reading and math with my mother so I would have a head start on other kids in my class. I had purchased my *Six Million Dollar Man* metal lunchbox and thermos almost a month earlier, and I had carried it around the house daily to be well-versed in its usage as a food-carrying device.

Before I knew it, the first day of school had finally arrived. It was a great Monday morning, and I had breakfast, got in the car with my father and was driven there. I remember he walked me into my classroom. He met my teacher, Ms. Hunt, and spoke to her for several minutes. As they spoke, I took a quick tour of the classroom. I remember wondering if this off-white colored space with very little decoration was all there was to look forward to. The room was very sterile and low-key. I began to feel a bit overwhelmed just due to these surroundings. As I had finished scanning the room, my eyes again fell upon my father and new teacher completing their conversation.

My dad came over to me and gave me a small hug and told me to not get into any kind of trouble, and then he left. I was alone in this strange room with strange kids and a strange grown-up, and I started to get anxious. I felt my heart start to beat quickly, and I started to sweat. I remember thinking that I needed to calm down and remember how much I had wanted to go to school and that I originally could not wait for this day to come. I had to focus on this and calm down. With that thought, I did just that, and the rest of the morning went by with no other issues. Before I knew it, lunch had come, and it was time to bust out my new lunchbox and thermos and show everyone what I had to eat, and more importantly, the awesome lunchbox. So I ate my lunch and then was off to play outside at recess.

I remember quickly scanning the school grounds. They were made up of one small classroom after another, each connected by a common wall. The entire area was then nothing but concrete and asphalt, with no grass or soil in sight. There were lots of kids of all ages throughout the playground. Some were running after each another and others were sitting and talking. I felt my heart start to palpitate at a tremendous speed. I started to think about the fact that I did not know any of these kids, had no friends and I was stuck in a concrete prison.

The people and buildings around me were now spinning, faster and faster, with no stopping in sight. I began to gasp for air. I felt my eyes start to tear up, and I felt this banging against the right temple area of my head. A teacher came over as she must have seen something was wrong and began speaking to me but I could not hear her. There was this awful ringing in my ears, and it continued to get louder as I started perspiring heavily, and it got very hot. She continued to speak to me, but her voice was garbled, and I could not understand her. I looked up at her one last time and then everything went dark and I fell to the ground, unconscious.

The next thing I remember, I was hearing voices and opened my eyes. There were popping lights and flashing streaks all around me. The lights started to subside, and I realized I was no longer on the playground but inside a building. A man was standing above me and shining a light into my face. He kept calling me by my name and asking if I knew what happened. I began to cry for my mom. I would not answer him but instead curled up into a ball and kept crying. Well, someone must have called my parents earlier because within two or three minutes of regaining consciousness, I saw my mom walking through the door. She spoke to the man who had been standing over me earlier. When she finished speaking with him, my mom came over to me, picked me up and hugged me as tight as she could. She then took me home. When we got back home, my mother gave me some water and then had me go lie down on the couch to take a nap. I slept for almost three hours.

When I got up, my father had already come home, and he and my mother were talking. I am pretty sure it was about what happened to me at school. After they had conversed among themselves for some time, my dad came over and checked on me. He had asked what happened, and I let him know that I was not sure. I explained what I was doing and then what I felt like right before passing out. I could tell he had a look of concern on his face and also one of disappointment, or at least it felt that way to me. We later ate dinner, and I then went to bed. I must have still been pretty tired from everything because I quickly fell asleep and did not get up until later in the morning when all the cartoons were done and only the boring adult shows were on television. My mom let me know that I was not going to school. Instead, I had an appointment to see the doctor. So I ate breakfast, took a shower, brushed my teeth, played a bit with my baby sister and was then driven to the doctor's office by my dad, who must have taken off from work as he was never home at this time of the day.

We pulled up to this small building and I realized that it was not my regular doctor's office.

"What place is this, dad?" I asked.

"It is a different doctor who can check you out for the issues you had at school," he said.

I immediately wondered to myself what that meant. I did not know I had issues at school. I just remembered getting scared, breathing heavily and then passing out. Whatever it was, I guess it warranted a trip to a new doctor.

When we walked into the office, I recognized that it lacked the toys and candy I regularly enjoyed at my regular doctor's office. This place did not have pictures on the wall, and there was not even a kid's book to read. There were only six chairs, and it looked to be the smallest office I had been to. I sat down as my dad went and spoke to the receptionist. About ten minutes later, we were taken back to a room that had several large reclining chairs and not a whole lot more. It lacked what I was used to seeing at other doctor's offices I had been to. My dad and I each sat in a chair and then waited for the doctor. Then this extremely attractive woman came in and sat in a chair next to me. She let me know her name was Dr. Hadley and that she was a child psychologist.

I had no idea what this meant and asked her to explain. She said she was a doctor who listened to children to find out what issues they were having to see if she can help them and their families change things or work around the issues to make the children be more comfortable in what they did and how they did it. I still remember not understanding what the hell she was talking about, even with this different explanation. About forty-five minutes went by as she asked me a bunch of questions, and I gave her the best answers I could. It almost began to feel like a test, and I was hoping I would pass. At the end of the session, she had me wait in the reception area as she spoke to my dad in her office. About ten minutes passed as I sat in one of the chairs in the waiting room before my dad came out, and we then went home.

After meeting with this doctor, I did not have to attend classes the entire week. The following Monday, my mom drove me to school, but it was not the one I went to on my first day. It was a new one – a place that was really nice-looking with grass and colorful buildings and a lot less students. I would later find out that my parents sacrificed a lot to put me into this private school. Whatever they had to do, I was very grateful as I enjoyed going to this place and had no issues like I did at the last school. As a matter of fact, that one day when I passed out was practically forgotten, and I went through that school year with no other problems.

The entire time I was in school, I did not once have a run-in with the flying figure. He did not make his presence known in any way, shape or form, and I had only a handful of nightmares about him. It almost began to feel like all that had happened with the dark flying figure was a distant nightmare I used to have, and I started looking over my shoulder less frequently in the house and having my parents be with me less often no matter where I went. I even occasionally went into a room at night without switching on every light I possibly could before entering. I truly felt like things were changing for the better.

Time continued to pass as we lived in Tustin, and before I knew it, I had completed first grade. The summer came and went and second grade started. Again, through this entire period, there was no sign of the Evil Pan. I did not even remember the last time I had a nightmare about this creature that once seemed to taunt and torture me nightly. Was it for real? Was my seeing him in the pool the last time I would encounter this creature from some other realm of existence? I sure as hell hoped so.

I believe I was into my second month of being a second-grader when I had another bad dream about the flying figure. I dreamt that night that the monster had gone to my father's place of work and set it on fire. I remember seeing it fly though the warehouse and touch parts of walls and boxes and desks, and wherever the flying figure touched was immediately set on fire. I remember that the figure would stop midway through his acts of arson and begin telling me something, but I could not understand. It was trying to communicate but nothing it was saying could be understood in my dream. After the warehouse was set on fire, the creature flew through the roof, and then it and I were in my room at the house.

I woke up scared and looked around. I could not find the creature anywhere. At that moment, I realized I was sweating to the point where my clothes were almost soaked. I then felt pain on the back of my right hand and looked down. The rear of my right hand was now throbbing, and I noticed it was burned. The pain was from fire, but the only fire or open flame I had been around was in my dream. I jumped out of the bed, ran to my parents' room and woke them both up, screaming that my hand was burned in my dream. My dad called me over to look at my hand. You could see this huge look of concern sweep over his face.

"Honey, Patrick's right hand really is burned. Quick, go check to make sure there is no fire in his room or in the rest of the house."

My mom looked and could find nothing. At this time, my dad was treating my hand with cool water and then some type of spray-on ointment. He then wrapped it with gauze.

My mom reported to him that there was no sign of open flames or a heat source hot enough to do that to my hand. I explained that it was not from anything in the house but that the flying creature had set fire to dad's workplace and then flown out of the roof of the warehouse and was suddenly in my room. I let them know that when I woke up, it was just a dream, and the creature was not in my room, but my hand was burned as if I really was in the warehouse. My parents told me not to repeat this story to anyone and that I should sleep with them that night. So, I spent the night for the first time in a long time with my parents and my baby sister. A short time later, I quit thinking about the thumping pain on my hand and fell asleep for the remainder of the night.

In the morning I woke up and found out that my dad had already left for work and that my mom and baby sister were going to take me to school. Apparently, my father got a phone call from his boss early in the morning and had to go to the warehouse right away. My mom let me know he had left about ninety minutes earlier. I asked her if she knew why he had to go into work early, and she said he did not say why. I then told my mother that I hoped the fire that the creature set at my dad's office was not too bad.

This comment got a quick response from my mom: "Shut up and quit speaking nonsense! That was a dream and not for real."

I went to school that day and had not given my dream another thought, even with my hand being burned. I guess I had been through so much of the supernatural that a burned hand had not been such a big deal. Before I knew it, school was out, and I went to meet my mom at the front gate where she usually picked me up, but this time, there was no mom waiting for me. Instead, a family friend from church was waiting for me and said my mother had asked her if she could pick me up. I knew the woman well so I went with her. I had asked her where my mom was, and she said at home, but there was an emergency. That answer really sparked my curiosity, and I now was wondering what had happened and if everyone was alright. I especially wondered if anything had happened to my baby sister or if some supernatural event had taken place at the house while I was gone. Before I knew it, we were home, and I thanked my mom's friend for driving me. I then jumped out of her car and ran into the house as quickly as I could. To my surprise, my father was already home, and he and my mom were waiting for me in the living room.

As soon as I got into the house, my parents stopped me inside the living room and told me to sit down as they wanted to talk to me. They told me that what was going to be discussed had better be kept between the three of us and the walls of the house. This was reiterated to me several times before the actual discussion began. My dad asked me about my dream from the previous night and he wanted to know exactly what happened.

"I told you, Pop. The flying monster boy was setting everything on fire. Whatever he touched immediately was burning," I exclaimed.

My dad stopped me and asked, "Patrick, I need you to be very specific. Tell me exactly what happened in your dream, step by step."

So I began to go into great detail as to what I had seen and how it seemed I was right next to the creature at my father's workplace the entire time it was setting the fire. I told my father about the path the creature took through my dad's workplace, what he touched, where he touched it and that he was trying to tell me something but I could not understand it. I also told my dad that after setting the fire, the creature shot straight upward through the ceiling of the warehouse. Once it left, he and I were immediately back in my room, and this is when I woke up and noticed the pain of my hand being burned. I asked my dad why he wanted to know, but first he and my mom were discussing something, and I could not understand them as they were whispering.

After they spoke to one another for a minute or two, my dad turned back to me and said, "Last night my office and the warehouse had a fire and burned down. The fire department believes it is arson as there were multiple fires started throughout the building."

I immediately replied, "Well, of course there was a fire at your office. I even told you how it was set and that I saw the flying monster do it."

All these happenings and my dream seemed a bit too much for my parents. Both my dad and mom had this look of frustration and fear.

"You must never speak of your dream, Patrick, to anyone," my father said in a stern and authoritative tone. He continued to explain that no one should know about how the fire was started and that for all we knew, I just had a dream and it was all a coincidence that an arsonist happened to break in and set my dad's workplace on fire the same night.

"Sure, Pop, whatever you say. I will not tell a soul what really happened."

That was the end of our discussing the incident.

The worst of it was not the fire itself but the fact that my dad was now out of a job during a time when the country was in recession. This meant he could not find work in Southern California. Because of this, he had to look for work elsewhere, and that elsewhere turned out to be Arizona.

# 5.

# Home in the Desert

We had been driving for approximately six hours when we finally got to our new rental home. I remember it was early afternoon in the autumn when we arrived in Paradise Valley. We pulled up to a small, typical looking home in the suburbs of Phoenix. Back then, there were not a whole lot of people in that area yet, and compared to Southern California, the entire valley area was lightly populated. The weather at that time of day and during that time of year was amazing. It was warm but not hot, and the sunshine was endless.

My parents, sister and I then went into the home and checked it out. It had a typical cookie-cutter tract home layout. It was nothing fancy and contained three bedrooms and two baths. One bathroom was in the main hallway and the other was the master bathroom in my parents' bedroom. Even though there were two additional bedrooms, my parents decided that my now two-year-old sister and I would share a room and the spare bedroom would be filled with boxes and act as a storage room. This was fine with me as it meant I did not have to sleep alone, and my sister always seemed to be good luck when it came to strange or paranormal occurrences. The initial walk-through of the house was cut short as we all heard the moving van pull up with our household items and went out to meet the movers. It took the moving guys about six hours to get our stuff into the house, where my mother made sure they put it where she saw fit. By the time the moving guys left, it was late, and we had little time to unpack. Because of this, the four of us spent the night in the living room on sleeping bags and blankets.

As the morning quickly came, light poured into the home through an ample amount of windows, including several skylights in different parts of the house. With plenty of light to guide me, I toured the house on my own and decided that my sister and I should have the room directly across the hall from the master bedroom. The front room would then make a perfect storage space for all the boxes my parents planned on keeping unopened as they always saw this move as a temporary solution to my father's current employment dilemma and need for leaving Southern California to find work.

Now we initially had arrived in Paradise Valley during the weekend, so as soon as Monday came, I was taken by my father to my new school. Remember that the school year had already been in progress, and I quickly found myself in a new second-grade class. The school was a private one right up against a large rock that people in the area called Camelback. The school itself was called Camelback Heights Private Academy, and it was amazing. There were several playgrounds on the campus full of amenities such as a miniature playhouse that had two different levels. There were seesaws and balance beams, monkey bars and even tetherball. This was the stuff recess was made for. I also seemed to be a perfect fit with my new classmates. My teacher was Ms. Porter, and she was one of the nicest people I knew. I quickly made some new friends, and class time became as exciting as recess and lunch. This was also the first time I did not have to bring a sack lunch or my lunch box to school. I got to eat food from the cafeteria. This was the coolest thing ever as I had always brought my lunch to school when I was in California.

Several months had quickly passed, and both school and home life were good. I was doing very well in school both academically and socially, and at home, nothing bad had happened, and the dark shadow creature had not been seen. We were coming up on the Christmas holiday, and that meant two weeks out of school, and I was ready for the break. While we were on vacation, I played a lot outside with the kids from the neighborhood. When I could not play outside, I did so inside, mostly with my sister Ann. Our favorite thing to do was go into the room that was being used for storage and climb up and around the boxes. We got yelled at for doing this all the time but it was way too much fun to let that stop us. My sister and I would move boxes and create mazes through which we had to follow one another in an attempt to catch each other. On occasion, we would be stepping on a box that would collapse in on itself, and this added to the fun as you could instantly find yourself stuck in a box or falling through multiple boxes that were stacked atop each other.

So there were two days before Christmas, and my sister and I were bored out of our minds. We could not go outside because it was raining, and the television was not working because the power had gone out in the neighborhood due to the windstorm we were having. The winds were fierce as one would know if he had ever lived in the Phoenix area. This day, the winds were clocking at 30 to 40 mph, and you could hear the continuous howl as they whipped around the house, banging against the windows and making anything that was not hunkered down seem like it was going to rip away from the Earth and be taken into the heavens.

With the weather like this, there was only one thing for my sister and I to do, and that was to head to the storage room and start stacking boxes and chasing one another. As we played, Ann and I continued to hear the wind pounding on the walls and the rain then smashing on top of the roof. What was great about this was we were able to be a little louder than usual without mom hearing us and stopping the fun. Around and around Ann and I went, jumping from box to box, crawling under others and leaping over smaller boxes. Ann stopped for a moment and asked me to stack several of the larger boxes to the ceiling. I had never stacked the boxes so high, but it seemed like a great idea at the time. I noticed the boxes were leaning sideways at the top as I did this, but being seven years old at the time, I did not think much more about it. It was at this time that Ann was chasing me, and in order to get away from her, I made a gutsy move. I jumped on the third box of that large stack I just created, and the boxes above it began to fall over. These boxes on top were heavy, and they were falling all the way down from the ceiling.

My sister being right behind me stopped dead under them as she, too, saw them falling and panicked. She now could only watch as multiple boxes were about to crush her. I could do nothing; these boxes were too big for me and full of heavy objects such as books, and I also happened to be too far away already to grab Ann or push her out of the way. I held my breath and watched as there was absolutely nothing I could do. I saw Ann's eyes get huge as she saw the top box about to hit her in the face. Some hardcover books even began to fall out of the top of the box and head down toward her. My sister was only two, and this was going to seriously hurt her and quite possibly kill her. Right as the first of many books and then boxes were going to pummel her, everything just stopped. When I mean stopped, I mean everything froze in place. Gravity no longer existed. Multiple books and huge boxes hung in the air.

Neither Ann nor I could believe it, and Ann just continued to look at the objects frozen in the air. She did not know what to do. This was her first time experiencing anything supernatural. Then I heard it. I heard that same voice – the same voice in my head that belonged to that shadow creature that had haunted me for so long.

"Grab her and take her now! Get her out."

With that, I grabbed Ann and pulled her toward me, and then we ran out of the room as all the boxes began to collapse. The initial boxes that fell caused a domino effect on the remaining ones. Before Ann and I knew it, anything stacked higher than three boxes up came crashing down on each other. We heard our mom yelling and cursing in her native language. For my mom to revert to her native language around my sister and I meant a good ass-whooping was imminent. But at that moment, neither Ann nor I cared. We were just happy to have gotten out of the room in one piece and also a bit confused by everything that took place.

Now, my mother was a larger woman from a foreign country. She spoke several languages other than English. Now I had her in my face screaming at me in several languages. Items in the boxes were obviously damaged, and some were most likely destroyed.

"What the hell have I told you two? What the hell were you both doing? Why the hell are you not answering me?"

This was my mom's response to us after what must have felt like an earthquake taking place. I attempted to tell her what we were doing and then what happened and how Ann was saved, but my mom did not believe me. She thought I was lying to avoid being punished or beaten or maybe even killed, seeing as how angry she was.

"Quit your lying and tell me the truth," she screamed.

Then my sister began to cry. With that, my mom looked at her and saw how terrified she looked, and this changed my mother's attitude immediately. She picked Ann up to comfort her. Ann then began to tell my mom exactly what I told her. My sister was so genuine and soft spoken with her story that my mom believed her and realized I was telling the truth and that what we told her did in fact happen and that this was the only reason Ann got out of that room without being seriously injured or killed. My mom began to cry, which in turn made my sister start crying again. For the next hour, my mom had us both explain everything that took place. She continued to ask me if I was positive that it was the same flying monster that told me to get Ann, and I continued to tell her that it was. This confused my mom and I as this creature wanted only to harm me. Why was it that the creature showed itself less and less as Ann came into our lives, and why had it not made its presence known to her except when it saved her life? This indeed was something that would truly bother me for a long time.

After this incident, the creature would come back only one more time while we lived in Arizona. With nothing else taking place after the box incident, time quickly passed, and with it, Christmas came and went and so did January. February was quickly upon us, and it ended up being a month I would never forget – not for the rest of my life.

I had been at school one morning doing the same routine that consisted of class, recess and then class again. Lunch came, and I ate and then went out to play. I remember that several of us were playing tag on the large playhouse in the middle of the main playground. Remember that this playhouse was two stories high. My friends and I had been chasing each other through the house, going up and down from floor to floor. I remember that my friend, Tiffany Reidman, was "it," and she was chasing me. I remember this part well because she kept telling me that if she caught me, she would kiss me and make me taste her bubble gum-flavored lip gloss. There was no way in hell I wanted that to happen. So I ran up to the second floor and what do you know, she cornered me, and I could not get to either the stairs or the slide pole that led to the first story. I was trapped, and she was ready to lay her lips on me.

So, being the seven-year-old boy I was, I walked out of the window and got on a long ledge that went around one side of the playhouse to another window. I began to walk along the narrow ledge to get away from Tiffany. While doing this, I failed to notice a rock on the ledge then slipped on it and fell off the playhouse. Down I went, and I did not land softly. As a matter of fact, someone had the amazing idea to leave a metal garbage can up against the playhouse, and I landed on the side of the trash can, half my body inside the can and the other half dangling out. This meant that the rim of the metal can caught me in the stomach region as I fell upon it. The can then fell onto its side and took me down with it. I could not breathe at all. I heard a loud-pitched noise in my ears that would not go away. It was an awful ringing sound. I could not breathe no matter how hard I tried, and I was panicking and did not know what to do. Suddenly, things started getting darker and darker until I lost consciousness.

I later awoke in the school office, on the ground and curled up. I had the worst stomach ache I had ever felt. The inside of my belly felt hot, almost as if something were burning inside me. I looked up, and the school coach was standing over me. Apparently, he was also a nurse or had been a nurse and was asking me questions. I tried to answer him but could barely get anything other than a gasp of air out of me.

"Patrick, we called your mom, and she is going to pick you up." He said. "You fell and got the wind knocked out of you, but you will be fine. You just need to rest at home the remainder of the day."

I thought to myself that the coach was a real idiot and I was only seven years old, soon to be eight. I had the wind knocked out of me before but it did not take this long to get it back, and it sure as hell did not hurt like this. "But who am I to know better than an adult, especially the coach?" I thought to myself. Well, for the next fifteen minutes, I laid on the floor, curled in a fetal position as any attempt of me to stretch my body in any other position led to the most agonizing pain I had ever felt. I just could not wait until my mom got to the school office so she could take me home to rest like the coach said. But I also thought, how was I going to get home if I could not move from this position? And with that thought, my father walked into the office, looked at me, looked at the coach and the principal, and began yelling with more anger than I have ever seen or heard from my father.

"Mr. Kilian, your son is going to be fine. He just fell and had the wind knocked out of him," The coach said to my dad. "I used to be a nurse, and I felt his stomach. He will be fine."

Then came my father's response, and it was not pretty. He was so fierce, so angry that he turned red, then purple as he yelled at the coach. He went on to tell Coach Crosby that he must have gotten his nursing license from a box of Cracker Jack and that any moron could see something was seriously wrong internally with me. He let the coach and principal know that there was no way in hell he was taking me anywhere else but the emergency room of the local hospital. With that, my father gathered me off the floor as I could only gasp in tremendous pain and he lifted me into his arms and took me to the car. My father cautiously placed me into the back and drove me to the hospital, which was less than five minutes away. I last remember looking out the window of the car, only to see the school gates go by. I then passed out.

Apparently, I had passed out for some time, because when I came to, I was already in the emergency room, and there were several doctors around me.

"Patrick, Patrick, can you hear me? I am Dr. Davenport. Your father brought you to the hospital, and we are taking you into the operating room."

This came from some man in a blue outfit as I slowly came to and felt the most excruciating pain in my stomach area. I was apparently on some type of mobile bed and being pushed into the operating room. I located my father off to the side of one of the doctors, and I guess he noticed that I finally became aware of his being there. My dad let me know that I was going to be fine but that I needed to have emergency surgery. He told me to listen to the doctors and follow their instructions.

"I love you, son."

That is one of the few times I ever remember my father telling me he loved me. I knew he did, it was just that he rarely expressed this in a verbal manner. With that being said, I was taken into a large room full of devices, some making sounds and others whirling with different types of lights. I was pushed into the middle of the room and under several large lights that made it hard to see anything else as they were quite blinding. At this point, I realized there was something stuck in the top of my hand, and it was connected to some type of clear tube. This device hurt a bit, but I guess I had overlooked the pain because of the other godawful pain coming from my stomach area.

"Patrick, I am Dr. Whitman. I am an anesthesiologist," I heard someone tell me. "You have an IV hooked into your hand, and this helps me and the other doctors administer medicine and other fluids into your body so that we can help you. There is nothing to be afraid of."

I remember thinking that I had no clue what he was talking about, but I nodded as if I did.

The same doctor continued to speak: "You are going to have surgery, and we are going to make you feel better. In order for us to do that, I am going to put some medicine into your IV that is going to put you to sleep. We can then start this procedure."

I nodded again and then watched as the doctor used what looked to be a needle to inject some type of liquid into the clear tube that was leading to the needle that then went into the back of my hand. He then told me to begin counting backward from ten, and by the time I was done, I would be asleep. I started counting, and by eight, I was out.

What had happened was when I fell off of the playhouse, the impact upon the metal garbage can caused massive trauma to my spleen. Back in 1980, not too much was known about the spleen, and to this day, it is still not fully understood what its full functions are. It does, however, play a part in the body's immune system and has an active part in assisting the white blood cells. But enough about the spleen's role. What is needed to be known is that it began filling with blood, and by the time I was seen by doctors at the emergency room, it was about ready to rupture. If the spleen ruptured, there was a good chance I would die, and that was the reason for the emergency surgery.

As I was in the surgery room and having my spleen removed, something happened. I am not sure if it was a dream or some type of flashback, and if it was a flashback, how and to what? I remember no longer being Patrick Kilian. I was somebody else, someone older, and I was definitely in a different time period. I remember things were so different around me. People were dressed differently; I was dressed differently; and buildings and the surroundings were completely different. The clothing everyone was wearing was almost from what seemed to be from a science fiction movie. The buildings were made of massive rectangular stones, far larger than anything I had ever seen in 1980. People were speaking to me in a different language, yet I understood them.

I remember them telling me that the time had come, and we have to hurry, but I could not figure out what was coming and what exactly they wanted me to acknowledge. Then I spotted her, to the left of several men who were speaking to me all at once. I saw her and realized she was everything in my world. She was blonde, blue-eyed and in her mid-forties. She yelled out to me and told me that I had to find her and we both had to remember for the sake of everyone and everything. She also addressed me as Adama, and this caused me to wonder if she had me confused with someone else.

The next thing I knew, I had someone standing over me and saying, "Patrick, you have to wake up. Your surgery is over and you are in recovery. Can you hear me, Patrick? I am Nurse Smith, and you need to wake up."

The dream had been interrupted, and I was regaining consciousness. What I had just experienced did not feel like a dream. It felt like a past memory or even as if I had traveled into a past that was somehow my own yet could not be as I was only a child who had just suffered a terrible accident. I quickly put the matter aside as all I could think about was the excruciating pain in my stomach area. It felt as if someone had just kicked me as hard as they could in the gut. I began to open my eyes in the recovery room and was in terrible pain. I was groggy and felt nauseated, too. The stomach pain was different now than before my surgery. Before, all the hurting was on the inside, but now it was on both the inside and outside of my body. While I continued to have all this discomfort, the nurse continued to stand over me and agitate the hell out of me. She was forcing me to wake up when all I wanted to do was go back to sleep and hope that when I awoke, all this would be a bad dream that could be quickly forgotten. That definitely was not the case, and eventually, I came to my senses and was awake.

The surgery had gone well and my spleen was removed. My surgeon later told me he had to place four staples inside of my body and that these would always be there. I also had five staples on the front of my stomach to close the incision that was made to remove my spleen. It ran from approximately five inches above my naval and ended to the right of the naval. These temporary staples would have to be removed, once the incision had time to heal. The doctor continued to explain that I would also have to spend between five and seven days in the children's ward to recuperate and get physical therapy. I was also told that by the time they took the spleen out, it had enlarged to the size of a grapefruit and that if my father had not immediately brought me to the emergency room, I would no longer be on this planet. Thank God for my dad. This was the second time he saved my life.

I ended up being at the hospital for seven days. It was difficult to walk and took some time before I could do so comfortably and without the assistance of my IV pole on wheels that doubled for several days as a crutch. I also had a lot of antibiotics over the course of those seven days and was told that I would most likely need medication throughout life, especially if I caught certain types of viruses or bacterial infections and could not get rid of them on my own due to my compromised immune system. They were right: this would become a constant thorn in my side through most of my life.

I was on day seven in the hospital and was going to be released the next morning, and I could not wait. I was sick of being stuck in a bed all day and tired of the food. I went to bed early that last night hoping that if I did so, the morning would come quickly. There was a clock in the room that I watched when I was awake, which was often, and I remember it being 2 a.m. when I looked up to the ceiling and realized the dark shadow creature was staring down at me. I quit breathing and froze in place. I had not seen the flying apparition for a very long time and had almost begun to believe that it was just an old nightmare. But here it was, hovering just feet above me, staring down with that face that was always veiled in darkness. It flew through my hospital room, back and forth, from one side to the other, and then effortlessly darted under the bed. I was frozen with fear and dismay that his was happening again and at a time when I was still in great pain and had a lot of trouble being ambulatory. It then shot up from under the bed and hovered just inches above me, staring at me with its face veiled in darkness, almost faceless yet making me feel as if it was staring right through me, piercing my body with its eyes that were so hard to make out, even being just inches away.

It began to move what looked to be its mouth, and I could hear it speaking to me but as if it was putting its thoughts directly into my head.

"I have been with you since you stole from me the most important thing in this world. You will know in time that you are not who you seem to be, and I want back what is mine."

The creature reached out and pinned my arms back against the bed and inched even closer to me as it hung in the air above my body.

"I don't care what you are, and know that you are not me!"

With that, it let me go, looked toward the ceiling, and faster than a bullet, it shot through the ceiling. It was gone, but I was still horrified from the encounter and still could not move, fearful it would return as quickly as it had left.

The creature did not return that night, and that was the last I would see of it for a long time. After several minutes, I began to move again and was no longer frozen in fear from the encounter. I began to think about what the creature had somehow communicated to me but could not understand the meaning behind it all, and with that, I stayed up all night, thinking about the encounter. I made no mention of the creature's visit that night to anyone. My final night at the hospital finally came to an end, and I left the hospital and got to go home.

I returned to school after being out for several weeks. Things did not feel the same. Something had awoken inside of me, and I dwelled a lot on the dream or vision I had while being operated on and the most recent encounter with the Evil Pan. I thought about all that took place and could come to no solid conclusion, just greater confusion as to what it all meant.

Before I knew it, I also turned eight. The biggest thing with that was being baptized in the church where my parents, sister and I were members. It was a big deal to my parents and all the other people at church, but to me, it never seemed that important. I just played the part as if it was a big deal and told all the grown-ups what they wanted to hear. For me, my friends at school, the pain in my stomach and the dream and encounter with the flying creature were what took up most of my time and thoughts.

Time now passed quickly, and before I knew it, second grade and half of third grade came and went. Then in the middle of my third grade school year, I was told by my mom and dad that we were moving to Colorado as dad had acquired a better job and we would be moving to a place called Littleton. I was sad to go as nothing bad had ever happened at our house, and I knew I would miss my friends at school, especially Tiffany. But that did not matter to my parents.

# 6.

# A Trip to the Basement

One thing I distinctly remember that was different between where we had lived in Arizona and where we moved were the surroundings. I was not a fan of the desert. I did not like how dirty things always were in Arizona, with the debris and sand blowing everywhere, and the summer heat in the Phoenix Valley verged on unbearable. But in Littleton, it was amazing. Everywhere you looked was green and beautiful, and the temperature was also a million times better. You could go outside and not feel like you were about to melt into the concrete or catch fire and burn up into ashes.

The house we were renting in Littleton was four stories when you included the basement. I never had a basement before as this was something very rare in California and Arizona. The home was amazing, except for the fact that I totally feared the basement as it was far away from where my family and I usually hung out and watched television and definitely far from where we all slept. Just so long I stayed away from that dark and desolate part of the house, I felt I would be just fine and have little to no issues. The school where I resumed third grade was also nice. Most of the kids I met were pretty cool, and having to take a school bus back and forth allowed me to get to know some of the ones who lived in my new neighborhood and become good friends with several of them.

This period spent in Colorado held a few important details and events in my life that need to be mentioned. The first of these happened almost toward the end of January in 1981. It was a weekday, and we had already finished dinner, and my sister was asleep in her room next to mine, and my bedtime was fast approaching. My father was showering and my mother was occupied in the restroom. I was sitting on my parents' bed watching television when the power went out. My dad started yelling at my mom to go down to the basement and flip the switch in the breaker box. My mom yelled back that she could not, and then guess what? I heard my father yelling at me to do it. This took me by surprise, and I felt my heart beating fast in my chest and the side of my neck pulsating with the same beat. Was he kidding me? There was no way on God's green Earth that I was heading down two flights of stairs, through two separate levels of the house, passing through a basement door, going down basement steps and into the black abyss at the bottom of our house.

With that thought in my mind, I quickly blurted, "No way will I go down to the basement alone. That is way too scary."

That statement incurred his wrath, and he began yelling at me that I would indeed be the one going down to the basement to click the main breaker back on so that power could be returned to the house and he could finish his shower. Remember, also, that the entire conversation was now taking place in complete darkness as it was approximately 8:30 p.m. in January.

My dad continued to yell at me to get the flashlight next to his dresser, which was on his side of the bed, and to hurry my ass up and get down there. Even my mom started in on me as she, too, was now sitting in the toilet room in the dark. With my heart beating furiously, I searched in the dark for the flashlight and located it behind my father's nightstand. I had to get down on my hands and knees, crawl under the back corner of the bed and extend my arm as far as it could go to reach the light. I got hold of it, turned it on and was able to see the parts of my parents' room where I directed the beam of light. I got up and then pointed the light toward the room's entry. I yelled to my parents that I had found the flashlight and was getting ready to go downstairs.

"I am scared," I yelled one more time to my parents.

"I don't give a crap what you are, go flip the breaker in the basement now!" was my dad's response.

With that, I headed out their door, turned left and headed down the first flight of stairs.

I moved slowly down the 12 steps. I knew there were twelve because I always counted them as I went up and down. As I slowly descended, I thought I saw all types of things moving below on the next level of the house. I told myself this was all my imagination and that I had to continue on because I had no other choice. I was sure that if I ran back upstairs and refused to do what my dad said that I would receive the ass-whooping of a lifetime once he got out of the shower and got the lights back on himself. So I proceeded down until I reached step number twelve. There I was, standing on the mid-level of the house – what was now seeming to be a mile or two away from my parents' room and the protection of my mom and dad. I turned right and saw the next set of steps. There were six more on this flight before reaching the main floor where the family room, kitchen and doors to the garage and basement were located. I took step one and heard it groan as I put my weight onto it. This scared the hell out of me, and I now thought my heart was going to rip out of the side of my throat, where I could also feel what seemed to be my heartbeat as blood was moving through the side of my neck. Then came step two, step three, step four, five and six. I had reached the main level of the house and was standing off to the side of the kitchen. I shined the light down what looked to be an endless hallway and saw the fireplace at the far end of the wall in the family room and a bit of the bar off to the right. I would have to walk down this hall and still turn right just before the bar. Then a sudden right turn would have me smack dab in front of the basement door.

I started slowly down the hall. I continued to try light switches in the hopes that it would immediately ignite the lighting in the area of the main level and hallway. Nothing happened when I flipped a switch. The main breaker really must have popped, and I knew now I really was going to have to do this on my own and go down into the basement, all the way down, and get to the breaker box and flip the switch. I continued one step at a time until I finally reached the other end of the hall and was in the family room. I never liked being down this far by myself, even with all the lights on in the house, and now there I was with just the light of a small flashlight. I turned to my right and shined the light everywhere – behind the bar, toward the guest bathroom and the door that led to the garage – to make sure nothing was down there waiting for me. I was good to go, and I did not see anything, so I rotated my body 90 degrees until I was standing in front of that white door that led down to the basement from hell.

With one large breathe and sigh, I put my right hand on the door knob, turned it and pulled the door back toward me. It squeaked so loudly that I nearly urinated in my pants. I then put one foot inward and down onto the first step that led to the bottom of the basement. I never liked coming down to the basement and had been inside it only three times before, so I had no clue how many steps there were until I would reach the bottom. I took the next step down, and I had to let go of the basement door. Slowly I let the door settle without fully closing, just in case I had to make a quick getaway from whatever lurked below. I was in the basement, and now I had to press forward with the most horrifying part of this ordeal: the descent into the darkest basement on this planet and then a search for a breaker box that I think I knew was behind the furnace. I had both feet on the second step leading into the basement and then took the third step, then the forth and next the fifth. I paused and began frantically shining the flashlight in every direction I could. I suddenly heard a popping sound and what sounded to be something being dragged along the concrete floor of the basement.

In my mind, I had to tell myself to stop this thinking and that I could do this. I was eight years old, almost nine, and had been through far worse when I lived in California. I calmed myself down and continued down steps six, seven, eight and the final step. Nine steps, I thought to myself; I would have to remember that for future purposes. I shined the light to the right and saw that in the far back corner where the furnace was and off to its side was what looked to be the breaker box. I shined the light all around and then to my left and also noticed that there were a large number of boxes all over the place that I would have to weave through as I made my final approach. As I slowly started walking in the direction of the furnace, I could hear all types of sounds coming from it. It hissed and popped and clicked. This only added to my fear, and I started thinking that demons or creatures were hiding behind the boxes, waiting for me to get close before they could reach out and grab me and take me from this Earth and pull me down to the greatest depths of hell, where I would be tortured and burned alive.

"Oh my God," I thought, "I have to quit having these thoughts and press forward."

I inched closer and closer to the furnace and continued to flash the light all over the area in order to see if anything was about to spring toward me. Closer and closer I got until I was only several feet from the furnace, and with that, I broke into a run and reached the furnace and the breaker box. I quickly put my back up against the cement wall and looked all around the rest of the basement, shining the flashlight in every direction. There was nothing. I turned around, opened the breaker box door, located the main breaker and realized it had tripped. I pushed it back up into the on position as my father had once shown me in the old house in Arizona and then quickly shut the box and turned around. Suddenly I realized I was still in darkness as I had forgotten to flip the light switch at the top of the stairs when I first walked in. I felt sick to my stomach as I realized I would have to do this all again backwards.

I began walking toward the stairs of the basement and felt myself starting to move faster and faster. Before I knew it, I cleared almost all the boxes and was just a couple of feet from the stairs when my flashlight started fading. The light started flickering, and I began to run, and suddenly, darkness fell. The flashlight went out, and I was standing in the pitch black void of the basement, not sure where the steps were, not sure where the last box or two was located. Then, I heard boxes moving and the tops opening, and I felt a rush of wind blowing through the basement as if windows on all ends were instantly opened. I began to cry and frantically put my hands in front of me in an attempt to locate the wall that would hopefully guide me to the steps going up. Nothing! I felt nothing in front of me, and then I heard it, I heard a laugh followed by what could only be classified as a snarl.

I seemed to see shadows or figures moving in the dark. Before I could think about anything else, something grabbed me around my neck and began to squeeze. I was lifted off my feet and then thrown head first into one of the large boxes. Then as I tried to turn myself in the box and move from being face down to at least face up, the box was closed on me, and I could hear it being taped up. I started screaming as if my life depended on it. I started pushing on the sides and then trying to push my fingers through them. As I was doing this, I heard laughter and screams outside of the box. Then it was knocked onto its side. I could then feel the box lift off the ground and get thrown as if someone picked it up from both ends and heaved it back and forth, letting go as it was in a forward motion in order to allow more velocity. The box crashed against a wall and fell against the cement floor. It tore open, and I kicked it open further to escape. As I began crawling out, something grabbed and yanked me out. I felt like I was in the grips of something, but I was not sure what it was.

As I became more adjusted to the light, I saw that I was being held up in the air as this man or what looked to be a man was looking right into my face. But this was no man; this was something that looked like an apparition, a body that I could clearly see through. It pulled me closer, and I could see this awful grin on its face. Then it attempted to speak to me, but I could hear nothing it said. This angered the apparition, and I found myself being shaken in a ferocious manner. My neck and head began to hurt as the apparition continued to shake me harder and harder. When I felt like I was about to lose consciousness, the basement lit up with this massive intense red light that had to be from a tremendous explosion. I felt an intense heat and then wind from this explosion. I felt it all around me, and I closed my eyes as it hurt to have them open. Then there was nothing. Nothing was around me – no creatures, no red lights, no explosions. I gathered my thoughts and noticed the flashlight on the ground had come back to life. I ran to the light, picked it up, located the steps and ran out of the basement.

I continued running through the family room, then the hallway and up both flights of stairs. I ran into my parents' room and jumped into their bed. I was sweating and crying and looked around only to find that little time had passed, and my dad was still in the shower and my mom still in the bathroom. I began to cry loudly, and both my parents heard me. They came out as quickly as possible to check on me. As I explained what happened in the basement, they both looked at me and then each other with fear and helplessness in their eyes, and their expressions also seemed to show frustration. They calmed me down and got me to stop crying. Then my mom got Ann from her room, and all four of us slept in their bedroom that night. The following day, my mom and dad went into the basement together only to find nothing disturbed: no boxes damaged and no hint of an explosion or wind of any type had traveled through the basement. Nothing at all could be found to back up what happened to me and what I told them happened to me. This only made me question myself as to what I thought happened and if anything at all in fact took place. Maybe I was imagining it all; maybe something was wrong with me, I thought. Maybe I needed help.

I thought to myself that maybe I was seeing things that really did not exist except in my head. But how could this be? It seemed so real, and I felt physical pain when the apparition or whatever it was grabbed me around my neck and also when I was tossed into the box and throughout the basement. I was still hurting this morning all over my neck, shoulders and back, and I imagined my pain was equal to having been in a pretty significant car accident. Needless to say, after the things my parents saw in the old house in California, they did not completely discount what I had told them, and they made sure the basement was off limits to me. My parents also asked for additional clarity as to the thing that attacked me as they wanted to know if it was the same flying figure from before. I told them it was not the same creature and that the thing that was choking me was completely different. This thing looked like a full-sized adult, and I was easily able to make out its face.

I explained to my parents that the ghost creature or whatever it was spoke to me, but I could not hear anything it was saying. One other odd fact I recalled was that as I stared back into the thing's face, I almost felt like I recognized who it was or what it had been at some point in time but was not clear as to how this could be or who it could be. Then there was the bright flash of light and the burning heat that came with it. It felt for one split second that my skin was going to be burned off my body, but that instantly it stopped, and there was nothing but me, the boxes and the flashlight that had turned back on.

"What is happening to me? Why is this happening to me?" I asked my mom.

"I don't know, honey. I don't know why this is happening to you or what exactly it is or what it all means."

I just wished it all would have stopped and everything would be normal like it was for so many other kids around me. But my life would never be normal and would never be free of crap like this.

March of 1981 had arrived, and I turned nine. This birthday was particularly exciting as I got a lot of very good gifts from my parents. I would later find out that the reason for such lavish gifts was that my parents had sued my old school in Arizona and that they had just received the settlement check from the attorney who was representing us. I loved the gifts and had just an amazing birthday, which really helped me stop thinking about everything that took place several weeks back and the fears I had of still being in the same house where the assault had taken place. It felt good to just be able to feel like a normal kid for a while and forget for a bit the strange things that had taken place in my young life of nine years.

April came and went, and so did most of May. School was almost out, and I remember that I could not wait for summer vacation to begin. There were four days left before the third grade was done, and I could call myself a fourth-grader. To help me celebrate this time of the year finally coming, I decided to get dressed up and wear a brand-new pair of golden brown cowboy boots that I got for my birthday. I had never owned a pair of boots before, and I was so excited when my parents had taken me to the mall in Littleton to pick them out on my birthday. I had not yet worn the boots out of the house and decided that today would be the perfect day to show them off. I remember walking off the bus, into the school and into my classroom with nothing else on my mind but wanting to show off the boots. I had been a huge fan of cowboy shows and movies, and when I wore the boots, it made me feel like I was one of those bigger-than-life movie stars, walking through the double saloon doors that you always see in the movies, and then everyone stops what they are doing and watches as the actor playing the cowboy enters.

Well, this was my day for getting to be the cowboy who walks through those saloon doors and everyone would stop and watch as I did it. But to my dismay, I got nothing, not even an acknowledgment from Mrs. Sampson, my third-grade teacher. I did not let that small hiccup in my expectations bother me and continued on with the day, constantly stopping to look down and admire my boots. It had not been more than fifteen minutes into class starting when Mrs. Sampson told us we would be doing speed drill math problems on the board. She asked for volunteers, and I immediately was the first to raise my hand. I figured that everyone would have to notice my new boots as I walked to the front of the class and up to the chalkboard and then stood as I worked out the math problem. Mrs. Sampson saw my hand go up and called my name.

"Patrick and Shauna, come to the board and work out the problem I give you," she exclaimed.

I knew this was my chance, and I practically jumped out of my seat and headed to the chalkboard. As I walked, I must have still been getting accustomed to the boots and how different they were from the tennis shoes I was used to wearing, because I suddenly realized one of my legs coming out from under me and then the other. Before I knew it, I had slipped and fell backward. I felt this tremendous pain as the back of my head struck the hard floor of the classroom. The next thing I knew, I was looking at the ceiling and could hear the tremendous roar of laughter from my classmates. I felt very lightheaded as I lifted my head off the floor and then that was it – lights out!

I now found myself outside in the countryside of some place I believe I was familiar with but could not recall how. I noticed that the sky was a deep shade of red. I saw electrical discharges traveling everywhere throughout it. I also realized that it felt like my skin was on fire. It was so hot that I felt my skin bubbling. I saw the ground lifting and huge amounts of new rock and dirt deposits coming up. Mountains were forming before my very eyes. I looked farther outward toward the horizon and could see a massive wall of water traveling toward me. The water went on forever. I looked around me and noticed others were staring at it and glued in amazement. I looked down at myself and realized I was not me anymore. I now was a fully-grown adult, and my skin was darker than my normal color. I shouted to a group of people to my left but I could not hear my voice.

"Adama, Adama, naum talac sheiklac," came from behind me.

I turned to see an adult female not too far off in the distance yelling and gesturing with her hand to come to her. I looked closer, and she was standing at the mouth of a cave.

Again, she yelled out, "Adama naum talac, talac!"

I do not remember ever seeing this woman before, yet I somehow felt as if I had known her for a long time and that she was familiar to me. Because of this, I began to run toward her. In the distance behind me, I could hear screams and shouting and the crashing of huge amounts of water against the local landscape. As I ran, I noticed a young girl and boy in front of me. I grabbed each of them and placed them over my shoulders as I continued to run toward the woman and the cave.

The children were screaming and crying, and one called out, "Talac Adama, talac."

I ran faster and harder, and all the while, I watched as the sky became a darker tint of red and massive arcs of electricity were coming down from the heavens and striking the land everywhere. Just as I was a few feet from the woman, I noticed her face and how familiar she looked.

Suddenly, I heard someone over me say, "Patrick, Patrick, can you hear me?"

I opened my eyes and was blinded by someone pointing a flashlight into them. It was some man dressed in a doctor's white coat.

"Patrick, I am Dr. Guiron, and you are in the emergency room at Littleton Hospital."

The doctor had now removed the flashlight, and I began to open my eyes more and more. As I did so, the back of my head felt as if someone had hit me with a baseball bat. I tried to get up, and the doctor pushed me back down gently and told me to remain lying down and resting. The attempted sudden movement of my body to the upright position brought about this awful feeling of nausea. I thought I was about to vomit and began to yawn in an attempt to keep from throwing up all over myself and those around me. I laid back down and slowly moved my head from left to right. As I did so, I noticed a nurse to my left and my parents on my right.

"You suffered a major concussion from falling and have a large bump on the back of your head from where you came into contact with the floor," the doctor stated.

What had happened was I slipped while walking in my boots and hit my head hard in the classroom. The paramedics and firemen were called, and I was taken to the hospital by ambulance. I had apparently been unconscious for approximately twenty-five minutes. My parents were called, and they both showed up soon after. I would later go and get a CAT scan and find out that I had minor swelling under the base of my skull that was putting pressure on a small portion of the parietal and occipital lobes of my brain. Due to the pressure, the doctor had me stay for several days in the hospital. So I was admitted and spent my last three days of the third grade in the children's ward of Littleton Hospital.

On that initial night in the hospital, my parents' had to leave at 9 p.m. as that was when visiting hours ended. After they left, I continued to play out in my head what took place that day. I was initially so excited to be at school, wearing my new boots and wanting to show them off. Then I was on the ground, staring up at the ceiling in the classroom with this huge thumping pain at the back of my head. The next thing I knew I was not me but some completely different grown-up, trying to get to a cave with two children tossed over my shoulders during what seemed to be the end of the world.

That portion of the day was what I was laser focused on. What had I dreamed, or what reality had I entered? It did not seem like a dream or hallucination because of the head injury. It seemed all too real, almost as if I were living the moment or had lived through the ordeal in the past, only to suddenly return there once more. It just felt too real to have been my imagination. I mean, I felt my skin on fire from the tremendous heat all around me and could feel the electricity passing through the air. I could also feel myself having to gain my balance over and over again as the ground continued to shift and new rock and land formations came bursting up through the ground. Something happened to me and I was not at all sure exactly what. I just did not know what to do about it or if I should even talk about it to anyone, even my parents. Something else also started happening to me after this experience. I began hearing voices – not all the time, just on occasion, and many of them were in a language other than English. There would be days when this would really upset me as I heard the talking clear as day and could not understand what the hell it meant.

After the third day in the hospital, the doctors felt that the swelling inside my head had subsided enough to not be a huge concern and that I looked to not have suffered permanent brain damage from it. Another CAT scan was done, and the results came back negative. I was released on that third day and went home. When we got home, I received some additional news from my parents. I was told that dad had gotten another job in another state and that we were moving yet again. This time, I was not so sad to leave as I hated the house we were in and feared being anywhere in it alone. It would be good to go elsewhere and be given yet another shot at a normal life, hopefully this time free of any demons, ghosts, flying monsters or end-of-the-world encounters. So, three weeks later, we packed and were headed to Odessa, Texas.

# 7.

# Texas Here I Come

I remember the drive from Littleton being excruciatingly long, and the entire time my sister and I were fighting in the back of the car, every now and then getting a death threat or two from my mom or dad that if we did not shut up and cut it out, they would pull over and leave us on the side of the road so we could be eaten by the wildlife that was apparently abundant where we were to be kicked out. My sister and I apparently were behaved enough after the threats as both of us made it to Odessa. When we drove into the city limits, I could not help but notice what a tragic place Odessa seemed to be. Maybe it would have been better being let out on the side of the road somewhere in Colorado, where there was scenery and greenery, not pump jacks, oil derricks and the smell of natural gas everywhere you went.

It was still summer when we relocated, so this meant I had the ability to ease into the move without being thrust into a new school yet once again. It allowed me to make friends in the neighborhood and at church prior to school starting. This helped me feel more comfortable with the move as I would already have friends who went to my new school prior to the first day. As it turned out, there were some great kids in the neighborhood, like Tommy and Bubba

Hicks and, each day left in the summer was spent playing outside or at a neighbor's home. The new house was also spacious, with an open floor plan and no basement. I felt safe and did not mind roaming through it at night on my own. It is worth mentioning that the entire time we lived in that house, not a single supernatural or other threatening incident by unknown forces occurred. I did not once get punched, thrown, strangled or beaten by something that was not supposed to be in our plane of existence. But this did not include some very strange dreams I would have.

One of these dreams took place just before I was about to start the fourth grade at the local elementary school. I went to sleep one night, only to wake up a few minutes later, except I really did not wake up but was instead dreaming that I had done so. As I rolled out of what I thought was my bed, I was actually getting up off of what was some type of animal skin, and there was that same woman as in a prior dream, lying next to me. This was the woman that was frantically gesturing for me to run to her at the mouth of the cave before I was overtaken by what could only be described as the end of times in some unfamiliar period and location. I almost felt as if I were dreaming from right where I had left off when I slipped and struck my head in Colorado. Up until that night, I had no other dreams about this and had only pondered what it all meant on occasion up until now.

So again, there I was in some unknown strange place. This time, it was what looked to be underground in what may have started out as a cave but was slowly being transformed into a complex or city. I looked at my hands and legs and again noticed I was no longer a nine-year-old boy but instead an adult male. I was very big and tall, and by this I mean at least seven-foot-plus with a large build. I got up and looked at the woman who had been lying next to me. I was not sure who she was but I had this feeling that she was very important to me and quite possibly my wife. This triggered a weird feeling that I was not in a dream but more of a memory. How, though, could a nine-year-old boy have a memory such as this floating around inside his head?

I then stood up and looked around. I concluded that we were in a small section of what could only be described as an underground city in progress. I had no idea what time of day it was as there was no sun, moon and sky to gauge this. There was, however, artificial lighting everywhere, and I do not mean candles or torches but some type of devices I was not familiar with. They glowed and provided immense light but were not battery-powered, and I could see no electrical wiring anywhere in the dwelling. I started walking and realized it must be early morning as the people in the structure were up and awake for only a short while or just now getting up as I had done. I moved toward what had to be the front opening of the structure and saw a massive circular rock or rock-type device blocking the entrance – or in my case, the exit. I approached what I concluded had to be a rolling door and started to feel what it was made of and tried to get a sense of how massive this stone wheel door was. I also realized just how big I was as I could now make a comparison of my height and size directly to another large object. What was this, and who the hell was I? More importantly, where the hell was I? Not just geographically, but now I also wondered what period of time was it?

I began pushing on the large door, and as I did so, another large man, almost my size, approached me from behind and began speaking to me in some unknown language. The only thing I understood was the word, "Adama." I know I have heard this word on multiple other occasions in my life when something strange was taking place or during another dream I had or during a dream state I had been in. As the man continued to speak, I believe I started to understand him. I had no idea how, but he was telling me I could not remove the stone door and go outside as the surface of the planet outside was still too dangerous and would be for many years to come. I wanted to ask the man what he meant but did not know how. Then I heard a loud crash and woke up. I now realized I was back in my room in our new house in Odessa.

I jumped out of the bed and ran to my window. A car coming around the corner of our street had just crashed into our neighbor's car. The person driving the car was attempting to take off from the wreck, and there were neighbors outside trying to stop him from doing so. Eventually, they got the man out of the car and had called the police as officers soon came to the accident scene. This accident outside my window late at night had scared the crap out of me but more importantly, interrupted the dream I was having – or maybe it was more than just a dream. I guess I would not know that night. The Odessa police ended up later taking the man who had caused the accident into custody for driving while intoxicated. The guy's vehicle was towed, along with the neighbor's damaged vehicle, and everything happening outside eventually settled down. The only thing then left for me to do was ponder the dream I had.

I woke up the next day and again thought about the experience. I decided I would consider this more of an experience than a dream, and I would start keeping a diary of the things that took place in my life, especially the strange, peculiar and supernatural occurrences. Time went on in Odessa, and life went on in a normal fashion. Before I knew it, fourth grade came and went. In the petroleum-rich Permian Basin we lived in, summer arrived, and I welcomed the time off from school. I spent most of my days playing with friends both from the neighborhood and church. We also did a lot of traveling that summer to other cities in the area as my mother had some type of high calling in the Mormon stake we were in. She was some type of Relief Society bigwig, and that meant she had to visit each of the wards that made up the stake.

Since this was a remote area in West Texas, the geographical portion of the stake was large, and travel was sometimes two or three hours in one direction. I remember liking it a lot as it got us out of the nasty-smelling Odessa area. One thing that always loomed in the air in Odessa was the odor of natural gas and petroleum being pumped or processed somewhere nearby. I remember this made many parts of the city smell like rotten eggs, and I hated that smell. So when we got to go to really nice places that were away from Odessa, I was ready and willing. I wanted to mention the travelling that summer because of one incident during the course of a trip on a Sunday morning to Alpine, Texas.

Alpine was this amazing small town surrounded by beautiful mountains. The area had both desert and a green plains area, and I always thought this was so different than most places I had ever been to. Well, we had been driving for some time and were very close to reaching our destination. We had just transitioned from the 385 highway to the 90 when I was looking out the car window, closed my eyes for what could not have been more than a few seconds and opened them again, only to see a bright flash of light go across the entire area. Instantly, everything in the sky turned brownish-red, and lightning lit up the sky and was striking the ground in almost every place you looked. I felt this massive static electricity building up in the air around me and then searing heat. I looked around and noticed I was not in the car anymore but standing outside in the exact area we had been driving through. I knew I was about to lose consciousness from how hot it was when I blinked, and everything I was looking at and experiencing was gone, and I was once again in the car with my family headed to Alpine.

Had I experienced a daydream or another episode of recalling some forgotten memory? Something about this area triggered a memory of a time when this location was having some type of cataclysmic event, and I was experiencing it firsthand. It was not a dream because it felt too real, and it hurt to the point where my skin, especially on my face, was still in pain from such intense temperatures. I did not say anything to my parents in the car and made no mention of this experience to anyone. I again had become so accustomed to the unexplained taking place around me that I just continued to analyze the experience in my head and made sure I logged it in my journal, especially the fact that there was a specific location involved where the cataclysm took place and I was there, just apparently in the wrong time period. I also had one other thought on the matter. Was this cataclysm in the past, future, or was it just the active imagination of a young boy?

The summer of 1982 passed, and I was now a fifth-grader. Nothing happened that entire year that was out of the ordinary, and life was good. My biggest concern of my fifth-grade year was winning marble contests at school and making sure I had some good cat's eye and boulder marbles that looked radical and awesome. I had really enjoyed the school I attended in Odessa and had not once had any type of panic attack or episode of fainting as I had been known to do when things at a school did not fit well with my construct of how school should be. I felt like I was growing up and that things in the past should stay there. I pondered the dark shadow monster that would menace me when I was a young child and the other creature that tried inflicting harm on me in the basement of our Colorado home. I decided that those things were in the past, and it looked like

I would not be bothered by them or things like them in my future.

Of course, I now had these weird dreams or memories to deal with, but at least they did not try to strangle me and toss me into a moving box or trip me and cause metal objects to get lodged into the back of my head. Whatever seemed to make that type of experience end in my life was just fine with me, and I now wanted to just move on and try to forget they ever happened. With that all being told, the fifth grade flew by, and we were once again at the best time of the year for kids of any age, and that was the summer.

I had been on summer break for two weeks when one day I heard my mother and father speaking in their room. Apparently, my father had gone to El Paso to interview for the position of President of a mid-sized bank in downtown El Paso. This was the opportunity of a lifetime that he and my mother had been waiting for. So yes, we were again going to move. This time, the move would take us to El Paso, which was less than five hours away. I remember feeling both happy and sad when I overheard this news. I would truly miss the school I was attending and all my friends in Odessa, but I would not miss this city that smelled so weird all the time and had nothing but oil rigs and pump jacks everywhere you looked.

# 8.

# Living in El Paso

El Paso was an interesting city because it looked so much larger than it really was. It had a sister city just over the U.S.-Mexico border. With Juarez just on the other side of a very shallow river called the Rio Grande, the city of approximately 450,000 people in 1983 looked more like 1.5 million people. The area also had an extremely different desert than the one I was used to seeing in Arizona. The desert area of El Paso was bare compared to Phoenix, with less types of cactus and darker dirt as far as the eye could see surrounding the city. But I remember as we drove into the outskirts of the city the amazingly beautiful desert mountains that seemed to box in Juarez to the left and El Paso straight ahead and to the right as one entered from westbound on Interstate 10. As we began to get farther into El Paso, I also noticed that a lot of signage was in two languages: English and Spanish. I remember thinking that this was such an awesome thing to see as I had often wished my mother had taught me the other language she spoke so that I could have been bi-lingual.

Ten minutes later, my father pulled into the driveway of one of the largest homes I had ever seen in my eleven years of life. We had arrived at our new home. I looked at the house closely, and it seemed to sit on two different lots, side-by-side. The house was massive, and all I could think of was how I was going to be by myself much of the time as the Spanish-style villa was too big for a family of four to always be in contact with each other.

As I progressed through the sixth grade, I remember always thinking just how awesome things had become and that not too long ago, I was plagued with strange dreams, sinister nightmares and supernatural events that grew real and physical. I had made it all the way to October with nothing out of the ordinary happening at home, school or any other place. I studied and worked hard in class, tried to hit on the girls as best as an eleven-year-old could, went to church as I was supposed to every Sunday, was in the Webelos with the Boy Scouts through a church program and practiced my drumming for band at least one hour per night. I even took up basketball and joined a local league. What ended up happening is I got relaxed and let my guard down, and that is when things began to happen again.

My father and mother had been invited to an evening function on the second-to-last weekend of October. I had pleaded with them to let me stay alone at home as I thought I was big enough to care for myself and no longer needed any type of baby sitter. Whatever I said worked, and they decided that at some point, I would need to be by myself and that now was as good a time as any. So, that evening at around six, my parents and sister went to a function for my father's workplace and left me home alone. I remember that for the first thirty minutes, I thought this was the greatest thing that could ever happen to me. I could do whatever I wanted and whenever I wanted to do it, and no one could tell me otherwise. I had the house to myself and started off by eating whatever I was not supposed to have. Then I turned on the television and started watching some rated "R" movie on one of the premium channels.

As I was sitting there in the living room, I looked out one of the windows and noticed it was getting pretty dark outside. This is when I looked around the house and noticed just how big, dark and creepy it was without anyone else in it with me. This epiphany of sorts immediately scared the crap out of me. I turned off the television, dumped whatever food I had left into the trash and ran upstairs to my room and locked the door. At least in my room, I felt safer than being elsewhere in the house. I knew I had made a big mistake and should have given this being home alone thing more thought, especially with knowing how I felt when it gets dark at night. I locked my door, put my desk chair under the door knob for extra security and then grabbed my drum sticks and started playing. I remember that just before I put the sticks to the snare drum, I thought I heard something outside in the house creak loudly and then something fall. I started playing the drums loud – louder than ever before to drown out any other noise and to help me forget or pretend that nothing just happened in the house.

I quit looking at my music sheet and started playing by memory. I was hitting as many flams as I could and crashing down hard on some major drum rolls. But as I continued to make noise, something in the house was also making noise, and the noise it was making was louder than mine. I was truly scared out of my mind! I did not know what else to do but keep on playing. There was no phone in my room, and even if there was, who was I going to call? I could not call my parents; there were no cellphones back then. I sure as hell could not call the police because my mom and dad would never again let me stay home alone, not even as an adult.

"Wait a minute," I thought, "Maybe the noise I am hearing is someone breaking into the house, and maybe the police are exactly who I need to call."

Up until that moment, all I thought the noise could be was some type of creature, demon or monster, here to hurt, capture or kill me. But just as I considered contacting the police, I thought that the more likely cause of the noise was someone breaking into the house. If that was truly the case, I had to do something about it. I could not let any burglar think I did not hear him with my drum playing and that my stopping and going outside might get them to leave or at least hopefully allow me the time to get to the phone down the hall and in the loft to call the police. So, I stopped playing the drums and moved my chair away from the front of the door. I then opened it and ran down the hall to the phone in the loft. As soon as I had exited my room, the noise stopped. I figured me opening my door may have scared the burglar or burglars into leaving the house. I was still scared of strangers being in my home, so I picked up the phone and began to dial the police. I heard an initial ringing out to the police department and then I heard nothing. The phone went dead.

"Hello, hello, is anyone there? Is this the El Paso Police Department? I have an emergency. I think someone is in my house."

Then I received a response on the phone that I was not ready for and sent chills down my spine.

"I am here; I am here with you in the fucking house you little piece of shit," a female voice said. "How dare you pretend to be Patrick! Don't think you got away with it because I know."

I dropped to the floor and was in a complete panic.

There was a single light on downstairs that lit up the house and allowed me to see, and I did not remember turning it on.

"I know you are there, and I know what you have done. Now I want you to know we are always here," the female voice continued.

It then stopped, and I heard what sounded to be wood sliding back and forth on a wall or some other type of surface. I slowly got some type of feeling back into my legs and was able to lift myself up from the floor. Slowly and quietly, I put the phone back on its stand. I then started moving out of the loft in an attempt to go down the upstairs hall and straight to my room that was at the very end. However, in order to do this, I would have to go past my sister's room to the left, where the door was wide open and there was no light on inside, and then the bathroom on the right side of the hall that also had the door open and was dark inside. Slowly, my attempt began to get to the safety of my room.

Seconds felt like hours – even days. I could not take my eyes off of my room that was straight down the hall and still had lights on inside. Out of the corners of my eyes, I noticed every shadow that was cast in the house because of the one light downstairs and the one that was on in my room. I continued to hear the scraping of wood downstairs and began seeing things move, but I think this was just my eyes playing tricks on me and my imagination in overdrive. I could barely keep moving, and each forward step now felt like I was in quicksand and having to wade through it. I had walked approximately eight feet, which was enough to now put me past the open loft and into the hall area. I quickly thought to myself that my room was no farther than fifteen feet away, and all I had to do was start running.

"Move dammit, move!" went through my head, and I started sprinting to my room. No sooner had I burst into full speed that my sister's door slammed shut with the force of a hurricane, then the bathroom door, and then to my horror, my bedroom door. I froze and fell to the ground. The safety of my room was gone, and now I did not know what was in there. Also, I had lost the light that was shining out from my bedroom. The last light was the one I did not turn on downstairs. As I was now on the ground in a semi-Indian-style seated position, I turned my head to the right to where the stairs began their descent to the first floor. I thought to myself, was I going to stay here in the middle of the hall, frozen until something came for me, or was I going to make an attempt to go downstairs and confront whatever it was down there and what had made its presence known to me on the phone? I could not allow this thing to come for me, and I decided that I would somehow, someway get downstairs and confront it.

I gathered myself together and somehow lifted myself up. I turned to the right and grabbed the top railing and began the descent down the stairs. As I approached the halfway point, I could hear something wooden scraping harder and harder against some other object. As I turned slightly to continue down the last set of steps, I could now see the downstairs area in front of me. Directly ahead was a wall that separated the den and the entry way. As I reached the bottom of the steps, I could turn left or right. Left would lead me down a short distance of a hallway, past the entryway and then to the doors of my parents' room. Turning right would lead me down the longer part of the hallway that led to the guest bedroom on the first floor and the entry to the garage.

As I was deciding which way to go I realized that the awful scraping sound was coming from my parents' room. I had already hated going in there alone because my father had a portrait of his mother hanging, and it was extremely creepy. My dad's mom had passed away years before I was born, so I never met her. He had a couple of photos of her that I had seen before, but it was the hanging portrait that continually had her on my mind. I had never seen the portrait until we lived in the Colorado home as it had been left in storage until then. From Colorado through El Paso, it hung in my parents' room, and I swear my grandmother would follow me with her eyes no matter where I went in the room. I had terrible, evil things happen to me, and this oil painting still scared me about as much as the flying shadow creature of long ago.

The other thing that scared the crap out of me in my parents' room was this cloth clown that my mother had hanging on their bathroom wall. If I ever was forced to use the toilet in their bathroom, I would sit there and not take my eyes off of that sinister, evil-looking clown. I truly had no idea what my mom liked about it. I think that damn thing even scared my dad as he had commented on it once or twice while in my presence. That clown had a face about eight inches in diameter, and the paint on it was black, white and red. It had huge red lips and this massive grimacing grin, where all its teeth showed, and the teeth were outlined in black. Then, instead of a regular body of two arms, a torso and legs, this thing had two arms, half a torso and then two long dangling tentacles that I guess were supposed to be legs. The outfit it was wearing was dark blue, white and black, and it had something in its one hand that was supposed to be a rolling pin or rod of sorts but looked more like a miniature meat cleaver if I had to guess. This is the reason I hated going into my parents' room, even when they were home, and I was now about to go into their room while I was home alone, hearing terrible scraping sounds and earlier having been yelled at by some unknown female on a phone that apparently had gone dead just before her rant began. I turned left and started walking down the hall, passing the entryway, then coming up to the double doors that were the entrance to my parents' bedroom. I turned left and began to enter. As I did so, I looked in and almost lost control of my bowels. I was terrified more than I had ever been in my life from what I saw happening inside the room.

As I turned and entered past the double doors, I was looking up the entire time. Directly ahead was the end wall where my grandmother's portrait hung. I continued to stay focused on the portrait as it was swinging wildly from left to right. Inside the painting I could see my grandmother's face turning and moving and then screaming at me. Her voice was the same one I had heard on the phone upstairs.

"I know who you are and you are not him. You leave this fucking house and get out now, you little lying piece of shit! Get out of this house or I am going to get you out myself."

My grandmother's portrait continued screaming at me while I just stood there and watched instead of running out of the room. I suddenly heard a huge crack as the painting separated itself from the wall, taking a large piece of the wall with it. Then that portion of the drywall crashed to the ground. The portrait flew right at me and smashed with intense force into my face and upper body, throwing me back and knocking me off my feet in the process.

This painting had to be about three feet by four feet, and it had a large and heavy ornate wood frame. "Get out – get out or I am going to tear your soul from your skin!" it screamed and then again slammed on top of me as I now partially lay on my parents' bedroom floor.

The intense impact this time caused me to get slammed back, partially up against the opposite side wall from where the painting initially hung. I could feel warm liquid running down the left side of my head and into my left eye. As the liquid entered my eye, it stung with a burning pain. I realized then that I was bleeding from my head and that my own blood was what had dripped down into my eye. I also had blood coming out of both nostrils.

"Stop hurting me, grandma. Why are you doing this to me?" I screamed.

"Don't you dare fucking call me your grandma, you thief of souls," the portrait replied in a menacing tone.

As it pulled back somewhat and continued to levitate, I saw this as my chance to escape by rolling to the right on the floor and crawling into my parents' bathroom. Once I was all the way in, I shut the door behind me and locked it. That very moment from the other side, I heard the painting crash into the door with such force that a portion of the back end of the door splintered out. I started crying and yelling for it to stop, but this just made my grandmother angry, and her portrait slammed into the bathroom door over and over until the door began to break open. I thought I was going to be killed; I gave up at that very moment as I could not take it any longer.

I was so scared that I shut down and gave up. It was that very moment when I heard my father yelling on the other side of the door, "What the hell is going on? What is happening? Patrick, son, are you inside there? Mom, what are you doing to my boy?"

With that, everything stopped. I heard the painting fall to the ground and then fall forward. I opened the door and screamed out for my dad as I ran into his arms and thanked him for saving me.

"I love you, dad. Please don't let grandma kill me; please don't leave me here with her again."

"Patrick, never would I let anything hurt you, and I don't know what the hell that was, but it was not your grandma. Your grandma passed away years before you were born. That is just some painting of her."

I had later found out that when my parents pulled into the garage, they had heard all the screaming and banging. So my mom stayed with my sister in the car as my father went inside to see what was happening. When he got to his room, he was horrified at what he saw taking place. Afterward, the four of us sat at the dining room table and discussed what had occurred. I told them what I had been told over the phone and when the portrait was screaming at me but that I did not understand what it had meant. Apparently my parents also had no clue in regards to the meaning of the event. What did it mean that I was not Patrick? That evening, before we all went to bed, my parents packed up the portrait of my grandmother into the painting crate that had stored it for so many years. They sealed it with two rolls of packing tape. Then my father placed it in the trunk of his car in the garage. The next morning, my father must have gotten up pretty early, and he took that painting to a storage facility several miles from the house. That was the last I ever saw of my grandmother's portrait.

It took weeks before I felt anything close to being safe. It also caused me to keep a heightened awareness of my surroundings, no matter where I was. It made me re-evaluate how I went about doing simple tasks at home and how I got from point A to point B inside the house. I also found myself needing plenty of time to overcome the nightmares I continued having about the encounter.

Days, weeks, then months went by from the night I was brutally attacked in the house by some unknown entity that seemed to masquerade as the spirit of my grandmother. I had plenty of time to ponder it all and had time to even learn how to overcome the portrait and entity in my daily nightmares. I focused more on the good things in my life like school, the girls in class and sports at school. I went to the movies with my friends and went to lots of church activities to surround myself with what I thought were things that could protect me from the darkness and creatures that few people experienced in this world. Church seemed like a great outlet at the time and even a protector for me as I was constantly being told in church how God could protect me from evil and its harmful ways. I was all about getting some protecting through God or any other way I could find it.

The year came to an end, and 1984 now continued at what seemed a remarkable pace. March came and went, and I turned twelve years old. April and May marched effortlessly by, and suddenly it was the end of the school year. The sixth grade was about to end, and I was deeply saddened by this. Don't get me wrong, I was definitely looking forward to having the summer off, but I was looking too far out and already starting to panic over the fact that I would be a seventh-grader, and this meant having to start middle school and go to multiple classes. This type of change scared me, and I got that strange, overwhelmed feeling that I did all those years back when I had first started school and passed out from the massive amount of anxiety with which I was struck. Oh well, I would just have to forget about it now and worry about it later. Now I thought to myself, this twelve-year-old was going to change his thought pattern and focus on the positives of the summer.

It was the summer of 1984, and that meant this was the first time I would be going to Boy Scout camp. I had been in Cub Scouts since I was eight. I advanced through all the stages of Cub Scouting and was now old enough to become a full blown Boy Scout. I had been looking forward to this for a long time as the church had its own scout troop in the El Paso Yucca Council. I had religiously attended the scout meetings and continued to do so during the summer. My first weeklong scout camp was going to take place during the second week of July, and I was so excited that I had been shopping for all my camping supplies weeks out from the event. I think I continued to go through the things I purchased and rearranged my backpack and other bags three or four times a day – and that was no exaggeration.

My troop had not raised a lot of money this year, so our troop leader and some of the parents decided we would go it alone and not go to an organized Boy Scout camp. The planned outing was scheduled for a remote wooded area above Alamogordo, N.M. The location was known as Dog Canyon. I remember thinking that with a name like that, it had to be full of adventures for scouts. There would be eighteen scouts going, all ranging from ages twelve to eighteen. Our scout master, Doug Farelong, and five fathers were also going to be in attendance. I was sure there was going to be plenty to learn, lots to experience and great memories to be made throughout the entire adventure.

The Saturday that would start scout camp had arrived, and everyone met at the church parking lot. It took about two hours for everyone to get there and for all the trucks and trailers to be loaded. There was so much stuff going with us that it looked like we were going camping for a month instead of a week. But I guess the moral of the story is to be prepared for everything. The drive time from El Paso to Alamogordo was two hours, and then it was another forty minutes to the canyon. I was riding up with one of my best friends, Ed Stague, his brother Dave Stague, and their father, Gary Stague, who was also one of the assistant scout masters for the troop. Only four of us fit into Gary's truck, which was a good thing as Ed and I did not want to be jammed in with a bunch of people like it ended up being in some of the other vehicles.

For the entire drive up to Alamogordo, we talked about girls that we liked at school and church and also what we planned on doing for the rest of the summer. Ed and I had also saved up a ton of money before the trip. Before we left, the two of us rode our bikes to the local Stop and Go mini-mart and purchased forty candy bars. We had planned on selling them for $2 or $3 each when we were in the canyon but apparently between the two of us, we ended up eating somewhere in the realm of eight by the time we got to Alamogordo. So much for being entrepreneurs and making some easy money off of the candy sales. At this rate, we would have to sell them for $4 each in order to make the profit we were hoping for. Whatever the case, getting to eat as much candy as I wanted without being told to stop by my parents was worth it.

A quick stop in Alamogordo took place for everyone to use the restroom and for the adults to fill the vehicles with gasoline since this would be the last opportunity until we returned one week from today. The last forty minutes of driving felt like ten hours as I just could not wait to get this adventure going. Also, whoever said it was only forty minutes past Alamogordo must have never been up to the canyon. It really ended up taking just under ninety minutes. All this added time was due to the fact that there was a single, one-lane road that led in and out of the canyon. That meant that every time another vehicle was coming from the opposite direction, all the vehicles had to get super close to the right side of the road in order for the other vehicle to pass. This was not just time consuming, but it scared the crap out of everyone. This was because we were just inches from a straight drop-down of approximately eighty feet to the cliff bottom. It took a lot longer than everyone expected, but as we finally rounded the last turn and saw high-altitude desert turn into amazing rolling green grassland and then into a semi-coniferous forest, it was well worth the added time. We arrived, and it was everything I had imaged it would be and then some.

Our initial objective as a troop collective was to get everything unpacked, get all the tents and canopies set up, put together the tables for the eating station and then unload our gear into our tents. This took about ninety minutes. I had purchased an amazing three-person tent that was going to be used by just two people; Ed and I were bunking together. Once everything was set up, Ed and I took our stuff into the tent and got everything situated. This included getting our air mattresses inflated, sleeping bags unrolled and toiletries ready to go. We got everything set up with still plenty of light left in the day. So, the troop came together for supper, and the adults whipped up some amazing hot dogs and burgers for our first night at camp. I remember thinking that the hot dogs I ate tasted amazing. I was told they were that good because they had been cooked on an open fire. More likely it was just due to the fact that I had eaten only candy bars for the last five or six hours and was starving for real sustenance.

After dinner, we were met by the local National Park Service Ranger. With the ranger leading, we took our first hike. It was magnificent. I had never seen so much wildlife that close to me, and the cooler air in the canyon sure beat the 100-plus degree weather that we had left behind in El Paso. As we finished the hike, the ranger bid us farewell. But right before he left, he warned of the possibility of some pretty bad weather that may head into the area for the next day or two. With that, the troop was left alone, and as the night overtook the day, the campfire got going and the adults started telling us all some damn good campfire ghost stories. I remembered thinking that they were good but that I had lived through some that were far worse than they could imagine up here in Dog Canyon. An hour or so passed, and it was time to head to our tents and the luxury sleep accommodations waiting for each of us.

That first evening, it took some time for me to get used to sleeping on an air mattress and in a sleeping bag after having been sleeping on a waterbed for the last year or so. Also, the wind picked up around midnight and made it difficult to fall asleep as it howled through the canyon. I eventually fell asleep and dreamt of fishing and hiking. The remainder of the night must have been uneventful because when I woke up, it was already 7 in the morning.

The sun was shining and someone outside was yelling, "Get up – get your lazy butts up and come get some bacon and eggs before they are all gone."

I threw my clothes on and was outside the tent before Ed could even get unzipped in his sleeping bag. I quickly ate several pieces of bacon and a couple pieces of bread. Afterward, I took care of personal business and walked around the camp area while the others ate breakfast and then got ready for the daily events. Then we headed to the high region of the canyon.

The plan was to hike deep back into the canyon and then up into the forested area above the canyon. The roundtrip was nine miles. I loved to walk and jog and thought I was in great shape, but unless you have hiked nine miles through very rugged terrain, nothing can prepare you for just how difficult and exhausting a trek of that nature can be, even on a twelve-year-old. Let me just say that I had never felt such exhaustion like I felt during this intense hike. It was some of the most picturesque countryside I had ever seen. The constant talking and banter between everyone really made me forget about how sore my body felt and how painful the water blisters were that had formed on almost every toe inside my boots. The entire hike took us about nine hours as it included the need to cross several large streams and go around one good-sized pond. We also had to make a detour at one point due to two large brown bears that were in front of us and had quickly become aware of so many people moving toward them. But when it was all over and we were all back at camp, the only thing everyone could talk about was how much fun the hike had been, what we had seen and the amazing photos everyone had taken with their 110 or disc cameras.

It definitely made for good times, and the stories I could now tell about the day and the hike would last a lifetime. The rest of the evening was spent prepping dinner, eating it and then the adults telling ghost stories around the campfire. I was having an amazing time because when I looked down at my watch on my wrist, it read 9:45 p.m. I took one last look up at the night sky and was still able to make out some amazing stars and constellations, even with the heavy cloud cover that had been forming above the canyon. The clouds made me remember the warning from the ranger the evening before about the possibility of foul weather. With that last thought, I headed to the tent before everyone else and fell asleep the moment my head touched my air pillow.

The night was uneventful, and I woke up feeling refreshed and ready for another adventure on day two of scout camp. Everyone that morning ate breakfast together as things were more organized on the second day, and almost everyone seemed to be fitting into the routine that was set up by the adults so that we could maximize the time we had at Dog Canyon. For day two, we all headed for a two-mile hike back up to that amazingly beautiful pond we had run into the day before. The plans were to fish for trout and catfish as the pond had been stocked by Fish and Wildlife Management two weeks before camp. It took about an hour to hike to the pond. Once we got there, everyone picked a spot, pulled out their poles, placed their bait of choice onto their hook and began to fish. It could not have been more than two minutes before everyone began getting bites and started reeling in trout and catfish. Within a couple of hours, all the scouts and adults had hit the daily limit for fish that could legally be caught. So, the next thing we all did was gut and clean them, and then we cooked and ate most of them right there on the edge of the pond.

The adults had brought all the needed supplies to broil the fish or put them in foil paper and cook them under the hot coals of the fire created by the adults earlier. I remember the meal as it was the best fish I had ever eaten. The rest of the day we worked on earning some other merit badges and played a lot of games for awards. At about five in the evening, we started the hike back to the campsite. While we were hiking back down into the canyon, the weather started changing. By the time we made it back to camp and were going to get dinner going, the sky was full of dark, ominous thunderclouds. The wind had also picked up, and gusts had to be going through the canyon at upward of 25 mph. We worked at getting dinner ready, and then we all ate. Because we could see lightning off in the distance, we decided to get our tents latched down as best as possible and then secure the rest of the gear that was outside or in the trailers so that nothing would get damaged or blown away if the storm we saw off in the distance ended up reaching us. By the time everything was secure, we were exhausted, and everyone had decided to turn in for the night to get some good shut-eye before day three.

As it turned out, there would be no day three at scout camp due to what took place that night. At around eleven in the evening, I woke up due to the tremendous howling of the wind. It was so strong that over half my tent was bent downward and blowing into Ed and I while we slept. Ed was up, as well, and he even had to move over to my side of the tent. We both popped up out of our sleeping bags and decided to unzip the front door of the tent, just enough to take a quick look outside. As we did this, all hell broke loose above us. At that very moment, it started raining and hailing, and the hail was the size of very large marbles. The top of the tent began to leak due to the intense amount of rain and hail that fell in a matter of a minute or two. It was truly one of those microbursts you hear about on the news. Then came the awful wind that was magnified to an even greater degree as it traveled down into and then through the canyon.

The wind had to be hitting in the upward of 60 and 70 mph at certain points. Ed and I looked at each other in disbelief after we somehow managed to close our tent door without being washed away. Then came the added and unexpected activity – the kind I had grown accustomed to but Ed had never experienced. As we could hear thunder just above us and see the crackling down of lightning very close to the camp and our tent, Ed and I watched as parts of the lightning slithered toward us on the ground outside – the same way that a snake were to move. We could see this happening even from the inside of the tent just due to the immense and blinding glare that the lightning was producing. We both watched, speechless as the lightning came from the bottom of the tent on one side, up alongside it and around to the front. Then as our tent door unzipped by itself, the lightening went into the tent through the opening made by some unknown and unseen presence.

Immediately, the lightning or whatever type of intense energy was acting like lightning was all over Ed and I. That is when all the screaming began. Ed was getting electrocuted, and his screams from the shock and the pain that came along with it was ear-shattering. Then I felt the same thing and was screaming in pain as loudly as Ed had been. The energy would not dissipate, and worse yet, no one else could hear us because of how loudly the wind was howling in the canyon and how loudly the thunder was crackling just above the camp. We were now both being shocked so violently that neither of us could say anything, and all the muscles in my body were so tense that every part of me felt like I was about to explode. Then, to my utter disbelief, I watched as Ed was raised into the air and was floating in the middle of the tent. Once he stopped being raised upward, multiple strikes of energy started hitting his body, and I watched as the clothing he had on started to smoke, and I could smell his skin and hair burning.

I then realized that nothing else was happening to me, and all of this energy was focused on Ed. What I did not know and would later be told by Ed is that as I watched him being hit with balls of energy or lightning, he watched me as three dark black figures swirled around me so quickly that at one point, he could no longer see me, and it looked as if I had left and that there was this area of void or pure darkness where I was supposed to be. This scared Ed so much that he had not even felt the lightning hitting him. He said he must have gone into shock at what he saw happening to me and could not believe that I did not see this happening. I later confirmed that I saw none of that and saw only the intense light that was bombarding Ed's body and causing his clothing to catch fire. Then, just when we both thought we were going to die, everything stopped, and I mean everything all at once. There was suddenly no rain, no hail, no wind, no thunder, and especially, no more lightning or whatever the hell the lines of energy were that slithered into our tent.

"Holy shit, dude. Are you all right?" I blurted out. "You were on damn fire, Ed – seriously on fire."

"Screw the lightning and fire – you had these devils or demons all around you, and they took you away from inside the tent. Patrick, dude, you were not here in the tent with me. There was just a black hole or space where you had been sitting at."

The two of us continued to discuss what just happened. We both got dressed and went outside to inspect ourselves while we were standing, and then we inspected the campsite. Other than some burns on our skin, singed hair and smoking clothes, we were both fine. Unfortunately, the same could not be said for the campsite and all our gear and supplies. The storm and whatever else came with it wiped out our campsite. Now that the others heard Ed and I talking outside, we watched as almost all the tent doors unzipped, and we were joined outside by about twenty others, all holding flashlights and trying to assess the damage.

It was still very dark out, and it seemed like the entire area was hit by a flash flood as we all were ankle-deep in mud. There was just nothing anyone could do in the middle of the night and under the current conditions we all found ourselves in. With that in mind, the adults told those who could still sleep in their tents to do just that. Those who could not due to their tents being too damaged were told to spend the night inside the truck cabs with their sleeping bags if they were not wet. So everyone tried to find a place to spend the night. Of course, sleeping was optional at this point.

At about five in the morning it was light enough that most of the scout masters or other fathers were already up and trying to see what made it and what did not in the way of supplies and gear. The outcome ended up being bad – very bad. There was not much left. Out of all the tents, only two had made it through the storm and would not require repair or replacement. Most of the gear and supplies on the open trailers could not be found. They were most likely blown away, or after what happened to me, quite possibly taken into another dimension. The gas grills were broken, and the tarps and plastic gazebo shelters were ripped in half or blown away, as well. Some people had left their backpacks and gear outside on picnic tables or up against the trucks or trailers, and they, too, could not be found.

A true assessment of the situation was that the place looked like a shit storm hit it hard. The entire area looked like it went through a major weather event, and our campsite incurred the most damage. Neither Ed nor I told anyone else about the extra happenings that went down the night before since no one would believe us, and secondly, everything was already bad enough just from the weather incident. About an hour later, the adults decided to end the camping trip and that it would be best for us to get back home. There were just not enough supplies, gear or food left for us to continue camping for the next four days. Approximately two hours later, we were packed up and headed out of Dog Canyon. The only place we stopped was at the ranger station to let them know what had happened and that we would be leaving early. With that, I bid an early farewell to scout camp and Dog Canyon.

As we began our drive down to Alamogordo, you could see that Ed was thinking as much about what took place in our tent as I was. It had to be harder for him as he had never experienced the supernatural before. For me, this was not as bad an incident as I have had in my past.

"Do you want to talk about it?" I whispered to him while he and I sat in the back seat of his dad's vehicle and Ed's father and brother were up front.

"There is nothing to talk about, and I just want to forget it happened," Ed exclaimed.

After this very brief discussion, I left Ed alone for the remainder of the drive to Alamogordo. After we had filled the vehicles with gasoline and everyone pigged out on whatever food they could get their hands on, we began the final leg of the trip to El Paso.

During the drive, Ed's dad and older brother were talking about the crazy weather at the camp. Ed and I mostly listened, unless we were specifically addressed during the conversation. During the time in the vehicle, someone started discussing the end of the world and that the weather last night felt like just that. The person continued on with how helpless he felt and how scared he was. It must have been Ed's older brother who was having this discussion. Whatever the case, Ed and his father were chiming in and guessing how the world would end and when. The topic quickly went from bad weather and cancelled scout trip to an apocalyptic ending of the world. I remember thinking how the hell that happened, yet it was the topic of discussion.

The three of them went on and on. Ed was saying he thought the end of the world would be around the turn of the century and that the twenty-first century would bring the second coming of Jesus Christ. His dad was agreeing but stating that it would be much, much later – after all of us were long dead and gone. Dave again took over the conversation and gave his opinion of the entire topic. He said the world was ending when the Mayan Indians said it would end: in 2012. With this, I began to listen more intently as I had not heard much about Mayan Indians in Mexico before, but for some strange reason, I had this feeling as if I had a discussion about this many times in my past and that I knew about this 2012 prediction already. It just felt like deja vu.

As Dave began schooling us on the end of the world according to the Maya of the Central Americas, I must have started to doze off or daydream as I stared out the back window of the truck. As I got more and more into a trance by watching the scenery go by outside at a side angle without looking forward, everything outside began to change. This was not a gradual geographic change but an instant one. I was again in a place I seemed to have been before and known well but did not know how I knew of such things. As I looked off into the distance, I saw the most beautiful blonde woman ever. She was trying to signal me from a distance and get my attention.

When I focused on her and she saw I was paying attention, she yelled, "You know the truth; you have lived it time and time again. The periods of time between incidents are always the same. Just tell them – tell everyone so they can prepare."

Suddenly, the scenery changed back to where we actually were in New Mexico, and that beautiful older female was gone. I am pretty sure I was dreaming this, but for some uncanny reason, I felt as if it was a real occurrence and I just did not understand how. Then I focused back on Dave's account of what he must have read or seen on television about this Mayan end of times in 2012.

All three of us continued to listen to Dave without interrupting him, and we were genuinely intrigued with what he was telling us. I also took him at his word as I knew Dave was a very bright fourteen-year-old who never lied about anything and was always quite serious. I also always saw him reading when I would be at his house playing Atari or ColecoVision with Ed.

Then Gary chimed in: "That totally gets away from what the church teaches us, and you should not listen or read about such nonsense."

I was thinking that is a pretty shallow comment. How is one theory wrong but his religion's theory always right? Why does everything have to end with gods and demons battling it out for good and evil? Why is it that everyone's soul always needs saving from damnation and hell?

Then Ed blurted out, "What do you think, Kilian? How and when is the world going to end?"

With some unknown force behind my answer and not knowing how it came out, I answered, "The world is not going to end. Humanity and society as we know it will end just as it has multiple times in the past because of how close it comes to Earth."

"How close what comes to Earth?" Gary asked.

I did not know what he was talking about. I did not remember what I said.

"I don't know – I don't know where my answer came from."

Gary and Dave stopped and looked back at me, and Ed looked over to me and wanted to know what the hell I must have been smoking in the back seat. Then Dave and Ed started fighting about something, and the conversation completely changed.

For five minutes, the conversation was no longer about the end of the world and had changed topics two or three times.

"2036!" I screamed out of nowhere. "The world as we know it today is going to end in 2036 and we have to prepare."

They all looked at me again, and I felt a bit uncomfortable with it.

"I don't know where that came from, either, but I had to let you all know. The true year for the end is 2036."

No one said anything else after that for some time. I kept quiet as I felt stupid with this answer firing out of my mouth and not knowing what I was saying. But then again, I flashed back to the end happening and my being there, yet why in the hell did I see the past and yell out "2036," which is decades into the future? Also, if the end of the world happened in the past, then why are we all here now? Before I knew it, we had arrived in El Paso, and Gary dropped me off at home with what gear I had left after the storm. Mr. Stague made sure my parents were home and explained what happened at camp and why the decision was made to come home early. I then thanked him, said goodbye to Ed and Dave and went into the house.

# 9.

# Grow Up

The summer was almost over, and scout camp felt like a distant memory of some adventure that took place a long time ago. After a few weeks had passed, I got more focused on the future, especially with the seventh grade right around the corner. The more I thought about it, the more it seemed to suck. Worse yet, I started to get that intense high anxiety again, and I could not understand why. I tried isolating this way of thinking that caused me to overanalyze everything, which in turned made me feel trapped and full of anxiety. Once this trapped feeling started, I would have flashbacks to being this older man who had been underground for long lengths of time and felt trapped due to being below the Earth's surface, not being able to see the outside. This thinking and daydreaming then caused even greater anxiety about the seventh grade.

Then I woke up one Monday morning, and it was the first day of the seventh grade at Desert Vista Middle School. One other thing important worth mentioning at this point is that before the summer ended, Mr. Stague was transferred with his company, and that meant that Ed and Dave moved to Midland, Texas, before school started. Another good friend of mine, Jim Espers, moved with his family to Scottsdale, Ariz., when his father got a new job with some petroleum company in the Phoenix area. Then finally, my best friend from the sixth grade, Rick Bottega, decided he wanted to go to a private Catholic school for seventh grade. So he ended up going to school in downtown El Paso. I would never see Rick and Jim again. I would see Ed and Dave again, but only later on when I could drive to Midland and visit them or when they would tag along with Mr. Stague when he was in El Paso on a business trip. But all this moving away by my close friends did not help me with the seventh grade. It made me feel isolated and abandoned since now I would be on my own in Desert Vista Middle School. So there I was, by myself frantically walking the halls of Desert Vista, trying to locate my locker and then my first-period class.

I do not know how I made it through the first day of school as it all felt like a blur. The only thing I remember was hyperventilating several times and breaking out in a cold sweat in the middle of August. When I got home, my face must have said it all as my mom immediately began asking what was wrong, and I broke out in a hysterical rant and then toward the end, I was crying. I truly had one of the worst anxiety attacks I could remember. During that time period, no one really called it anxiety disorder or had anxiety attacks, so I just simply freaked out! The next day, I did not go to school. As a matter of fact, I did not go back at all.

The following Monday, my parents enrolled me into the same school that my sister had started to attend. It was a brand-new private school that went from first through eighth grade. For some reason, after going into this private school, I had no other issues. I felt fine there and had no feeling of being trapped. With that big issue taken care of, the rest of the seventh grade went without a hitch. Nothing happened the entire year that was out of the ordinary or worth mentioning. I had no creature attacks, no spirit attacks and no portrait painting attacks. I did not lose consciousness and have some bizarre dream and did not find myself in someone else's body, running from a massive deluge in an end-of-the-world storm. I went to school, did homework, hung out with friends at school and out of school, turned thirteen in March and completed the seventh grade in May.

During summer 1985, not much really happened. I stayed home most of the days while I was on summer vacation. I read a lot. I did finally get to go to an organized Boy Scout camp in New Mexico with my scout troop, and this was the highlight of the summer. I remember learning a lot while I was at camp. It was well organized and allowed me to learn first-aid, cooking and camping skills that I continued to use throughout the rest of this lifetime. I even got to earn my archery and shooting merit badges as the camp had both archery and real rifles. Those two were my favorite badges to earn.

When I got back from camp, I still had most of July and August left for my summer vacation. I read a lot during my time off from school. For some reason, when it came to reading during that summer, most of what I was interested in dealt with the solar system, its planets and what scientists do and do not know about gravity. I wasn't sure during the time why this was such an interesting subject to me, but it had truly piqued my interest, and I devoured whatever books I could on the topics. I also read a lot about reincarnation and the differences this had versus life after death in Christianity.

While reading book after book during the last half of summer vacation, I came across one in particular that talked about the fact that ancient and long-lost civilizations, such as the Maya and Sumerians, knew about the farthest planets in our galaxy but did not have the tools we have to see or study them. I thought that if they did not have our technology, such as the large telescopes, how did they know about these planets in the first place? In my mind, I felt that something was wrong with what history was telling us, but I was not sure what or how to proceed in researching the topic. Remember that there was no instant search in 1985 on the Internet. You had to go to a library and do research or send away for what you needed. Well, I had written all this down, and by all means, had done so with the intent on following up and finding answers to my questions. But summer vacation ended, and eighth grade was about to begin. With that, I forgot about wanting to know why civilizations of long ago seemed to know as much as we did in the twentieth century.

I had done a lot of growing up in the last year. While I read about reincarnation, I also ended up reading and learning about several Eastern philosophies, and in those philosophies certain forms of meditation and coping techniques that were common practice. I had started meditating daily upon returning from scout camp and continued with my journal writing I had started a long time ago. Now I also included my daily thoughts on what troubled me and would jot down possible ways to cope with these thoughts that found their way into my daily journal. I learned to identify what was bothering me and then focus my thought on this matter during meditation. My goal was to meditate and reach a level of thought where I would forget about those things that caused me great anxiety and attempt to wash them from my thoughts. In so doing, I had built up greater tolerance with my troubles and in handling anxiety issues in my life, especially when things did not go my way or when I had that gut-wrenching feeling of being buried alive, deep underground and not being able to get back to the surface.

With all of this, I came to the conclusion that I was going to go back to Desert Vista for the eighth grade. I was going to find a way to make it there without running away from fears that seemed to overtake and cause me this feeling of helplessness and the need to get away from it. So that is exactly what happened. I went back to Desert Vista for the eighth grade. I had to use a lot of coping tools the first few weeks that I went, which included coming home at lunch so that I had a break from the school each day. I lived just around the corner, so this was easy to do daily. I also made a great effort to interact with everyone around me and in so doing, made some pretty good friends, a couple of which remained my friends for a long time to come.

During the eighth grade, I excelled in school work, especially science and math. It was as if something inside me clicked and I knew a lot of what was being taught without having learned it yet or read the subject matter. I would see some things being taught in the chapters we were on or on the board by the instructor and had this uncanny feeling like this was not the first time I had come across this material. But I could not remember ever reading about these science and math topics before.

I also need to mention one incident during January 1986. My parents and sister were at a church function, and I was home alone one evening. As I had said earlier, I was growing up, and with this came my ability to cope better with what had happened to me in my past, especially with the supernatural. So yes, I was still scared to be alone and always fearful of something supernatural happening that would cause both physical and mental pain, but I came to the realization that it would occur no matter what I did. I concluded that I could then just deal with it when it transpired.

I was home alone that evening and meditating in the loft on the second floor. As I had almost reached that level of consciousness where I was partly in a dream state, I felt something touch my shoulder – no, put its hand on my shoulder. I opened my eyes and lurched forward, away from what was behind me, and then quickly jumped to my feet and turned around. There in front of me was a dark shadow creature that was completely black. Actually, a better description was that it was shrouded in darkness. It stood as tall as me and projected itself in the form of an adult male, although it was difficult to make out any physical features. I was holding my breath. I also noticed I was beginning to take a bit of a defensive stance as this figure started moving toward me. It was not walking but instead slowly advancing as it levitated.

I am not going to lie – I was so afraid I could not speak, and I had not taken a breath for a good period of time. The creature stopped advancing and was about two feet away from me. It began to speak, and again, I could not hear anything it was saying. This often was the case when these creatures spoke. I started to think that it was not their lack of trying or lack of speaking but that somehow they were out of sync with our plane of existence, and where man interacts with time and space in a chronological order was not where these creatures typically existed.

My being able to see them may have been something of an anomaly. I definitely would not call it a gift or a skill but more of a curse. At some point, the creature saw that I could not understand what it was saying, and I now felt as if my mind was being invaded. This thing in front of me was in my head, and now I could clearly understand what it was projecting into my realm of understanding. It did not need to communicate in a verbal language, and I was not hearing talking. Instead, I understood what it was thinking and felt. I knew it was angry with me for something I had done to it long ago.

The shadow figure made me understand it was very old and had been in this form for a long time and that it partly blamed me for this. Somehow, I must have communicated with it as I had wondered what the hell the creature meant being as I was not even fourteen years old. I quickly felt the creature become frustrated, and it placed into my head its thoughts that I was not always in this time and in this place and definitely not just age thirteen. Then the figure grabbed my arm. I pulled back and broke free.

It came forward again, and when it did, I yelled, "Tarak li rew alqadim."

This surprised both me and the shadow figure. I had no idea what I had just said, but the creature understood. It looked very angry and made one more sudden advance toward me.

I again felt the urge to yell at it and wanted to tell it to get out of my house, but instead, I again spoke in some unknown language to myself, "akhraj min bayti!"

The figure turned around and flew off the upstairs loft, across the living room and through the rear wall of the house.

This interaction did not leave me afraid. Instead, I was more confused as the creature seemed to know me. I seemed to know it, too, and I could understand it, and then I spoke a language I had never spoken before directly to it. While I still remembered what I told the creature, I wrote it in my journal as best I could write something I did not even know I could speak. As I wrote the words, I realized I clearly understood them but did not know how. The first part that I told the shadow figure was to tell the ancient spirit to let go of me. The next part was for it to get out of my house. But just because I knew what it meant did not mean I knew how I could know its meaning or even what language it was. I continued to document the incident so I could review it at a later date if needed. When my parents got home, I kept silent on what happened upstairs because I did not want to freak them out or upset Ann. I also still felt that I could handle being left alone and did not want this otherworldly run-in to put an end to that or being able to go places without my parents feeling they needed to go, as well.

Another year of school had come to an end. It felt as if the eighth grade flew by in a blur. I was glad to have attended Desert Vista, and looking back, I knew this was the best decision I could have made. My being able to stick it out and not run from anything this time around showed that I was maturing and better coping with life changes. I had met some great people, some becoming friends who would continue as such to a later time in my life. I also had some speed bumps during my travel through the year but got over them and moved onto the next challenge. I took time to reflect on not just what I did at school during the year but also out of school. I learned that there were things in my life that I did not yet understand but knew they would make themselves known to me at the proper time. With middle school now in the rear view mirror, I also welcomed the coming of high school. I welcomed the thought of nearing adulthood and having the growth experiences that I was sure would come with the next four years.

# 10.

# High School Life

August of 1986 came quickly, and with it came my high school years. In 1986, there were two high schools on the Eastside of El Paso, and I went to the one closest to my house, which was a good two miles away. When my freshman year started, I had to walk to and from school each day as my father had already gone to work earlier each morning and my mom did not wake up until after my first period. I could not take the school bus as the house was too close. It gave me plenty of time to think about things. Most of the time, I liked to cut across the golf course as this saved a good five to eight minutes, and in August, El Paso reached 100-plus degrees each day. During the winter, it grew very cold and windy, and there also was a good amount of snowfall.

The first few days of school were hard, and I was just trying to find my way to where I needed to go and make it there on time. As for friends, I gravitated toward a few people I knew from my ward at church, but they were already sophomores and juniors, and it was hard to hang out with them when our schedules were so different, and this included having different lunch periods. One great thing about lunch was that you could go off campus, and there were a lot of places to eat within walking distance.

But I could not go it alone. So, I ended up hanging out in the cafeteria for the first week, eating as quickly as I could and then heading to the library. Soon, though, I ended up with two friends that I had met in physical education class. Their names were Jim and John. I also had English with Jim, so it made sense to become friends as we could not only hang together but also get answers from each other for class. There was also Chris Martinez, with whom I became friends as we had two classes together. Last but not least was Douglas Upchurch. He was one of the few friends I had made in the eighth grade, and I continued to be friends with him even later into life.

During the first few months of school, there was nothing that separated me from any other freshman. I did not participate in any athletics and was not part of any school club or program such as band. I went to my classes during the day, hung out with Jim, John or Chris at lunch and then headed home when school ended. Anything I did out of school always seemed to be some church function, such as a dance or a basketball game. Since I did not do anything after school, it gave me plenty of time to do my homework and then practice my meditation techniques or read up on ancient history.

I had no recent run-in with any type of supernatural creature. I had no strange dreams and did not find myself instantly elsewhere. I just had a huge desire to learn all I could about ancient cultures and also about the solar system, planets and our solar system's travel patterns through the Milky Way Galaxy. I was not sure why I found a desire for this other than I always was searching for something that I was not quite sure of at the time. I was searching for answers to questions I had yet to ask.

School continued on and the holidays were fast approaching. One thing that happened in November alerted me as to what I was truly capable of.

It was a regular day at school and I had gone to my morning classes. At lunch, I went with Jim and John to the Whataburger down the street from the school. Jim and John loved to go to this place, but when we would get there, I would get in line to order my food and the two of them usually disappeared for about ten minutes. They would come back and then order their food and join me at one of the booths in the restaurant. So on this day they took off when we got to the Whataburger and I again stood in line waiting by myself. What happened differently this day was that I had to use the restroom. I was in the men's room washing my hands when I heard something above the ceiling tiles. I turned the water off and listened closely. I could swear I heard voices in the ceiling. I then heard people crawling above the ceiling. I waited in the bathroom and listened as the crawling went from past the main walls, back over the men's area of the restroom and then just above one of the stalls where the door was locked.

The stall door stood about eight inches off the floor and spanned toward the top of the ceiling, so you could see only a small portion of the inside. I then heard what were tiles from the ceiling being moved and then people shuffling out of the ceiling, crashing and clanking as shoes were landing on the toilet tank and then the seat, and then I heard it all over a second time. Suddenly the stall door opened, and Jim and John came out.

"What the hell were you two doing in the stall together? Were you both in the ceiling?"

They looked at each other and then they both looked back at me.

"We might as well tell him, dude. He isn't going to say shit to anyone," Jim exclaimed.

"I guess you are right. He can even do it, but that means we will have to go twice," John replied.

"Again, what the hell are you two talking about, and what were you doing up in the ceiling?" I asked.

Jim and John ushered me out of the bathroom, and we went to order lunch.

When we sat down to eat, they explained that the reason they would disappear every day for several minutes was to climb into the ceiling, go across to the other side of the wall and above the women's bathroom. Then they could watch the women through the ceiling tiles as they used the restroom. When they told me this, I thought they were two of the biggest perverts on the planet. How could anyone get off by watching as a woman went number one or number two in the restroom? What sick kind of entertainment was that? They then asked me if I was in and if I wanted to do it with them the following day.

"Absolutely not! Why would I want to see something like that? I believe that would scar me for life."

I continued to tell them they were crazy, but I also told them I would not tell anyone what they were doing as it was not just disgusting but also illegal. The two of them continued to converse among themselves as I could not stop thinking if this was the absolute best I could do friendship-wise. Was I destined to have the pervert squad as my school friends?

After the lunch incident, I could not wait to get back to campus, go to class and get away from Jim and John. During the rest of fifth and sixth period, all I could think about was what I saw at lunch and what Jim and John told me. I knew that I would be seeing both of them again at seventh period as this was our last period for the day and the three of us had P.E. together. As we were in the locker room, the two of them changed and said nothing to me about lunch period. I, on the other hand, continued to look at them as if they had just committed one of the worst sex crimes known to a high school student. I finished changing and went to the tennis courts as we were playing tennis for this portion of the year in physical education class. About forty minutes later, I was back in the locker room cleaning off and then changing back into my regular clothes as I had planned to go do some research for my science class in the library. I had sat down on a chair to put my socks and shoes on. Unbeknownst to me both Jim and John had come up behind me and then had grabbed the back portion of my chair and yanked the chair out from under me. It was a bit larger and higher up than a regular chair, and this meant that my fall to the ground was that much greater.

As I heard the two of them laughing uncontrollably, I fell back and hit my tailbone and it cracked. I would later find out I had a hairline fracture because of the two of them and their prank. But that was not all. I also struck my head on one of the lower lockers. I felt a sudden urge to throw up. This was compounded by the room spinning. Those two fucktards continued to laugh and had not realized just how badly I was injured. I did not get up for some time and did not say anything else about it as I was in a lot of pain but had to play it off because of where I was. There was no way I could lose my composure at school and especially in the locker room. I eventually got some help from one of the other guys in the locker room and got up off the floor.

Jim and John had already left the locker room and said nothing to me about what they did. I could barely walk and knew there was no way I could get to the library, yet alone walk home. I had to do what no freshman likes doing and that was calling his mom for a ride home. My mom picked me up from the front of the school twenty minutes later. She took me to the emergency clinic, and I got an X-ray. This is when I found out my coccyx was hairline fractured. I also had a mild concussion and was told to be careful sleeping that night and for my parents to wake me every hour on the hour and make sure I was alright. We ended up getting home a couple hours later, and I went upstairs to get some rest. I ended up missing the next two days of school as I had a lot of trouble walking.

That evening, I felt very tired and groggy. I quickly fell asleep and began dreaming. During the dream, I was no longer Patrick Kilian but was a very tall individual who people in the dream referred to as Grom Sarrum. I stood approximately nine feet. I saw everything in the dream out of the eyes of this Grom. Even more bizarre was the fact that as I was dreaming, I felt that this was not just a typical and senseless dream but more like the ones you have about places you have been to and the things you saw while you were there. This dream again was more of a recollection that is replayed by the mind in an unconscious state with great amounts of detail about past experiences or events. I also recognized during the dream that I was not that other person who had been underground after a great deluge and apocalyptic event from past dreams. I was Grom, and I was living in a mountainous area that could have been close to the same area as in my prior dreams or recollections but apparently not during any catastrophic event.

The land was lush and green, and the mountains above the alluvial plains were stunningly beautiful. I also realized that everyone else around me was also of large stature and could pass for being called a giant. I knew this was not some fantasy dream or one where reality mixes with part of a TV show you watched that same night or the one before.

This felt like an honest-to-God memory of my being this giant named Grom, living among a group of tall humans in ancient Mesopotamia thousands of years ago. In the dream, two other giants approached me and asked what they should do about the clan to the south of us that had been conducting raids at night on our village. Again, I had another epiphany and understood that I was in charge of these people and that Grom was the chieftain. The three of us created a plan to ambush the next raiding party that came to our village in the dead of night. We were to terminate most of the other tribe's warriors and also capture several of them to use as pawns in a trade to get back the items that were taken from us in prior raids.

We were lying in wait to set this plan into motion when I heard, "Patrick, wake up; you have to wake up, son, and let me check on you. Patrick, wake up now!"

I came out of the dream, opened my eyes and saw that my father had been trying to get me up. I let my father know I was feeling fine and that there was nothing I needed. He then went back downstairs so he could go back to sleep. I laid awake in bed thinking about this Grom and how this dream was another memory of yet another life I lived that was not a part of my being Patrick Kilian. This was just a strange feeling, and I started to recall all I had been reading regarding reincarnation. I remembered thinking that what I was going through was similar to reincarnation. But it was not identical to it and was something not known to present-day man. I then thought about the fact that it was very early in the morning and that I had just suffered a pretty good shot to the head. Maybe my early-morning theorizing made sense at that moment, but come morning, I would have regained my senses and realized everything I was thinking about was just me in a semi-conscious state of mind and was really nonsense. Grom; how could I have ever thought I had a past life where I was a giant human named Grom?

Then I also remembered something else for which I needed to create a game plan. That something was revenge.

There was no way on God's green Earth that I was letting Jim and John get away with what they did. I decided that for the next few hours, I would figure out how I would seek retribution on them, and I swore to myself that I would never let anyone treat me like that again. Something awoke that day in me – something that had remained dormant for a very long time. I could feel this rage inside me grow, and I realized that my being a vengeful person was not a new concept for me but one I had suppressed and not allowed to be felt for a long time.

For the next two days, I stayed home trying to recover as best I could, not only from my physical injuries but also my pride being hurt. I had been embarrassed at school and in front of a lot of people in the locker room by those two guys I thought were my friends. Had I been so desperate to have friends that I latched onto whatever I could? Then a wicked thought raced through my head, and I knew just how I was going to get back at Jim and John, and when I was done with them, they weren't going to be able to mess with anyone like that again.

Thursday through Sunday came and went and I stayed home to heal. When Monday came around, there was nothing that would keep me from going to school as I could think of nothing else but putting my plan into motion and seeking retribution. So I got up early and got ready. Then I had my father drive me to school and drop me off at the front of the building. I went to my locker and got my stuff together for the day and even had time to go see my teachers and get the makeup work for the two days I had missed. I then went to first period. It was second period where I had Jim in my class.

He came up and talked to me like nothing had happened in the locker room and asked why I missed Thursday and Friday. I played along and said nothing about the locker room incident and told him that I was sick and stayed home. I asked him what he and John were doing for lunch, and he told me they were going to Whataburger. I asked if I could go, and he let me know to meet them in the same place as usual and that we would all walk over during lunch period. When class ended, Jim and I went our separate ways. Third and fourth period took forever to end but lunch finally arrived. I walked down to the end of the senior locker bay and met Jim and John. The three of us then walked to Whataburger. That walk was painful because of my injury, but I sucked it up and thought just how sweet payback would be and that a little pain was well worth the rewards I was about to reap. Just like clockwork, I got into line to order lunch, and Jim and John told me they would be back in a few minutes. I nodded my head and then turned back around to face forward in the line as they went to the men's bathroom. I watched as the two of them entered the restroom. Immediately, I felt this huge grin come over my face as I was about to exact some revenge.

For the past four days I had been working out in my mind how long it would take two kids my age to go into a bathroom stall after making sure they were not seen doing so and then crawl through the ceiling to the women's room, pausing for a few to get their rocks off and then coming back. At the point where they would reach the women's restroom, I was going to approach the assistant manager of the Whataburger, who happened to be a woman, and let her know that I believed there were people in the ceiling above the bathrooms and that the ceiling tiles looked to be giving way and were about to collapse. Now remember that I always ordered alone and sat down alone, so the assistant manager would never recognize that I had been friends with them.

Once I let her know what was going on, I had planned on walking out of the restaurant and letting some of the female patrons there also know what was happening so that they could catch Jim and John in the act. Later at school, if nothing happened to them, I would tell them that I took off after I saw people and the manager going into the men's bathroom and then people talking about guys up in the ceiling. Well that was the plan, at least, but on that day, fate was on my side. I know that on occasion the El Paso Police would go into the restaurant to make sure everything was alright during high school lunch hours. So right about the time I was going to approach the assistant manager, two officers entered. One of them stood near the entrance door, and the other went into the women's restroom. Yes, the officer going into the women's bathroom was female. I immediately went to the assistant manager and stopped her as she was about to exit from behind the counter.

"Excuse me – I just wanted to let you know that while I was in the men's restroom a second ago, I heard people get up into the ceiling in one of the stalls, and they sounded as if they were crawling across the tiles. I also wanted to let you know it looked like the tiles were about to fall down because of it."

She asked me if I saw who it was, and I said that the stall door was already locked before I went into the restroom. She thanked me and then got one of the male employees, and together they went into the men's restroom. I then calmly walked toward the exit, passing the police officer as I did so. I went about two hundred feet from the restaurant, where I then stopped and turned around to where I could still see inside the front windows. As I watched, I saw the assistant manager walk up to the officer at the front door and engage him in conversation. Then, both the officer and the employee went into the men's restroom. I stood there for a good five minutes and watched as large crowds gathered inside the Whataburger and out front of the Whataburger. There were so many people up front that I could no longer see what was going on. Just then I saw two more police cars drive up to the parking lot of the restaurant. Two officers exited from the cars and they went inside. Another five minutes had gone by, and I realized it was getting close to lunch period being over, and I did not want to stick around too long to have someone recognize me as being with Jim and John. Plus, I figured I would hear about whatever happened later at school. So, I walked back to campus and barely made it to my next class period on time.

The class after lunch ended and I went to the locker bay to get my book and homework for my next class. As I did, everyone was talking about the two guys from school who had got arrested at the Whataburger for climbing into the ceiling to watch women in the restroom. People were even talking about the fact that a female police officer was in the bathroom at the time, and that was when the two were cornered up in the ceiling between the men's and women's restroom. As I opened my locker, I overheard that Jim and John got so scared they forgot to balance their weight among multiple tiles and ceiling rafters and that the ceiling above the stall that the female officer had just come out of gave way, and the two of them fell and landed on top of the toilet. They were then arrested and taken away in two separate police cars.

I thought to myself that it could not have gotten any better than that. When it was time for P.E., there was no Jim or John to be found. The entire period ended up being about what happened at the Whataburger, and Coach Gomez told everyone that Jim and John were arrested for burglary. I did not know they could be arrested for that. Apparently, since they entered a portion of the restaurant that was off limits to the public with the intent to commit a crime, burglary was the charge. This was some great news. Now no one remembered or at least they never brought up what happened to me the past Wednesday, and no one else asked me where I had been on Thursday and Friday as the fiasco at Whataburger trumped absolutely everything. "Vengeance is truly precious," I thought to myself. After P.E. class, I walked home, and I felt elated that the plan turned out so well.

The rest of the week went by, and there was no Jim and John. Both had been suspended from school for two weeks. It turned out that neither one of them ever came back to school. I would later find out that they enrolled in a private school downtown so that the suspension would not show on their record. That was just fine, because I also would later find out that both of them ended up with a juvenile record for the burglary and that they had to perform an immense amount of community service as part of their probation. This entire event made me unusually happy. I got a tremendous amount of pleasure for what I did. The entire experience changed me and set me on a different path than the one I currently had been on. I would never settle for mediocracy again, not in the friends I was with and not in life. I was meant for bigger and better during this lifetime and I finally recognized it. I was going to find out and accept what this life had in store for me.

There were only a few weeks left in 1986, and Christmas vacation was fast approaching. In school, I was now hanging out with my friend Chris and his friend Andrew. I also started hanging out more and more with Doug Upchurch. As a matter of fact, this truly was the beginning of one of the best friendships I would have, and Doug and I would continue to be friends well into adulthood. Doug was absolutely one of the liveliest individuals I would ever know in this lifetime. He truly was larger than life. He had failed the seventh grade years ago and was about a year or two older than everyone else in freshman class. This is the same Doug I knew in the eighth grade. He was this big, tall and strong black guy that everyone loved and knew. He played football in the eighth grade and played this year on the freshman team. He was the starting defensive end. The thing I liked most about Doug was he genuinely was a nice guy and cared about the people around him. He had this laugh that was so contagious that it was almost impossible to be around him and not find oneself also laughing about whatever it was he was laughing about. He was a true friend, and I really credit him for having made my high school experience something amazing. So, for the last few weeks up until Christmas vacation, I hung out with Chris, Andrew and Doug and started meeting a lot of their friends, and that made my friend pool a lot larger.

The week of Christmas was one to remember. I found out at the beginning of the week that my parents were getting divorced. I will keep it short and just say that at the end of the separation period, my father ended up moving back into the house, and my mother moved to another state. My sister moved with my mom, and I stayed with my father. My father quickly got remarried, and I was now living with a new stepmom. The dynamics of life were soon about to change, and for me, they changed in a very positive fashion.

I had been getting used to the new living arrangements. I was grateful to still be living in the same house I had been in for a couple of years and continuing to go to the same high school. This made the change easier to digest. My father had also quit going to church. He told me it was hokey and that I did not have to go if I did not want to. That was all he had to tell me as I always felt like it was fun to socialize at church and hang out with people, but in regard to organized religion, I somehow felt like an expert and knew that it was created to control the masses and allow for the rich to keep their control over society. Religion gave the poor something to look forward to after death and therefore they rarely questioned their current status in life and the hardships it brought to the majority of the human population. So I nixed church and freed my mind from the control that religion had over me.

Another thing that changed was my father quit his job at the bank and opened a restaurant with his new wife. Life became fantastic after this as my father and his new wife were usually at the restaurant fourteen or fifteen hours a day, six days a week. They had Mondays off, so I was out of the house and at school most of that time. I saw my father and stepmom about four or five hours a week, total. Since they were gone most of the time and the restaurant was on the other end of El Paso, I had no way of getting rides to and from where I needed to go. I also could not run errands for my dad when it came to things he needed for the restaurant. My dad and I came up with a solution that was illegal, and I loved every bit of it. He and my stepmom took my birth certificate to a person she knew who created fake identifications. I never asked her how she knew this type of person and I just went along with the amazing plan. So this friend of my stepmom took my birth certificate and changed my birthdate by one year, now making me about to turn sixteen in March instead of fifteen. With this in hand, I went with my stepmom to the Department of Motor Vehicles on the Eastside of town, and we looked for an employee behind one of the counters who looked least likely to question anything. We soon noticed a young woman working at the front who looked to be fairly new. My stepmom began talking to her, and before you knew it, they were best of friends. A few minutes later, we provided the altered document to her and she questioned nothing.

She had me take the eye exam with her and then gave me the paperwork for the written test. I passed with flying colors. We went back to the same woman as before, and minutes later, I had my temporary driving permit. These were issued to youths who were about to turn sixteen and were going to start driver's education classes. The youth could then get his license upon turning sixteen and passing the driving course. Also, during the entire time we spoke to the woman behind the counter, I had brought up the fact that I wanted to also get my motorcycle license. She was kind enough to add a class M to the permit with a K restriction for moped only. This meant the engine had to be under 49cc. This was good enough, I thought, and could later be changed by working some additional magic at this DMV location. So I left with a driver's permit in hand.

My stepmom drove me to the local motorcycle dealership, where we purchased a Honda Elite 80 scooter. It was over the 49cc limit, but I figured I could weasel my way out of any issues that may come up, especially if I were stopped by El Paso Police. I then drove home on my first motor vehicle, and it felt great. I could now go as fast as 52 mph in the El Paso area, and this would include being able to get to school in record time and get whatever I needed to my dad when he was at the restaurant.

I now drove to school, and the scooter was quickly noticed by a lot of people. This meant that people I did not even know were stopping me in the halls and asking about it. I also started giving Upchurch a ride back to his house each day, and this got me noticed even more. School became a much better place for me, and before I knew it, March had arrived, and Upchurch told me I should try out for baseball with him. Up until this point in my life, I had never played organized sports outside of church ball. I had become very good at softball because I played it so much at church. So I figured what the hell and went to tryouts with Doug.

Tryouts were Monday through Thursday. I worked my ass off that week and hustled like never before. On Friday, I found out that I made the junior varsity baseball team. Doug did not make it but just went back to off-season football practice. Starting that Monday, I was taken out of physical education class for the last hour and placed into JV baseball. I was practicing from 2 in the afternoon until 5 or 5:30 in the evening. I was playing left or centerfield and I found myself having to play catch-up on the game of baseball.

I was way behind the curve as everyone else on the JV and varsity team had been playing for years. But I studied the game, gave it everything I had at every practice and hustled day in and day out. I also had to eat lunch in the cafeteria with the team and then go to study hall so that my grades remained above a seventy percent average. This was easy for me as I had little issues with the school curriculum and was often bored by what was being taught. But study hall was mandatory, and I made sure I never was late and never missed the period. Now, not only did my life change in school and in athletics, but it changed with my friends, the groups I would hang out with and the life I would live outside of school. This all started with two very good new friends.

As luck would have it, the other person who played outfielder on the JV baseball team was Miguel Puebla. Miguel and I were out on the field for about three hours a day together, and this caused us to not only become good teammates but also good friends outside of baseball. Before I knew it, Miguel and I were hanging out all the time together. Then I met a friend of Miguel's whose name was

Bryan Vostic, and Bryan was close to crazy. It also turned out to be a small world as Bryan's mom ended up having worked for my dad at the bank before my father quit and opened the restaurant.

Bryan, Miguel and I were doing everything together outside of school. Sometimes, the logistics were hard, but I would pick up Bryan on the scooter, take him to my house and then get Miguel. We would then hang out at the house as my dad and his wife were always gone. Also, as fate would have it, I passed driver's education, and on March 18, I passed my driving test and got my driver's license. I never told anyone at school that I was really a year younger. I let everyone think that I was as old as Doug. I kept this a secret in case I pissed someone off so that they could not rat me out.

My mom and sister had moved out of the state. In so doing, they flew in an airplane, and my mom had all her stuff shipped to her. This did not include her 1985 Nissan Maxima that was still sitting in the garage. Yes, I will say it again; I suddenly had access to a 1985 Nissan Maxima that was never being used, and there was no one around to know if I was taking it or not. I began driving it at lunch and picking up my friends. I started lunch by driving my scooter back to the house, making sure my dad and his wife were not there, taking the car, going back to school, picking up my friends, going where we needed to go, dropping them back off at school, taking the car back to the house, getting my scooter and going back to school. This routine was tight on time due to lunch period being fifty minutes, but no one cared, and I was the only one of my friends who had a driver's license and access to a scooter and a car.

Later, I was taking the car in the late afternoon and evenings while everyone was out at the restaurant. Since the restaurant had a bar, the earliest my father or stepmother got home was 11 or 11:30 at night. I would pick up Miguel, Bryan and their other good friend Brent Ward. The four of us began doing everything together and going wherever we wanted. We often got people to buy us alcohol and then would go back to my house and get wasted.

They spent the night often at my house. We also went out to the desert a lot and had massive bonfires while we drank. If we could not get anyone to buy us alcohol, we were sometimes able to get liquor from my parents' house as they often kept supplies there for the bar. My dad did not seem to care, just so long we paid him for what we took. I am sure my father knew we were also using the car, but he never said anything about it. I also never drove after drinking. This may be the reason why he never said anything. We also would go over to people's houses and hang out with them or call all the girls who Brent, Bryan and Miguel knew and hang out with them. Other times, we had our good friend Franky Castillo with us and even had Upchurch with us on occasion. Through these last few months of my freshman year in 1987, I ended up also making friends with several girls who were still going to Desert Vista Middle School. They were in the eighth grade, but this did not matter much to me. Apparently, these girls knew Bryan and Brent when they were eighth-graders and the girls were in the seventh grade. One of these girls lived just behind my street. She was so close to my house that Brent and I often went out the window of my room and would sit on the roof and watch her while we spoke to her on the phone. Her name was Heather Howard, and she would turn out to be a very important part of my life and in many more ways than I currently understood.

During the last couple of months of school, I not only became great friends with Miguel, Bryan and Brent, but I also ended up becoming very good friends with Heather.

When I did not have study hall for lunch, I would pick Heather up at Desert Vista, and she and I would go to my house to eat and hang out together. There were days when she would also bring her friends. Not only was Heather amazingly good looking, but her friends were, as well. So there were some days when Lea Luchard, Paula Stucky, Nicky Stevens or Cassy Beltran would also be at my house for lunch.

Heather was beautiful, and there was something about her that I did not quite understand at the time that made me feel very close and comfortable with her. She seemed to be a person I had known for years – no, centuries – and it was as if we hooked up in this life and just continued from where we had left off in a prior existence. This feeling I had around her was one of nausea and pain mixed with care and love. Whatever it was, we talked for hours at a time on the phone or at my home, and we could tell each other absolutely everything. So this led to her telling me she had the hots for Miguel, and then I told her I was crazy about her friend Lea Luchard. Then her friend Paula was completely in love with Brent, and Nicky Stevens was completely in love with my friend Franky Castillo. Brent wanted to have sex with all of them, and Bryan felt the same way as Brent. Miguel liked Heather, as well, but also wanted to hook up with Cassy Beltran. So toss all this together with raging fourteen- and fifteen-year-old hormones, and the last couple of months of my freshman year turned out to be – well should we just say fantastic!

My relationship with Heather grew and by May, I could not tell if I was better friends with Miguel or her. Miguel and I also finished up baseball and had a pretty good winning season. The coach then asked me if I wanted to play football the next year, and I told him yes. So there I was, in off-season football practice and weight training for the last few weeks of May and signed up for JV football my sophomore year. I had worked out a few times during my lifetime with weights, but these last few weeks were a true eye-opener into the power of the weight room. I ended up becoming hooked on weight training. Those weights helped me get bigger and a lot stronger. My physical gains came in leaps and bounds.

With our freshman year all about to end, Miguel, Bryan and I thought it would be a great idea to go out with a bang. We decided to have a party at my house on a Friday night when my dad and his wife were out of town and we did not have to worry about being out of the house by 11:30. We kept the invite list short. For the guys, it would be Bryan, Miguel, Brent, Franky, another one of Brent's friends named Chris and myself. For the girls, we invited Heather, Lea, Paula, Nicky, Cassy, and four more of their friends who I had met once or twice. More girls than guys were fine with me, and I knew Lea would come as she was best friends with Heather. We also got someone to score us about ten packs of Bartles & Jaymes wine coolers and a couple of six packs of beer.

So everything was set for the second-to-last weekend of the school year. The girls told their parents they were spending the night at someone's house and vice versa. I picked the guys up, and they were at the house a solid hour before we told the girls to come over. We set up for the party, meaning we basically got the wine coolers and beer on ice. By 9 at night, Heather and five other girls showed up. I lent the Nissan to Bryan to pick up a couple of the other girls who were coming but did not have a ride to Heather's house or my house. Suddenly, I was hosting my first party, and it was going to be one hell of a night.

Initially, the girls gathered in the living room, and the guys got them wine coolers. We had purchased a ton of them because this was the drink of choice for the girls in 1987.

There was a lot of picture-taking. I remember 110 camera and disc camera flash bulbs flashing everywhere. The alcohol started taking effect, and about an hour later, the music was playing loudly, girls were mixing with guys, people were laughing and acting stupid, and slowly guys and girls started going off to other parts of the house together. Now at about 10:30, I was sitting on the couch with Heather on one side and Lea on the other. Bryan was bombed out of his mind and lying on the floor in front of us. One of the girls I was not too familiar with had passed out and was lying on the tile in front of the fireplace.

Lea asked to see the house, so I took her for the full tour. The first stop was upstairs. As we went up the staircase, I noticed my sister's old room had the door closed. We stopped and opened it. Inside we saw Franky and Nicky going at it. She was topless with just her skirt and heels on.

Lea commented, "I guess that confirms what Heather and I were talking about downstairs."

I just kept staring at Nicky because for her being fourteen, she had to already be a solid and perky D-cup size. Lea closed the door, and we moved down the hall to my room. The door was open, so she and I walked in. We did not turn on the lights. Upon entering, we heard something coming from my walk-in closet. It sounded like someone moaning. Lea and I smirked at one another and walked to the closet door, which was closed, and I never close my closet door. I turned the doorknob and peeped inside. There, in between Cassy's legs, was Miguel's head, and she was moaning like I had only heard on movies at night on HBO. Miguel looked out the closet door.

He smiled and then said, "Close the damn door! Can't you see we are busy in here?"

Lea and I chuckled and closed the door.

"I guess we are running out of rooms," she said.

"I guess so," I replied.

We then went downstairs to the back room that had been converted into a game room. It had several large video games and one cocktail table Ms. Pac-Man machine. I learned how much Lea loved the game, because for the next thirty minutes, she and I played while drinking more wine coolers and getting to know one another. I liked Lea a lot, and many of my conversations with Heather were about how I liked her and how Heather liked Miguel. Well, obviously Heather was not ending up with Miguel that night, and here I was getting to know Lea.

She told me how Heather was always talking about me. Heather apparently had let it slip to Lea that I liked her, but Lea continued to tell me that this was not what she always discussed with Lea when it came to me. Lea continued to tell me that Heather constantly brought me up in almost every conversation. She said it was not always about who liked who but many times about how Heather thought she and I could easily have been together in another lifetime. Heather also told Lea that I was like no other guy on the planet and I was easy to have a relationship with. Lea went on to say that she was pretty drunk at that moment and wanted to do more than play Ms. Pac-Man with me but felt that both our relationships with Heather could be affected, and not in a good way. Now I was damn horny and I liked Lea, and she was very easy on the eyes, but somehow I agreed with her, and all I could think about was Heather, and especially the comment of Heather feeling like she and I had been together before in another lifetime.

It was strange as I have had many dreams and flashbacks to what I can only consider to have been other people's lives seen through my eyes. I caught myself thinking about reincarnation and also how I had seen a couple of women in my dreams with whom I seemed to be very connected. I then tuned back to Lea who was talking to me. Lea and I then returned to the living room.

Heather was still on the sofa, and she was talking to Paula. Brent was also back from being absent. Brent signaled to me that he and Paula had been in my dad's room going at it. Apparently, he and Paula did not get as far as Franky and Miguel did upstairs. Now Lea sat on the sofa with Heather and Paula, and we all continued to drink and talk while the others were still upstairs and Bryan and that one girl were still passed out. For another hour or so we, all talked and played some drinking games that led to everyone getting drunker. Finally, Franky, Nicky, Miguel and Cassy came down and joined everyone. A few minutes later, most of the girls left and walked back to Heather's house. They had all planned on sneaking back into Heather's house and up to her room by climbing up the trellis on the side of her house.

Brent had not had as much to drink as everyone else, and he drove several of the girls to one of their homes, where they were all spending the night. Brent also drove Franky and Chris home and then came back to my house, where we all talked about everything that took place that night. Miguel turned out to have the best story as he ended up having sex with Cassy in my closet. He told us she would not do it in my bed because she was afraid someone would walk in. Brent ended up getting to second base with Paula Stucky, and Brent said that Frank had told him that Frank and Nicky had sex several times upstairs. Bryan did not say much as he constantly was running to the bathroom to throw up. Then we all ended up crashing for the night. The following morning, we cleaned up and went out to breakfast before I took everyone home. Overall, it was a great night and one I would never forget. I still had questions in my mind about what Lea told me Heather had said. I wanted to talk to Heather about these things but was afraid of asking her as I was not sure what her answers would be or even if she would think I was crazy if I told her about some of the things I had dreamed about or experienced while being awake. I would have to think about what I was going to discuss with her at a later time.

The last week of school came and went. I was living a completely different life than when I started out the year as a freshman. I had new friends with whom I loved hanging out and getting into trouble with. I had a new mom and no sister. I was playing high school sports and loving it. I took up one of my greatest passions in life of weight training. I grew up and gained a year overnight. I was growing up and transforming from a person who always walked a straight path into something else. The strange thing is that none of this felt new to me; none of it.

# 11.

# My Eternal Flame

The house phone rang.

"Hey, it's me," the voice on the other end said when I answered it.

"What's going on, Heather? You sound strange."

It was Heather, and she asked me if my parents were home, and if not, could she come over and hang out tonight. I let her know that it would be fine and asked if she wanted me to invite anyone else.

"Only the two of us, if you don't mind," was her response.

I agreed but was wondering what was wrong as she did not sound her usual perky self. She let me know she was going to tell her mom that she was spending the night at Lea's and then come over at 6. After hanging up with Heather, I realized that since the party at my house, I had spoken only once with Heather, and it was a quick call for me to ask her a question, and that was it. I did not think too much of it as I had several errands to run.

One thing I wanted to do was to go and look at new cars. My mom was having her Nissan Maxima shipped to her as she had just gotten a new job in the Los Angeles area and needed the vehicle. People from the shipping company were coming Monday morning and picking up the car. So out of a necessity, as my father still needed me to run several errands a week for the restaurant, he was going to get me a new car. The scooter just could not hold the amount of items he needed me to bring to him and my stepmom while they were working at the restaurant.

I finished my chores, ran my errands and ended up going to several car dealerships in the Eastside of town. I had looked at a Pontiac Fiero, Dodge Shadow and a Chevy Camaro. The Camaro was way too expensive, and the insurance would be out of this world, so that was out. I liked the Dodge Shadow as it was a new vehicle type and no one else on the road looked to own it. But the Pontiac Fiero was just a sweet-looking ride and cost just a couple of hundred more than the Shadow with its turbo engine option. So I figured I would present all the paperwork the salesman at Pontiac gave me to my father the next time I saw him and see what he had to say about getting me a two-seater that looked like the closest thing I could get to a Ferrari. When I finished at the dealerships I saw that it was already 5 in the evening. I remembered that Heather wanted to come over at 6, so I rushed home to take a shower and clean up the loft and my bedroom.

I had showered and just finished vacuuming the upstairs when I heard the doorbell ring. It was exactly six o'clock, and I was kind of surprised that it could be Heather as I don't think she was ever on time for anything. This piqued my curiosity. I went downstairs and opened the front door. Sure enough, it was Heather, and she had a small overnight bag. She walked into the house, and I asked her if she wanted to go get something to eat or rent a VHS tape to watch.

"Can you make us something here at the house, and can we watch one of the movies you have already? I just want to hang out, and I don't want to go anywhere," she told me.

"Are you OK? You don't sound like your usual self."

She had tears in her eyes and came over and hugged me. This I was not expecting. I had hugged Heather a couple of times before, but never like this.

She latched on and would not let go. I put my arms around her and hugged her back.

"Heather, what's going on?"

She began to tell me as she sobbed that her father was being transferred in his job and that her entire family, including her, was moving back to North Carolina where Heather was originally from. When I heard this I quickly got emotional. I never pictured her any farther than a block away. I had known her only for a few months and had expected to have many more years of being with her. I sat her down, and she told me that her family was moving in a week. She had known for a few days and had already told all the girls but she said she didn't know how to tell me. For some reason, I was the hardest one for her to tell. I did not want to lose her. I was not sure yet what our bond was, but it was strong – more so than just two kids who had just recently met. For a few minutes, neither one of us said anything. I took this time to make some food and grab some chips and drinks. We picked up the food, grabbed a VHS tape and headed up to the loft to eat and watch the movie.

As we ate, I would catch myself staring at Heather. At one point, I moved from this existence to a place and time where nothing looked like the modern world. There was very little around, and the land was different. I was outside, and the sky also looked different. Next to me was this woman in her mid-thirties, and she was stunningly beautiful. As I stared at her, I could see that this woman had the same exact side profile and features as Heather. I mean it was not Heather, but somehow, it was her or her in a previous existence or in a different body and as a different individual. I was not sure which of these it was. Suddenly, the woman smiled at me. She took my hand and told me that everything would be alright and that I had done the best I could or that anyone could. Then, I was back in my loft, and Heather was staring at me.

She had this huge smile on her face and was holding my hand. I stared into her big blue eyes, as blue as the most beautiful sea that I had ever seen, and then she said something that caught me off guard: "Now you know what happens to me when I am around you. I am lost in another time and another space and yet somehow you or someone that does not look like you but is you is always there."

It dawned on me that my attraction to Heather was not just physical but far greater than anything anyone could imagine. She experienced the same things I experienced, and somehow, this linked us together in a way that neither of us yet understood.

"Patrick, I have grown old with you before. I have lived with you, and I have loved you in many other lifetimes. When I touch you, I am instantly nowhere and everywhere at the same time. I am me, then not me but many other people that were me."

I did not know how to respond as I was having trouble understanding what the two of us were experiencing, and I had lots of questions running through my head with regard to knowing if she had things happen to her as they did to me in the past and as far as the supernatural. For the next few minutes, neither of us spoke but just got lost in each other. I swear as I looked into her blue eyes, I saw her having lived many lifetimes as many different people. Some of those women I recognized, and others, I did not.

I was excited and nervous around her and blurted out, "Let's go drink! I think I need to drink."

She laughed as she got up and followed me downstairs to the bar, where there was a small fridge with wine coolers and beer.

Heather and I had been drinking now for about an hour and the movie was close to being over. We did not speak about what happened earlier as I believe neither one of us knew what was taking place between us. We drank until I was pretty wasted, and I knew Heather had to be the same way.

"What do you want to do now?" I asked her.

She asked me if I had a deck of cards, and I let her know I did. I went downstairs to get them and hurried back up. By the time I got upstairs, Heather was not in the loft. I walked down the hall to the other side of the house and into my room. She was there sitting on the floor in the dark.

I went to turn the main light on, and she quickly blurted out, "Not that light. Turn the small one on that is sitting on your desk."

I did what she asked and then joined her on the floor. She asked me if I knew any card games, and I told her I knew how to play poker. She liked this answer a lot and said she wanted to play but it had to be strip poker. Of course, I agreed with her choice, and before I knew it, both of us were down to our last few pieces of clothing. We played another hand, and I won, and off came her last sock. All she had left was her bra and panties. I was down to my boxers and nothing else. Another hand was played, and I won again. She smiled and undid the back of her bra.

"Do you want to remove it for me?" she asked.

"Is that a trick question? Of course I want to remove it for you."

Slowly, I leaned over and took one of the straps of her bra in my hand and gently pulled it toward me. I became focused on her breasts and how soft and sensual they looked; she was the most beautiful person I had ever seen. She put the cards down on the floor and stood up, slowly extending her hand out to me. I gave her my hand and she slowly helped pull me up to her. As she stood there topless and smiling she moved right up against me and placed her arms completely around me, embracing me with her bare breast now against my chest. I could feel her warm soft skin, her breasts against me, and I could feel her breath on my lips. I looked down at her and could smell her amazing scent, and I could not look away from her blue eyes – blue like the early-morning sky. I put my arms around her and pulled her closer to me, and as I did, I bent down and kissed her on the lips.

We kissed for several minutes as we stood in this embrace I hoped would never end. I did not know what passion was in this lifetime until that very moment. Her lips and breath made me feel lightheaded and made the room seem to spin. Then she pulled back and I let her go. She put her hands on her hips and then slowly started pushing her panties down until they were to her knees, then her ankles and finally down on the floor. Before me Heather stood completely nude, and I looked upon her and could not believe this perfect creature wanted to be with me. I removed my boxers and we got into my bed. That night with Heather was one of the greatest and most passionate nights I have had in this lifetime or any lifetime before it. I will always remember it and the true eternal bond between her and I that crossed over many lifetimes and seemed to have no boundaries of space and time.

We had been in bed for a while when she asked me if I see them, too.

"See who?" I asked.

"The dark figures. The ones that hate us," she responded.

"You mean you see dark flying creatures, as well? I thought I was the only one who saw them."

She told me that when she was a little girl, she had accidently been electrocuted, and that her heart stopped beating for several minutes. She was not resuscitated until the paramedics got there. She said that ever since then, she had this creature or dark shadow monster constantly haunting her and wreaking havoc with her, more so when she was younger than in recent times. She described the exact type of creature that haunted me when I was young and that had caused me so much physical pain when I was a child. She also said that there were others like it that came to her, as well. As soon as she was done telling me this, I shared with her what had happened to me, from drowning to the attacks by the dark figures to the strange dreams or daydreams that felt too lifelike to have not been real.

A lot immediately made sense for the two of us. We were somehow interwoven into each other's existence, and our attraction to one another had to be more than physical. The rest of the night, we discussed everything we had both been through and also talked about what each of us saw in our dreams and daydreams. The similarities were uncanny. At some point during all of this, we fell asleep.

When the morning came, we got dressed, and I then made breakfast for the two of us. She had to get home before her parents thought of calling Lea's house to check on her. I realized during the conversation that she was a bit distant from me but I did not want to bring it up. I figured last night would have been a lot to handle for anyone, and I did not want to mess anything up as I knew I had precious little time left with her before she moved away. As I remembered this portion of what she told me from the night before, I got that sick feeling when someone you care for or love is suddenly gone, and it did not feel good. I kissed her goodbye, and we quietly walked outside through the back door. As we walked around to the front of the house, she stopped and looked at me.

"I am not sure we were meant to be together in this lifetime," she told me.

"What does that mean?"

She shook her head and told me to forget it and that she was just being stupid. We said our goodbyes, and I watched as she walked down the street, turned left and was suddenly out of view. That would be the last time I saw Heather Howard. I called her many times a day, every day for that entire last week, but was told each time by her mom, dad or one of her siblings that she was not there. I even drove over a couple of times and was told the same thing. I was so angry at her on the day she was supposed to move that I did not attempt to go over when I knew she had to be at her house, packing and getting ready to leave. I should have gone because I never saw her again.

My life at the moment felt shattered. I had found my counterpart with whom I had a bond that crossed over into unknown realms of a reality I still could not comprehend. I ached for her and felt a passion that seemed to have been created and developed over an indefinite period of time. But she was gone, and worst of all, she did not want to have anything to do with me during her last few days in El Paso. I was in a dismal emptiness and did not know what to do or how to fix the way I felt. I yearned for her and was helpless in being able to change the situation. She was gone, and I was not prepared to handle it.

The next day I got a phone call from Lea, and she asked how I was doing. I did not respond as I did not know how to answer that and also, Lea never called me before. Never!

"Patrick, are you there? You need to come over to my house and pick something up that Heather left here for you. She told me to wait until she was gone before I had you come and get it."

I wondered what Heather could have left for me.

"What is it?" I asked Lea.

"It is an envelope, so I am assuming there is a letter in it from her," she said sarcastically.

I told Lea I would be over in a few minutes. When I got to Lea's house, she let me know that she was pretty upset, as well, over Heather leaving so quickly. She had considered Heather her best friend.

"I guess we both got fucked!" I told Lea.

It was not her fault. I thanked her for calling me and being available for me to pick up the letter. I then took the letter home. When I got to the house I opened the envelope and saw her letter with my full name on it, Patrick Kilian, and I then went on to read it.

"I know you must hate me right now, and I don't blame you; I would hate me, too. I did not speak to you during this last week because of something that happened that night we were together in your room and while you were asleep. I wanted to tell you. I did. But I didn't know how. Please know that I am truly sorry and that all I really wanted to do was be with you every minute and every second that I was in El Paso but I could not. When you slept that night, they came to me in your room and there were many. Patrick, there were so many of those dark-figured creatures in your room that I was terrified. They were around the bed, in the closet, up around the walls and all over the ceiling. I couldn't see anything but a sea of demons. When I was going to wake you up, they stopped me. Somehow they spoke to me as a collective. I know what they are now but I can't tell you. I can't tell you because they told me not to, and I am afraid of them all. Patrick, you have a greater destiny in this lifetime, and this time around, I am not supposed to be a part of it. You and I have done this before, and at some point in this lifetime, you will understand what I mean. This, again, is just one of those times when I cannot interfere, and I must allow you to accomplish what needs to be done. They did not tell me exactly what will happen, and even though I tried to remember from the past, I cannot. I just cannot recall what it is they knew about you. Please understand when I tell you that I love you and that we will be together again, but not yet – not yet. Please do not try to find me or contact me, just let the short time we were together be one that we will always remember, and in some other plane of existence, we can later build upon it. Promise me that you will remember me and promise me that you will try to put it all together and figure it out before it is too late.

Eternally, your Eve,

Heather"

It is rare that I cried or showed outward emotion. At that moment in my life, I did both. For the next few days, I did nothing but stay in my room, only coming out to use the bathroom or quickly grab something small to eat. I read the letter over and over and had mixed feelings of sadness and anger toward not just Heather, but others who were in our lives and those goddamn dark shadow creatures. I took up my journal again and read through prior entries and made a lot of new ones. It had been a while since I even picked up the spiral notebook, but now, at this time, it felt like a necessity to have it with me and to actively read it and update it. I had to figure out what these things were in my life. I also decided to respect Heather's wishes as I understood the creatures as well as she did, and I feared them in the past. But after this I despised them. At this point, I no longer feared the dark but welcomed it. A burning anger had grown inside me. An erupting volcano had taken over my emotions.

"So help me God!" I said out loud, "I will never fear these goddamn creatures and will never allow them to control my life or the world around me!"

Then just like that, my closet door slammed shut so hard that the wood of the door cracked down the middle, from top to bottom. It then quickly swung back open, and standing in the dark shadows of the closet was not one but two of these dark Pans.

One I knew immediately was my Pan of old – the one that wreaked havoc with me as a child. The other was taller and larger, and its face could be seen more clearly than my Pan. They came toward me as I sat up in my waterbed. As they did so, the bed furiously began to ripple and it felt as if I were on a small boat in the middle of the ocean during a great tempest. I turned as best I could toward my right to face them as they now both stood or levitated at the edge of the bed. Both began to speak in unison but nothing could be heard from either one. At that moment, I realized it was not that I couldn't hear them but that they were not in sync with this time and space and because of it, could not communicate with three-dimensional creatures such as living humans. It then dawned on me that I didn't need to hear them but just open myself up mentally and hear them as thoughts in my head, just like I did when I was young.

Sure enough, the moment I took the time to just open myself up to these creatures, I heard them loud and clear. There was no need for a language to be spoken. On some subconscious level, some level of thought in the human body and in my mind, I transmitted and received what needed to be said. I heard them communicate not as two separate entities but as one. I recognized that they were letting me know that what I could do and what I have done in the past is ancient and rare among mankind. They told me that what Heather saw and did was what had to be done. They let me know that I must mature and evolve in this lifetime. I would need to be strong and weak, good and evil, loved and hated, and at the right time, I would just know and it would overtake me like a thief in the night. As this was being communicated to me, I got up off the bed and stood before both of them, not afraid but empowered, beginning to grasp my destiny and beginning to understand my power. Then, just as they had come from nowhere, they were gone. I wrote everything down that happened and studied it many times over. I found new inner strength and understood that things in this life happen for a reason and would have happened no matter what I did. I was going to continue living my life and letting this body and mind evolve. I would allow it to experience anything and everything so that I could grow and at the right time, remember and understand what it is the supernatural phenomena around me already seems to know.

Through life, I would constantly see Heather, not just in my dreams but even while I was awake. I would be lost in a moment of thought or deep meditation and see her, not just as she is today but as a woman in her thirties then her forties and so forth. I saw her as other women in what I believed were past lives, and she always looked at me the exact same way, and I knew they were all her. I felt her presence because of that bond we shared at some higher level of existence and that I had experienced only with her. But later on in this life, there would be another. There would be one more person with whom I would cross paths who was just like Heather and just like me.

Several days passed, and I was close to being back to my normal self, at least on the outside. I was again hanging out with my buddies, and we were again getting into trouble and doing stuff we shouldn't have been doing. I even went with my father to the Pontiac dealership to test drive the Fiero. There ended up being issues with purchasing a vehicle at the Pontiac dealership. So my dad and I went to the Dodge dealership and ended up getting the Dodge Shadow.

I was glad everything turned out the way it did as I now could fit more than two people into the car, and that meant being able to shuttle more friends around. The Dodge Shadow was also fast, sometimes too fast as I got more than one or two speeding tickets while I owned it. It was definitely a hit that summer as now the gang and I were no longer limited as to where we could go due to not having the proper transportation.

When August came, it meant two-a-days for football practice. This was my first time to ever play organized football. I loved the game but had just felt physically too small to play at the school level. However, that all changed with baseball my freshman year and then with my love for weight training. That summer of 1987 saw me put on twenty pounds of muscle between May and August. I worked out six days a week, once or twice a day, and each time in the gym for anywhere between ninety minutes and three hours. I became a gym rat at the local Gold's Gym. All of this combined made athletics in my life a positive experience.

One unfortunate thing that came from playing football was I drastically quit hanging around Bryan and Brent as neither of them played on the team. Doug Upchurch was there, and I started hanging around with him almost as much as I had done my freshman year before baseball. Miguel Puebla also was on the JV football team, and I continued to hang around with him. But there was also an upside to all this, and that was the amount of new friends I made from the football team. These guys turned out to be the friends I would keep through my entire high school adventure and some even past high school.

Now I did not make friends with everyone on the team, and I sure as shit did not hang out with them all, but there were some of us who hung out so much, we later would form a crew. Not everyone in the crew played football, but the majority did at some point in time. That crew became famous – no infamous. We sure did do a lot of fun crap together – some of it stupid and some of it illegal – but be that as it may, it was a big part of my life at that time, and I will always remember those friends that made up the crew and the stories that came out of it all.

Now during this time of my sophomore year in high school, there were several events or occurrences that were important because they impacted me with regard to my higher purpose or why so much craziness and unimaginable events took place or were going to take place in my life.

The first of these events happened in late September during a football practice.

I was playing the safety position on dummy defense against the first-string offense. The coach had the offense run a play where our quarterback handed the ball off to the fullback. Now the fullback was this huge Hispanic guy named Jose Aguilar who had a full beard by the time he was twelve and looked like he had eaten several children earlier to get as big as he was. So Jose was supposed to sweep all the way out and then cut back at the last minute in between the right tackle and the tight end. The tight end was my good friend Miguel. So Jose did this, and the tackle executed the play so well that Jose went right past the defensive line and into the backfield. Since Miguel did not have to help block out the end or linebacker as that person went the wrong direction on the play, Jose and Miguel were headed straight into the backfield and toward the safety, namely me. I had two large bodies coming at me, and they were traveling at full speed. Now pride kept me from fake tripping and falling, and pride had me line up directly and open field tackle Jose. However, in the process, I got run over by Jose as I brought him down. His two hundred and forty-pound body came down on my neck and head and knocked me out cold. People told me later that it was one of the most intense tackles they had ever seen, and it sounded like two vehicles colliding. Miguel told me that I was out cold before hitting the ground, and my eyes rolled all the way into the back of my head. He said that there were a lot of coaches and trainers huddling over me for some time and that they were just about ready to call 911 for the paramedics. I do not remember any of this.

To this very day, the last thing I remember happening on that football field was making eye contact with Jose and then our helmets colliding. When I thought I had regained consciousness, I realized I was no longer on a football field in El Paso, and the year was no longer 1987. I awoke from the impact wearing some type of clothing made out of leather, wool and flax with leather sandals on my feet. I immediately recognized that I was in ancient Mesopotamia. I was no longer Patrick Kilian. Instead, I was fully aware that I was Nippuro, king of the Mat Umerai or what history would later call the ancient Sumerians.

I could see that I was much darker-skinned than I was a few seconds ago. I was confused as I had full recollection of being Patrick, but also was fully aware that I was now Nippuro and it was the year of Uruk mu in my period of ruling over the Mat Umerai. I recognized from this experience that everything scientists told us, especially archaeologists and anthropologists, were wrong. The year of my reign would convert into 4,812 BCE. I could see that I was in the process of still rebuilding all that had been destroyed from several hundred years back and that had been due to a catastrophic event that I was trying to recall but just could not. I turned to my left to look out over the courtyard and gardens at the palace and saw her – my queen, my wife, my Puabina. The moment I saw her, even with her dark skin and completely different features, I knew it was Heather, or Puabina before she would become Heather. She approached me, and I began to walk toward her as I could think of nothing else at that moment but wanting to hold her in my arms.

As I reached out I heard someone speaking: "Patrick, Patrick –can you hear me? Open your eyes; you have to open your eyes."

It was Coach Ritchie, the trainer. He had just put smelling salts under my nose, and I gained consciousness and was now in the training room on one of the bed mats. I slowly came to and could tell I was back at school. The coach asked me to move my neck and I did. It hurt like hell, but I was able to move everything and could feel all my body parts, from my head to my toes. He helped me up so that I was sitting on the bed. As I did this, I still had my helmet on. The coaches did not want to remove it until they knew my neck and head were alright. Slowly I took the helmet off and looked around. As I did so, I became dizzy, and then before I knew what I was doing, I hurled down the side of the bed. But I was fine – just a bit shaken up and sore. I later walked to my car and drove home.

When I got home, I got bags of ice and put them all over my body. After thirty minutes of icing what I could, I went to sleep. The next day, I did not go to school as I could barely get out of the bed to go to the bathroom. So that day as I was in bed staring at the ceiling, I had lots of time to think about what happened to me after the injury. I swear to the gods that I was back in ancient Sumer and that I was someone different. What was so different about this than from any prior experience I had where I was suddenly elsewhere was that this time, I knew about things happening around me. I had some type of high-percentage recall. I had full memories of both lives I had lived, both Patrick and Nippuro. I remembered far more, understood more about the place I was at and was aware of the time period I was in and who I was with. But this was crazy; how could I have these memories embedded inside of me? This had to be some crazy dream or I was delusional from the impact to the head I had just suffered. But then again, this has happened before, and what I read about reincarnation or other people experiencing their past lives somewhat matched what continued to happen to me. Now I thought that maybe I had read or watched something that could have had me associate these experiences to myself while in a dream state, but I did not recall anything like this, and the recall I had of such very specific places and people and feelings made no sense other than I had to have lived it before.

The winter was fast approaching in El Paso. Football had just ended with our JV team putting up a winning season, with only two losses under our belts. I continued working hard in school and looked forward to winter break. I did well in my classes, and over the weekends, it was one big continuous party with my friends, either at my house or in Juarez, where all the high school kids went. This again was because they never carded or really cared if anyone was eighteen or not, just so long you had the money to get in and bought plenty of alcohol while you were there. So I partied a lot and was drunk most Friday nights, Saturday nights and even an occasional Sunday afternoon. My friends and I also liked to go to the dog races in Juarez and bet on the greyhounds while we drank our body weight in alcohol. This continued week in and week out, and then before I knew it, half of my sophomore year was over, and winter break was upon us.

I have to mention that during this time, The Crew, as we called ourselves, was made up of a lot of different types of people. Most of us were sophomores, except for one or two freshman. No one in The Crew was allowed to be from outside our school. Many of The Crew were football players. The Crew started out with an original nine. Greg Upchurch and Miguel Puebla were part of the original nine, as was I. The Crew was really the first of any organized group at our high school that was recognized as a group outside of the regular curriculum or after-school group programs. There had not been gangs or tagging crews or crews of any kind in our middle-class neighborhoods of the El Paso Eastside. So on this one particular night, with nine of us altogether, The Crew was born.

So it was the first Friday of winter break, and we had all just gotten out that day from school, beginning our two weeks off for Christmas and the New Year's holiday. Nine of us that night got together in two vehicles. There was my car and a pickup truck that belonged to the quarterback of our JV football team, Shane Hines. The "Original 9" as we would later be called, met up at my house and hung out there for an hour, playing foosball and Nintendo. We began drinking, and I don't think we ever stopped. I no longer condone drinking and driving, but back then, I was a stupid, naïve teenager who did not think about the dire consequences of driving drunk. So we drank and drank and continued drinking. Greg got tired of getting his ass handed to him on Nintendo Baseball and suggested we all go out and do something.

The first thing we needed to do was get more alcohol. The nine of us piled into our two vehicles and drove off to the nearest 7-Eleven, and we could score nothing as no adults we asked would buy alcoholic beverages for us. We headed to the Stop and Go, and the same thing happened. Buzzes were starting to wear off, and Upchurch suggested we go park around the corner, and he and Chris Nickel would go down to the Stop and Go and try one more time to get someone to get us beer. Seven of us stayed by the vehicles.

Not more than five minutes had gone by when Shane yelled, "Look, Chris and Greg are running this way."

I looked up and I saw both of them running toward us with bottles and boxes of beer.

Upchurch yelled, "Start the car, start the fucking car, get in the car and start the fucking car!"

All of us piled in the vehicles, and Chris and Greg jumped into the back of Shane's pickup, and we sped off.

We drove back to my house knowing those two bastards just did a beer run at the Stop and Go. We got to my house, and everyone went inside laughing and talking shit about what just took place. I know it was illegal, but there was something fun and exhilarating about what had just gone down. Those two walked into the house laughing and telling the story of how they both slowly walked into the Stop and Go, both walked to the back where the beer was, took out several cases, walked to the front, told the cashier to have a great night and then bolted out the front doors. I knew right then that this was just the beginning of what was to become one crazy and adventurous night.

The nine of us ripped through the six cases in about an hour, and when we were done, we agreed it was time to go do more crazy shit. So we piled back into the vehicles and headed to the local Alpha Beta supermarket. It was a good four or five miles from my house and not anywhere near where any of us lived. We all decided to go to this market as it was far enough away from where we usually shopped, and hopefully no one would recognize us there. About ten minutes later, we pulled up into the parking lot and decided who was going in, who was driving and who was going to run as a blocker in the store in case something went wrong. I was pretty wasted by now and immediately volunteered to be part of the beer runners. So I was a runner and Upchurch was running. Chris and Eddy were going to be blockers, and Shane was driving his truck and John was driving my car. This was finalized, along with where we were going to meet, the getaway route and where we were going to drive. It was decided upon before everything went down that we were headed next to Album Park. So with everything worked out and a plan coming together, Chris, Eddy, Upchurch and I headed into the supermarket.

It was about 10 at night, and the store had very few patrons and employees inside. I feared that the four of us walking in together had to send up some type of red flag to the employees, but I still walked in and began walking toward the back of the store. I headed up one aisle, and Greg went up another. Eddy and Chris took up blocking points back toward the front registers and pretended to be reading magazines. As I walked to the rear of the store where the beer was, I did not run into Upchurch or even see him come near the beer aisle. I wondered a bit where he could be but still remembered my role in everything. So without waiting or looking around, I grabbed a case of beer and headed back down one of the aisles to the front of the grocery store. As I did so, midway down the aisle, I quickly saw why Greg did not make it to the back of the grocery store. He immediately began being followed by several of the employees. I could only think it was because he was black as we had both entered into the store together, yet not a soul followed me. I figured that meant Upchurch was now a blocker like Chris and Eddy.

So I continued down the aisle and stopped toward the front, right before it opened up into the front of the store and the cash registers. I looked around and decided to just see if I was being watched. As I did this, I picked up a large case of toilet paper and then slowly started walking to the front registers. I am not sure why I kept the toilet paper, but I did. I ran out the front doors, turning to the left and heading toward the back of the building where John was waiting with my car. I jumped into the front seat and John took off like a bat out of hell, headed toward Album Park. I was laughing, and everyone else in the car was laughing, as well.

"Why the fuck do you have toilet paper?" John asked.

"I have no fucking clue!" I replied.

Everyone continued to laugh at the fact that I had come running into the car with the biggest damn case of beer the store had and a package of twenty-four rolls of toilet paper.

Several minutes later, we got to Album Park and parked on the inside residential street where we could quickly exit in either a north or south direction if we needed to. The four of us who were in my car got out and took the beer with us. We walked to the meeting place, which was decided to be the playground area. The four of us busted open some beers and began drinking while we waited for Shane and the others to get there. About five more minutes passed when we saw our five friends coming toward us laughing and calling out my name. Eddy and Chris came up to me and asked what happened to the toilet paper I ran out with. I let them know it was still in my car. Once I let them know that, the two of them started talking shit and let me know that once I had run out the doors, they went to the front register and paid for two candy bars.

They told me that the cashier looked up at me then continued to ring up the candy and the only thing he said was, "I guess that guy really needed to take a shit!"

Upchurch then came over and told me he had to pull away from grabbing beer as he immediately had everyone in the store following him. I had seen what had happened and figured that was the perfect time for me to bolt. So for the next twenty minutes, we all drank that case of beer, laughed about the crap we had done and wondered what the hell we could do with 24 rolls of toilet paper. Miguel then suggested we go and toilet-paper someone's house. This was another excellent idea, I thought. With that set as our next objective for the night, we headed back to the vehicles and were off to Letty Brionna's house as this was the girl of the week who Miguel liked.

Before getting to Letty's house, we had stopped at another grocery store and purchased another forty-eight rolls of toilet paper and for some stupid reason Chris purchased several bottles of shaving cream. Nobody knew why, but then why did I grab toilet paper and run in the first place? We then drove by Letty's house and ended up parking a block away. We split up into three groups and headed in different directions but made sure we met up in front of Letty's home. When we got there, several of us started throwing toilet paper through the big trees in the front. Others started toilet-papering the bushes and two cars in the front driveway. Tony and Miguel got the bright idea that they would get on top of the roof to toilet-paper and spray shaving cream all over it.

"What the hell are you doing on the roof? They are going to hear you from inside, you fucking idiots. Get off the roof," Greg quietly called out.

Just then, lights went on in the house, and the rest of us scattered like roaches. We then booked back to the vehicles and slowly started driving away. The last two to come running were Tony and Miguel, and they jumped into the back of Shane's pickup, and we all sped off to the desert, which was the outskirts of the Eastside.

When we got out to Zaragoza Road, we started yelling at Tony and Miguel for being dumb-asses and getting on the roof. Of course, it then turned into laughter and great story telling as rarely does a roof get toilet-papered and shaving creamed during a TP party. We used seventy of the toilet paper rolls before we had to run from Letty's place. I knew I was going to have to check that house out in the morning. Then again, maybe not as it would be a bad idea to return to the scene of the crime. So now we found ourselves out in the desert, on the outskirts of town, and asked each other what else we could do?

Shane blurted out, "We should take all these damn street barricades and their blinking lights."

Everyone looked around and noticed all the street work going on as they were being expanded due to the city's growth. We realized we were standing in a sea of barricades, each with its own blinking orange light. With everyone in agreement, the next part of the evening was in full swing.

Shane had a toolbox in the back of his truck, and he handed out hammers, screwdrivers, pliers – you name it. Armed with these tools, the nine of us hastily got to work. The first thing we did was take several of the barricades in their entirety, tossed them into the back of Shane's pickup and covered them with several blankets so the flashing lights could not be seen. Then we all went to work removing another fifty to sixty of the blinking lights and placed them into the trunk of my car. Whenever a vehicle would drive by, which was rare, we would hide behind the dirt dunes on the side of the road. Once the vehicle would pass, we got back to work. About twenty minutes went by when we realized there were no more blinking lights for almost a block and a half. When we got ready to leave and tossed the last of the lights into my trunk, it was quite the scene as it looked like the inside of a Las Vegas casino in the trunk of the Dodge.

With blinking detour and caution barricades at our disposal, we went to the rival high school and placed the signage on the road in front of the school. It took about fifteen minutes to do so as this area of town had a lot more traffic than where we had gotten the barricades. We made it where the signs led the vehicles to a dead-end street behind the school. After the barricades were all in place, we moved the vehicles several hundred feet back and watched as one car after another drove into the dead-end street. Since we were all pretty buzzed, this did not get tiresome to witness for a good thirty minutes. As a matter of fact, Chris and John did another beer run so we could keep drinking while we watched our project unfold. The beer later ran out, and we finally left. We did not bother to remove the barricades.

It was now approximately 2 in the morning, and we decided our night was still too young for it to end. We cruised by Chris Nikkel's house and he snuck in through his bedroom window to get a couple of pellet guns he owned. He went through the window of his bedroom so that his mom would not know he was home and make him stay. Soon after, he came out with two pellet guns and a whole lot of pellets. We decided to do drive-by shootings on several of the car dealerships that had those huge inflatable advertising animals in the front of their buildings.

The first place we went was a dealership on Airway Boulevard as this had light traffic this early in the morning and no security cameras outside as far as we could tell. The first victim of the night was a huge inflatable ape in front of the local Chrysler dealership. Let me tell you, we shot the hell out of the thing, and it took over one hundred shots before it came tumbling down. Because it was so much work, the ape became the only victim to the pellet guns that night as this was no longer seen as fun teenage entertainment for the early-morning hours. Next thing up on the agenda was mailbox baseball, and the lucky street we chose was one of the more expensive neighborhoods of the local golf course: Leo Collins Drive.

I had two baseball bats in the trunk of my car, and it was just a matter of digging through all the blinking lights to get to them. Once we did, Shane took one for his truck and I the other for the Dodge. We drove to the end of the straightaway on Leo Collins, just before it turns into a large circular continuation. Each of us then lined up our vehicle on a different side of the street. Shane was driving his truck while Doug was in the pickup bed with the bat, and I was driving the Dodge while Miguel was hanging out the passenger window with the other bat.

"On your mark, get set, go!" Shane yelled from his window.

And we were off, down the street swinging away at each and every mailbox. Things were going well for Miguel and Doug until the two geniuses came up against stone and brick boxes. Since both of them were pretty wasted, they took a swing at the mailboxes. You could hear a massive crack on both sides of the car, and then you saw splintered bats flying all over the street.

"Oh shit, man, I didn't see it was a brick mailbox," Miguel blurted out.

"Go pick that crap up out of the street so they don't have our finger prints," I told Miguel.

He jumped out of the car and grabbed what was left of both bats right when the owners of the homes came out to see what the hell all the noise was from.

"Oh, fuck, get back in the car and drive, drive, fucker!" Eddy yelled from the back seat of my car.

I sped up to meet Miguel in the street, and he jumped in, and Shane and I peeled out of Leo Collins and headed to Pellicano Drive.

Now you would think that with us almost getting caught that we would be done for the night, but no! We were drunken teenagers, and for us, the night was not over. Earlier it had been brought to our attention by Chris that he had seen an abandoned vehicle off of Pellicano, where they were getting ready to start building but had not yet put in the paved streets. He remembered again after the mailbox baseball competition, so we headed to the abandoned car right after a quick beer run. This was carried out by four people at once, and yes, that, in turn, meant we got a lot of beer. Once everyone got back to the two vehicles, we headed to Pellicano Drive and located the abandoned car. We had to drive on a dirt road for about two thousand feet. The car was in an area that had already been cleared of the desert brush by bulldozers, but no construction had started in the area. So, we pulled out the beer and started drinking. Several minutes into drinking and figuring out what we wanted to do with the car, the dumbest idea of the night came out of Eddy, who had been pretty quiet until then.

"Hey, let's blow that shit up!"

Everyone nodded in agreement.

"How are we going to blow up the car?" Shane asked.

"Fuck if I know," Upchurch said.

Miguel then had an idea. He suggested we tie several rags from Shane's truck together and then douse it in gasoline from the spare gas canister Shane had. Miguel then suggested we pour the rest of the gasoline all over the interior of the car and the back end where the gas port was located. We would then push the cloth down into the gas port and keep a portion hanging out of the port. So we went ahead and did what Miguel suggested. Eddy then had four M-80 firecrackers with him that he had wanted to throw at cars all night as they drove by but never had the chance. So we taped the M-80s together with duct tape that I had in my trunk. The M-80 bomb, as we were now calling it, was placed on the top of the gas tank cap area of the car, right where the rag stuck out. More gasoline was poured over the top of the car and the interior. Then my dumb ass lit the vehicle on the inside with a lighter, and that car quickly caught fire. Who knew the interior of a vehicle was so flammable?

Before we knew it, the entire vehicle was on fire, and that meant it spread to the gas tank area before I could run away. I heard one small explosion and then heard another as I felt the air around me drastically change in pressure. I then felt the air get sucked out of the vicinity and then blown right back toward me. I was blown off my feet and right into Shane's truck as the windows on the left side of his truck blew out. Everyone was on the ground from the explosion. Now all anyone could hear was this massive ringing in their ears. We knew we had to get out of there quick as half the Eastside had to see the explosion and the huge fire ball it made. As we slowly got into the vehicles, we drove away while the abandoned car continued to burn. I did not drive as I was still feeling the effects of the explosion, and instead John drove the car.

We got back to my house and parked my car inside the garage and parked Shane's truck behind my car in the driveway. We removed his rear license plate just in case someone got the plate number and let El Paso Police know about it. Then we all went inside and began recovering from one of the craziest nights of my life. Now I know I suffered a concussion and head trauma from the explosion as I had some blood coming out of one of my ears. I vomited several times during the night, and I knew it was a combination of the concussion and being drunk. Everyone crashed at my house that night, either in my room or what used to be my sister Ann's room. At some point after heavy projectile vomiting, I passed out. Lo and behold, when I awoke I was no longer in my house, and the year definitely was not 1987.

I closed my eyes for a second and then opened them again, hoping I would find myself in my room, barely able to get out of my waterbed because of how drunk I was. This was not the case. As I opened my eyes, I was in a different part of the world. At first I was not sure where I was since there was nothing around but mountains and green hillsides. But then as I continued looking, I slowly recognized that the mountains were in an area of the world that would eventually become known to modern-day man as Peru. But how could I recognize this location and know the time period in which I found myself? I saw that the sky was very different-looking, and this was not due to me being in the southern hemisphere of the planet and not recognizing anything other than a northern sky. This was because something was happening at that very moment, and it was not good.

The sky had a pink and red hue to it, and the clouds were a dark, even dirty-looking brown. As I looked up, I saw balls of fire descending from the heavens. The fireballs were of all shapes and sizes, and all the land around me was set ablaze. I felt the ground fall away from below me and watched as new rock shot up from the Earth. Mountains of tremendous size were being built around me in a matter of minutes instead of millions of years as we were all taught to believe. To my right was a great city made out of massive stone blocks. These blocks were not from our modern time period. The technology and master craftsmanship were far more advanced than anything within the twentieth century. But how could that be? This incredibly well-built city of the past was being ripped apart, and these massive stones were tumbling off of each other and falling onto the new earth that was rising out of the old.

I looked out toward the horizon and saw a wall of sea water coming toward me and the city. It was something I had seen once before in another dream or recollection I had, but that was a different time and place and not where I now stood. The mountains continued to shoot up to new massive heights, none of which existed just a few moments ago. The city I saw was overtaken by the waters, and people and vehicles and machinery I had not seen for a very long time were washed away. The only thing that remained were those large stone walls and blocks that made up the city and the landing docks. However, now these parts of the city would be located at the tops of wherever these new mountains formed once they were done in their sudden and instant rise toward the heavens. Then it happened: the wall of ocean waters reached me, and I was no more.

I awoke back in El Paso, so certain I was crushed by water that I had to make sure I was in one piece. I was alive, and there was not one bit of me that was wet. I do not know how as it felt so damn real. I thought that this had to be another person's life I saw through the eyes of that individual, a long time ago in what now looked to be a past lost to our current population. Was what we were being told by scientists, archaeologists and historians a fabricated lie regarding humanity's past? Did they just not know the truth, destined to only regurgitate the misinformation they were taught in school by a professor who in turn was also taught the wrong information? It felt like we were stuck in a vicious cycle of a made-up history – or at least a good part of it that someone did not want us to know about. This was way too much for me to take in at this time after almost being blown up earlier. I had to give it up and try to go to sleep. That is exactly what I did: I joined the other eight around me who were in a deep drunken slumber.

The following morning, I awoke to blinking orange lights all over my damn bedroom. As I wondered what the hell was happening, I heard a ton of laughter from everyone else. Apparently, I was the last to get up, and the rest of my friends thought it would be a great prank to get all the blinking lights out of my car trunk and decorate my room with them. It was definitely interesting, I thought. Those lights stayed in my room for a few weeks before I got around to disposing of them in a Dumpster in back of some commercial property. Slowly over the next few days, we heard about some of our misdeeds from friends or the local news. Weeks later, when Letty found out it was us who toilet-papered her home, she was not angry. She also told us of how her little brother and aunt had been at the house that night and thought people were breaking in and were on the roof. The police were called, but they obviously got there too late. Letty never told her family that it was our group.

The holidays came and went, and we celebrated the coming of a new year. 1988 continued on, and we continued to live life at a fast pace. I had another birthday and turned sixteen for real and seventeen to all those around me. Instead of playing baseball that spring, I decided to focus on weight training and power lifting. The two became an obsession, and I could almost always be found at the gym when school was not in session. In May, one other strange thing took place just before school ended. I was at home alone on a Friday night. I had let my friends know I did not want to go to Juarez that night but instead had to study for several classes. No one else was home at the time. I looked up from where I was sitting in the living room on the couch and saw a shadow figure walk from the upstairs loft to the center of the hallway that led to my room and suddenly stop. It looked down at me, and with what looked to be its hand, signaled for me to come upstairs and follow it. Now I was scared, I am not going to lie, but I was also curious as the shadow figure was not aggressive and seemed to want only to communicate.

It did not move and continued to signal me. I cautiously went up the stairs and toward the figure. As I was getting to the top of the stairs, it started floating down the hall and into my room. I got to the upstairs and turned right to follow the creature. I could see it in the dark, standing at the foot of my bed. When I got into the room, it motioned for me to look up. As I looked up, the ceiling to my room vanished, and I saw nothing but millions upon millions of stars, the likes of which I had not seen before. The figure spoke to me in my mind and told me I had been here before and will soon be here again. I must prepare not just myself but all who will listen and follow. When I asked the figure what it meant by this, it again motioned for me to look up. As I did, I saw something large enter the sky, and it was travelling fast. I was about to ask what it was but realized I was alone in my room and again standing below my bedroom ceiling. I was now standing in the darkness, not sure what took place and why. "Where had I been before?" I thought to myself. I did not want any of this crap to happen to me anymore as I was sick and tired of things that didn't make sense and things that were not of this world. But it would never really end – never.

# 12.

# Vacationing With Crazy

My junior year of high school was just as crazy as my sophomore year. The Crew did a lot of foolish stuff, and we were all lucky to make it out of school without being arrested or convicted for some of the more illegal things we did. I continued to do well that entire year in my classes. I ended up dropping high school sports and focused on powerlifting and bodybuilding. In regards to my being able to report on any supernatural occurrences that year, there were none.

During the school year, seven members of The Crew, including myself, threw some huge keg parties at my house once or twice a month to raise money for a trip we wanted to take during summer vacation of 1989. This meant that the seven of us would front enough money to purchase three or four kegs of a mid-range beer and would then stage the party in my backyard. We charged $4 or $5 per person and usually walked away with $400 to $600 a night in profit. By the time April came around, we had already saved up a little over $5,000. With that money, we purchased airline tickets and a hotel room in downtown San Diego. We would also end up using the money for transportation, food, alcohol, entertainment and other miscellaneous expenses that would come up. The most expensive part of the trip would end up being transportation to where we wanted to go as no one would rent a vehicle to any of us. So once July came around, the seven of us headed to sunny San Diego, and what would end up being one of the worst times of my life.

When we originally got there, everything was great. None of us could believe we made it and that everyone's parents agreed to it. We were all seventeen or eighteen – me seventeen but pretending to be eighteen. From the airport, we took a minibus to our hotel in the downtown area. We had selected this location so that we could walk to many of the places we wanted to go without the need for two taxis or using public transportation. We checked into the hotel, and the place was pretty shady. However, it was one of the few places that would rent to an eighteen-year-old and allow seven guys to stay in one room. That night, we smoked some weed that Chris had scored from some random guy outside our hotel room door. Then we went and had one heck of a steak dinner and headed to a local night club, where we got shit-faced and then proceeded to strike out with the women.

There is also one additional piece of information that needs mentioning. We were able to get into all the clubs and get alcohol as all seven of us had gone to Juarez and got real Mexico driver's licenses from the uncle of a friend of ours. He charged us $400 for all seven, and since they were all real government identifications, no one back in 1989 questioned them. As a matter of fact, I don't think any of the bouncers or cashiers we came upon had seen a Mexico driver's license before. Some of them did test our Spanish-speaking ability, but enough of us spoke it fluently or partially to make sure we got into the club and were able to purchase alcohol. So that first night, we had fun together, but from there on out things got progressively worse, until it all culminated into one of the worst vacations I have ever had.

That night, I found out just how hard it was to sleep with six other people in the room and half of them snoring. Not to mention there was a single bathroom. This, too, had been overlooked in the planning stage of the vacation. This meant that there were times when I had to use the bathroom at the Jack in the Box down the street as a line had already formed for the usage of ours. There also was the constant dog-piling on top of me in the early-morning hours by a bunch of drunk and stoned assholes. Other things happened that just took away from the experience. One of these times was when Don decided to get his ear pierced by a street vendor. We told him not to, but he didn't listen. Hours later, his ear was showing signs of infection. So he went into a local pharmacy to get an antibiotic ointment. We waited outside for him for more than ten minutes. He finally came out, and his hands were empty. That was because Don decided not to pay for the ointment but instead shoplifted it. The next two people who came out were loss prevention employees, who stopped and arrested him.

That ordeal lasted five hours as the San Diego police did not want to take him into custody. But in order for them to give him a citation, they had to contact his parents and get their permission as Don was still seventeen. Also, he happened to have his fake Mexico driver's license with him, and that, too, was confiscated. Now one of us could not get into the clubs, and this caused conflict as others wanted to stay with him or do something else so that Don could be included. Now no one could decide on what we would do in the evening for entertainment. Then that second night I was again unable to sleep because I was with people who snored.

On day three, we took a tour bus up to Orange County and went to Disneyland, "The happiest place on Earth," or so they say. I was excited to be there. It made me feel like I did when my parents would bring me when we lived in Orange County so many years ago. But apparently, I was the only one who felt that way. The rest of my friends began to complain that it was for children and that we should have gone to Six Flags Magic Mountain or Universal Studios Hollywood instead. This pissed me off because I had originally wanted to go to Universal Studios but was outvoted. Now that we were here, I heard nothing but complaining. The only two things everyone wanted to do was ride Space Mountain or Star Wars. The Matterhorn Bobsleds had been closed for repairs that day.

Then there was the other issue of all the shoplifting taking place. Except for Don and I, everyone else was taking whatever they could fit into their pockets. The only reason Don was not stealing was because he had already been caught the day before. All I could think of was, when would this day end and when would we get back to the hotel? We ended up getting back to downtown San Diego at about 7 at night. Everyone else just wanted to go to the Jack in the Box to get food and bring it back to the hotel room. Their big plan for the evening was to smoke pot and then maybe make a second trip to Jack in the Box.

I was pretty much over it and left. I had decided to get a taxi cab and go to a bar and pool hall I had seen earlier while the bus was bringing us back into town. The taxi ended up dropping me off at the bar at around 8 in the evening, and I was there for a couple of hours shooting pool with a couple of girls I had met. They turned out to be lesbians, and I knew nothing other than playing a few games of pool was taking place for me tonight. I ended up leaving at 10 and got a cab down the street about ten minutes later. From the moment I got into the taxi, I knew something was wrong; something did not sit right with me.

This taxi I got into was like every other one I had seen in the city, but the driver seemed very off to me. I watched him in the center rear view mirror as he continued to watch me and barely monitor the road. He had asked me where I was going and who I was going to see. This question made me wonder why he would need to know. Now I was just a teenager in a large city by himself, but I had some amazing street smarts about me. As I began to watch where I was being driven to, I noticed that we were not going in the direction of the hotel, but instead into a shadier part of the downtown area with lots of back alleyways. I knew I was going to get robbed by this cab driver. Sure enough, he made a quick right into a back alleyway with no lighting and stopped. In the shadows and up against the wall of one of the buildings, I could see movement, and it was from more than one person.

I dove across the backseat to the other side of the car, pushed open the door, got out and started running. My feet hit the ground and never stopped. I heard several people yelling at me and lots of shoes hitting the pavement as this was a good indication that I was being pursued by more than one individual. As I continued to run, I attempted to get my bearings location-wise based on some of the larger buildings, and I knew my hotel would be past a couple of large skyscrapers I recognized. Suddenly, I heard glass smash up against the wall to my left. I then heard another and another. My pursuers were throwing bottles at me. Then I felt something hit me in the back of my head, and it instantly hurt. Something pierced my skin, and then I felt warm liquid running down the back of my neck and then my back.

I ran that much harder and picked up the pace. I started weaving in and out of streets and did not run in a straight line. Before long, I ditched my assailants. A couple of more minutes of medium-paced jogging turned into quick walking, with me looking back about every three or four seconds. I finally saw a building I recognized and estimated that I was still about a mile from the hotel. I was now getting dizzy and knew it had to be from blood loss. I could not just pass out anywhere as I knew I may wake up in someone's trunk or naked with all my belongings taken or even worse. I saw that just up and to the left was a small shop with Chinese writing on the sign above the door. It was still open, and I figured I would go in and ask for them to call the police and an ambulance. I got very dizzy as I got to the front door and had to hold onto the door handle so that I would not fall back and onto the sidewalk. In the store, I saw an old Chinese woman, an even older Chinese man and a very attractive Chinese girl who looked about my age.

"Help me, please," I said. "I have been attacked. I am bleeding and need help!"

That was the last thing I remember just before I blacked out.

"Adama, Adama – you must wake up, Adama! Wake up now, Adama – now!" said an unknown female standing above me in what looked to be a large cave or subterranean structure.

I tried keeping my eyes open but could not and blacked out a second time. I slowly started to wake and felt groggy and disoriented. As I began to open and focus my eyes, I could see that I was in a dim room lit by twenty or thirty candles. As I gained my bearings, I could see that the old Chinese man and woman were directly above me and that the old man was tending to the back of my head. I lifted my head off of a pillow and began to reach my arm and hand back behind my head to feel my injury when I heard a soft and young but now scolding voice say, "Stop! Don't touch it. Grandfather just removed the glass and stitched you up. Now he needs to cleanse the wound."

"OK," I told her. "Where am I, and who are you?"

The beautiful teenage girl told me that her name was Lynn and that she just happened to be visiting her grandparents when I barged into the store and passed out with blood streaming out of the back of my head. She told me that she was going to call the police but that both her grandparents stopped her and said she could not and that they would help instead. When she asked them why, her grandparents told her that I was an "Ancient" and that I needed their help and later their counsel.

"What do they mean by my being an Ancient, and why would I need their counsel?" I asked.

Lynn said she had asked them that same question when they first told her and that their response made no sense to her. They went on to tell her that I am older than much of time itself and that my powers are of a time long ago.

"Are you shitting me?" I accidently blurted out.

"I shit you not!" she responded.

Neither of us said anything more as her grandfather was just then finishing up on bandaging the back of my head and the base of my neck. When he finished working on me, he began to speak to his granddaughter in Mandarin. Lynn was just about to tell me what her grandfather said when all of a sudden I responded to the old man in his native language. For several moments, I lost track of time and zoned out. To where I zoned I do not know, but I do remember hearing myself speak Chinese back to the man and his wife for some time, and I understood everything they were telling me. Lynn looked perplexed this entire time as I seemed to be more fluid in Mandarin than she was. After several minutes of conversation with them, I grew tired and must have again blacked out.

I later awoke and looked at my watch. The time was 3 in the morning. As out of it as I was, I knew I had to get going as I knew my friends were probably freaked out by my having never returned to the hotel. When I got up, I realized the room and building I was in was shut down and abandoned. This really threw me for a loop. If it were not for the fact that my head was stitched and bandaged up, I would have thought I hallucinated the entire event from the point of stumbling into the open door until now. But how was any of this possible? I know I was speaking to the old couple and their granddaughter earlier, but this building looked like it had been abandoned for quite some time, and there was no way everything in the shop could have been taken out while I slept for such a short period of time. I did not know what was happening to me or how. Somehow, someway, someone or something came to my aide in this abandoned building and it manifested itself in the form of an elderly Chinese couple and their granddaughter Lynn. Once I was up I realized I was somehow locked in the building and had to break the glass on the door to get outside.

About thirty minutes later, I was outside of the hotel and started getting scolded by my friends.

"Where the hell were you, Patrick?" Chris yelled from the second floor of the hotel.

All of them came out and looked seriously perturbed at my having left without telling them where I was going. I could not believe that I was the one getting scolded for having ruined the night and morning when they had spoiled the entire trip for me almost from the get-go. They saw my head and asked me what happened, and I told them the story but left out the part about my three guardian angels or whoever it was who helped me. I continued to take criticism from everyone for having left in the first place, as if getting high in the hotel room and then wasting another $40 at Jack in the Box would have been the better alternative. Well, maybe in hindsight it would have been.

The last few days we were in San Diego were just as bad, and I was elated when the day came for us to board the plane at San Diego airport and head back to El Paso. I remember getting home and not wanting to do anything with those six people. My relationship was never the same with them. I even believe some of the other six may have even been upset with one another and their relationships also were strained to a degree. But as for me, I could not put up with any of them for too long, and if more than one of them was together at a time, it made for that much more displeasure while in their presence. The Crew even broke into factions after that point. There were times when some of us no longer cared for the other, and hanging out felt like an amicable relationship maintained by a divorced couple for the sake of their children.

Fall of 1989 quickly passed, and things just never felt the way they had during my sophomore and junior year with my friends in The Crew. Most of my days out of school were spent hanging out with Shane or Doug. I tried just doing stuff with the guys who had not gone to San Diego, but if they were hanging with those other six or even a couple of them, it became uncomfortable and not even worth the effort. Also, during my senior year, I partied a lot with Luis Escondido. He was from Juarez and would come to the United States to go to school. His father was financially well off and could afford to get him transportation and an apartment down the street from our high school. He and I had a blast together. This included doing a lot of weed and speed and shooting up the occasional steroids before a workout, but the experiences with him were always memorable and he genuinely cared about the people around him. As a matter of fact, for a few weeks, I stayed at his place and had not even gone home. Of course, we were rarely at his pad and could usually be found drunk at the Corner Bar, The Copacabana Bar or the Tequila Derby in Juarez, just off of the Santa Fe Bridge.

Before I knew it, high school was coming to an end. Four years went by in the blink of an eye. It felt like this high school experience was just a page in a long novel and one that had many past pages that were somehow forgotten. I know I did a lot of bad things during my high school years, but I had to experience both the good and the bad as there always was this driving force in my head that screamed out all the time, and the voices always seemed to be different. I know some people would think I was crazy, but that was not it at all. I constantly felt that no matter what I did, whether good or bad, it had already been done before, and I was stuck in a loop and could not escape that feeling of "been there and done that." So school ended, and I had no plans for the future.

Almost everyone I hung out with was going to college, and Doug and I looked to be the only ones not going. I did not want to lounge at home or get some crappy part-time job or worse yet, a full-time job that paid me well enough to get me used to having money, and before I knew it, I would wake up twenty years later with the same piece-of-shit job. So what did I do? I talked to a U.S. Navy recruiter. Then I took the Armed Services Vocational Aptitude Battery test and scored in the top ninety-nine percentile. I ended up having my choice of any job in the Navy I wanted because my line scores were also off the chart. So, I decided to enter Navy Intelligence. One week after I graduated from high school, I was headed off to boot camp in San Diego. I hoped that city would be better for me the second time around.

I have to tell you that basic training came very natural to me. At first I had thought I may have high anxiety issues like I did in the past as you are basically stripped down in basic training and re-built as a soldier – a drone that the military can control. I made for one hell of a soldier. I easily memorized everything that was put in front of me. The physical fitness part was a piece of cake, and the metamorphosis into a soldier again felt like I had been there and done it many times before. Before I knew it, I was graduating boot camp and did so as the best recruit out of my class. After this, I then went to Virginia Beach, Va., for A-school. I did exceptionally well. I almost felt as if I knew how to do something before being taught, and my assessment of intelligence documentation and intelligence gathering was second to none. I also caught the eye of many officers from the Office of Naval Intelligence due to my exceptional talent of picking up almost immediately all crypto communication techniques and also my ability to receive and translate code. I think this came from my love of reading ancient history and being so genuinely interested in symbols and glyphs from past cultures and societies. One thing that changed a lot during my stay in A-school was what took place on Aug. 2, 1990. Iraq invaded Kuwait, and a lot changed in a matter of days at Virginia Beach.

A-school was thirteen weeks long, and once most of us were finished, we were told that not everyone would be going to C-school as would usually be the case. Because the U.S. and its coalition partners were starting to amass troops and supplies in and around Iraq, most of us would ship out and be stationed in what eventually became termed Operation Desert Shield. Only four sailors would stay and continue in C-school, and they were staying only because their skills and abilities put them in high demand for what looked like a quickly approaching war with the fourth largest army in the world. I happened to be one of the four who went to C-school. Due to the situation in the Middle East, I was not told what I would be doing until I got there. That time quickly came, and I was now training for IS-3913, counterintelligence. I will not go into too much detail as to what my training entailed, but what I will tell you is by Christmas Day of 1990, I was onboard the USS Nicholas and part of a Special Operations Force made up of a SEAL team out of San Diego and a United States Coast Guard law enforcement detachments unit (LEDET).

What most of the public was told about Operation Desert Shield was that it was a buildup of coalition forces before Operation Desert Storm began on Jan. 17, 1991, with most of the war phase taking place in the air. But this was not entirely the case. The fact of the matter was there were a lot of oil derricks off of Kuwait's coast that also had been taken over by Iraqi forces. Command was afraid all those derricks would be destroyed if given the command to do so by the Iraqi soldiers who were strategically placed on the derricks. So, to prevent the loss of this high-value resource and spillage of large amounts of crude oil into the sea, my unit was directed to infiltrate the derricks and neutralize the enemy before they would damage the derricks.

This, mind you, was no easy task. No one knew how many Iraqi soldiers were on each derrick, what communications systems they had or what weapons and ordinance they possessed. A SEAL team was trained to insert and destroy many types of targets in various settings, but it was the US Coast Guard LEDET units that were specially trained to make assaults on ships and sea-going vessels and platforms. This was the reason they were pretty much loaned to the U.S. Navy and stationed on the USS Nicholas with us.

My function for the unit was to be incoming and outgoing communications and all intelligence gathering, including on-the-spot interrogation if need be. Not only did I have my Navy training for this assignment, but I also had a three-day crash course from a CIA operative and CIA analyst who accompanied me to the USS Nicholas. All intelligence was to go from me in the field to the analyst aboard the Nicholas. Then the analyst was to immediately transmit all incoming information back to the Pentagon where there were military, CIA and NSA intelligence officers. I also took a three-day crash course in special weapons and tactics by both the SEAL team and the LEDET unit. Let me tell you, I fit right in, and this training came naturally to me. I absorbed everything and was told that I could pass for a Deployable Operations Group team member by the end of the crash course in SWAT training. The operation was codenamed as Operation Essential. The team trained for three more days on the ship and in the water. Then on Jan. 10, we were given the green light by the CIA operative and Navy Intelligence Officer on board the Nicholas and Operation Essential was a go.

Everyone was in black tactical response uniforms that included night vision. I was armed with a shotgun and my side arm. The shotgun performed better in the close quarters situations in which we would soon find ourselves, and it also had a better chance of not damaging the machinery on the oil derrick, which translated to less chance of causing a fire or blowing up everyone on the platform. The team broke up into three units, each on their own inflatable assault vessel. There was also a larger patrol craft that went with us that was armed with the standard Ma

Deuce – a .50-caliber machine gun – and several handheld surface-to-surface missile modules. The derricks we were assaulting were owned by the Kuwait Oil Company and Kuwait Petroleum Corp. I had met with engineers from both companies prior to Operation Essential so that I could get intelligence on locations of the derricks that were essential for the team to capture and hold so that the Iraqi soldiers could not plant and detonate explosives in those locations as that would almost immediately destroy the platform while we were on it. So, we had final weapon's check, and I had a final intelligence briefing.

That night, we operated in the northern part of the Persian Gulf, just off the coast where Kuwait and Iraq met. As fortune would have it, the soldiers on the first two derricks we came upon must have been actively waiting for us to show up, and this was not to fight or blow up the derrick but instead to surrender. As we took the Iraqi soldiers into custody, we learned that they had been starving and had not eaten much of anything but rats and other creatures they caught. They were actually excited to finally be taken as prisoners of war that they cried and thanked us for finally rescuing them. They were also very receptive to giving up all kinds of intelligence. The only thing was there were no high-ranking officers on board the derricks, and we soon learned that the mid-level officers knew very little and had depended greatly on most of the orders and intelligence from their superiors. I did learn that on one of the larger oil derricks we would be assaulting in the next day or two, there were specially trained Iraqi guard on that platform, and they were very loyal to Saddam Hussein and would most likely fight to the death. With that piece of intelligence now known, the Pentagon decided to move up the assault on that derrick. So the next day we headed to what we knew was going to be our first true battle of the war on the sea.

As we approached the larger derrick, I immediately could tell this platform stood higher up than those we had come across before. It was also longer than the ones farther north. Our approach formation was one inflatable would flank on the left, another on the right, and my inflatable was on a vector straight ahead and in the middle. The larger patrol craft was directly off the port side of our inflatable and was directed to draw the fire of any enemy weapons if we were spotted before reaching the platform and boarding. Everyone was in the dark, and night vision was being used upon the approach. As we came within fifteen hundred meters of the platform, all motors were reduced to minimal output. We were slowly making final approach and were now within one thousand meters of the platform. At this point, units one and three were closer to contacting the platform from flanking positions. Both our inflatable and the patrol craft were now approximately four hundred meters from the platform. Then, both our inflatable and the patrol craft were lit up by flares fired from the platform. Immediately after that, we came under heavy small-arms fire. Tracer rounds were going off everywhere. I could hear bullets whizzing by my head and others striking the water. The patrol craft and our inflatable throttled the engines and cut in a starboard path so that the gunner on the patrol craft could now return fire on the Ma Deuce.

Just as the gunner began returning fire on the .50-caliber machine gun, we saw a flash from the top of the platform, and in rained the rocket fire. The first handheld rocket just missed the bow of the patrol craft. With rockets now in the equation, the patrol craft fired a single missile at the platform but missed. Those in my inflatable were also returning fire. I could do nothing as I was armed with a shotgun that was useless at this range. Then another flash of light was seen from the platform, and the next thing I knew, I heard a tremendous explosion as the rocket impacted the upper deck corner of the patrol craft. Mind you, the patrol craft was just feet away from the inflatable when it was struck. I saw a burst of light as the rocket came in contact with the patrol craft. Then a shockwave hit me, and I was lifted off the dinghy and thrown into the water.

"Man overboard! Portside, portside. There he is!" was the last thing I remember hearing.

"Anhu Nox Zule! Anhu Nox Zule!" the voice said to me.

I opened my eyes and was not in the Persian Gulf. I got up and saw two men standing near me; one of them was calling me Anhu Nox Zule. We were in a large chamber room that was furnished with items you would see only in the ancient Egyptian section of a museum. These two men again spoke to me in a foreign language. I could understand everything they were saying, and then the light bulb in my head went off and I knew I was in ancient Kemet or what would today be known as Egypt.

The two men were telling me that I was late to the engineer's meeting that I was to preside over. They were also bickering among themselves as to what size the entry should be to the new solar facility being built into the cliff walls. I closed my eyes and hoped that when I opened them again, this dream would all end, and I would be back on board ship, but it did not end. Since I could do nothing else, I followed the two men out of the chamber, through the center gardens and then outside the wall of the palace. As the two men continued to converse with me, I realized that I was Anhu Nox Zule, lead engineer of the Pharaoh Shendjw. I was way, way back in very early Egypt, most likely the period of its pre-dynastic rulers. Things were very different than what modern-day archaeologists would have you believe. There were machines at work powered by solar panels, and I watched as several people used a heating device that was shooting a green flame, and the flame was being used to shape and fit massive stones next to other stones.

Then, straight out from the road we were walking down, I saw the Great Pyramid of Giza, and it stood by itself. Well, not completely, as what looked to be the Sphinx was in front of it, but it did not have a human head. Instead, the head was that of a lion, and on the front of the lion's face, just above its eyes, was the sculpted constellation of Leo. But the constellation looked different than how it is today. The stars were in a slightly different arrangement.

I spoke to the two men, and sure enough, I easily spoke in their language. I asked them, which came first, the pyramid or the sphinx? They laughed and answered that no one knew as both were there longer than the people and city around it. After walking for approximately ten minutes, we entered another building that was still under construction. I was led to a room full of men who looked like they were right out of an old movie that took place in ancient Egypt, and it all seemed to be the real thing.

I was escorted to the front of a large table, where I sat down and had several pieces of parchment placed before me. I looked at the parchment and could understand that these were plans I had created for a large solar collection building that was to be constructed into the side of a cliff, some distance away. The building was to collect and store energy for the lighting of most underground facilities in the area. I thought to myself, "How could this be? How could there be solar power, machinery that did things we could not do in the twentieth century and artificial lighting this far in the past of Egypt?" We really had it wrong in the twentieth century, and those archaeologists, especially the Egyptologists, should be fired from their positions for having misled the public.

I also noticed one other fact as I looked over the documents, and that was that most twentieth century scientists put the pre-dynastic rulers somewhere around 3,200 BCE. But clearly, these documents suggested the time period was more like ten thousand to twelve thousand years ago. What is even crazier than that is we were told that the Great Pyramid was built around 2,560 BCE. However, that, too, is just another error by a bunch of men and women calling themselves Egyptologists yet know nothing about the true past. I know for a fact that I was truly in Kemet and either reliving this somehow or recalling an ancient memory passed down to me or stored deep within my mind. Then there was a brilliant flash of light followed by lots of sounds and voices, and I was now on board a modern-day naval medical ship.

I am not sure what was going on, but I was looking down from some vantage point as doctors and nurses worked on a soldier on an operating table. The soldier was without a pulse, and the doctors were attempting to resuscitate him by bagging him and doing chest compressions. I realized that it was not just any soldier, it was me. I began to panic and then started trying to figure out where I was and how I was able to see myself. Something was wrong, and I did not know how to fix it.

Then, one of the doctors yelled, "We got him back; he has a pulse. Quickly, set up the oxygen and bring in the paddles in case we start losing him again."

With that, I could no longer see myself and realized I had returned to my body.

I woke up days later and was told I was in Landstuhl Regional Medical Center, just outside of Ramstein Air Base in Germany. I was also told that I had been put into a coma due to injuries I sustained in the Persian Gulf. I had been hit by the concussive force of a blast wave from an explosion and thrown into the water. Luckily, I was immediately pulled from the water by another sailor and then rushed to the naval medical ship, the USNS Comfort, where I had to be resuscitated three times. I had suffered a nasty head injury and was told it would take several months to return to normal. There went my military career. I was going to be honorably discharged due to injury. And just like that, my military intelligence days in the Navy came to an end.

It took me some time before I could function halfway normal. I required some physical rehabilitation and psychological assistance. The issue was not just with my constant feeling of being helpless after the blast, but I was also having flashbacks while awake of the last few minutes in the inflatable dingy before being hit by the blast. There were times when people were talking to me, and I would drift back to that night on the water. When I would come to my senses, I would usually be drenched in sweat and terror-stricken. The psychiatrist I would see on an outpatient basis from the VA hospital said I was suffering from post-traumatic stress disorder and that it would take time before I learned to deal with it appropriately.

There was also one other thing that was happening to me that I did not mention to the VA psychiatrist. I was constantly hearing voices in my head, and the voices were of many different people and speaking many different languages. I could not get them to stop no matter what I did, and many times, there was more than one voice speaking at a time. Sometimes, I understood what was being said, and other times, I had just an inkling of what was taking place in the conversation. Many times, the doctor would give me one or two types of medications that made everything go away, including my sadness, my rehashing of the explosion and even the voices. But the medication also had awful side effects, and after a short while, I decided the sadness and voices were not as bad as the major mood swings the meds caused or the anger I sometimes would feel. After months of this, I finally was able to quiet the voices to a whisper, and I started dealing better with my fears of helplessness and loud noises. I started functioning enough on the outside to where people who came into contact with me would never know how disturbed or haunted I was from what happened during the brief time I was in the military.

One thing I did start doing early on with the voices was I kept track of what I could understand. I used multiple journals to log everything and follow-up on them for patterns or hints as to what was going on. Nothing immediately became evident in all the data I logged, and after a while, it felt like my journal entries were more of a way for me to cope than anything else. All of this was taking place in El Paso as I came back home after I was discharged. I even got a job delivering pizza with my friend Shane from high school. He was doing it only for a short time before he left for college in San Antonio. For me, it was therapeutic to be doing any type of work that allowed me to keep my mind off of the recent past.

One day I also decided to try something different to assist me with the voices I was hearing and all the experiences I had where I seemed to be different people and living their lives in past time periods. I flew to Phoenix and saw a hypnotherapist I had read about. She was a licensed psychologist and dealt with patients who had some type of past life experience that caused distress in their lives. Her name was Angela G. Smith, and her office was in Scottsdale. I had read that Dr. Smith had been able to help a lot of people with all types of disorders, and when I had called and spoke with her prior to traveling, she seemed very positive that she would be able to help me. Since I had flown in from El Paso, she was kind enough to schedule two ninety-minute sessions on consecutive days. When I arrived in Scottsdale, I first went to the hotel that I booked and checked in. I then went to Dr. Smith's office for the first appointment, which was at 11 in the morning.

Her office was not big at all, and there was no waiting room or staff to greet and check in the patients. What was in the entry area was a light on the side of Dr. Smith's door that told patients whether she was available. Once inside her office, I noticed it was more like a room and that the space consisted of three chairs, a couch and two tables. Everything was decorated to make one feel cozy and comfortable. Dr. Smith then told me to take a seat. I introduced myself and went over the reasons why I was there. I also let her know some of the results I was hoping to gain from the sessions. She gave me a brief description of herself and her background and then explained what takes place in the session, especially if hypnotherapy is used.

Then she told me I could move to the sofa and relax as this is what worked best for most people on whom she performed hypnotherapy. She also asked me if I would like the session recorded in case either she or I wanted to go back to review it. I decided it would be a good idea. She then had me relax and do some breathing exercises, followed by closing my eyes and trying to focus on times in my life when I felt most happy and secure. Once I found that memory, I was to focus on it and her voice. As I did so, I felt much of the anxiety from the traveling I just did leave me, both physically and mentally. She continued speaking to me and coaching me into a deeper and deeper relaxed state, free of anxiety and other negative emotions until I felt like I had reached a state of consciousness between being awake and asleep.

She then began having me remember my past until I reached my young childhood. Up until this point, she had me focus only on going backwards in life to recall my past but not to get too detailed as she felt my issues were farther into the earliest part of my childhood. It was at this time period when she had me start focusing on specifics and what I could remember starting around the age of four or five. I must have become very comfortable as I no longer remembered Dr. Smith in the room or this being connected to a hypnosis session. I then felt that I was back at that age and started recalling traumatic experiences, including my dark shadow creature.

Then I went farther back. I remembered the ambulance ride and the trip to the hospital after drowning. I recalled coming to and seeing people around me after drowning, but that is where things stopped, and older memories, including those leading up to my drowning, were more like me watching this portion through a different vantage point. Dr. Smith attempted to get me to go back before the drowning, and I could not because there were clouded memories prior to my being brought back to life by my father.

Dr. Smith then began speaking to me: "Patrick, I am going to try something a little more direct in our session. I want you to focus on my voice and only my voice until there is nothing else in this room and nothing else in this world but my voice. Focus in on my voice and the quiet and peacefulness of the darkness as you keep your eyes closed. Slowly push back further into your mind and deeper into your memories, deeper into the void and step through the darkness. Cross to the other side of the darkness that is blocked by your consciousness."

That was the last thing I remember as I must have either fallen asleep or crossed into that deep void. I remember nothing else that had to do with the session after that. The next thing I do remember is opening my eyes and feeling refreshed. I could recall the good and bad experiences she had me focus on all the way up to drowning but no further than that. It took a moment for me to focus my eyes because of the lights in the room, and when I looked at Dr. Smith, she had this look of total disbelief. I asked her what happened after my memories of being resuscitated by my father. She began to tell me what sounded like one amazing fictional tale but was actually what she had just experienced with me during the session.

At the point where things got foggy for me, she stated that when she asked what happened next, I told her I died at the age of fifty-nine and had to find my next host. When she asked what I meant by this, I explained that my host passed away at the age of fifty-nine and I needed to skin-jump immediately into my next one while that new body could still sustain a life force. She asked me who I was, and I had responded that my name was Heinrich. She asked me when I was born, and my response was in 1915. When she asked where I was from, I told her that Heinrich was born in Deutschland during World War I. She then asked me what I died from, and I told her I had a congenital heart issue that caused my heart to quit, and that is why I jumped. Patrick had just died so I jumped into Patrick's body and used it for my new host.

Dr. Smith told me that as she continued with the questions, I told her of four other people I had been prior to Heinrich and Patrick. She then asked me who I originally was and when that person was born, at which time everything in her office began to shake, books began flying off shelves and lights started flickering. As she told me this, I looked around the office and saw a minor earthquake having struck. Dr. Smith stated that she got scared at this point and tried bringing me out of the hypnotic state but that I refused and began speaking to her in a foreign language she did not recognize. I then asked her if she really wanted to know who I was and I stated to her that I had lived many lifetimes over the course of thousands of years.

Just when I was about to tell her who I was, the room filled with darkness, and it was not due to the light going out but to hundreds of these flying apparitions instantly in the room. As I spoke to her, the room filled with screams and curses in many different languages all at once. At this point Dr. Smith stated she began to cry. As she did this, all the flying creatures stopped, looked at her and at me, and then there was nothing. The room quit shaking, nothing was flying around or falling to the floor, and I began to come out of my hypnotic state. The two of us continued to discuss everything that took place, and she told me nothing like this had ever happened to her before. She had people speak to her in foreign languages before and think they were someone else before their current life, but nothing to where the physical realm was altered or where energy not from our current existence could affect our space and time. She told me she always kept an open mind to everything, but up until just a few minutes ago, she was very skeptical of there being any truth to what her past clients had told her or what she had seen and been able to confirm with her own eyes. She now had to re-evaluate everything she thought was impossible in our world.

I asked her if this could all be true or if it could be due to me having watched television or read a science fiction or horror book. She said it was possible, and what happened in the office she saw with her own eyes.

"How can what is in your head have affected the environment around us if it was all made up and not real memories on your part and energy from you or something tied to you?" she asked. "Patrick, you have got to consider the true possibility that you are a living testament to reincarnation or something along that line that the rest of us are not aware of and did not know exists."

This was a lot for me to take in and analyze. I thanked her for her time and asked if we were still set for my appointment at 11 the next day. She said she no longer felt safe around me and did not want to put herself in harm's way again. I let her know I understood. I paid for the session and gave her my address and phone number one more time so she could send me the recording of the session once she had a chance to evaluate it. Once I was back at the hotel, I evaluated everything she had told me. How is it possible that I could make up such an intricate story while in a hypnotic state and not remember any of it myself? Who the hell was this Heinrich, and what the hell is a skin-jump? I left Arizona far more confused about everything in my life than before. This only made my anxiety issues worse.

Several days had passed since my return to Texas, and I had heard nothing back from Dr. Smith. I wanted to know about the recording as I was very interested in at least hearing what took place, not just with my answers but with what was happening in the office as I was in this hypnotic state. As soon as I had this thought, the phone rang. It was Dr. Smith, and she wanted to let me know that it took her a bit longer to send the tape as she had a lot to review from it. She wanted to have a colleague of hers listen to it but needed my permission. I said I would not be giving my consent as I first had to know what happened, and this meant listening to the session myself. She said she understood this decision but that I may be able to get additional help and answers by allowing others to review what took place.

Dr. Smith also told me that something else bothered her and even scared her slightly while reviewing the recording.

I asked her what this was, and she said that toward the middle of my explaining who I was before being Patrick, that other voices could be heard yelling at me in the background. She said that she did not hear this during the session but that it was clear as day on the tape.

"Mr. Kilian, there was one last thing I wanted to let you know about the tape," she said. "When I asked you during the session who you originally were, something else in the room answered."

I quickly replied, "What responded, and what name did it give?"

"I am not sure what it was that responded or where the response came from, but I am almost positive it stated that you were originally named Adama."

With that, I thanked her for the call, let her know I looked forward to reviewing the tape and then sat down as that name was definitely not new to me. How could I be Adama when I know I am Patrick Kilian?

# 13.

# Witches and Mushrooms

For weeks after I met with Dr. Smith, I could do nothing but think about what transpired during my session. After listening to the tape, I walked away with more questions than answers, especially with so many other voices and languages being heard in the background. At first I thought it might be a hoax on the doctor's part, but there was no way she could have known about certain names that I had already heard in my past, and there were languages heard on the tape that I was sure had not been spoken for hundreds if not thousands of years. I had considered researching names, languages and locations I had come across not only in my session with Dr. Smith but also in my dreams and flashbacks prior to the hypnosis. But in late 1991, there was no Internet, and you had to know a bit about what you were researching in order to find out more about it at the library. So again, I let it go without any kind of follow-up. I also had a lot in my personal life going on. Work sucked, and my parents had a fire at their restaurant and lost everything. My father and my stepmom decided to move to Monterey in Central California, where my stepmom had lived for over twenty years. I really had nothing keeping me in El Paso, and I decided to also move with them.

I sold almost everything I had and drove the Dodge to Monterey while my parents drove their vehicle. The trip was thirteen hours, and when we got there, I was exhausted, but not enough to realize how beautiful Monterey and its surrounding sister cities were. The Monterey Peninsula had beautiful forests that led up to some of the most amazing coastline this planet has to offer. I was living in paradise and loving every minute of it. We had already rented a two-bedroom apartment, so the living arrangements were taken care of upon arrival. What I did next was go to the local community college and sign up for classes full-time. I was able to get enrolled for twelve units, even at the last minute, but I had to pay a pretty penny as I qualified for only out-of-state tuition. Still, I figured this would be worth it.

The next thing I did during the first week was land a job at one of the local resort hotels, working in their room service department. I then went to the local surf shop and purchased a used wetsuit and seven-foot surf board with decently placed rails and fin. For the first couple of weeks, all I did was work early-morning shifts at the hotel, go to classes on three days out of the week and surf for two or three hours each day. I had met a couple of people at work and a couple of people at the college with whom I started hanging out, but it was not until I was surfing one Thursday evening at Asilomar State Beach that I ran into an amazing individual, Nicole Honda.

I will always remember Heather and share a bond with her that I cannot explain, but the moment I bumped into Nicole in the water, life for a while became one crazy and exciting experience. Nicole was a year older than I and she was half Japanese and half American. Her father owned several of the farms north of Marina, so money was not an issue for her, and she never cared that I had very little of it. She was beautiful, about five-foot-seven, light brown hair, a golden tan and hazel-green eyes. Also, when I said I ran into Nicole I really ran into her and her board while she was trying to surf the same set of waves. At first she was pretty pissed off and cursed me out for a good five minutes. But after surfing together for two straight hours, we could not get enough of each other.

From that point on, we did almost everything together. Nicole was passionate about everything, and that led to everything she did being taken to the extreme. So we were constantly doing crazy shit like jumping off cliffs into the ocean near Big Sur or racing motorcycles at Laguna Seca racetrack when it was open for public use. I even remember we went up to Santa Cruz on a day when there were multiple reports of surfers spotting several massive great white sharks. We still paddled out and surfed with a handful of other crazy, diehard surfers. That was up until a fifteen-foot-plus great white shark swam directly under us. I seriously thought I was going to shit myself as being eaten alive by some massive animal tops my list of how I do not want to die. I remember Nicole and I trying to keep our bodies up on our boards until we could no longer see that massive dark shadow that crossed beneath us in the water. We then made a break for land and paddled as hard as we could. We made it safely to shore, and I told her it would be a long time before I went back into the water.

"You big pussy," she said. "I'll be back in the water tomorrow, and you better be there right next to me."

Sure enough, the next day we were surfing, and all I could think about was some massive shark shooting out of the water and eating me or at least taking off a leg or two and causing me to bleed to death in the ocean.

Things were good between Nicole and I for several months. We practically lived together as she always wanted me to spend the night with her at her apartment in Pacific Grove. I went back home only to get clothes or other personal belongings. But finally, her extreme personality and behavior began to take a toll on me. I was realizing that everything had to be what she wanted to do or how she wanted it done. I cared about her a lot, and she truly was an amazing sight. However, she started becoming psycho-possessive, especially about me being at work when this one girl named Virginia would be on the same shift. She had met Virginia one day when she stopped by to see when I would be done so that we could head to the Santa Cruz Beach Boardwalk. From that moment on, I started getting accused of flirting with Virginia then doing other stuff with her until Nicole even accused me of sleeping with her. This was not the case at all, but this crazy behavior from Nicole was a big turn-off for me. It also had me worrying that she may do something either to Virginia or me. One day I was just finishing up my shift at work and was walking out to my car. There at my car was Nicole, and she was intoxicated. She began screaming at me and accusing me of things that were not true.

"You're screwing her, aren't you? I know the two of you are sleeping together, you asshole. I know it. I smell her on you when you come back to the apartment."

Nicole went on and on this way for a good ten minutes. To make things worse, a crowd had formed around us, and that included Virginia. I figured there was no reasoning with Nicole, and I had to leave. I knew she was drunk, but things were only going to get worse if I stuck around. So I quickly moved around Nicole, got in my car and left. Later that night, I went to her apartment and told her I was breaking up with her. She pulled a gun out on me and told me that if this is what I wanted, then neither one of us needed to continue living. I told her to quit being stupid and think about what she was doing. Lucky for me one of her neighbors heard what was taking place and called the police. As I continued to speak to her and try to calm her down, several officers from the Pacific Grove Police Department got there and began talking to her while they had their weapons pointed in her direction. They had me leave and go to the police car with another officer as they continued to converse with Nicole and attempt to get her to give up her revolver. Eventually, she did so, and the police took her into custody and then to the local hospital for a seventy-two hour psychological evaluation. After that, she was released from the hospital. No one pressed charges, so she was free to go home. Maybe it would have been better if someone did place her in jail for a while, or maybe it would have been best if she was committed for longer than seventy-two hours. Nicole went back to her apartment, took out a 9mm handgun that I did not know she owned and committed suicide that day.

I did not find out that Nicole had taken her own life until her mother called me and let me know the next morning. I cried that entire day and blamed myself for it. I should have seen the signs and helped her more. I should have recognized that she did everything to the extreme because something was wrong and she had to fill a void with reckless behavior. I have had to live with her suicide every day of my life, and it never gets easier.

Christmas came and went, and Nicole's funeral was the day after that holiday. I remember her father and mother speaking at her funeral and letting everyone know that there was nothing anyone could do as Nicole was always a stubborn person and did what she wanted to do no matter what anyone told her. This still did not make my pain go away or the guilt I felt any easier to carry around. She will forever be remembered by me, and I hope she finally found the peace she lacked in this lifetime.

New Year's came and went just as Christmas had done. I worked extra hours so that I had less time to remember everything that had transpired in the previous couple of weeks. Then, during the following week, Virginia from work began talking to me and checking to make sure I was doing alright. Virginia was a very interesting person. She had this super bubbly personality that always made me smile, even in my current state of being. She was tatted down one arm, and her choice of clothing always made me think she was into Goth or witchcraft. At least that is what I pictured her doing in the outfits she would wear. But she was being super friendly, and right now I really needed someone to hang out with and speak to.

One night, we both worked a late shift and did not get off until after midnight. She asked me if I would walk her to her car because of how late it was, and I thought nothing of it. The next thing I knew, I was back at her apartment. I think having sex at this time helped me detach myself from the weight and burden I was carrying around. I ended up spending the night at her place and confirmed she was in fact a practicing witch. She had been practicing shadow magic, which was kind of like walking the fine line between light and dark magic. She told me that the moment she first saw me, there was an aura around me that she had never seen around any other human before. She said that it looked as if my aura was constantly being manipulated and changed and that this was almost unheard of. I jokingly told her that I have been many different people over a large time span and that I have lived for thousands of years.

She responded, "Have you been told this by others or have you seen this in your dreams and memories?"

I looked at her a bit confused and then let her know it was both.

"Don't take these things lightly, Kilian," she said. "You seem to me to be a lost elemental and don't even know it yet. Some call them wanderers and others call them soul thieves. But if this is what you are, you must have a reason to be doing it, and you really should find out."

I responded, "Do you really believe such a thing is possible? I have read about reincarnation, and I have experienced some strange things in my life, but I still have trouble believing something like this is possible, and more so for me to be one of these wanderers."

She said that she had seen demons and spirits conjured, as well as other things that she is still unable to identify, and that people like me do exist, and it has been documented through time. She told me about a famous person by the name of Edgar Cayce who was a well-known mystic who believed in reincarnation, and that our past lives directly affected our current life. I thought this was interesting, but still, I was not sure what to believe.

It was easier for me to believe in spirits and ghosts as I had many encounters with entities in my life that were of the supernatural realm, but for me to have lived as different people through the ages; this was harder for me to grasp. Virginia then explained that there was one sure way to experience it. This immediately grabbed my attention.

"What way would that be, Virginia?" I asked.

"I have a simple answer for you, Kilian. Amanita muscaria or a combination of ayahuasca and Banisteriopsis caapi will do the trick. That stuff will have you remembering everything as it will help you journey wherever you need to go," she said.

The next morning, both Virginia and I had to return to work at the hotel, and our schedule was the same, so we decided to go in one car. Virginia said she had lots of connections that could get us all three of the hallucinogenic substances she had told me about the night before. She could administer it to me that night and watch after me as I went on a vision quest. She also let me know that I should have no meat or fatty foods that day and stick to simple liquids and light salads that way I would not get sick after ingesting the hallucinogenic substances. The two of us then went to work. At around noon, she stopped me in the hallway at work to tell me that she was able to get hold of someone who had the mushrooms and that we could go pick them up after work.

When work ended, we went to her friend Samantha's house. She also was a practicing witch and got some very nice-sized mushrooms. They had already been dried out so they did not look like the awesome colored shrooms I had expected to see that were red with white dots, like those seen in *Alice in Wonderland*. But according to Samantha, they were potent and had helped her reach multiple altered states of reality. Now instead of going to Virginia's apartment and shrooming there, Samantha insisted we stay at her place, and she would prepare everything for me. Apparently, she also was very intrigued with me the moment I walked through her door. Samantha had practiced traditional British witchcraft for some time and told Virginia and I that she had never come across a person such as me who gave off this exceptionally unusual aura and was full of intense universal currents of divine thought. I smiled when she told me this to be polite but secretly was thinking she must have already been taking the shrooms before we got there. I guess I really had no clue what she was talking about.

We initially sat and chatted with Samantha for almost an hour. She and Virginia had not seen each other in several months and decided it would be the perfect time for catching up. While they were talking, I was secretly drifting into my own thoughts. As I lay back on Samantha's couch, I could not help but think about Nicole and the fact that she was gone from my life and that I would not see her again. Then I suddenly saw Heather. It had been years since we were together, but I could not help wonder where she was and how she was doing.

"Patrick! Patrick, are you with us?" Virginia called to me.

I zeroed back in to where I was and politely let her know that I was among the living. Virginia said that while I was off in my own world, Samantha had headed to the kitchen and was preparing the Amanita muscaria for me to chew and some for me to drink as a warm tea. Virginia explained that it may take a while to work on me due to my size but that I would eventually feel its effects and definitely know when it kicked in. While Samantha prepared the Amanita muscaria in the kitchen, Virginia and I started kissing and touching and maybe got a bit further than that. We heard a polite cough, and I looked up and saw Samantha watching us and smiling.

"There will be plenty of time for that with this stuff, and who knows, maybe we will all get lucky tonight," Samantha stated as she smiled.

This made me smile at her and caused me to get an elbow in the chest from Virginia.

Samantha began to reiterate what Virginia had told me about the mushrooms. She explained what their effect might be like and that everyone is affected differently in some way. With finally having received all the instructions on how to properly get stoned, I ingested about four caps of dried Amanita muscaria and then drank an eight-ounce warm mushroom tea. Let me tell you, the shrooms may make for a great spiritual awakening or coming to Jesus, but they made for shitty-tasting tea. I just remember thinking to myself that after having downed the nastiest tasting tea ever that this crap had better work.

The three of us discussed what makes for good and evil witchcraft and where lines must be drawn while one practices one form or the other. I did a lot of nodding and agreeing to things I really knew nothing about. Right at about that twenty-minute mark, I began to feel warm, and then I started having trouble keeping my eyes open. The mushrooms had started to kick-in. Initially, I started hearing all those voices in my head yelling at me. This I was not happy with, as it took great effort for me to control them in the first place. Those voices then started making sense, and they were talking among themselves and occasionally to me. Then the room began to spin and was filled with white lights popping all over the place.

I looked around, and Virginia and Samantha were gone. Next thing I knew, Samantha's place was gone, and then the city was gone. This was followed by me flying through the sky and leaving the planet. I was hurdling through space so quickly that almost everything around me was a blur. I then remembered that I had experienced this before, a long time ago, when I had drowned and felt as if I were traveling through the void of space. This continued for some time until I could see a planet approaching. It was a burnt orange or reddish-brown and slightly smaller than Earth. For a split second, I closed my eyes, and when I opened them again, I had already reached the planet's surface and was standing on what I could only believe to be Mars.

I remember thinking that maybe NASA should give these mushrooms to their astronauts so that they could get to Mars a whole lot quicker than if they were to take a spaceship. The surface of the planet looked so real, and as I bent down and touched the dirt, it sure seemed to be the real thing. I slowly walked toward something on the surface that was massive and triangular. As I walked closer to the object, I realized I had no issues breathing on the red planet, and I also felt a lot lighter as I moved around on the planet's surface. I quickly was approaching the triangular object and stopped in my tracks when I knew what it was: a pyramid. Yes, a pyramid that looked identical to the one in Giza, except for the fact that at the top, it was capped and coated with pure gold or a combination of gold and copper.

I felt the ground shake and move. It was an earthquake, I had thought, but then I watched as the pyramid came to life. It was somehow attached to the planet or at least something below it was attached, and it was charging the pyramid. Somehow, what was happening below where I stood and below the surface of the planet was being converted into some type of energy inside the pyramid. As the shaking grew stronger, a whirling or whizzing noise was building up inside the pyramid, and as this continued to get louder, the top portion of the pyramid began to emit some type of energy waves that I could barely notice while I stared at it. It almost looked like the heat waves that rise off the desert floor on a very hot day. Then, a multitude of people were instantly standing around me and conversing. They dressed differently than we did on Earth but were just as human.

One elderly man stepped away from the people and approached me. He was speaking to me, but I could not hear him and could hear only the voices in my head conversing. The elderly man became upset with me when he noticed I could not understand him. So he bent over and wrote with his fingers in the dirt. I looked down and saw that he had written 27.510948N 117.475122E. I was about to ask him what it meant. Unfortunately, I could not as I now was back on Earth, and this time, I was standing on top of the Pyramid of the Sun in Teotihuacan, Mexico. It was dark out, and as I looked up into the sky, there were no stars or moon. As a matter of fact, nothing at all but darkness could be seen. When I looked back down, I was surrounded by what had to be over a hundred of the dark shadowy figures from my childhood. They had surrounded the pyramid and were looking at me and trying to speak to me in synchronicity. I closed my eyes and screamed for them to stop and leave me alone. When I opened my eyes, everything was gone, and I was now back in Samantha's home, but this time, I was laying in the prone position on the floor.

"Patrick, Patrick – wake up; you have to wake up!" Virginia screamed.

Suddenly, I opened my eyes.

"Holy shit; I thought we were going to have to call 911 since you quit breathing," Samantha added.

I slowly regained my faculties and lifted my head from off of Samantha's rug.

"That stuff is amazing!" I told the girls.

"You completely scared the crap out of us! We thought you were dead," Virginia said.

"I've been told I have this bad track record of dying or coming close to death; my breaking body parts or getting injured is also a pretty high statistical possibility," I sarcastically replied.

I apparently had another brush with death or close call with the reaper. I would later learn that Samantha thought we were kidding about me being a newbie to mushrooms and that she should have given me only a single cap and a few ounces of tea. I was not upset with her because I think that amount helped me experience the things I did. I later told Samantha and Virginia about my experience, and I had them write down the numbers and letters the unknown older man in my vision wrote for me. I had no idea what they meant or even if I had remembered them correctly, and I knew it was going to be difficult figuring out what they were or if they meant anything at all. At a later time, I would place the numbers and letters into the journal where I documented all the crazy stuff that happened to me, and it would become yet another piece of the big puzzle.

Both of the girls were interested in the fact that I could somehow use all five of my senses during the out-of-body planetary travel. The girls told me that my experience lasted a good thirty minutes and that I started having issues with my breathing only during the last few minutes. This correlated with the time that the dark shadows entered the picture and surrounded me on top of the Pyramid of the Sun. Samantha also asked me about the people I came across during my trip, and I could tell her only that those people seemed familiar to me, at least in how they dressed and the way they carried themselves. I also told Samantha that I was pretty sure some of the voices in my head correlated to the people who were conversing around me when I was near the pyramid on what I was pretty sure was Mars.

"Why do you think it was Mars?" Virginia asked.

"I honestly cannot tell you that it was. But at the same time, I felt like I knew the place I was in or at least remembered something similar in a memory that I do not know existed until after this mushroom trip."

I explained in detail how there were a lot of similarities between this Mars pyramid and the Great Pyramid on the outskirts of Cairo, Egypt. I also told the girls about the top of the pyramid being different but explained that it could be that the top of the pyramid in Egypt used to be the same and was just removed, damaged or lost at some point. The energy being created resonated from within the planet and then was converted to this usable form through the pyramid. I understood that the creation of the usable energy was done through forced vibration, and this dealt with the principle of resonance vibration.

"The fact that I know about this stuff and understand it is seriously scaring the crap out of me this very minute!" I told Samantha and Virginia.

I stopped with the science lecture and told them that I was then back on planet Earth and standing on top of the Pyramid of the Sun outside of Mexico City. I shared that I felt all the pyramids were somehow connected but could not explain how this was at this moment. I told the girls about the dark shadow people and about my experiences with these supernatural beings. As I was talking, Samantha suddenly stopped me. She then started explaining that one of the other witches in her coven had the same type of being attack her during a spiritual session with a woman who said she had just recently found out she was on her fourth human lifetime due to reincarnation, and that the dark shadow spirit was her prior past self.

The shadow figure attacked her sister witch because she apparently was allowing the woman to recall too much of her past life and stated that this was forbidden. I explained to Samantha that I, too, had this weird feeling that the figures had something directly to do with me or were attached to me somehow but that I did not believe they came to keep me from learning about any past lives. I also had this strong inclination that I had offended these spirits either in this lifetime or a past one. I was hesitant using this term of a "past lifetime" with her but as things continued to happen in my life I could not help but believe they were past lifetimes and that somehow I am intermingling them with my present life. This, too, was something I felt I would have to follow up on but at a later time.

By the time we finished, most of the night had passed, and I decided to spend the night at Virginia's place. The next morning, we were both so exhausted that we both ended up calling in sick at work. The two of us instead hung out together that day, and for a short part of the morning went to the local library to see if we could learn anything about Mars or the Pyramid of the Sun in Mexico. We learned very little about Mars as little was known about it in the early part of 1992. We also learned that very little was known about the area of Teotihuacan in Mexico. Again, Teotihuacan was where the Pyramid of the Sun was located, but the city had been abandoned for hundreds if not a thousand years, and next to nothing was known about how or why it was built or who it was built by. What little was known seemed to be wrong to me, and somehow, I knew that most of what these archaeologists and anthropologists were peddling about the place was bullshit. It was nothing more than a continued lie or a wealth of incorrect information, passed down from teacher to student in an endless line of misinformation based on what people thought they knew in the nineteenth century.

One thing I also want to explain is that I was fascinated with ancient history and culture, and my biggest hobby was learning as much as I could about things that dealt with the social science of anthropology and archaeology. Both of these sciences dealt with the study of humankind and the existence of modern-day man. I am fully aware that archaeology is a form of anthropology and one that focuses on past human cultures instead of current ones. I knew I had to learn about these practices in order to follow up on everything taking place in my life and quite possibly past lives. Virginia and I later had lunch together, and then I headed back to my place.

For the next several months of 1992, I continued to work at the resort hotel, and Virginia and I continued to see each other. I had several more mushroom experiences, but we never graduated to the usage of ayahuasca to have what I was told would be an even greater experience with dreams and visions. When I took the mushrooms the other times, the amount was nowhere near what I had taken the first time accidentally. Because of this, it had only minor calming effects and mostly visual effects that consisted of colors changing in the room. After a while, I just stopped using the amanita muscaria.

March and April came and went, and the Monterey area no longer seemed to be a place I wanted to be. Even with Virginia being around, I constantly thought about Nicole and her having taken her own life. I knew that I would not be able to escape these thoughts or the mild depression I think I was starting to suffer unless I left Monterey. Before doing so, I discussed my leaving with Virginia, and she understood and hoped that very soon I could somehow find peace and find answers to the things that were happening to me in my life. I put in my two weeks' notice at work, let my dad and stepmom know I would be leaving, and on May 10, 1992, I was headed back to El Paso.

When I got back, I moved in with two of my friends from high school. I got a part-time job at a big-box electronics store, where they, too, were working, and I had also signed up for classes at El Paso Community College. I purchased this old Pontiac and remember having to pray a lot that it would make it from one place to the next. I had not been to church for a long time and even started going back. What was great this time around was that there was a young single adult ward, and that meant plenty of people my own age were available to hang around with and hopefully do more right than wrong.

My decision to return to El Paso ended up being the best thing I could have done at that time. If I was not hanging out or clubbing with my roommates, I was playing in some type of sporting event at church or going to the dances and other activities the single's ward was constantly putting on. I even fit full-time college classes into the schedule when the fall rolled back around and worked about twenty-five hours a week.

I was having some serious fun, and as the months went by, I thought of Nicole less and less until I finally made peace with everything that happened in Monterey. I even hooked up with a nice girl for once from the single's ward. It took a little getting used to in terms of what a Mormon girlfriend would and would not do compared to the women I was used to dating, but she made me laugh, and we did a lot of things together I would have never thought of doing since sex, drinking and drugs were not an option with her.

Unfortunately, it did not end up lasting too long. Another guy from the ward, who I thought was a friend, ended up weaseling his way in with her, and the next thing I knew, they were madly in love and talking about getting married. The biggest issue with the situation was that I had not gone on a mission for the church, and this other guy did. Apparently, this was a big thing with LDS church girls. You were definitely not long-term relationship material for these Mormon girls.

So I figured out a way around the fact that Mormon girls had long-term relationships only with returned missionaries. That workaround was to date the bad girls in the ward. They may have acted all pristine and morally upright on the outside, but some were worse than me, and yes, I am talking about how sexual they were.

I still kept going to church because that is what these women wanted to do, and I lied all the time about keeping commandments and faith. It really seemed that the more I attempted to believe in faith and organized religion, the more I knew it was all a farce and a creation by man. I constantly had this strange feeling that I had attempted to go down this path of religion many times before, and somewhere in my mind, I felt it was nothing more than a creation of the rich and powerful. The elite controlled whatever society was on this planet, and religion was their greatest asset in keeping control over the population. The elite just had to convince people that not conforming to their rules and regulations was a sin against a higher being and that if the typical peon or plebeian did live according to these bullshit rules, they would be rewarded with a greater life and higher standing in the next world. How could anyone who has the ability to think and reason fall for this?

So I went to church, went to work and went to school. I would zone out when I was at work because it was mind-numbing. School at the community college level challenged me in no way, shape or form. It was just too easy. By the time winter break rolled around, I thought I had everything fitting in the right slots and tuned exactly the way everything in my life needed to be. Then sure enough, this is exactly when Murphy's Law kicked in, and life threw me a huge curveball.

On Dec. 23, 1992, the annual Christmas basketball tournament was at the Mormon stake center on the Eastside of town. This was a huge deal in El Paso, and winning brought bragging rights to the men of that ward for an entire year. I had been asked by one of the brothers from my old ward where I attended church when I was a kid to play for them that night. I accepted as I had nothing else to do that night and figured I would get a good cardio session out of the whole thing. I thought I was ready for this game. It was against the ward that had won the tournament the last two years in a row. I was a very competitive person and absolutely wanted to assist in ending that streak. What I did not know and had not given much thought to was what happened to me the night before at work.

The night before, I had closed at work, and the store received a big shipment before the last couple of shopping days before Christmas. The store manager asked if I could help unload the truck as they were short several people. I could think of no excuse that moment, so sure enough, I helped unload the truck. I was taking a small dishwasher to the sales floor on a dolly cart, I did not see a solid metal beam in front of the box I had on the dolly and ended up running into it. Obviously, that beam was not going to budge, and I instantly went from a fast walking pace to a dead stop from the impact. The back of the metal dolly cart struck the shin area of my right leg. I remember the instant pain and my releasing some F bombs in the process. Still, I shook it off, sucked it up and kept unloading the truck for another hour. By the time I went home, I did not even remember hitting my shin or my leg ever hurting. Well, unknown to me was the fact that I got a hairline fracture in that part of my leg from the impact. I would not even remember this happening or put two and two together until a couple days after the basketball tournament. So the ward for which I was playing got on the court first that night to warm up. I shot a couple of free throws and then took several shots from other parts of the court. I dribbled the ball back and forth and even did some stretching before I began getting more aggressive with my warmups. Then came my first practice layup of the night. I dribbled with the ball, went up for the layup and found my target. The ball went right in, and I came down on both legs, and that is when things quickly got ugly.

I heard a massive crack that was so loud it sounded as if someone broke a wooden board in half. I looked around as the sound traveled through the cultural hall due to the acoustics.

One of my team members looked at me and said, "Oh my God, bro – look at your leg. You broke your leg!"

He leaned over and threw up on the court. I looked down and saw the lower portion of my right leg swinging back and forth. My toes would at first be facing forward and then swing back. Bones were sticking out of the top of my lower leg, just below the knee area, and bones were sticking out about four or five inches above the ankle. As my leg swung back and forth, and apparently as my heart pumped blood to my lower extremities, it would shoot out of my leg and across the basketball court approximately three feet. In a matter of seconds, the court looked like the site of a mass murder.

Several people who were sitting around the court and watching the practice also began to throw up. Once I realized what happened, I went to the ground and tried to pin my leg against the court floor so that my leg could keep from flipping back and forth. I still felt no pain at this point; I am sure because of the amounts of chemicals my body was releasing to deal with the extreme trauma I just suffered. Since I had shorts on, I took my warm ups and wrapped them around the upper break, from where most of the blood shot every time my heart beat. At this point, another one of the older men on my team lifted my foot into a better position and held it there while another one of the church brothers from the ward we were competing with got several towels and applied some pressure to the spot from where the blood was shooting. The moment he touched my exposed bones, I felt the most intense chills run up and down my spine. This was followed by some of the most intense pain I have ever felt. It was equal to when I fell on the playground and ruptured my spleen.

I began joking around with everyone, saying that I guess I would not be the top scorer for the evening. I think everyone laughed in order to keep me thinking about anything other than my leg. I could think only that I must seriously be cursed with some of the worst luck as I just constantly got injured or had something pretty damn awful happen to me. I wondered how long my new injury would take to heal and how long I would be out of commission. It took about five minutes for the firefighters to show up and begin administering first-responder care. Next on the scene were the emergency medical technicians. As the firefighters and EMTs began to stabilize my leg using a wooden two-by-four, the pain began to intensify. It then became almost unbearable when they began cutting my shoe off. Luckily, I was somehow getting some blood flow all the way to my toes, and the paramedic told me this was a very good sign. Still, they had to rush me to the hospital so medical staffers could stabilize my tibia and fibula since both looked to have broken at both ends. After ten minutes of the first-responders stabilizing my leg, getting me on the gurney and into the ambulance, I was taken to the hospital, which just happened to be about a quarter of a mile from the church. The ride was so quick that the crew did not even turn on the lights or siren. I remember feeling a bit shortchanged because of that.

Once we got to the emergency room, I was prioritized and immediately had several doctors attempting to stabilize the break and clean the exposed bones. A portable X-ray machine was brought over, and within a couple of minutes, I found out that my tibia and fibula were compound-fractured at both ends. The doctors told me this was a rare break that destabilizes the entire leg as I now had no weight-bearing bones. Two of the emergency room doctors continued to work on my leg, and they let me know that a very good orthopedic surgeon was on his way. Approximately ninety minutes went by before the surgeon arrived and introduced himself. He looked at my leg and then looked at my X-rays. He left for a few minutes and looked to have gone to where the emergency doctors were and looked to be consulting with them. Five more minutes elapsed before he came back and let me know I had two options. He said he needed to perform surgery ASAP. He said that it could go one of two ways. The first option would mean a shorter surgery and shorter recovery time but that I would have multiple metal rods and screws placed into my leg and bones in both the top and bottom areas where the compound fractures were. The second option was a surgery that would take longer and result in two or three times the amount of recovery time but would require no foreign objects being installed in my leg.

The doctor went into more details about each option and then gave me ten minutes to decide as he prepared for the surgery and let the hospital staff know to get the operating room ready. I thought about the additional information he gave me in regards to possible future pain or issues with the hardware and that at some point, my leg may require additional surgery to take out or replace hardware. This made me decide to go with the longer surgery and recovery times. So I went with that option, where the surgeon would set the bones and try to attach them at both ends, and then I would rely on a longer cast that would extend up to the top of my hip. Over an extended amount of recovery time, the doctor would take off each cast and replace them with one that was shorter in length until finally, I would use only a soft walking cast. He said this process may require me to be in a cast for almost a year, compared to the three months at most if I had rods and pins placed into my leg. I stuck to my decision of letting the leg naturally heal.

When we got into the operating room, the orthopedic surgeon and anesthesiologist were waiting. The anesthesiologist placed a general anesthesia cocktail into my IV and told me to count backward from thirty. As the general anesthesia entered my blood stream through my IV, I could remember how it felt like I was on fire from the inside out. The pain in my arm from the drug was intense. I tried to not think about it and started counting. The last thing I remember was the number twenty-seven.

What happened during surgery was simply amazing, and the fact that I remembered everything upon waking was even more amazing. I woke up at the base of a large mountain. Snow was covering its peak. From past experience, I expected something like this to happen to me if I ever found myself again in an operating room and drugged up with potent narcotics. As I opened my eyes, I was lying in a grassy field below the mountain Subar-Ki, which became known as Mount Ararat. I could tell that it must have been autumn as it was cold but not yet freezing, and there was snow only at the higher elevations. As I got up, I looked down at myself and noticed I was wearing clothing that would only have been acceptable in the distant past. I looked around and noticed that there was a large community approximately two hundred yards away.

I headed in that direction, and as I did, I looked up to the sky. Almost directly above me, I saw a massive fireball and what looked to be a huge tail of fire on the trailing end. I thought it looked like a dragon. If I had to draw what I saw, I would have drawn an actual dragon. At the end of its tail were huge charged particles of electricity being released into the atmosphere. I also noticed that something looked wrong with the moon. It did not seem to be where one would expect it to be. It looked a lot closer to Earth. As I approached the city as it was too large to be considered a village, I was met by at least two hundred people who looked to be waiting for me. Once I was within a close proximity of them, they began asking me questions in a different language that I thought I did not know. But as I listened, again as in these same types of past experiences, I understood what was being asked and was able to reply in what I recognized was an ancient form or dialect of Hun-Magyar.

People were addressing me as Magog, and I was considered a prophet or seer. For them, the fact that I could see the future and that I had apparently lived many past lives were of little issue and almost considered necessary to have the position of seer in the community. I had entered the crowd and had to stop when I now was before a quorum of nine older men. Everyone quit speaking as the men began to speak to me.

Several of them took their turns asking me if I knew where the dragon in the sky came from and if this was the dragon of old that brought damnation to the human population in the past. I was asked what the people of the city should do.

In perfect ancient Hun-Magyar, I responded, "Quorum of the Nine, hear me and take heed. Those of Japhetic Stock, direct descendants of Japheth, I being his son, come before you and let you know that this is not like past times but something very unique and to my recollection, singular in occurrence. Never before have I seen a dragon of fire in the sky that spews lightning from its tail, and never have I seen an object in the sky pull on the moon and take it farther away from our sky. I am troubled greatly by what I see happening and plead with the Quorum of the Nine to have those within our city of Madzhar Agadzor run and hide in the deep caves to the west as was done in my past lives when the world ended. I fear that as the dragon gets farther and farther away and takes our moon farther from us, that this could only spell disaster among the people of our lands."

The Quorum of the Nine then began discussing the matter. As I watched, I felt a soft hand begin to hold my hand, and I began to smell what could only be fresh flowers. I turned and saw one of the most beautiful creatures to ever walk this planet. I recognized her as my wife, Olivana, and also recognized that aura or spirit bottled inside her as being the same as Heather, millenniums before she would walk this planet as that incarnation.

As the people in the crowd continued to discuss the situation and the Quorum continued their discussions, Olivana and I snuck away and went around the corner of a building where no people were to be found. She asked me if I was able to recall any of my past lives and verify that indeed this was a new apocalyptic event, and I stated that I did have recall days earlier, and that this is nothing like before when it was the end of times. Olivana also stated that she still could not remember much of the past and would try to work toward recall, but for now, I was the only one who could help make a sound decision on what to do next.

"Olivana, have you noticed how the days seem to get longer and longer and how the moon seems to move farther and farther away from our sky?" I asked her.

"Yes, I have noticed, and I have noticed that the earthquakes have grown stronger each day. What do you believe is happening?"

"I am not sure, but somehow, I believe this fire dragon is taking our land with it and moving our moon farther away from our sky and our planet farther away from our sun. I wish I had the technology and tools of the ancients that allowed for calculations of the celestial bodies in the sky. Unfortunately, they were destroyed in the past cataclysms and the technology lost forever," I replied.

Olivana and I then returned to the crowd, and as I approached, Madzhar Agadzor began to fade away, and with it went my love, my Olivana.

"Mr. Kilian, Mr. Kilian; my name is nurse Stevens, and I am here in recovery with you. I need for you to open your eyes. You are in the recovery room, and your surgery went very well."

I realized I was back in December 1992, and everything prior had to be some type of past life experience. I was sure of this now. I then noticed I could not move. I began speaking to the nurse and had trouble hearing myself but apparently got a response.

"You have a cast on your right leg that goes completely up and over the hip. This is the reason why you feel immobile and are having trouble moving your lower body. Just take it easy, and let's first make sure you come out of the current state you are in. You need to breathe on your own and not need that oxygen cannula you have on right now," she said.

It took me another thirty minutes to come to and not feel like I was in a stupor. At this point, I began feeling extreme pain. I also felt caged due to the cast and the mobility issues. This caused my anxiety to go through the roof, and I began getting combative and thrashing around. I was being held down as a nurse put a needle into my IV. Someone began telling me that I was getting morphine in my drip and would soon be back to feeling good. Moments later, I had no fight in me and no anxiety. I was smiling and laughing as I was wheeled away in the bed to my hospital room. I was now in a private room alone in the dark and feeling fantastic. This is when I got a visit from one of the dark shadow figures.

The creature flew from a corner across the room up to my face. It was also levitating above me in a prone position, with its face directly in front of mine. I smiled and laughed as I did not seem to be bothered by these creatures any longer, and the morphine contributed to my relaxed take on the situation. The creature began to communicate with me and entered my thoughts.

"You have had more recall now than ever before, haven't you?"

I answered aloud, "I sure did, but right now, I can't remember where I am or why I am here, and I sure don't know who you are!"

"In due time you will remember who I am; you will remember who all of us are," the creature replied telepathically.

Then I blinked, and the dark figure was gone. Soon after I fell asleep.

A short while later, I felt someone touching me who continued to tell me I needed to wake up so staff members could take my vitals. As I opened one eye, I noticed there was this very attractive Asian nurse telling me to wake up as she put something tight around my upper arm and something cold just below it. I started to smile as I saw how good-looking she was.

As she took my vitals, I blurted out, "How are you doing?"

I had no idea what I was saying, and luckily, she laughed and did not take offense. When she was done, she smiled back at me and walked out of the room. I never saw that nurse again, and I was in the hospital for one week, which included Christmas Day.

I was awake and staring up at the wall when I began feeling something vibrating on my leg. It started to hurt a lot, and I felt a burning from ankle to hip. I searched for the nurse assist button and began pushing it. Within a minute, a male nurse came in and asked what was wrong. I told him my leg has something moving inside of it, and it burns. He said there was a muscle stimulator unit inside the cast and that it was programmed to go off every hour to help prevent major atrophy. I asked if there were any other surprises I should know about, and he stated that he would save all the others for the surgeon to tell me about in the morning when he came to check on me. He asked how my pain was, and I told him almost to the point of unbearable.

A few minutes later, he came back with more morphine, and within a few minutes, I was feeling fantastic. As he left, he notified me that this was the last of the morphine I would be getting since the doctor had switched me to Demerol that way I would not get addicted. I was fine with that, just so long I was getting some type of medication to relieve the torment I was going through. It turned out to be a brutal night, and I had a hard time finding comfort because of the pain and the hourly intrusions so nurses could check my vitals. I again felt anxious and caged up, and I could do absolutely nothing about it since I could not get out of the bed. I did not think about what happened to me during my surgery as for now I could focus only on trying to get through the night.

It finally began to get light outside my hospital window, and soon, the clock in the room registered 8 in the morning.

A few minutes later, the surgeon who performed my surgery came strolling into my room. He spoke to me as he checked the cast and my chart. He let me know what took place during the surgery and that it lasted six hours. This was due to how difficult it was to get both sides of the break into alignment and set in the correct fashion. The casting also went well on the surgeon's first attempt. He let me know how I would need to see him at his office every four to six weeks so he could remove the old cast, check my leg and then put a smaller cast on each time until it was healed. He also let me know I would be in the hospital for Christmas and most likely for five to seven days total. It turned out that I was there for the full seven days. I was lucky I had good friends and roommates as a multitude of people came to visit me that day, which was Christmas Eve. The same was true with Christmas Day. Everyone taking time away from their family to see me made that Christmas a little easier to deal with.

For the next couple of months, I rarely left my apartment. I learned to hop around on my other leg when I needed to get somewhere inside my place. I had a lot of friends who took the time out of their schedules to drive me to the doctor or other places so I could do simple things such as get a haircut. Before I knew it, six months went by, and I now had a walking cast. I felt good enough to get back to work, and the store was gracious enough to let me come back and accommodate me with my temporary disability. I also began heading to the gym and started my own rehabilitation. During the six months I was in a cast, it took a heavy toll on my leg from muscle atrophy, and I was determined to get back into the great shape I was in prior to breaking it. Within two months of starting my own rehabilitation, I became stronger than ever and no longer used the walking cast. My leg healed better and quicker than the orthopedic surgeon had anticipated.

While I was healing and working only part-time, I was able to finally spend time on attempting to investigate or solve some of the weird phenomenon in my life. I had started creating charts of the events in order to log my visitations by supernatural beings, as well as dreams and flashbacks I had. I also was charting what I considered to be the locations and time frames of these occurrences. With the supernatural beings, I also attempted to create sketches of each one. The other thing I was doing at this time was going through the hiring process for the El Paso Police Academy. I figured that being a cop in El Paso had to be one of the better paying jobs in a city that offered little in the way of employment opportunity. So I started the process in July 1993, and by October, I had only the oral boards and polygraph exam to go through.

I was very good at conversing with people face to face, and even though the officers at the oral board tried to get me fired up and grilled me on some issues regarding my background, I made it through and was notified to take the polygraph exam the next day. Now with the shit I had done in my life, a lot of it bad, some of it illegal, and the fact that I heard voices in my head, would make most people think I had no chance in hell of passing. That turned out not to be the case, and I aced that polygraph and showed no negative results as I lied during the entire examination. I knew I could do a good job as a cop and felt that things in the past should remain as such. A week later, I received a phone call from El Paso's Police Department. I was told I had been accepted for the next police academy. On Oct. 18, 1993, I reported to the academy on Scenic Drive.

The academy was much like military basic training, and because of this, I did well. Training was Monday through Friday from 7 in the morning until 4 in the afternoon, but many of those days ended at 5 or 6 instead. Plus, once you left, you had to go to the main police station for weight training or practice your boxing skills before going home. Once you got home, you had to memorize laws, codes and ordinances, and that meant another two or three hours of study time.

We had three to five classes a day that consisted of learning city, state and federal laws and ordinances. There also were tactical and hands-on procedures training and physical fitness classes. I excelled at everything during the academy.

The academy was fantastic and taught me how to handle most types of situations and to question and investigate whatever looked to be out of place. I got to be good with the Texas penal code and vehicle code. I learned to drive a vehicle from an offensive and defensive position, improved my shooting capability with a pistol and shotgun, learned boxing skills and martial arts, and by the time it was over, I was in the best shape of my life. We were taught not to win a fight immediately but instead to outlast our opponent and overcome them at the end.

We had ax handles swung at us that had to be blocked with our PR-24 control baton. Two and three people would attack us at one time, and we had to learn to survive and not allow for our sidearm to be taken and also how to fight off a crowd if need be. Tuesday became known as Terrible Tuesday as this was when we would have physical fitness for two or three hours straight and were pretty much tortured by officer Toraya. He would tell us this was for our own good and safety, but I know that son of a bitch got off on watching people pass out from exhaustion or be on the verge of wanting to quit because they were at the brink of physical failure. I felt bad for the four women in my class as he really liked to pick on them, and many times, it became uncomfortable to watch. But they all sucked it up and got through the academy.

After all this pain and suffering and intense schooling, twenty-two of us made it to the end, and on a Thursday, we graduated during a ceremony at the Chamizal National Memorial in the downtown El Paso area. I was now a rookie on the El Paso Police Department, making a whopping $24,000 a year. With this minor amount of money, I had to also purchase my own 9mm sidearm and bulletproof vest. I ended up being stationed at the brand-new Eastside Pebble Hills Regional Command Center, and I was on graveyard shift for my first thirty days. I was assigned to my field training officer, Cpl. Miguel Fernandez, who was a five-year veteran of the force and a former solider in the U.S. Army. I would also later learn that he was burned out and wanted to do as little as possible during his shift. He was best known as the "Skater" on the watch I was assigned to. He became a field training officer so he could be paid more money for training rookies incorrectly. Much of what I ended up learning came from other officers who filled in for him as he almost always missed one or two days a week.

Even with a field training officer like Miguel Fernandez, I still tried to make the most of the job and help as many people as I could. During my first week, Officer Sanchez and I located several subjects who were coming in and out of an abandoned townhome off of McRae. We pulled our patrol car up to a home about six houses down and then walked back to the townhome, where we waited at the entrance of the adjoining property. When two of the suspects came out again to look around, we stopped them and began asking questions. Both of the men were Mexican nationals, and Officer Sanchez spoke to them in Spanish as I searched them for weapons. During the interview, one of the men broke down and told us that they were drug mules and had a van parked in the garage that was full of narcotics. We ended up arrested three suspects and finding a Ford van full of marijuana, cocaine and heroin, with an estimated street value of $7 million. I received an accommodation for the bust on my very first week. I remember being very happy that my field training officer called out sick that day because he would have never listened to me when I noticed the subjects initially outside the townhome and would have kept on driving.

By my fourth month, I began driving alone on graveyard shift while my field training officer was close by in another squad car. On my first night alone, I got a call to a local Denny's restaurant on a possible aggravated sexual assault. I pulled up to the Denny's about five minutes later and met a Hispanic woman who told me she had been to a local country nightclub earlier and met this guy there with whom she ended up leaving. When she got into his Ford Bronco, she stated that two of his buddies were waiting inside the truck. When she got in, they pulled her into the back seat and raped her. While she was telling me this story, Miguel pulled up in a separate squad car and was now also on scene with me as I was taking the woman's statement.

The woman then notified us that after they were done taking turns raping her, the three suspects dropped her off at the Denny's and left. I called dispatch for a female officer as she was going to have to take the victim to a local hospital for a physical exam and for personnel to collect evidence with a rape kit. Once I was done calling dispatch, I asked the victim to describe the vehicle the three men used. As she was describing it, someone on the highway that was about two hundred feet from the Denny's, began honking as they drove by. I happened to look up and noticed that the vehicle fit the description of the suspects' vehicle and that they must have been honking at the victim, not knowing that police had shown up. I ran to the squad car and pursued them, code 3, with lights and sirens. While

I was entering the I-10 onramp, I was calling dispatch to clear the air for emergency traffic.

"Dispatch be advised, I am in pursuit of a Ford Bronco with three felony suspects inside headed westbound on the I-10 at a high rate of speed toward the Hawkins off-ramp."

I could not see any trucks on the highway, so I exited at Hawkins and located the Ford Bronco turning left and going into the lower valley with no lights on. I lit the vehicle up with my side spotlight and was now approximately two hundred feet behind the Bronco, which was traveling down side streets at a high rate of speed. About two miles down a straight road, the Ford slowed enough for me to attempt a pit maneuver on the Bronco. I notified dispatch that I was conducting a pit maneuver as the vehicle was traveling at an unsafe speed and that because of it, I feared that a civilian may be injured if I did not stop the vehicle. I got approval from the supervisor on duty and moved into position on the rear left of the Bronco. I impacted the Bronco, and the rear wheel blew out but the driver gained control before spinning out. The suspects continued down the street, driving on a rim for another mile before they could no longer proceed and came to a stop in the middle of the road.

By this time, ten other police units were on scene and had surrounded the vehicle. I got out with my weapon out, and from behind my open door and window, I began yelling for the suspects to exit the vehicle one at a time. I attempted to get them to exit on three separate times, but no one left the Bronco. The bad part about this situation was that the windows were tinted so dark that no officer could see inside. At this point, I called dispatch to request a tactical unit for an assault on the vehicle. Just as I no sooner finished making the request, the passenger door to the Bronco flung open, and a male in a cowboy hat, cowboy clothes and boots exited with an Uzi submachine gun, and he began firing at my vehicle.

My door was riddled with 9mm rounds. At this point, I heard approximately twelve to fifteen shots fired back at the suspect by other officers, and the suspect went down to the ground. I looked down at my body, thinking that I was going to see blood coming out of me. Thank the gods there was none. The door to my unit ended up stopping approximately seven rounds that would have otherwise hit me in the torso, head or arms. The other two suspects eventually came out of the Ford and were taken into custody. The injured suspect survived and would later receive twenty years in a Texas penitentiary for attempted murder of a police officer. When the Ford was processed, we found several additional handguns and a shotgun in the truck. I was very lucky I got to go home that night.

This was the first of three occurrences when I was on duty that would eventually lead to my quitting before my rookie year was up. Exactly thirty days from the day that my life almost ended at the hands of an Uzi, I would again tempt fate and have a second near-death experience while I was on the job. This time, I was at the end of my shift when I worked the evening watch. I thought I was going to get through the night with no other calls as I had only ten minutes left. But some brand-new piece-of-crap dispatcher ended up sending me to a fight in progress at a topless bar on Montana Avenue, which was outside of my district. I was one pissed-off officer as it had already been a long night. Even worse, my piece-of-crap field training officer decided to leave. Lucky for me other officers who had just gotten on duty knew what a skater Miguel was, and two units let the dumbass dispatcher know they were headed to my location as backup. I was only two minutes from the bar, and my backup was approximately five minutes away. I was tired and wanted to clear the scene quickly as most of the time, the fight is done before police ever get to the scene. This would not be one of those times.

I pulled up to the nude bar parking lot and saw no fight taking place outside. The dispatcher never stated if the fight was happening inside or outside of the bar, so I knew I would have to go inside and check it out. Then I would have to locate the caller and see if a report was going to be needed. I called dispatch and said I was headed to the front entrance of what was a very shady topless bar and pool hall behind the main set of buildings that lined Montana Avenue. I was still pretty pissed for having been called at the end of my shift and did not think to grab my baton. So back in 1994, the only other thing on my Sam Brown belt were two pairs of handcuffs, a portable two-way radio, my flashlight, which doubled back then as a better baton than the real one, and my Glock 9mm handgun.

The El Paso police did not carry pepper spray or a Taser at that time. I reached the front door, which was blacked out. I then opened it and walked in. The call for police was a setup, and several of the patrons that night were drunk and thought it would be a great idea to call cops out on a fake fight call and then fight the police officers who showed up. The moment I walked through the door, I felt something hard, like a bat hitting me across my face, and I instantly was knocked off my feet and fell to the floor. Someone had hit me with a cue stick.

I was immediately elsewhere, where a massive battle was taking place, with explosions going off and bullets whizzing by my head.

"Corporal, corporal – get your head down; get back in the fox hole. We are taking heavy fire!"

I was a soldier in World War I and the language being spoken was German. I was a German soldier. Then something hit me, and I was decapitated. The next thing I knew, I was back in the bar, and I fought to regain consciousness. I was laid out on the ground. Instinctively, I curled into a ball and put all my weight down on the left side of my body, where my gun was. With my one hand, I put as much force as I could on my gun to keep it from being taken, and with my other hand, I activated my code 99 emergency button on my two-way radio.

As I fought to secure my weapon, I was being punched in the face and kicked in the lower extremities.

I was barely conscious but aware enough to hear one of the seasoned dispatchers call out my radio designation, "1SAM-273? 1SAM-273?"

There was a quick pause, and I heard the third call out, "1SAM-273? All units in the vicinity of Menos Topless Bar, I have a code 99 activated and no response from the officer. All units available respond code 3 to an officer down. I repeat all units available respond to unit 1S273 as that officer is unresponsive and code 99 is active."

Even though I was almost unable to stay conscious, and just at a point where I almost no longer cared, I slightly grinned as I heard the cavalry on my radio. I lost track of how many units responded, and they were on their way from as far as the northeast side of town.

As I felt my hand that was holding my gun being broken, I heard the two units that were already initially backing me up clearing the air for emergency traffic as they pulled up to my vehicle outside and entered the bar. Once I saw the officers, I blacked out. I later woke up at the same hospital where I had my leg surgery. I would later find out that I had my left wrist and some carpal bones broken, several cracked ribs and a concussion. I found out that I had been jumped by four drunken bikers who had decided they were going to ambush some cops that night. They had called 911 themselves and planned on fighting as many cops as they could, and I was the lucky officer who received the original call. I also was told that thirty officers responded to my location and that all four of those bikers were at Thomason Hospital in ICU and in critical condition. They would end up going to prison, and the one who hit me with the cue stick was given twenty years to life for the attempted capital murder of a police officer. It took me twelve weeks to heal, and I did not return to full active duty until my ninth month of being a full-time officer.

I eventually got back and was again solo in a vehicle, but this time, I had a new field training officer as Miguel was disciplined for having left me alone the night of the bar fight and was suspended for two weeks with no pay. He would never again be a field training officer, and this I could not agree with more. My new partner and field training officer was Henry Quintana, and he was an exceptional officer who taught me more in thirty days than I had learned in my first five and a half months. I appreciated his direction, and he and I worked toward getting me to pass my rookie year and make it through my probationary period. Unfortunately, month eleven would be my last as an officer, and eleven months would be the full extent of my career as a patrol officer.

I remember that Henry and I were working on a Friday night, and it was a graveyard shift. There was only one vehicle available for us that night, so we rolled together on our shift as 2F376. For some reason, as we started out that night, I kept flashing back to when I saw myself as a German soldier in World War I, right before I was decapitated on the battle field. I should have taken this memory as a bad omen. The shift started out fairly simple with only one report being made and one arrest being conducted for a person I stopped who had an outstanding warrant for his arrest. Henry and I were almost halfway done with the shift and were about to request our lunch break when dispatch notified us of a domestic disturbance in progress, and we were to respond code 2.

I had been called out to this home several times before due to domestic issues. It was in my old district, and tonight we seemed to be covering for everyone else as all the other units were busy in their districts, and the seventy-six district was pretty slow all evening. We pulled up and notified dispatch that we had arrived. It was a standard-looking two-story house in a typical Eastside neighborhood of El Paso. The homeowners were also your typical neighbors who just had marital problems that many times escalated into a shouting match. The fighting would get too loud for the neighbors, and they would call police. The husband and wife had three kids, two girls and a boy, who were between the ages of twelve and fifteen.

The last time I was at the location was with Miguel, and we had warned the husband and wife that if police had to come back again and if there was any physical violence to anyone, then police would arrest them, and they'd be going to jail for the night. As I approached the door, I could hear yelling and some crying. Henry hung back to make sure no one came around from the backyard or pulled up behind us. I rang the doorbell and announced that it was the police. The wife opened the door and recognized that I had been there before. She let me in, and I walked to the family room, where the father and three kids were gathered. I told the wife to have a seat and began speaking to all five of them.

"I thought my old partner made it clear that if there were future issues and we had to come out here again that there was a good chance someone was going to jail. Did he not make himself clear?" I asked.

The father responded, "I remember what the other officer told us, and I promise you we have been trying to do the best we can and have really cut back on the fighting. There has been no physical contact between my wife and I or the kids."

"How about all the yelling and screaming coming from the house that the entire neighborhood is sick of hearing; you can't tell me that has stopped. I heard it walking up to the front door."

At that point, I noticed Henry behind me and to the left.

"You would not believe us if we told you officer what is happening, and I sometimes have trouble believing it myself. What the neighbors sometimes are hearing is not us; it is not anyone in our family," the wife exclaimed.

This comment of hers really piqued my interest and got me thinking something else was wrong, and it was going to be one of those unusual calls.

Sure enough, everyone in the home, including myself and Henry, heard someone upstairs yell, "Get the fuck out of the house, you mother fuckers! You pieces of shit are as bad as the rest. You all deserve to fucking die, and no one will fucking miss you."

I turned to the family and asked them who else was in the house as I knew that it was usually just the five of them. The dad said no one else was with them.

"Then who is yelling from upstairs?" Henry asked the dad.

"I don't know what it is, but it seems to only have gotten worse as Janet and I have gotten uglier with one another."

"What do you mean by you saying that you don't know what it is?" I asked, as what he said insinuated it was something other than a person.

The father again said that none of them knew, and sometimes, even they were pretty scared.

At that moment, someone upstairs again began yelling, "I thought I told you piece-of-shit pigs to get out. You are not wanted here. There is nothing you can fucking do. You are few and we; we are many!"

That was the last straw for Henry, and he began walking up to the second floor.

I slowly backed up to the bottom of the stairs and kept an eye on the occupants in the family room. I also kept glancing up the stairs to keep track of Henry. This whole time, the yelling got worse from upstairs, and suddenly, it sounded like there were crowds of people on the second floor, and none of them was in a pleasant mood. I yelled up to Henry to see what was going on, and I got no response. I could see he was in the hall at the top of the stairs and was not moving. He had his flashlight on as the hall was dark, but the light was pointed to his feet. He was staring back and forth from one side of the wood walls to the other.

I could see Henry was looking at something on the walls that featured 1980s-style laminated wood panels. The yelling became deafening, and I thought there was a huge group of people about to attack Henry. I called for backup on the radio and heard two units responding. I told everyone in the family room stay seated, and then I began heading up the stairs. As I did so, it got so loud with yelling that I could barely hear myself think. When I reached the top step and walked forward, I quickly saw what Henry was looking at and what had him so scared that he was not able to move. On both sides of the walls of the hall, inside the paneling where you usually see the ovals and circular patterns of the wood, were hundreds of faces, and they seemed to be part of the laminate wood panels. The faces were moving and staring and yelling obscenities. It felt like something out of a horror movie.

I had been in contact with the supernatural before, and I was not as bothered by it as Henry was, but I recognized that this was different than anything that had ever happened to me. These things, these faces, were a multitude of minions or an army of angry spirits that were screaming and feeding off of the negative energy in the house created by the constant fighting and anger. I watched the faces in the dark for a few seconds and then took my flashlight off of my belt and began to shine the light on the walls. This angered whatever these things were that much more. I then walked to the end of the hall and flipped on the light switch. When I did this, I noticed that every face on both sides of the wall instantly swung toward me and began to stare in my direction, and I noticed that it became silent. Then one of the faces closest to me on my left side pushed itself out past the wall barrier and gained three dimensions to its features.

Then it spoke: "You – you are not what we know. You are not like the rest. You have escaped us for many millenniums, but your time on this realm of existence is not infinite, and at some point, you will be among the dead."

I understood that the comment by this demon was directly meant for me. I understood the implications behind what this demon was saying and that I may truly have a soul that never remains dead. I was also pretty sure that no one else in the house knew what the demon meant. As it finished speaking, two officers walked through the front door downstairs and asked what was going on, and when Henry and I again looked back at the walls around us, there were no longer faces.

I notified the other officers that we thought there were additional people upstairs and needed possible backup but we were unable to locate anyone else. The officers cleared from the call and went back out on the streets. Henry sat down near the family, and we all discussed what just took place. I let the family know that apparently all their fighting and anger was causing other things to enter this physical realm. I told them that it could only get worse, especially for the kids, if they kept things up. The family promised they would seek counseling and that they may even start attending church. They did not seem to care what church that was, just so long as they attended. I gave them my card and told them to call me if there were any other issues like the one upstairs. They thanked me, and I then practically had to pick Henry up off the couch and take him out to the patrol car. Once we were inside the car, I cleared us from the scene, and Henry and I talked for a while. We discussed what just took place and said that it was probably best we not mention the demons. The two of us also decided that when we were ready to write up the incident report, that we would stick to the standard domestic violence call that ends in a good way for all involved. He agreed, and I then drove off. This may seem like it was the third incident that caused me to no longer want to be a police officer, but it was not.

As soon as I had driven away, dispatch contacted us and put us en route to our second domestic disturbance call. This would be the call that changed my outlook on life and made me no longer want to be a police officer. Again, we had been dispatched outside of our district and to a location I had never been to. Several neighbors had called regarding this domestic disturbance, and apparently, it was still in progress as we pulled up. Henry and I watched as this small Latina woman was punching one of the largest black men I had ever seen in person. The woman seriously had to be no taller than five feet, and the man she was hitting had to be at least six-foot-nine or six-foot-ten and with the physique of a pro football lineman. The woman punched the man one more time in the gut and then walked into their townhome, slamming the screen door behind her.

As Henry and I exited the squad car, the man tried getting the screen door open and realized the woman had locked it. That did not stop him as he put his fist through the screen, put his other hand in the hole and then ripped the screen door open and walked through the entry he created. Henry and I opened our car doors, reached in and got out our PR-24 side-handle batons and attached them to our belts. We then headed toward the front door. I remembered thinking that Henry could not be taller than five-foot-six as he walked in front of me. He reached the door first and announced that we were the police as he knocked. There was no answer, so Henry knocked again. The Latina woman came around the corner, cursing in Spanish, and she opened what was left of the screen door. She told us to come in, and we entered into what was the living room of the townhouse. As we began asking the woman questions, we learned that she and the man were husband and wife, and that he had come home that night with the smell of another woman's perfume on his clothing. She had started yelling at her husband and then started hitting him. She stated that he grabbed and held both her hands and forearms in one of his hands to keep her from hitting him but at no time did he hit or push her. After she explained this and again started yelling at her husband, he came down the hall and was now also in the living room with Henry, myself and his hysterical wife.

The husband was pretty calm, and when I asked him what had happened, he began to tell me that one of the women at his workplace happened to give him a hug for helping her out. Apparently, she had some heavy perfume on that rubbed into his clothes. I asked him what he did for a living, and he told me he was a high school football coach at one of the local schools. Henry and I began de-escalating the situation. After talking to the husband and wife separately for a couple of minutes, Henry and I thought we had a good grasp on the situation. Unfortunately for my partner and I that night, we were going to have to take the woman into custody and arrest her for assault and battery. This was the policy of the El Paso Police Department when violence takes place between domestic partners and it is witnessed by the officer.

Somehow, I knew the night had already been bizarre and that this scenario was not going to end well. Sure enough, Henry notified the woman that he was placing her under arrest and calmly grabbed the wrist of her right arm. As he did so, the woman went into what can only be described as berserker mode. She started assaulting Henry.

I grabbed her, and as I did, I heard the following from her husband, "You are not laying a hand on my wife tonight – not in my house!"

I felt myself being lifted off the ground and thrown across the living room just like a rag doll. This monster of a man had just picked me up and tossed me a good ten feet across the living room, and I hit hard against the back wall. As I fell to the floor, a medium-sized painting came crashing down on my head. One hell of a fight for survival for my partner and I quickly ensued.

The woman punched Henry square in the jaw, and he fell backward and stumbled over some furniture. Henry landed on the ground of the living room. I got back up in time to see the woman run down the hall and lock the door to a room she had just went into. Before I knew it, the husband was again on top of me and had my head in between his massive hands. I felt him crushing my skull from both sides. I was lifted off the ground, and my feet were dangling in the air. I did the only thing I could in this situation and that was to kick the husband as hard as I could in his groin. He let go for a moment, looked at me, smiled and then grabbed me by my left arm and swung me across the room. I crashed into his glass entertainment center. I could hear glass shelves crack and break. I pulled away from the shelves but was immediately tackled and had this massive guy on top of my back. I could feel him then push me to the ground and slam my face into the tile on the floor. As he was doing this, my partner had been able to get up and pull his baton from his belt. He got behind the husband and started swinging as hard as he could, with the large part of the baton now striking the husband multiple times in the kidneys. This did nothing to the man, and he continued to crush me into the ground.

This went on for a good ten or fifteen seconds until the man must have finally gotten tired of Henry hitting him, and he then got up off the floor and off of me. He then turned toward Henry. Again, in the mid-1990s, El Paso police had no Tasers or pepper spray. These items had not yet become standard issue for most police departments. What I did have was my Mag flashlight and my PR-24 side-handle baton, which I could not find as it went flying somewhere when I was tossed through the air, and I also had my 9mm Glock semi-automatic pistol. I slowly got up as the man had turned his attention to my partner. I got back to my feet just in time to watch as the man lifted my partner over his head and slammed him several times into the ceiling. After doing this for a while, the man then threw Henry out the front window, shattering the glass in the process. We were now fighting for our lives, and my partner may be out front bleeding to death. This was not a good situation to be in.

The man then turned back toward me. I pulled my Mag light from my belt, held it in my left hand and cocked my hand back. The husband then began charging me. As he was coming at me I could hear my partner outside clearing the air for emergency traffic, then reporting that there was an officer down and that we were requesting backup. The husband reached where I stood, and I hurled my hand forward and caught the subject in the jaw with my hand and the back end of my Mag light. This caused the husband to stop in his tracks. I took another swing at him with my flashlight and caught the right side of his head. My flashlight found its target just above his right ear, and blood now started flowing from his head. All this did was turn this monster of a man into one pissed off fighting machine.

He lifted me and body slammed me through his glass-top living room coffee table. I remember hearing glass shatter all around me. I looked down at my torso, and I had large pieces of glass sticking into me everywhere. Luckily, I was wearing my Kevlar vest, and it stopped the glass from entering into my body. The guy grabbed me by the neck and yanked me out from the middle of the table. As he did this, I pulled a shard of the glass out of my vest and used it to slice the husband's wrist open. Blood gushed out of his arm, and when he saw this, he released me from the choke hold. I stumbled backward to put some distance between us.

"I am going to kill you, mother fucker!" he said.

I could do nothing else but shoot him to save my life. As I began to unholster my sidearm, he came for me. Two shots rang out, and he fell to the floor in front of me. Henry had fired his weapon and struck him both times on the right side of his torso. I quickly turned the husband on his side, and cuffed his hands together behind his back as I was not taking any chances. It took both pairs of my handcuffs to accomplish this. Henry then notified dispatch that shots had been fired, and emergency medical services and a supervisor were needed at our location. Afterward, I continued to pull shards of glass from my vest and made sure I had none sticking out of me. The man ended up surviving and was later sentenced to ten years in prison for the attempted capital murder of a police officer. I ended up with bruises, scrapes and some minor cuts that night, but I was alive and able to continue with my journey through this life. Henry sustained a punctured lung and blown-out knee. He ended up on medical retirement because of what took place that night. I quit the next day and never again would be a patrol officer, at least not during this lifetime.

# 14.

# So Much in California

My two roommates had continued to work at that big-box retail store where I was employed part-time before becoming a police officer. I was told that the company was going to enter the Southern California market by opening eight new stores all at once, with grand openings scheduled for May 1995. I ended up applying for the District Loss Prevention Supervisor position and got the job. I was in charge of loss prevention for three of the new locations. With about seven weeks before the grand opening of the new stores, my roommates and I sold our vehicles, packed our stuff into a moving truck and headed to sunny Southern California. I was headed back home and could not wait to get there.

We moved into a three-bedroom apartment off the Pacific Coast Highway in Torrance. That was where my main store was located and where I based my headquarters. I also ended up having the stores in Hawthorne and West LA. I purchased a used Honda Civic so I could travel to work and cart my roommates around since the two of them ended up purchasing motorcycles for their transportation. For the next seven weeks, I worked an average of sixty hours per week as I had to learn my job duties, which were different than what I had done before with the company. This time spent working included having to hire and train the loss prevention staff at all three stores I oversaw. It was not easy, and I had never managed anyone before, but I caught on quickly, and in no time at all, I established myself as one of the go-to managers for the new district.

During our off-time, which was very little at the beginning but gradually increased, my roommates and I would hit up the clubs and bars in the Redondo Beach, Hermosa Beach and Torrance areas. Nights after work consisted of a lot of partying until the early hours of the following day. I was having a great time as there was never any kind of nightlife like this in El Paso, and I wanted to make sure I experienced it over and over again. At some point within the next few months, I ended up meeting a few women who turned out to be one-night stands and nothing serious. That soon changed when the Torrance store where I was based soon hired a new Customer Service Supervisor, and she was attractive, intelligent and classy. Unfortunately she was also engaged. I figured if I could not end up with her, I might as well become friends with her.

As time passed we ended up getting closer and closer in our relationship until the next thing I knew, she no longer had an engagement ring on her left hand. When I asked her what happened, she told me that her fiancé turned out to be the wrong person for her. She then told me that she did end up finding that Mr. Right in her life and that he was standing in front of her. For the next three months, this amazing woman and I did everything together. By the end of 1995, I was getting married at the local county courthouse. A couple of months later, we got married in the Catholic Church as she was Catholic, and this was a very important process for her and her family. Once we were married, the two of us transferred to several newly opened stores farther north in the Ventura County area. My wife worked in the Oxnard store, and I was based at the

Thousand Oaks store due to the nepotism policy the company had regarding a regular store employee and loss prevention employee. This area of California was simply one of the most beautiful and amazing I had ever been to, and Ventura County ended up being called home for a long time.

When we first moved north, we rented this awesome loft apartment on the harbor in Oxnard. It was so nice to walk every morning and be surrounded by boats and ocean. I had fallen in love with the ocean during my short time in the military and never thought I would end up back around any body of water, especially living right on the edge of the Pacific Ocean. After our first year of marriage, we ended up moving to Ventura and getting an apartment across the street from the local mall. I was still working for the well-known electronics store and continued to supervise the loss prevention departments at the Oxnard, Thousand Oaks and Woodland Hills locations. My wife ended up going to work for one of the local police departments as an intake officer. We both also started going to the local community college, and before you know it, I had an associate of arts degree.

It was a big accomplishment, and something I never thought I would get around to doing. Unfortunately, work for me began to be a nightmare. Before I let it get to me any further, I went to work for one of the largest and best known retail clothing stores that happened to have a location in the Ventura mall. I ended up loving the loss prevention position that I landed. I had a great time and ended up meeting a lot of people and making many new friends. Unfortunately for my marriage, the new position did not help it as my wife began to grow jealous of the women with whom I worked. She started accusing me of sleeping with them while she was at her job, which had her working graveyard shifts. My wife never really had a lot of friends, and she preferred to spend time only with her family. I was OK with this at the beginning, but it eventually began to grow old, and I got tired of being unable to do anything with anyone else other than her family members. Because of this, we separated several times. But in the end, she could not get over her jealousy issues, and it got so bad that she began spying on me in the evening when she was supposed to have been at work. By Christmas of 1999, I could not take it any longer; I knew that she was not the one for me and that what I thought to be love was just lust this entire time. I did not want to continue living what had become a miserable life. I still cared for her deeply but knew we could no longer be together. Six months later, we were divorced.

From 1995 through 1999, nothing had happened in the way of the supernatural or my dream states or even daydreams and flashbacks. I had started to forget about so much that happened before in my life, and it rarely came up in any discussion with my wife during those years. It seemed as if the last few years were somehow lost to linear time as I knew it. And because of this, I seemed to skip from 1995 to what was June 2000. After the divorce, I continued living in the same apartment complex where my wife and I had lived, but I now had a new roommate who worked with me at the department store in the mall.

My new roommate and I hit it off well. This new life and freedom led to partying and doing things I never would have were it not for this urge of sorts to make up for the last five years, which felt to have slipped away. I had gone off into a detour of sorts that took me away from what I was supposed to be doing in life and a destiny that cried out to be fulfilled. With so much in my life now changed, I began to feel like the person I was before, having moved back to California. I again began hearing those voices in my head that had gone dormant for years. I started having flashbacks about places I had not been to and dreams of being other people in a past that extended through what I could only explain as thousands upon thousands of years.

I kept everything to myself but again logged it in a journal. What was better this time around was the fact that I now had at my disposal this amazing invention called the Internet that allowed me to start researching things that were happening to me, and this helped me begin to get a grasp on what I may have been experiencing through my lifetime. One of my big research topics dealt with the collapse of societies in the distant past that history, historians, anthropologists, archaeologists and others seemed to forget. Maybe they did not want to remember or take the time to possibly research the possibility that these lapses in history and losses of ancient cultures could indeed be factual. But if the scientists had to admit to this and say that they had been wrong, then the belief system they created for themselves would be wrong, and what they did for a living would be senseless. Then everyone would see them for the fakes they truly were, full of wisdom and information that turns out to be complete bullshit.

My friends and I frequented the bars of downtown Ventura, and I ended up being there so often that I became good friends with the staff at several of the bars or restaurants in the area. Before I knew it, anything and everything I did required that alcohol be involved. By the end of that year, things had spiraled out of control. I was spending huge amounts of money on alcohol and who knows what else. I was filling my time with one-night stands because I feared having another relationship that would accomplish nothing and lead to a bitter end. I became selfish and worried only about myself. I knew that in order for me to stop this downward spiral, I had to make some big changes and figure out what I was supposed to do in this world. I knew that no one could help me but myself and that I had to start now. Otherwise, later may turn out to be too late.

The first thing I did was apply to the University of California, Los Angeles, and I got accepted. I decided to major in anthropology as the study of mankind fascinated me, and I felt that I knew more and understood the past better than those idiots who went around calling themselves anthropologists and archaeologists. I would go to a satellite campus three nights a week and go to labs at the main campus in Los Angeles on the weekends. I also ended up applying for a position with the Bureau of Investigations for a local district attorney's office as an investigator and was hired four months later. My normal work hours were Monday through Friday, 8 in the morning to 5 in the evening, and this worked out well with my school schedule. I worked hard at getting the best education I could and learning as much as I could about other cultures, past and present, that had left some sort of footprint on human history. I learned how to properly research historical matters and also began cataloging anything I would come across that looked familiar to me from past cultures, known or unknown. I especially was fascinated with anomalies in history that scientists purposely ignored because they did not fit into their falsified history of mankind's timeline.

As I was in school and working for the local district attorney's office, time flew by, and before I knew it, it was May 2003, and I was graduating with a B.A. degree in anthropology from UCLA. I never thought I would get my B.A. and had somehow always thought I would just stay a cop in El Paso and worry about doing something else after twenty-plus years on the force. It is truly interesting how things change and how the future seems to write the present, which instantly makes your past. After having graduated, I decided that the next thing I wanted to do was go to Argentina. I always wanted to go to South America and was not sure why. So I purchased my airline tickets and got my hotel set for six weeks out. This meant that I would be going in the last week of June, which was the start of winter in the southern hemisphere. I got approved for two weeks off from work. During the six-week period before my trip to Argentina, a lot of things went wrong. Things happened that would lead to a transformation in me and in the knowledge I apparently possessed that came from somewhere I did not yet know existed.

It was Thursday, May 29, 2003, when everything would begin to take shape in what I would soon find out was going to be life changing, not just for me but for those who would listen to me and heed my call. That Thursday, I was told to execute a felony arrest warrant on a woman named Adroa Tabares. She was wanted on felony narcotics charges, and an informant notified the DA's office that she had been staying at a cousin's home in the back hills of Moorpark. Adroa was supposed to be a local witch who belonged to a coven that practiced dark magic on the outskirts of the county. I figured her coven was more of a social club that allowed these men and women to get together and do all types of drugs as they chanted and then had sex with each other and called it dark arts. But what the hell did I know about this kind of thing?

I went to the cousin's home with two sheriff's deputies who were going to assist me with the arrest. The home turned out to be off a dirt road approximately one thousand feet away from the main paved road. We approached it at a high rate of speed as there was nowhere to hide. Anyone driving up to the house from this dirt road was going to be immediately seen because of all the dust that the vehicle kicked up. There was also nothing around the home but vacant fields. So as we started exiting the vehicle, a woman who matched the description of Adroa opened the front door and began running out of the house and into the fields. The two deputies had already exited the car and were in pursuit of the woman. I finished parking the vehicle at the front of the home and exited with my weapon drawn. Once out of the car, I could see that the two deputies and the woman were a good several hundred feet away from the house and both deputies had almost caught up with her.

As I began to turn toward the house, I could see there was someone looking out the screen door. As soon as that person saw me looking at them, they retreated into the home. I began to approach the front door when the two deputies radioed that they had the woman in custody and that she did not look to be the correct wanted subject. I radioed back that there was at least one other individual in the home and that I was going to attempt to locate that person. I banged on the front door and identified myself as a police officer. I said I was executing an arrest warrant on Adroa Tabares and that she needed to exit the home and surrender herself at this moment. Of course, there was no response, and that is when I turned the knob and the door opened. I looked into the first room, and there was no one. As I entered the house, Adroa must have been waiting just off to the side of the door and near the corner of the living room.

I turned to my blind side and saw Adroa as she blew some type of dust or other substance into my face. I wrestled her to the ground. I then began handcuffing her when the room started to spin and I started to get hot flashes that made me feel like I was on fire. As I finished handcuffing her, I started to lose the ability to see, and before I knew it, I could see only massive amounts of vivid colors around me with what looked to be bubbles of light popping all around. I called out to the deputies that the remainder of the home had not been cleared yet and that the suspect had blown some type of chemical into my face and I was losing the ability to focus. Suddenly, I could not see anything around me.

"Don't fight it, traveler. Let it take you where you need to be. Consider this a gift from Adroa," the woman in handcuffs was apparently telling me.

"What did you do to me? What did you blow into my face?" I replied.

"Something that will open your eyes to your reality and invite you to see the real you."

"What is happening to me? I can't focus, and I cannot see."

"Your aura is different than everyone around you, and we know your kind; we have seen you travelers before, and most of the time, you just need to awaken to what has been dormant inside your life force. Let the devil's breath awaken who you really are."

"What the fuck is devil's breathe, bitch? What the fuck did you do to me?"

At that point, the deputies took Adroa into custody, cleared the rest of the home, making sure no one else was inside, and then called dispatch for emergency medical services for whatever was happening to me.

I could hear things happening around me as I began to hallucinate. Even though I felt awake, I could not move or talk. I felt like I was a zombie, stuck in a state of mind between being awake and asleep. All those voices that I had pushed back into some closed off part of my mind were awakened and became very loud. I could hear and sense what had to be at least thirty voices or remnants of other conscious thoughts speaking to me in what now was a different reality. I knew I was not crazy but instead almost hearing recordings of past thoughts or experiences that somehow I was keeping in my head. It almost seemed that I was sharing my mind and soul with other beings. As the drug that was blown into my face began to kick in, the voices I heard now started forming pictures in my mind. Then memories were forming, playing out in my head in a manner that made me feel as if I were watching television through the eyes of one of the characters on a show.

I watched this play out as I was one person or character, then another and another. I was living their lives one after the other, and it would not stop. The memories started overlapping and playing in my head faster and faster until I could not separate them. I heard screaming, laughing and crying. I felt happiness, anger, sadness and pain. I had all these emotions and memories bombarding me, and I felt like my head was overloading and I was about to explode from the inside out. I was losing my mind and could not remember who I was, where I was or what any of this was about. I was in darkness, spinning around and around, farther into the middle of nothing. There was a lot of light popping everywhere. I could feel intense heat, followed by intense pain, and then nothing.

I must have passed out because at some point, I began to wake up with a massive headache. I opened my eyes and was now at the Ventura County Medical Center. I was in the emergency room and had all kinds of tubes hooked to me or stuck inside me and had an oxygen cannula attached to my nose. I frantically started thrashing around as I had this feeling of being buried with all this stuff attached to me.

"Calm down, officer; you are alright. You are in the ER at Ventura County Medical Center, and I am Dr. Rashad."

I looked up and saw a man standing over me in a blue shirt.

"What happened to me?" I asked.

"You were serving a warrant when a substance was blown into your face. The substance is known as devil's breath and most likely comes from the nightshade plant. The deputies who were with you have been trying to confirm exactly what the drug was from the woman that blew it in your face."

The doctor said he wanted to keep me at the emergency room for another eight hours so that I could be observed. He wanted to make sure nothing else happened and that the drug's effects were out of my system. So for the next eight hours, I lay in an emergency room bed and had plenty of time to think about the awful trip I had on this drug. I tried to remember what some of the voices were trying to say or what had played out in my head. There were just so many voices and so many memories flooding my mind, everything was jumbled and made little to no sense. It all just served as the cause for me of getting another headache as I thought about it all. Once the eight hours were up, I was released from the hospital and told to self-monitor how I felt and if anything felt wrong, to come back immediately.

I went into the office the following morning to complete paperwork on the arrest and be debriefed on what took place. I found out that deputies located LSD, heroine, marijuana and scopolamine hydrobromide, which is a medication used for the treatment of motion sickness and postoperative nausea and vomiting. A side effect of this narcotic is drowsiness. I was also told that they believe this scopolamine mixed with several other ingredients may have been what was blown into my face. After being at the office for three hours, I went home sick as I began to get the headache again. I ended up staying in bed that entire weekend and even calling in sick the following Monday and Tuesday. I went back to work on Wednesday but did not feel quite myself. For the next couple of weeks I went to work, exercised at the gym and performed my regular routines but at what was half speed. I always felt tired and had also developed a cough that would not go away. I went to the doctor twice and was treated for bronchitis both times. The medications did not work, and I continued to feel lethargic and have what now was a hacking cough. I finally had enough and went back to the emergency room at Ventura County Medical Center.

I ended up seeing another physician who was working in the ER that night as Dr. Rashad had been on vacation. He reviewed my charts from several weeks earlier and then had me get a chest X-ray. About forty-five minutes later, the doctor notified me that I had walking pneumonia and due to my not having a spleen, he wanted to treat me immediately with a strong medication. He prescribed an antibiotic for me that went under the generic name of Moxifloxacin. He let me know that I should take it easy for the next week and make sure to finish the entire treatment of antibiotics. I then checked out of the hospital and got the prescription filled at the pharmacy down the street from the hospital. I went home and let a new roommates know about the trip to the hospital and that I was diagnosed with walking pneumonia.

My new roommate Kirk started laughing because of all the crap that always happens to me.

"I am going to start calling you Mr. Glass, dude. You have the absolute worst luck. I am surprised you are alive with all the crap that happens to you," Kirk said.

Then Kirk's girlfriend, Jackie, who was also at the apartment, began to laugh.

"Seriously, man, I don't know how you choose to be a cop with all the shit that happens to you. I bet if you were on an airplane and it crashed, you would be the only one who survives. Except that you would have broken every bone in your body and would be in the hospital having to recover for months," Kirk commented.

"I know, dude, I know," I replied. "You don't have to remind me as I am the one who has lived it."

"Who knows what is going to happen to you next. But whatever it is, man, it is going to make another hell of a story to tell everyone," Kirk said while Jackie and I laughed.

I told them I was going to start taking this Moxifloxacin and then crash early. I took the medication and then headed to my room while the two of them headed to Kirk's bedroom. I got to my bedroom and closed my door. I went to my bathroom, washed my face, brushed my teeth and then laid on top of my bed while I listened to some music. Approximately twenty minutes had gone by when I started to have this slight itch in my throat and then started coughing more than usual. A few more minutes went by, and I began having some trouble breathing. I felt myself starting to have tingling in my arms and legs, and then I felt my face swelling up. Next thing I know, I had a lot of trouble breathing. I could not believe my luck; I was having an allergic reaction to the medication.

I quickly got my pants and shoes back on, grabbed the medication and went down the hall to Kirk's bedroom door. I frantically knocked as my throat and tongue had swollen so quickly that I could no longer speak. A few seconds went by and he opened up the door and looked pissed off for me having bothered the two of them while they were obviously doing something or about to. However, he saw what was happening to my face and noticed I could barely breathe.

Kirk then yelled to Jackie, "Quick, Jackie, Patrick looks like he is having an allergic reaction to the medication he took! Grab my keys and let's get going to the hospital!"

Kirk helped me to his truck, and the three of us sped off to the hospital, which was no more than five minutes down the street. Kirk pulled up to the main entrance of the emergency room, and Jackie helped me out of the truck. I then stumbled into the ER as the two of them parked. I got to the front counter and tried speaking to the woman sitting behind the check-in desk. Unfortunately, I could say nothing and could barely breathe.

Since she was not looking up, she did not see me at the counter and looked to be filling out paperwork. I slammed the medication bottle down on her desk and then I collapsed to the floor.

I could hear her get on the intercom and then heard the following over the ER speakers: "I have a code blue at the front desk in ER! I have a code blue at the front desk in the ER and need emergency response, stat!"

Within seconds, I was being placed on a gurney and then wheeled through the emergency room doors. I could no longer see much as my eyelids had become so swollen that they blocked most of my vision. I no longer could breathe as my throat and tongue were swollen. I started panicking and thrashing around to the point where I had to be restrained.

The last thing I heard was from one of the doctors: "I need .5 cc of epinephrine immediately. I have an adult male having an anaphylactic reaction to what looks to be Moxifloxacin I prescribed him earlier!"

I knew it was the same doctor I had seen earlier for the walking pneumonia.

"Quick, Nurse Bennett, get the crash cart from down the hall! I believe we are going to have to resuscitate the patient."

That was the last thing I heard. Apparently, I went into cardiac arrest, and I was no longer breathing.

I was floating above the doctors and nurses who were frantically working on me in an attempt to save me. I was now in spirit, having no physical body to house what is more accurately known as life force or our vibrational energy that houses our thoughts and perception of reality. Beings exist in this state of energy forever. There is no human concept that can correctly explain this since when we are in human form, we experience linear time, and our physical form feels and vibrates through a present time that then enters into a future time period. But as vibrational energy alone, time is not experienced, and we are one, and one are many.

Out of nowhere, I now had full recollection that I am from an ancient race of beings, separate from humans, who were genetically created. I am an Ancient, a watcher of mankind and in order to do so, I am a skin-jumper. My life force was originally born into a human body that was initially my own in what would be just over fourteen thousand four hundred years ago. When being measured my modern man's Western calendar, also known as the Christian calendar, my initial birth would have been around 12,400 BCE. Every time my host body dies, I have recollection of my true form and nature of existence for the purpose of serving humanity. After my original death, I parted from my physical body and realized that I was given the ability by unknown means to skin-jump into another human's body, right when that human had died and their spirit, their life force, permanently separated. I can take over any human body that is empty of vibration, but I look for those that give me the possibility of long life. In the process, some residual memories are transferred to me from the chemical reactions still taking place in the physical brain structure of my new host. Many times, I never remember who I truly was or what my purpose was as my ability to do so has degraded over the many millenniums that have separated me from my original birth into this human existence as one of the few watchers. I am one of the few Ancients here to guide mankind as mankind is truly a new species in our vast expanse of vibrations and in the physical realm that humans comprehend and call the universe.

During this time period, I have been known by many names and lived hundreds of lives. I have been many different races, creeds and colors but always male. I have been a giant before their races were wiped out on this planet and lost from human history. I have been of a small-statured race of humans who were not known to have existed to current man. I have lived on all the continents and on this planet when it looked different, with land where oceans now prevail. I have lived where the land was so lush and green that no one would believe me if I were to tell them it is in the same lands that are now nothing but desert. I have lived on land that no man has seen for thousands of years and is currently covered in snow and ice. I have walked this planet when there were gods among men, the very creators of humanity. I came into being when man was originally known as Adama or first of the species. The Bible later records this in Genesis with Adam and Eve as over time, the oral tradition and stories were changed and origins lost. Eveh were the original females of the human race.

I have a purpose among humanity and one that I must remember to fulfill my mission for this species to survive on this planet. I had so much trouble remembering as I was in the body of Patrick but will make every effort to do so in the next host that I seek out. I understand the true nature of the black phantoms that haunted me when I was Patrick, and I know what has happened to this planet time and again; this is why I am here and why I must remember my calling as an Ancient, as a Watcher of man.

"We have a pulse; he's breathing again, so keep bagging him, and stop compressions," I heard someone say.

"Mr. Kilian, Mr. Kilian – can you hear me?" asked some unknown male voice.

I opened one of my eyes slightly and was able to see a little better as the swelling of my face was starting to subside. "Oh my God!" I thought to myself. "I have been resuscitated and I am still Patrick Kilian."

I recognized that I did not transfer into another person who was about to die, and for the first time in thousands of years, I did not skin-jump but was brought back to life as who I was before, and this time, I have complete recollection of what I am and who I am not.

# 15.

# Watchers, Ancients and Adam and Eve

I was conscious now and knew for sure that I was still in Patrick Kilian's body. I felt tingling still in my arms and legs and a lot of pressure on my chest, but I started taking my own inventory of how I felt and what was and was not still damaged or gauging the effect of my allergic reaction to the new medication. When I looked coherent enough for the doctor to have a meaningful conversation with me and one that I would remember, he told me that I suffered from anaphylaxis due to the strong antibiotic I was given for my pneumonia. The emergency room doctor notified me that I had to be given epinephrine twice and that my heart had just about given up due to lack of oxygen. They had to shock my heart back to a regular rhythm as I had gone into atrial fibrillation.

"Mr. Kilian, we are going to keep you here in the emergency room for eight to ten hours to make sure you have no delayed reaction of any sorts to the Moxifloxacin. I will also prescribe you another antibiotic but one that is not in the fluoroquinolone family of antibiotics," the doctor explained.

I spent the next several hours napping here and there and constantly running to the restroom.

Apparently, my body was trying to get the drugs out of my system, and over the next few hours, I must have gone to the bathroom twenty times. After four hours had passed, I began feeling better and confident that nothing else was going to happen. I now had time to start playing back in detail everything I experienced earlier. If I am to believe this experience and all the others during the last thirty-plus years of my life, I must conclude that I am not or at least have not always been Patrick Kilian. I became Patrick only when he drowned so many years ago, and his body became available after my last host became deceased. "This is crazy-insane," I thought to myself. I experienced something that goes beyond reincarnation and what very well could be what the premise of reincarnation is built upon. All these dreams, visions and experiences while I am unconscious were not fantasy but actual past life experiences.

I had to remember what I recalled when I had the out-of-body experience. I continued to process that original humans were Adama and Eveh. I was originally something known as a Watcher or an Ancient. I have lived on this planet for over fourteen thousand four hundred years as I apparently skin-jumped into human bodies that had just died, and their bodies were free of a life force for a few moments before true physical death. I somehow understood that I skin-jumped only into a body that could continue to support life and my soul and continue to let me live through the ages of man. "Oh my God!" I thought in my head. "I finally understand what the black phantoms are that have haunted me and at times physically harmed me." This all made sense.

The dark shadow figures were the souls, the life forces of people who had died but were not yet ready for death or prepared to go onto the next plane of existence where the life force goes once separated from the body. These life forces then saw me enter their prior human form and were upset that I did so. They felt that they should have been allowed to return into their body and that I kept them from that or they were not yet ready to accept their death in this world and sure as hell were not going to let me get away with hijacking their human skin and continue on in life being who they were. Now I know why my Evil Pan tormented me all those years ago. That Pan was the real Patrick Kilian, who died too young and just did not want to give up on his life – the life I took over. No wonder he protected my sister Ann that time in the Arizona house. He was really protecting his own flesh and blood. The other shadow figures were the same. They were prior lives I commandeered, and they could see when I skin-jumped, and they continued to follow me through time in this human existence.

"I am so sorry to all of you – I truly am," I said aloud.

I apparently do what I do for humanity and so mankind can continue to exist. I am just not sure how I do this and what the nature of this help or assistance is. I figured this knowledge would come to me in time.

About nine hours later, I was told I could check out and head home. I called my roommate, who had returned to the apartment once he found out I had not died and was going to be alright. Kirk picked me up from the front of the emergency room. Once I got home, I quickly pulled out all the journals I had kept, and for the next ten hours or so, poured over them and started piecing the puzzle together. I also began to research online anything that had to do with ancient cultures, reincarnation, Watchers, Ancients and Adam and Eve. Then something hit me out of nowhere: I had a random thought that was now stuck in my head. There is a reason why I chose to go to South America, and it came from somewhere deep inside of me that knows things to a better degree than my conscious and thinking self. I needed to go to South America, and I needed to go soon as there must be answers waiting for me to questions I have yet to ask.

I was able to get my general practitioner to sign off on my need for an absence from work due to my physical health. I then submitted this to human resources and was even able to get short-term disability benefits. I told my roommates what I was doing and where I was going and gave them enough money to cover rent and other bills for about three months. I made my hotel reservations, and before I knew it, I was headed to Buenos Aires, Argentina, with a one-way ticket. I had no clue where I was headed or what I was supposed to do; I just knew I had to be in South America. Once I was there, I would then worry about the specifics. Fifteen hours later, I landed in one of the most amazing cities I had ever laid eyes on.

Once I collected my bags and cleared Customs, I got a taxi outside the terminal and in half-broken Spanish, asked the cab driver to take me to my hotel in the Recoleta district of Buenos Aires. I had not slept for the entire fifteen-hour trip, so I took a two-hour nap to recharge my batteries but nothing more as I wanted to get used to the time change and avoid jet lag. I also knew I would need to get acclimated to the weather as it was just about winter time in South America, and that meant it was raining and cold outside.

I had gotten up from my slumber, taken a shower and was ready to head into the city to figure out why I was so enthralled with a place to which I had never been before – at least as far as I could remember. After all, I was starting to remember more than I ever thought possible and recall things I did in another lifetime. The first thing I did after leaving my hotel room was stop next door at this small bakery, and I ended up having some of the most amazing empanadas ever. I liked the fact that Argentinian food was not overly spicy like it can be in other Latin countries. I purchased a city map, a map of Argentina and then a map of South America. I then went to a local café, ordered an espresso and dessert empanada and began to pour over the Buenos Aires map.

I was not sure why I was doing this other than some of those voices in my head were guiding me in this direction. Then all of a sudden, something in Recoleta caught my attention on the map. The Cementerio de la Recoleta or Recoleta Cemetery, not more than four kilometers away. I was not sure why but I was headed to the largest tourist destination in the city. I finished my espresso and then hailed a taxi as I did not want to walk in the rain. Once I got to the cemetery, I did the first thing tourists do, and that was take a lot of pictures with one of the disposable cameras I had brought. As I walked up and down the many different paths of the cemetery, I guess I lost track of where I was and started to daydream. I was once again on that battlefield in World War I and once again a German soldier in the trenches, somewhere in Western Europe.

I heard something in German being yelled at me, and I immediately felt this tremendous pain and then I was staring at my own body in a German uniform as I had been decapitated by some type of ordnance that fell in the trenches directly where I had popped my head up. I found myself floating around or at least had the feeling of doing so but not in a reality that required any type of visual processes. I was in spirit, in life force, and I was anywhere and everywhere all at once. I had this feeling of peace and a higher existence that I just cannot explain as there is nothing to compare it with among the living. I realized at this point in the daydream that I could choose any male human body in the world that was about to die and skin-jump into it. I did not have to physically be near the person dying. I had to only think of entering it. So moments after being killed in that battle in 1915, I located a baby who had just died of Sudden Infant Death Syndrome in Munich. The next thing I knew, I was an infant named Heinrich Schneider.

I was not sure why I was daydreaming all of this as I strolled up and down the vast walkways of the cemetery, looking over each crypt and tomb as I passed. But I was, and my visions did not stop. I watched in my memories as Heinrich grew up from a child to a man. I watched as he found love and lost it. I was remembering or having visions of my parents, or at least Heinrich's parents, as he told them the news that he was joining the Third Reich and was going to be in the Kriegsmarine, also known as the German Navy. I saw Heinrich, or should I say myself, as I fought valiantly for Germany and Hitler in World War II aboard the U-977 VIIC class U-boat. I then watched as we found out Germany was about to surrender the war and we were called back to the motherland on a secret mission. As we approached Northern Germany on April 30, 1945, we sadly got word that Hitler had been killed or supposedly killed himself. On May 1, 1945, we pulled up to the coast of Cuxhaven in Northern Germany in the middle of the night. Two of my fellow crewmen and I took a large inflatable to shore and picked up four unknown passengers.

When we reached the passengers, it was extremely dark and I could not see who they were until I was face to face with them. I was shocked to have now been standing before my Fuhrer, Adolph Hitler, as well as Eva Braun and two other high-ranking Nazi officers. I quickly got the four onboard the inflatable raft and transported them safely to U-977. I continued to pace up and down in the cemetery, a bit distraught by what I was remembering. The crew would later be told that the suicides of our Fuhrer and his wife were faked so that their escape could be made. I am sure at some point in history that Russia will let the rest of the world know that the DNA for Hitler and his wife did not match and instead were the burned remains of two unknown German women. I continued to watch as one of my past life's memories unfolded like a television drama show.

We continued down the West Coast of Europe. We then took a long trek across the Atlantic and into Argentina waters. At some point, Hitler and his wife left the crew and supposedly headed to the Andes Mountains. The rest of the crew had the option to stay onboard the U-boat or escape into South America. I chose South America and lived my life in Argentina, from where I traveled extensively to other parts of the continent. For some reason, I could not see what happened next with Heinrich. Those memories could not be accessed, and I just could not remember anything more other than I had this feeling that I died sometime around 1974, and that is when I skin-jumped into Patrick Kilian's drowned body. Then, at that very moment, I looked in front of me in the cemetery and there was a tomb whose epitaph was in both Spanish and German. I was for some reason easily able to understand both and it translated to, "So many worlds, so many lives, the course is laid out and repeats itself - Heinrich Zerpa – 1915–1974," and then was followed by a symbol of what looked to be a helical motion spiral galaxy.

I knew this is where I was buried and remembered that I had to change my name from Schneider to Zerpa to avoid being discovered as having been a Nazi. This is why I was drawn to this cemetery, and this is what I was destined to find. In death, I apparently left a clue for my future self. The epitaph was interesting, and I wrote it down. I also took several photos of the drawing and recognized it as a petroglyph found all around the world and used by almost all known past cultures. I rummaged around the tomb for some time and wanted to make sure I did not miss anything, especially if there was possibly another clue. When I was good and ready and felt there was nothing left at the cemetery to discover, I headed back to the hotel, where I hung out in the restaurant and then the bar until late in the evening. I later headed to my room, where as soon as I laid down on the bed, I was out cold and off into the world of dreams.

While dreaming, I was visited by many of my dark shadow figures. During this particular dream, the figures were not out to harm me in any way. They instead wanted to let me know who they were, and even though they were angry at my having taken over their body and life, they had come to the realization that they passed onto the next realm, and it really was no longer their life to live. Then there were other phantoms that continued to stay in this plane of existence and still could not let their death go, especially seeing their physical bodies continue to walk around with my life force. Obviously Patrick was extremely upset about this for the first few years, and this is why he continued to terrorize me for so long. When he made himself seen to our parents that one night, he was not trying to harm them as much as communicate with them, and he never once put my sister, I mean our sister, in the way of harm and protected her as much as he could.

Those in my dream had passed into the next realm of existence as pure energy and total vibration. Over the course of the dream, I became aware of others who were skin-jumpers and learned very few were left. See, the initial group of Ancients, these Watchers, came to Earth around the same period that spanned between twenty-five thousand and fourteen thousand years ago. I was one of the last to be born into a human form on this planet. We were here to help humanity, and in order to do so, we carried advanced knowledge. But as we died and continued skin-jumping, our memories, knowledge, reason for existence and powers dwindled. As the ages came and went, many Watchers forgot who they truly were. At some point, they may not have jumped but instead crossed into the next life. Since I was one of the last, I could still remember, but it was difficult, and memories of everything were in bits and pieces.

I also learned that indeed, Heather, too, was an Ancient. She was a Watcher and learned from the shadow phantoms when she and I spent a night together in my room years ago. She was not allowed to tell me as this could have affected my ability to recall all this on my own or to purposely block this knowledge so that my calling in this lifetime may not have been fulfilled. I also learned that Heather and I were destined to meet in this lifetime, if nothing but to strengthen our bonds as Ancients, but this did not mean we had to stay together during this lifetime.

Just as the dark figures in my dream were about to tell me if there were any other Ancients left, I was brought out of my sleep by a large bang I heard from outside the hotel. I went to the window and looked out. I saw that two men had collided in a motor vehicle accident. Instead of exchanging information, they started fist-fighting. I learned later that this apparently was an acceptable way to make amends for colliding into each other as I saw this behavior on more than one occasion while I was in Buenos Aires. I then went back to bed and fell asleep but could remember no other dreams when I got up the next morning.

I got ready in the morning, went downstairs and had breakfast and coffee in the hotel's restaurant. As I had breakfast, I poured over the multiple journals I had brought with me to Argentina. I continued to play out my experience in the cemetery from the day before, and as I did so, I continued to have multiple flashbacks of me as

Heinrich, and all the memories were in German. Something else hit me as I was having the flashbacks. Heinrich also had this huge gravitational pull to South America. After the war and while living in Buenos Aires, he, I mean we, traveled mostly to see places that popped into his head, really our head, and that he, too, swore he had been to these places before, even though that seemed impossible. I also remembered that while I was Heinrich, I did not start remembering the true nature of my existence until coming to South America. Before that, I thought I was just a bit delusional while I wore the skin of Heinrich Zerpa.

I had additional flashbacks of places I had gone in my prior life and wrote down these places or clues of them so I would not forget. After breakfast, I went to a local camera shop that could develop my photos of the cemetery. I had to pay extra, but the woman behind the counter said she would have them ready in less than two hours. In the meantime, I had a taxi take me to the local library, where I was able to look up a couple of the places I remembered going to when I was in Heinrich's body. One of them was in the Amazon rainforest of Ecuador. The other was in Peru and was at an extremely high elevation, and I could see only the location in my mind. I was not able to remember the name of the place I saw. In my journal, I wrote everything I could about the spot in Ecuador and then left the library and went to pick up my photos. Once I had them, I went to a local bookstore that also had a café. I ordered an espresso and started to browse the books on Peru. I came across a large hardback that was almost completely photos of sites in Peru, and this book was different than the others as it did not focus on Machu Picchu, but instead, it had hundreds of photos of places around the country. So I purchased it and then headed back to the hotel.

For the rest of the day and evening, I hung out in the small café in the hotel lobby. While eating and drinking, I studied the photos I took at the cemetery and pored over the book I had purchased. I read the notes I took at the library and came to a conclusion: Ecuador was the next place I had to get to. With my mind made up about the next leg of my South American journey, I went to bed early and got a good night's sleep. The next morning, I went to a travel agency around the corner. This attractive young travel agent made my flight and hotel bookings for Quito, Ecuador. I then went back to the hotel, packed my stuff, checked out at the front desk and headed to the airport. Three hours later, I was on my way to Ecuador.

The flight took just over nine hours. By the time we had arrived, it was just before 2 in the morning. Once I cleared Customs, I got a taxi and headed to the Sheraton Hotel in Quito. I was exhausted by the time I arrived and was beyond grateful to the front desk staff for accommodating me being as I had no reservation and my arrival was late. I went up to my room, unpacked a couple of things and then fell into a deep sleep due to how long the day had been.

Upon my waking up the next morning, I had breakfast brought to me in my room. While eating, I reviewed my notes about Ecuador. Something here in the jungles was important to me, but I had no idea what it was. I had this profound feeling that it was something I had insight into from a lifetime in the distant past. I looked for it when I was Heinrich, and I was looking for it again as Patrick. Unfortunately, I had no idea where to start. The jungles in this country were extensive, and nothing I had in front of me told me where to begin. I had reached a dead end, and I was not sure what to do about it.

I got dressed and headed to a library six blocks from the hotel. As I was walking, a boy no older than twelve approached me and asked if he could have an American dollar so he could buy a Coca-Cola from the local vendor in front of us. In Spanish, I asked him what his name was, and he told me it was Jose. I let Jose know that instead of giving him $1, I would walk with him to the vendor and get him a Coke and a couple of empanadas to go with it. This made him very excited. As the vendor got Jose his drink and empanadas, Jose asked me what I was doing in Quito, and I told him I was looking for something ancient. Jose asked me in Spanish exactly what it was I was looking for, and I told him I was not sure. Suddenly, Jose started speaking to me in English.

"What do you mean, American, that you are not sure what you are looking for? How could you come to Quito and not know?"

"Jose, you didn't tell me you spoke English!"

"You didn't ask me if I spoke English; you only started speaking to me in Spanish, so I answered back in Spanish."

"You are right, Jose, I did not ask you if you spoke English and assumed you spoke Spanish only. Where did you learn to speak English?"

"I learned from Miguel, my older brother. Miguel got to go to the United States for a year as an exchange student, and when he came home, he taught me and my sister English."

"He did a fine job of teaching you. Your English-speaking skills are excellent."

This embarrassed Jose a bit, and he began to blush.

The two of us continued to speak as Jose drank his Coke and ate his empanadas. He was still fascinated with the fact that I came all this way looking for something that was important to me but not knowing exactly what it was.

"See, Jose, I know I am looking for something ancient. I believe it is a location of sorts, and I think it is in the jungles of your country. I believe I have been there before, but I think it was a long, long time ago, and I just do not remember anything more than that."

"Well, mister, if it is ancient you look for, maybe my bisabuelo can help you. He is very old and knows the sacred ways of the Cayambi people of Ecuador. But I must warn you: he speaks only in Quechua, and I do not know that language."

While Jose told me this, he seemed like a guardian angel sent my way and that I was supposed to befriend him so I could meet his great-grandfather.

The fact that his bisabuelo spoke only Quechua might be a big problem, I realized, but I would work that out.

"Jose, my speaking to your great-grandfather would be wonderful. Could you introduce me?"

"Of course, American – anything for a Coke and empanadas. My bisabuelo's name is Manco, but most people call him Paqo."

Somehow, I again had this knowledge that I had spoken Quechua in a distant past and I knew that "Paqo" in Quechua translated into priest or mystic. This meeting between Manco and I was destined to happen. I knew again that the future was already written and had helped create this present moment. Once Jose was ready, the two of us walked about two kilometers to a much older part of the city, and Jose led me to a small wooden shack at the end of a street.

"We need to go inside here. My bisabuelo stays here with his buddies during the day," Jose told me.

Jose and I entered the shack. He then told me to wait at the front door and that he would get Manco and Manco's friend, Pino. About five minutes had elapsed when he came back with two elderly men.

"American, this man in the blue shirt is my bisabuelo, Manco, and his friend is Pino. Just to let you know, Pino speaks Spanish and Quechua, and he will be able to translate for you. My bisabuelo told me that he has been waiting for you for a long time and he was beginning to think you were not going to come. Maybe he was the ancient thing you were looking for."

With that, I thanked the boy for his assistance, and he left the shack. As I stood before the two elderly men who both had distinctive indigenous features, I concluded that they were from the Cayambi population of Ecuador. I could also see that tears began streaming from their eyes.

In Spanish, the older gentleman, Pino, explained that Manco and the other paqos had many dreams and visions of my arrival. He said my spirit had walked these lands thousands of years ago. They knew I was of the Watchers and I came to them as Mene-ach, general of the Atl-Antis people of these lands when these lands were known as Atl-Antis, Peru was known as Coya and the Middle Americas were Tyrambel.

Then in the Quechua language, Manco yelled, "Who stands before me, and who asks the Paqo for help?"

In perfect Quechua, I responded, "I stand before you, Mene-ach, commander of the Atl-Antis legions, defender of the sacred realm, and I require your knowledge to assist me with my task as Watcher over mankind and humble servant to the Adama!"

I stood staring at the two men, not knowing where that came from but suddenly being flooded with memories. There were so many of these memories coming all at once that I became faint and had to sit down on the dirt floor of the shack. Manco walked to a small area of the shack that looked to possibly be the kitchen, and he took a glass jar off the shelf. The jar contained a reddish-brown liquid. He brought it over to me and sat down on the floor next to me. Then Pino sat down next to Manco and I. Then I watched as four other elderly men, all with the same indigenous features, came out of the back room and sat next to the three of us.

In Quechua, Manco said, "Drink this. It is the sacred drink of the gods. It will fill you with knowledge and clarity. Your body will resonate with the Mother Earth, and your life force will again join up with your planet and connect you with your kind."

I asked Pino in Spanish what I was about to drink, and he told me it was ayahuasca. As I drank it, the men began to sing in Quechua. The song was hypnotic, and I found myself singing along. This continued for fifteen or so minutes, and as time progressed, I began to feel so hot that I felt as if I were going to drown in the sweat coming from the pores on my body. I became nauseated and ended up vomiting into a small metal bucket near the entry of the shack. Then I began to have hallucinations and started to see many of the dark shadow people in the room with the seven of us.

"Do not fight it, allow it to happen!" Pino blurted out. "Allow the shadow people to help you recall your past lives and find again what it is you are searching for."

This made me realize that I must not be the only one who sees the shadow figures, and that Pino and the others must have experienced them, as well, or were experiencing them as they came into the shack. Then, I watched as one of the dark shadows ran toward me and jumped into my body. As it did so, I felt a freezing cold overtake the heat I was experiencing just moments before, and then I fell on the floor and was unable to move. My eyesight then left me, and I was in total darkness. Then out of nowhere, I was pulled from the darkness and was standing in the middle of the Amazon jungle next to a large river. I felt and knew it was no longer the present but instead many thousands of years ago in the distant past, when the lands were known by their original names. This land represented the remnants of where the gods once lived among man and was called Atl-Antis.

The continents were different back then, and there was less water among the surface of Mother Earth. As I stood there, I saw there was great upheaval taking place in the world and this was the first time I experienced this destruction upon the face of Mother Earth but it would not be the last time. I saw off in the distance a group of my soldiers diving into the river with crystals. I approached them and asked what they were doing.

One answered in an ancient language, which has not been spoken for in at least fourteen thousand years, "We are doing as you commanded, Gen. Mene-ach; we are taking the crystals that store the library of knowledge within them and placing them into the Tayos-hun Caves far below ground. You said they needed to be stored there for future generations to find so that once again the knowledge of the gods could be made known to those who survive this destruction."

I now was standing in the jungles where I once had the Library of Ancient Knowledge deposited in hopes of it surviving the apocalypse taking place. Only deep underground would these sacred crystals that contained the complete knowledge of our creators possibly be given the chance to survive for future humanity to use again to better mankind. All of a sudden, everything around me began to darken, and I knew I was returning to the present. I looked around in every direction in the hopes of being able to remember the location and get to it once I was back in my present time. Next I was in darkness, then again with the shadow people and finally waking up in the shack as the elderly men continued to chant. As I came to, I began to ask many questions of the men.

"How did you know I was coming to see you if I only met Jose earlier today?" I asked Manco.

"We, too, communicate with the gods and other Star People through the ayahuasca. It is through the sacred ayahuasca that all stories of men are told, and yours has been a long one in the making, Mene-ach," Manco said.

"Watcher, the path you take now has already been written in the future. You will remember your path in due time and know what it is you must accomplish in your lifetime," Pino added.

They answered my questions as best they could and at the end, let me know that they would have several of their tribesmen escort me into the jungles. They hoped that together we would be able to find the caves that may still house the crystals containing the knowledge of how humans came to be on this planet and other lost wonders, possibly forgotten on purpose due to how painful these past catastrophes must have been. I thanked them all for their time and for opening my eyes to the spiritual tools available in guiding me on the path I needed to travel.

"Remember, one final thing, son of Adama. We may look like the elders in the group, but you, you are the true elder in the quorum today. It is you and only you who in the end will know what must be done and how to fulfill what the gods have shown you to be your destiny," Manco said.

With that, I took leave of the elders and was escorted by Jose to a group of younger men waiting for me two blocks from the shack.

I was handed supplies to put into a backpack that was also given to me by one of the three younger men of the Cayambi people. As we were getting ready to begin our trek into the Ecuadorian Jungle, I learned that my guides and security were Hector, Armando and Jorge. Hector was one of the best guides in all of Quito, and he would be able to assist me in possibly locating the part of the jungle I saw in my vision earlier. Armando was security for the trip. He let me know that the locals in the jungle are pretty hostile to outsiders. Jorge would be the driver as he owned the old-school International Scout we would be using to get us through some difficult terrain. So, the first thing that needed to be done was locate our destination with only the bits and pieces of the area I saw in a vision. If someone had told me to do this, I would have thought he was crazy and left without him. But to these three young men, my vision and the words of the elders of their tribe were as real as if I had pulled out a map of the location to tell them where we were to go. They never thought that I was crazy and believed that where I was shown to go in my vision was where they needed to take me.

Ecuador may not be the largest country in the world, but when you are looking for a small area of jungle that you saw for a few moments in a dream, it feels like you are looking for a dot on a map of the entire world. I began to feel anxiety-ridden as I thought about this and started to feel uncomfortable. Hector and Armando must have noticed, and they told me to relax and close my eyes. They instructed me to become aware of my breathing pattern. I was further instructed to think about each breath I took and each time I exhaled. Then I was told to focus on who and where I am and what I saw in the dream. As I did this, I seemed to suddenly become a bird flying over Ecuador. I noticed an interstate number that was marked as 45. When I saw this in my mind's eye, I began to tell Hector and Armando what I was seeing.

"I see a large road marked with an Interstate 45 sign, and it is headed to the area known as Morona-Santiago. I also see a figure standing along the edges of the Rio Coangos. The Shuar ancestors are helping to protect the location while I am away."

As soon as I said "Shuar," Hector interrupted and said, "You are talking about the Tayos Cave system and the metal library that everyone knows about and has been looking for."

I opened my eyes and looked at him, "What did you say about a metal library?"

Hector again responded, "The metal library is what everyone has been looking for since the 1960s. They say it contains metal plates like those found by the Mormon leader in the United States and that there are other riches with the plates that are supposedly mostly made of gold. But no one has yet to find it."

I began having another vision about a long time ago when I was Mene-ach. I saw that I had stored metal plates at another location farther down river and that these plates were not as old but contained the history of my people for a few centuries. Some gold and other precious metals were stored with the plates in another cave system to throw off anyone looking for the true prize, the crystal library.

"No, Hector, that is a different location, but very close. Can we head down to that location and speak to the Shuar leaders?" I asked.

"If that is what is needed, then that is what we will do," Hector said.

So the four of us piled into the International Scout and were on our way to the Morona-Santiago Province of Ecuador.

It was a long trip, and due to a couple of accidents on the highway and some off-roading required to get to the small town where the Shuar Indian leaders were, we did not reach our destination until ten hours later. When we got to the town, I realized it was not so much a town as it was a tribal village with the bare necessities and nothing else. Hector was greeted by multiple men of the tribe who did not seem too happy to see us pull up to their village at such a late hour. Hector was the first out of the truck and began shouting back at the men who were now slowly surrounding him. Things got ugly quick, and one of the men pushed Hector to the ground from behind. Several of the other men held him to the ground as another pulled a large machete from behind his back. As he did so, two elderly men walked up to Hector and started speaking to him in the Shuar language. Hector knew a little and was speaking back as best he could. But you could tell he was physically shaken and had trouble communicating with the tribesmen.

Jorge, the driver, turned back to face me as I sat in the back seat of the truck. Jorge then spoke in Spanish.

"I know this is a bad time to bring this up, but the Shuar are known for still being headhunters and shrinking the heads of their victims. I think we are in a world of shit right now."

The yelling became fierce outside, and the two elderly men were speaking among themselves and deciding what would become of Hector. I could not take any more of this and I unrolled the back window of the Scout and crawled out. I was grabbed by several of the Shuar tribesmen and yanked around to the front of the truck, where I could be seen by the two elderly tribesmen. Then I began to speak to them in a much older Shuar language known as Achuar.

Again, I was just as perplexed to hear this language come out of my mouth as were the tribesmen. The two elders dropped to their knees and put their heads to the ground. The other men let go of Hector and did as their elders were doing. The yelling that was taking place was replaced by silence by the time I finished speaking.

I then continued in Achuar and said, "Rise and come before me, for I am Mene-ach, general of the Atl-Antis armies and humble servant of the Adama. Many thousands of years ago, I placed the crystal library in the care of your ancestors, and I am here once again to bring the library back to the lands that are once again populated by man."

One of the two elders replied in Shuar, saying, "My lord commander, forgive me, your humble servant, Patyo, chieftain of the Achu Shuar. We knew you would return one day in another form as it was told to us by our ancestors. We must humbly tell you that many years ago, the cave that housed the great knowledge of the gods was destroyed by a massive quake that shook the ground for many minutes, and much devastation took place upon the land. Only a single crystal survived, and it has been with me and my brother, Totoyo, for the last forty years."

I was saddened to hear of the destruction of the cave, and Patyo went on to tell of all the things the Shuar had done for so many centuries in protecting both the crystal library and the metal library. He said that much of the metal library was still intact and hidden deep within the cave system below where we stood. But I let Patyo know I was not interested in this and that I wanted him to bring me the last remaining crystal. Patyo spoke to one of his younger tribesmen, who went to fetch the crystal from Patyo's home. Several minutes later, the tribesman came back and presented to me a clear crystal, about fourteen inches long and one inch in diameter. The crystal looked polished, and upon closer inspection and with the light of the truck shining through it, I could see tons of dots neatly in rows. That night, I stayed with Patyo in his home, and he and his brother relayed a wealth of information to me. I later fell asleep and again had dreams of the last time I stood upon this ground.

I woke up the following morning and was treated to a feast by the tribe. I had asked Patyo if he knew how to read the crystal, and he told me that he was not aware it contained any information until the night before, when I told them what the crystals were. Patyo, Totoyo and I continued to discuss what else needed to be done before I left the Shuar.

"Patyo, you and your people must continue to protect the metal library and everything else that is with it. Let no one remove the plates as they still contain ancient records of man. Already, some of the plates were removed and taken all the way to North America, where they were later found by a boy who started his own religion with the knowledge he gained from them. He also must have stumbled upon one of the hologram recorders left by the Ancients as he believed he was visited by angels and spirits when this piece of equipment must have activated. So this is why protecting the plates is still of the utmost priority for the Shuar. Do I make myself clear?"

Patyo and Totoyo affirmed that they understood.

"It is just amazing as I think about it now and have all these memories returning, that this same boy, named Joseph, made the world aware of one of the most important gods who lived among man and was originally from the stars," I told Patyo.

"Who was this god among men?" Patyo asked.

"His name was Melchizedek, and he lived among man thousands of years before my original birth. He commanded great knowledge and power, and it was told that with just the sacred words of Melchizedek being spoken, that mountains could be moved or new ones created. I wish I could remember more about this, but everything about the past is still in this big hazy cloud that does not allow me to fully see my past just yet."

I continued to tell Patyo that all this knowledge of history, medicine, weapons, science and so much more was exactly what was contained on the metal plates and crystals; the crystals just contained far more amounts of knowledge that spanned the length of at least several million years, and not just several centuries like the metal plates.

I continued my conversations with the two elders and found out that at one point, it was said that the cavern system below us stretched as far away as the eastern waters, now known as the Atlantic Ocean, and as far south as the deserts of Patagonia. The elders continued to tell me that oral tradition and stories say the Shuar are related to Indians in the Peruvian mountains who lived in massive cities underground in the distant past and that these people had the ability to travel all over the world by walking through special doorways. This was of great interest to me as I clearly remember having lived underground in the past, and I seem to remember that this was as more than one person and at different periods in the past. These thoughts and bits of memories made me sad, as well, because I realized all this history was lost to current man and mankind today wanted to purposely ignore just how much greater and longer our history was on this planet. It also may have been that modern man and their scientists did not want to acknowledge they had been wrong as they were too proud to admit it or wanted the lies to continue in order to keep control of what people knew about humanity's origins. From this discussion with the elders, I knew I needed to head to Peru quickly. So I finished up with the Shuar and headed back to Quito, where I thanked the Cayambi people who helped me find my way through Ecuador and locate what looked to be the last remaining ancient crystal of knowledge. I got my ticket to Peru, and several hours later, I was on a plane to Lima.

I took this time to process what I had learned while in South America so far. I also processed the fact that I was starting to recall more and more from my past lives and that they have all been attached somehow. I understood that humanity's past is long and had its origins well before I was first born, and I have apparently lived on this planet for over fourteen thousand years. I knew that the science of earlier man was far more advanced and that there are things in this world that do not make sense because of this lost science. I also hoped that at some point in the near future, I would remember all of it, everything that had happened to me and what it was I still needed to do.

I had made it to Lima and settled into a subpar hotel for the night. I scattered my notes all over the bed and had the book I had purchased on Peru by my side. I combed through the notes and must have gone through the book five or six times. I got nothing in regards to where I needed to go and what I needed to find. For two hours, I continued this process and still gained nothing from it. I took the crystal out of my luggage and went over it, hoping to find out how to access the information it must contain. I tried shining a flashlight into it and got nothing. I tried reading it up against the lamp in the hotel, and this, too, yielded negative results. I ran it under water, spun it around in between the palms of my hand and still nothing. I had the most important piece of knowledge in my hand and had no clue how to get the damn thing to work. After a while, I became frustrated and put the crystal back into my luggage. I also took everything else off of the bed and shoved it back into my duffle bag. I had a couple of beers from the mini-bar in the room and then fell asleep for the night. My hope was that I would dream about what it was I needed to do here in Peru. Unfortunately, the next thing I knew, the sun was coming through the curtains of the room, and the light caused me to wake up sooner than I had hoped.

Not a single dream took place that night that was of any use to me on my fact-finding mission in Peru. I had breakfast in my room and then headed into Lima, hoping to run into someone who would end up helping me out the way Jose did in Quito. Hours went by and nothing. I had gone to seven sites in Lima and went to three bookstores and a library. I rummaged through tons of information, photos and periodicals about locations in Peru and still nothing. I did learn that Peru had a vast network of historical sites that had scientists perplexed as to their origins. I also learned that Machu Picchu got way too much recognition as a site when there were many more in Peru with far greater potential of being more mysterious and of more important origins. Unfortunately, Machu Picchu was what the media had latched onto. Because of this, the site had become world-famous, with almost everyone wanting to see it. This has caused tourists to skip over fifty other sites in Peru that would have been a better option to visit. Too bad I could not remember any of these sites I came across so far from a memory or daydream, and not one picture I have seen so far has triggered any type of recollection of having been there or needing to get back.

I stayed in Peru for three more days and took two excursions to other areas of the country and still nothing. I had zero visions, no visitations by supernatural forces and no chance run-ins with locals who had the answers I was looking for. Nothing at all triggered a memory and when I slept, and I did not remember my dreams or even if I had dreamt at all. By the fifth day, I had to call Peru a bust, and on day six, I headed back to the United States. One scary thing happened at Customs in Miami. I was stopped because of the crystal and had to lie my ass off to get it into the country without it being confiscated. I ended up saying that I purchased it at a flea market in Peru and that it cost me only four American dollars. I told them that it helped me with my chakras and balanced my yin and my yang. At that point, they began to think I was just a crazy New Age practitioner and let me pass. Luckily they did not question me any further because I had no clue what a chakra really was and could have been arrested for violating the Archaeological Resources Protection Act. From Miami, I headed home to Los Angeles and then back to Ventura County. I was disappointed with what happened in Peru, but at the same time excited to try to figure out how the crystal worked and what type of information it contained.

# 16.

# Remembering

The rest of 2003 was interesting indeed. I did very little in regards to finding out about my past lives and what it was I was supposed to do as far as this unknown calling I assumed I had. My mom and sister had moved back to El Paso, and I had gone to visit them soon after I returned from South America. While I was there, I happened to be forced into going to church by an old friend. We went to the old stake center on Sumac Drive in the Eastside of town. This was the same location where I broke my leg years earlier. While I was there with my friend, the Spanish speaking-ward happened to be having its meetings, as well. I ended up bumping into one of the most amazing women I had ever met. Well, needless to say, I fell head over heels for her, and because of this, everything was put on the back burner. Up until this time, I truly loved only one woman, and I knew I had loved her many times as many different people. The woman was Heather, and I would always have a bond with her that death could not even destroy. But with this new girl I had met at church in El Paso, I knew that she and I were compatible in every possible way. We dated long distance for some time until I finally moved back to El Paso.

El Paso did not make for the best place for the two of us to start our new life together. So, in late 2004, she and I got married in Las Vegas, Nev., with a few good friends and family attending the wedding. Then my new wife, three-year-old stepson and I moved to Tempe, Ariz., where we began our new life together. I went from being in law enforcement to insurance, and it turned out to be a work option I could live with for the time being. We originally lived in a two-bedroom apartment and then moved into our first home, which we purchased ourselves. It was an amazing time in my life, and I did not mind that everything else was put into a hold status.

I never told my wife about my past lives or the things that had happened to me – the things I had seen and the places I had been, as well as the reasons for going. I did not want to scare her off and for her to think I was crazy. Hell, if someone told me those things about them, I would leave them alone because I would have thought they had bats in the belfry. Instead, I decided I would gradually explain my beliefs and start with distant history that had been forgotten or hidden. Then over several years, I could tell her the strange and unbelievable things about my life. So that is exactly what I did, and you know what? She must love me because she didn't leave me, and she believed what I told her. And more importantly, she experienced some crazy and supernatural incidents, too, and that has helped her believe in the things that I have told her.

By 2008, my wife was familiar with most of my past. She even told me that on some nights, it was difficult to sleep with me in the same bed as I could be very vocal and many times, I was having full-on conversations with other people. She even recorded me a few times as I would be speaking in a language other than English, and she had no clue what most of the languages were. One night, she really got freaked out as I was dreaming. Because of what took place during that dream, my wife believed what I had been telling her all these years. Apparently, I was having a verbal confrontation in my dream with several of the dark shadow spirits whose bodies I took over when they were apparently not yet ready to accept death and move on. It got loud, and I was screaming at them. At some point in the dream, I told them all to get the hell out and to never come near me or my household again. When I said this in my dream, every door in our house slammed shut. This scared my wife so much that she started crying and attempted to wake me up. But I would not come out of the dream.

My wife told me that I was still having some type of confrontation with one of the spirits that refused to go when the others left. I started speaking in a deep voice that sounded nothing like me, and my wife said that I invoked the power of Melchizedek or so she thought as I was still speaking in a foreign language. When I invoked this power in my sleep, my wife told me that she saw a dark figure exit my body. The shadow figure then turned toward her and grinned. Even with the figure being cloaked in darkness, she could tell that this creature's face looked like it had been badly burned. She was crying and was so scared that she could not move as the spirit slowly moved closer to her. Just when it was about to come in contact with her, I turned on the lights in the room, and it changed course and came toward me. I must have come out of the dream and been awakened as soon as the shadow spirit exited my body. It flew toward me, but I again spoke in an unknown ancient language, and whatever I told it made it stop in front of me. It then disappeared right before our eyes. My wife had a lot of sleepless nights after this, and only after some time passed did she begin to feel comfortable sleeping in that house.

Several more years passed, and before I knew it, 2012 was upon us. It was this year that I had become so fed up with my career in insurance claims handling that I quit without finding another job. I had saved a lot of money over the years and was not too worried about being unemployed for a short period of time. My wife was making great money at her job, and she even had encouraged me to take some time off and again follow the path of my past that I had put on hold years ago. So I left the pathetic insurance industry behind. For so many years, I felt like a robot just going through the motions of life. I have to say that I had recalled other past lives, and some were as a pauper or as a servant to others. But at no time were any of those lives as meaningless as what my current one had become. I must say that the way we live as humans today is a miserable excuse for a life. It is amazing how we have been conditioned to sit in tiny little cubicles all day, barely scraping by as a few people in the world control everything. The powers that be have put capitalism, globalization and current social constructs into place to the point where we as a society go along with it and live our lives like drones. We wish the days away in the hopes of just getting to the weekend or to the two weeks of vacation out of the entire year that we only hope we can take. And even then, that is not always the case. We should be ashamed of who we have become as a species. This was not the path meant for humanity, and I should know.

So I began meditating a lot and taking a lot of hallucinogenic drugs in the hopes that I would be able to find my path and learn what was needed from me during a walk with the gods or other greater beings. Many times, I had minor details given to me during my vision quests, but nothing that was big enough to finally get me to realize what all this was about and why my life had become so important. One thing that also bothered me during 2012 was what everyone was saying about Dec. 21, 2012. The Maya supposedly had predicted long ago that this day would usher in the end of the world as there was nothing past this date in the Mayan calendar. I refused to believe this and knew something was drastically wrong with this prediction, but I could not remember what it was. I felt like I was privy to some type of important information on this matter but still did not know what that missing piece of the puzzle was. This was a constant in my life, always having a feeling of deja vu but not quite being able to piece things together.

Then one day, something happened to me that was bad. I got up one morning and went to the restroom. That was when I noticed I had some large growth in an area that was very sensitive. I was immediately freaked out by this and went straight to the emergency room at the hospital in the Phoenix area. During the course of the day that I spent there, I was diagnosed with having some antibiotic-resistant bacteria that was just a step away from MRSA. I was admitted into the hospital and quarantined. I was started on a huge cocktail of antibiotics and was watched closely due to not having a spleen. Over three days, I did not get better. My doctors then decided that it would be best for me to have surgery and have an abscess and fistula removed as this is where the bacteria was located. The surgery was scheduled for the following morning. The night before the surgery was pure hell. I was in a lot of pain, and not even the Demerol I was being given in large doses did much in the way of alleviating it. Somehow, I made it through the night, and the next morning, I kissed my wife and son goodbye, told them I loved them and was wheeled into surgery. This day of the surgery was June 21, 2012. It would turn out to be one of the most important days in my life as Patrick Kilian.

Once I was in the operating room, a nurse checked on my intravenous infusion and verified that the vein into which it was stuck was still good and had not collapsed. The anesthesiologist asked me questions about prior surgeries I had that required a general anesthesia. He said he was going to give me a newer drug that made it easier to awaken from, and there was far less nausea associated with it. So he prepped the drug and then administered it through an IV push. As soon as he injected it into my IV, I could feel my hand beginning to burn on the inside. This narcotic I was given was no joke, and it was causing me extreme physical discomfort. I decided to just deal with the pain and not say anything. As I was laying there waiting for the anesthesia to kick in, several other people came into the operating room, but none of them was the surgeon who was performing my surgery. Suddenly, I grew drowsy and had trouble keeping my eyes open. Then, just like many times before, I was out cold.

I was now traveling through darkness. Then the darkness turned into deep purple canyons, mountains and cliff walls. I was flying at a tremendous speed, and my velocity toward these purple walls increased. I next noticed I was decelerating and then came to a stop. I was once again at the foot of that great pyramid, on what I knew was Mars. This was not a dream but instead was me traveling in some type of alternate dimensional energy that can easily be achieved once our physical bodies were shed. I was fully aware that somewhere on Earth my physical body was undergoing surgery. But because of that potent narcotic, I was released from my physical body, and the bonds that kept me on Earth were no longer in effect. I know some people will find this hard to believe and they most likely made fun of those that talked about out-of-body experiences, but it is real, and I have had them hundreds of times over many lifetimes.

So here I was in front of this colossal, alien-made structure. I am convinced that it will be found in the near future by NASA, but of course kept a secret from the human population. As I looked at the pyramid, I felt a presence come close to me, and I turned to look around. I realized that I was in some type of shadow form. "Oh, my God, I am exactly like the shadow figures that have constantly come in contact with me my entire life," I thought. Now I know what they must be experiencing when they come into our physical realm and I am able to see them. I saw a giant apparition before me. Its energy force must have been at least twelve, maybe thirteen feet tall. Once in its presence, I recognized that I was standing before one of the gods in the form they took in the existence that comes after life in a physical form. This was an Adamian soul, a parent to mankind and a creator of life as we know it on Earth. I bowed my head before it and did not look up.

"Look upon me, Watcher, as your kind are older than our species are, and your abilities to travel through space and time are greater than ours," it told me.

I then responded to the Adamian, saying, "I have been told I am an Ancient and a Watcher among man, but I am not sure what exactly this is as I find myself to be in human form back on Earth. I am beginning to understand my abilities to skin-jump and in so doing, able to live for a long time, but what good is this if I cannot remember who I am or what I am every time I have to jump into another human being?"

The Adamian answered, "Being your kind must have its challenges, and I am sure remembering what you are and the reason for living for so long is difficult, if not impossible, as linear time passes for man. But your ability to communicate in the next realm of existence is an amazing gift your kind possesses, and because of it, I am here to explain to you so much and help you understand the quest you are on and how you have had to fulfill it time and again."

All of a sudden, I was inside the pyramid, and the Adamian was inside with me.

"What I am about to tell you is nothing new to you. It has just been temporarily lost as it was in your past because you sometimes remember more and other times less in each new human body you take over. But it is now one of those lifetimes where human time is again important, and this lifetime of yours happens only once every three thousand six hundred eight human years. Over one hundred fifty thousand years ago in current human measurements of a year's time on Earth, the Adamians were not on Earth but lived on this planet; the planet now known to humans as Mars. This planet to the Adamians was known as Har. The Adamians had lived on Har for hundreds of thousands of years, and our people were far more advanced than humans currently are. One day, the great planet now known to humans as Jupiter ejected a large mass out of its center that hurdled toward the inner planets. The mass was not just gases but was also made up of hardened materials, such as those the Earth and Har are made of. That mass collided with what was a sister planet of Har known by the Adamians as Tiamment. The Adamians had also populated Tiamment for thousands of years, and when the two large masses collided, Tiamment exploded in a violent manner, and what was left of Tiamment then became the asteroid belt that separates the inner planets from the outer planets. But this was not the end of the tragic ordeal. The mass that was ejected from Jupiter was still mostly intact and had now changed course due to the impact and was headed into Har. The Adamians had less than forty days in current Earth time to figure out a plan to stop the destruction of Har. The counsel at the time that lead the Adamians decided that nuclear weapons would be used against the mass to either destroy it or change its course. Special nuclear weapons were quickly made, and the plan was set in motion. The nuclear weapons were launched at the ejected mass, and the impact detonations helped change the mass' course and kept it from colliding with Har. However, something just as terrible ended up occurring to Har as the scientists there had waited too long to launch the weapons and allowed the ejected mass to come too close. Even though a collision was diverted, the nuclear explosions and ther impact on the mass caused Har's atmosphere to be ripped away and the magnetic field around the planet to almost become nonexistent. With Tiamment now destroyed and Har quickly losing its atmosphere and protective shielding, the Adamians had to abandon their home world. From a population of nearly three hundred million Adamians, only six thousand were capable of boarding available spacecraft that could carry them to the next inhabitable planet. Those six thousand fled to what is today known as Earth. They were all that was left of a once amazing race, and I was among those six thousand. I was known as Ra."

The Adamian then paused for a few minutes as he seemed shaken and saddened as he told me the history of his people, the destruction of his home planet and the birth of civilization on Earth. The Adamian continued to tell me that the mass ended up being captured in the gravity of the sun and Earth, and it became known as the planet Venus. The Adamian said that our solar system is really in a vortex shape, and the planets and everything else in the solar system move in a vortex pattern around the sun as it hurdles through the galaxy. Because of this, Venus was still not in a fully captured orbit in the solar system, and the new planet would continue to wreak havoc among her sister planets.

Once Ra and his fellow Adamians arrived on Earth, they realized the gravity was different, as was the air. So, the first thing they had to do was terraform the planet. They also had to wipe out certain large species of dinosaurs that still roamed the lands and were a nuisance to the Adamians. It was at this point that Ra explained to me that much of what humans think they know about Earth is wrong and that human scientists are too proud to admit it. Ra explained that the amount of carbon was drastically changed in the entire solar system when Venus came into being and also when the Adamians terraformed the planet. Ra explained that the carbon dating used by Earth scientists is senseless on Earth as Venus continued to cause conflict with planet Earth.

"Now the Adamians were a mighty race of large-statured humanoids, with average heights of between twelve and fifteen feet. But even with being such mighty physical specimens, six thousand Adamians were not enough to get things done on the new planet alone. This was when we decided to create a slave race that would perform the manual labor that we were no longer capable of doing or wanting to perform ourselves. So the scientists among us took two of the species already on planet Earth, the Homo habilis and the Neanderthal, and mixed their genetic coding with genetic material of our own race, the Adamians. With some additional tweaking, our scientists created early man, and we then attempted to get this slave race to do our bidding. Sadly, this early man turned out to be extremely low on intelligence, and the Adamians found them almost impossible to control. So this first group of men was exterminated, and our scientists this time took only the genetic material of Neanderthals and Adamians and created man as they are today. This first man was called the Adama. The females were later created, and their ability to procreate was activated in their genetic code so that we would no longer need to create man in a lab but instead could breed them. The first females were known as Eveh. Modern man and woman lived among their creators, serving and worshipping us from the moment they took their first breath."

As Ra finished explaining about the Adamians and mankind, I had a question in my own thoughts as to whether this was where Adam and Eve came from in the book of Genesis.

Apparently, my thoughts were not just my own, because Ra answered, "Watcher, this indeed is what Genesis speaks of. Man at the beginning did not understand what their creators knew, so they wrote it down as best as they understood – and only after having originally passed down this knowledge and history by word of mouth for over a hundred thousand years. The Adama and Eveh species did become known in religion as Adam and Eve – the first of humanity and the father and mother of the human race."

Ra then continued explaining the history on Earth. "When we initially got to Earth and terraformed the atmosphere to our liking, we divided the lands among six groups of Adamian. There was more land on Earth and less ocean. Continents were not as far apart, and an entire continent in the Pacific Ocean area existed where it does not in your modern day. The six groups separated and grew out the Adamian population, and the human slave population with it. Our airships were beyond modern-day man's capability, and we could travel the distance of the Earth in a matter of minutes, not hours as the human race does today. We also were able to go into space as needed, and one immediate change that was necessary was the main satellite of the Earth had to be moved farther away from the planet. So, over several centuries, the moon was slowly pushed away so that the gravity change between the two celestial bodies was lessened."

I had again formulated another question in my thoughts, and Ra answered immediately.

"Yes, Watcher, the Adamian lifespan was in the thousands of current Earth years. Humans, too, lived to be a thousand years old. This was due to there being no genetic faults at the time in their DNA, something that later was added by the Adamians to control the human population that at times exploded too quickly, making it difficult to control. Also, Earth was at a closer distance to the solar star in our system, and the year cycle was only two hundred and sixty days, making life lived and counted in years much longer for the original Adama and Eveh. This, too, is seen in your book of Genesis and also in the few historical documents that survived the multiple catastrophes that were soon to plague the planet."

At this point, I asked a question aloud: "Were airships the only transportation that the Adamians had?"

"No, we had land vehicles and sea vessels and also could instantly travel through space-time portals that we did not create but have been in our known galaxy for millions of years. The portals work within aether gravity, and magnetic fields hold them together, allowing great distances to be traveled in a matter of moments. Three of these portals existed on planet Earth. We could instantly move from one to the other on this planet or could go to a multitude of planets so long they were properly set up and attached to the other side's portal."

As Ra spoke, I had this feeling that these portals were going to play a meaningful part in my future, and I sensed the crystal back on Earth would be a key to this.

"You are right in your thoughts, and in due time, this will make itself known to you, ancient one. Your race, the

Watchers, may have been the creators of this technology as your kind has existed for a much greater length of time than the Adamians," Ra said.

"Watcher, I sense your time with me is almost at an end. You are going to be pulled back to your realm of existence, and once again, back into your physical human form. Quickly, remember that the key to the past is in you and those like you. There are ways to recall this past, and you must learn to activate this ability. Also, remember that catastrophes have fallen upon Earth time and time again. Some are anomalous in nature and others happen at regular intervals. This is due to the location of the vortex that carries the planets and space around your solar star as it travels through its own path in the galaxy."

Ra paused as he sensed I was being pulled from this realm and time. He would quickly find me gone.

"Finally, Watcher, search for information in the oldest of places, and use that which you have already found."

As Ra finished, I began traveling at tremendous speeds in pure darkness. I was now waking up in the recovery area after the surgery I just went through.

"Mr. Kilian, Mr. Kilian – you need to wake up. Your surgery went very well, and you are in the recovery room. As soon as you are fully awake, the doctor will be in to see you," said a person I gathered was a nurse.

As I began opening my eyes, I noticed my lovely wife was sitting by my side. She was watching me as I struggled to open my eyes. When I was coherent enough, she told me that while I was attempting to come out of the drug-induced sleep, I was repeating certain numbers and continued to tell her to write them down, which she did. They were 16, 10,

18, 69, 32 and 28. Later, I would realize what these numbers were.

The doctor later came in and let my wife and I know that the surgery was a success. The abscess was removed and the fistula cut apart. I spent a couple of more days in the hospital before being released, and it then took several weeks at home to fully recover. During this time, I spent hours researching ancient cultures, such as the Maya. I also researched anomalous items found in the Earth that should not have existed and researched ancient structures whose creators were unknown. It was crazy just how many there were and how little we knew about the past. Here I was, with a wealth of knowledge as to how man came into existence, and I could tell no one. Even if I did tell someone, would they really believe me over scientists? My dreams and visions also were off the charts after the surgery. I was recalling two or three of my past lives on a daily basis. This meant I would find myself elsewhere all the time. My journal entries became voluminous, and I even began sketching things I saw in my dreams, such as locations, buildings and symbols. I learned during this time that I lived past lives that ranged from being a king to an engineer, from a thief to a soldier. I was rich and poor, wise and ignorant, sometimes living a long life and other times my life being cut short. But it was not until I had a dream where Heather communicated to me that pieces of the puzzle began to fall into place.

It was early August 2012, and I stayed home that day because I had this feeling that something important was going to take place, and in order for it to happen, I needed to be home. Sometime around noon, I became tired and decided to take a nap. As I slept, I was whisked away to some city that had to be on the East Coast of the U.S. I was walking along a naval shipyard and as I did, I saw a beautiful blonde-haired woman standing as if she were waiting for me, not more than a hundred yards ahead of me. As I approached, she began to smile, and I knew that this woman, who looked to be about forty, was Heather.

"It took you long enough to get here and I was starting to worry that you would not let me in."

"Into where?" I asked her.

"Into our world and our realm of existence, smart guy. If you haven't figured it out by now, we can communicate with one another and other Watchers in this unconscious realm and over any amount of distance, here on Earth or elsewhere. You just have to think it, believe it and execute the out-of-body energy transfer, as I have come to label it. For it to work, both parties have to be thinking about the other at the same time that each enters into this other plane of existence, and you finally timed it right with me."

I asked her why we were here together after all this time. As I did this, she reached out and held my hand, and I swear it felt as if it were really happening. I tingled with energy as if I had just grabbed a live electrical wire.

"You and I are always meant to be, sometimes as lovers, sometimes as friends, and other times, we may miss each other completely. But Patrick, this is one of those lifetimes where you have to become fully aware, and that is what all the help is for, not just from me, but from everyone or everything else that has been reaching out to you. The great reckoning is here. A time of catastrophe is upon us, and I don't have all the answers. I was not chosen to be the Watcher who saves humanity time and again."

She said that if we came together at this moment, she could transfer her knowledge, and it would hopefully jumpstart everything else in my life force. I asked her how we were supposed to come together for this to take place.

"Take my hands, pull me close to you and kiss me. It is that simple."

She then reached out to me, and I pulled her body toward mine until we came together as one. As I did, our gazes at each other never faltered, and I began to see the past while staring into her eyes. Then I leaned into her, and we began to kiss. As this happened, I closed my eyes, and I suddenly saw through Heather's eyes, or through the vantage point of so many other lives Heather had lived. In a matter of seconds, I had experienced hundreds of lifetimes and her knowledge and my forgotten knowledge combined. The flood gates opened, and my past memories came pouring out.

I woke up from whatever it was that just took place. I now remembered who and what I was and that I have lived in a different realm of existence that I cannot explain for hundreds of thousands of years prior to my history on Earth. I have walked through different dimensions and been to galaxies near and far. My race, the Paa Talen, even watched over the Adamians in their infant stages of evolution. Around fourteen thousand five hundred years ago, I was tasked by the Paa Talen leaders to be born among the humans of a small planet known as Earth. It had been suffering great catastrophes, one after the other, and the human race was about to go extinct if help was not offered. So I was tasked with becoming a Watcher, a group of Paa Talen that looked after other species in many galaxies and were able to continue doing so by transferring their life force from one body to the next when death overcomes them.

So I was born among men right before a time of great upheaval in the Earth's history. I was given special abilities as a Watcher, many of which unfolded on different realms of existence. This still required my remembering who I was and what my calling was. This was something that was not always easy as a Watcher skin-jumps, and after a long period of doing so, has a high rate of degradation in memory of the past. I was born the first time to good parents and was originally named Adama, after the gods of old. As I grew up for the first time as human, I had total recall of what I was at a very early age. By age twelve, I knew I was on Earth to help man survive what was soon to come and what had claimed the lives of most of the Adamians by that time.

History repeats itself, and that was due to happen in the year 12,396 BCE. Even when I was originally born, a lot of the past history of mankind and the Adamians had already been lost due to catastrophes that plagued Earth. When the Adamians first came to Earth, there were no issues with the new planet of Venus. The Adamians lived as gods among humans for over one hundred thousand years with only minor localized catastrophes taking place. During this time, the Adamians created huge empires such as Atl-Antis and Kadesh. The Adamian sciences and culture flourished, and with it, came amazing inventions and technology, such as the pyramids that provided clean energy by harnessing the energy deep in the Earth, converting it to usable energy and transferring it effortlessly by way of obelisk transmitters. The energy was then stored for later use at collection sites that were partially above and below the Earth's surface.

What information survived until my time taught us back then that the Adamians continued to have bases high above the Earth and on the moon. These sites were used by the gods for reasons lost to humanity. Then I was taught that something terrible took place around thirty-six thousand years ago. Somehow, the infant planet Venus became active again and left the orbit it had been in for almost one hundred thousand years. Something pushed Venus closer to Earth, and when this happened, humans saw the great fire dragon in the sky rain fire upon the Earth and strike the Earth with massive electrical charges. In a single day and night, most of the surface of Earth was scorched. This was followed by electrical charges that damaged or destroyed almost everything in its path. The world was said to have flipped over, and the ground fell away from where there was land, and water took its place. The heat from the fires brought darkness to the sky for almost one hundred years. The greatest land of the gods, Atl-Antis, was destroyed in a matter of hours.

Parts of the land and city fell deep below the waters of the new sea, and other parts shot up to the highest points of the land on new mountains that were created in a matter of hours. Great deluges washed away the Adamians, humans and most other species of Mother Earth. A few of the Adamians were able to seek refuge deep within the planet in cave systems that went on for miles, and some were deeper than a mile underground. Some privileged, select humans also were allowed to survive among their gods deep in the bowels of Earth. When all the turmoil and destruction subsided and Venus moved farther from her sister planet Earth, the face of the lands were not the same. More water was among the planet as large pieces of ice and snow had melted. The Adamians and humans alike lived for almost one hundred years underground until it was again safe to come up. During this time, huge cities were created underground as populations grew. Some of the underground cities in the current region of Turkey and Armenia got to a point where they housed over two hundred thousand souls.

It was a sad time as so few Adamians survived, and most of those who did were not the scientists and engineers or doctors of the Adamians. Never again would the vastly superior technology of the gods be known and used to create amazing inventions and technology. The few

Adamians who survived were more like the fallen of the species, the ones who knew the least about Adamian science and culture. And after this point, those Adamians could create only basic technological devices from the limited knowledge they possessed. Still, these few who survived were looked upon as the elite of the gods, the ones who survived. Some of these Adamians are still remembered today, and many people would be amazed to find out that they were called Thor, Quetzalcoatl, Shiva, Yahweh, Zeus, Lei-Kung and so forth. These few Adamians still outlived humans by hundreds of years, and they still possessed some of their old technology that was spared in the great catastrophe yet could not be reproduced. They continued to use their lightning and thunder weapons. Humans continued to worship them and do as their gods told them. This went on for thousands of years until once again, Venus left its orbit and wreaked havoc among man and gods.

As had happened before, the world was cast into fire, and again, this was followed by massive electrical storms that killed all form of beasts, Adamians and humans. The sky once again was darkened by the rising smoke, and the ground shook and fell apart in some places. In other areas, the ground shot up and created mountains in a matter of minutes. The only thing that was lacking this time around was the deluge as the water upon the land was still in a free-flowing form and not kept captive in the clutches of ice. Once again man and the Adamians went deep into the depths of hell to seek refuge inside Mother Earth, and this time, had to live underground for over two hundred years.

From the even fewer records that survived this time around, humans in my original time period learned that a pattern seemed to be forming when the catastrophes were taking place. It seemed to those who paid attention that things went wrong, and they did so quickly – about every four thousand years. With this knowledge, those humans who survived and no longer had gods among them used what little knowledge of the gods they knew to watch the stars and track the war that was waging between the planets in our solar system. Some Adamians did survive, but there were so few that they began to take the daughters of man as their wives. As the two species mixed and interbred, hybrids were created who were half god and half man. They were smaller than their fathers and mothers and lacked the wisdom and knowledge of their forefathers.

Time continued on, and Venus continued to punish Mother Earth about every four thousand years. Eventually, several other things happened over time. First, most of the Adamian knowledge and technology was lost. There were very few books and crystals that had survived that contained this ancient wisdom. Those that did survive were being kept and protected as best as possible by the humans who saw enough into the future to determine how important this history was. Second, the gods were gone. On occasion, a giant among man would appear, but he or she was a lost remnant of the past and now more of an anomaly no one remembered as far as how or from where it originated.

Ruins also now existed throughout the planet that were being worshipped or altered by man. How they got there and who built them was almost unknown by this time. Many other animals were gone, never to return. They, too, were wiped out by the catastrophes. And their creators, the Adamians, who had genetically created them, were no longer around to replenish those creatures. Also, the Earth was pushed farther from the sun, and days became longer. Some places grew colder and others hotter. Lush green lands were swallowed up by the powerful sands of the desert that began to blow almost everywhere. Water again began to recede, and great sheets of ice formed farther north and deeper south.

Around this time, man began to rule over man. Those few who had some remaining bloodline connected to the Adamians became the ruling class, and they forced those around them to worship them like the gods of old. The population of humans exploded since there were no gods to keep the slave race in check. There was also a greater diversity of humans and cultures and languages. The privileged and upper class now controlled the little knowledge that remained of the creators. Secret sects formed from this, and the power that came from this knowledge created a distribution of dominance that was unbalanced among the masses. Mega structures were again being built, but they were only poor copies of those of the past, and they were being created only to show the power and tenacity of the ruling class.

As man looked to be reaching a pinnacle, Venus came back and destroyed all that man created, and the world was once again flipped upside down as had happened during the first great catastrophe. This time, those who could seek refuge below ground did so, and it would be another three hundred years or so before their posterity was able to come back out of the pits of hell and live upon the land and see the sky, the sun and the stars again. And this time, much of the stars and sky were different than before.

My time upon Earth was fast approaching. My species saw that mankind was stuck in an endless cycle of devastation and that man could not quite prepare for what had now become a common occurrence in the solar system that Earth and Venus shared. Humans on Earth were not advanced enough to understand the cosmic catastrophes taking place, and most reverted to believing it was angry gods who wreaked havoc among man as they were sinners and deserved to be punished. Some stability had to be secured on the planet, and if these catastrophes were going to be common, then someone was going to have to watch over humanity. With this, the Paa Talen sent the Watchers.

I was one of the last Watchers to be born into a human host body, and as I had said before, I came to be among man around 12,450 BCE. I prepared man for the great catastrophe in 12,396 BCE. I was able to get a large group of people to safety underground and to do this in more than just the one location where I lived. I did this three more times, and it was always three thousand six hundred and eight years from the last catastrophe. During this time, I came to finally realize that our solar system was in a specific part of the galaxy at these same intervals and also that the planets travel around our sun in a vortex pattern. Something in the galaxy comes into contact with our solar system at this same interval every three thousand six hundred and eight years and has a tremendous ability to disrupt the planets and their orbit, especially the newest inner planet, Venus.

Venus then is pushed or pulled dangerously close to Earth, and its inhabitants subsequently suffer. Other anomalous events have damaged Earth and its inhabitants, as well. I remember that somehow, the moon was ripped farther from Earth approximately five thousand years ago, and a lot of devastation took place because of it, but nothing like when Venus is disturbed and battles with her sister planets. With this being said, this means that time is fast approaching for the day of reckoning. In a way, the Bible is correct, and those who wrote Revelations knew what I knew and prophesized the beginning of the end. That end – that time of pain and suffering – will be in the final days of October in 2036. I will be sixty-four years old. This will give me twenty-four years to prepare mankind for the end and hopefully allow for some of us to again survive deep within the bowels of the planet. Of interest with this timing is that people said the world would end according to the Maya on Dec. 21, 2012. They were right, and they were wrong. The Maya did know about the end of days as they, too, had been wiped out over and over again by Venus as it battled its sister planet. They correctly wrote it down and made it known to man in the future. The only problem was with the scientists of today. These scientists did a poor job of converting the Mayan time and past Mayan dates to current time. And with the changes from Julian calendar to the Gregorian one, they failed to correctly line up the dates prior to these two forms of date keeping. So, the Maya never said anything about Dec. 21, 2012. The actual date for the end of the world that was predicted by the Mayan elite and with what I know from having lived through this catastrophe four times will be Oct. 22, 2036.

# 17.

# A Beginning to an End

I later told my wife about what I saw and remembered. She began to cry. I tried to comfort her, but she was too upset.

"Patrick, are you sure the things you saw are for real? Are you absolutely positive about your past and the end of the world in the very near future?"

"I know that it is hard to believe and even stomach the things I spew out of my mouth on occasion. But I know for certain that what I have seen and lived is the truth and that what I am and how long I have lived is for real. We have to begin preparing for the end to come, and not just for us but for all our immediate family. In past catastrophes, it took years to prepare to live underground as people had to stay there for a long time so the damage on the surface could subside. Remember also that some of the catastrophes were worse than others, and this looks like it will be one of those worse times."

My wife then asked, "Why do you think that?"

"Because look at how much ice is locked up in the north and south of the planet. All that ice is going to instantly melt, and there will again be a massive deluge like that of Noah. Also, the world has not been turned upside down in some time. There may very well be a magnetic pole shift, and while this happens, there is no protective magnetic field around the planet. The Earth will be bombarded with massive amounts of radiation, and this means we will have to get everyone that much deeper underground."

I told her of all the issues I felt were going to manifest this time around. I explained to her that I believed that some other star or massive planet was quickly approaching our solar system. I felt that the star or planet was in the perfect location to cause major havoc on our planets because of the weird vortex trajectory the planets travel around the sun as our sun yanks them with her through space.

My wife, being the perceptive individual that she was, asked, "How did Noah and his family just survive in an ark when others supposedly had to live underground for such a long time?"

I told her that the Noah's Ark story was not real and that the deluge story had been told many times before the real Noah was born. I explained that the real person was called Ziudsura, and that the deluge Ziudsura lived through was regional, due only to a massive tsunami around 6,000 BCE. I explained that the tsunami was caused by a portion of the moon that was ripped from the moon's surface by something unknown. When this happened, everyone on Earth was able to see this as a massive explosion on the moon's surface. Hours later, a massive streak of fire was seen entering into the skies. Seconds after that, there was a deafening explosion almost immediately, followed by a wall of water that destroyed most of the area that would later become Sumer. I went on to tell the story of how Ziudsura and his family finally reached dry land at the top of what were before even taller mountains in the Caucasus mountain range and that I would later skin-jump into a teenager named Akron who lived in the city of Portasar, which was founded by Ziudsura.

"And just in case you are really curious, my love, the ark of Ziudsura was more like a submarine, capable of surviving below and above the massive flood waters that overtook that fertile valley area that was so heavily populated by humans at that period in history."

For the next week or so, my wife and I did a lot of researching on the internet. The research included locations in Arizona and New Mexico where there were deep cave systems. We researched properties that were around these known cave systems. We also researched supplies, food, seeds and things of this nature that twenty-first century humans would need to survive underground for extended periods of time. The two of us worked out lists of people we would invite to remain with us. We laughed about how we would approach people, telling them the end of the world was going to take place. I told her that in the past, it was easier to explain this as most people were very religious. Because of this, people back then accepted my words as prophecy and accepted the possibility that the world could end because one god was angry with man. But in today's world, everyone is a skeptic, and most people will probably think I am a lunatic and that my wife is also a lunatic for believing me. But that is why we start with immediate family and then work our way out from there.

For the last remaining months of the year 2012, my wife and I went about our usual routine that included going to work, coming home and making dinner. After dinner, we prepared for Armageddon, which would be the battle between Venus and Earth. There was so much that needed to get done and with only two people doing the work part-time, it was going to take years for us to accomplish our goals.

One night I stayed up extremely late as my wife had gone to bed hours earlier. I had been up trying to locate known caves or tunnel systems in Arizona or New Mexico that had water running through them or water pooled below ground to form natural watering holes. I ended up locating more than I had thought existed, and this was very reassuring. While I did this research downstairs on the couch, I must have fallen asleep. I entered into another level of existence that falls between our physical and natural world and that of a spiritual realm. It is here where all beings can instantly communicate with one another if they happened to be tuned in to the right frequency. I must have been vibrating at the correct level that night as I again found myself back on Mars and was able to communicate with those other life forces that existed in that time and location so very long ago.

"You were given the coordinates before to this location on Mars. The ancient pyramid is still at that spot, 27.510948 N, 117.475122 E," explained one of the prior inhabitants, who now existed as some form of energy and no longer required a physical form.

It continued to communicate with me: "The same coordinates on Earth will put you in your modern-day China, close to the Longhu Lake. Inside those rugged mountains is a sister pyramid to the one on Mars. Travel between the two is possible. You just have to know how to activate the gate and portal system. There are others like it on Earth and endless doors and portals throughout the galaxy."

Without warning, I was no longer in this alternate state of existence but instead back on Earth.

"Patrick, Patrick – are you coming to bed?" my wife asked.

She had come downstairs and shaken me to get me to come to bed. I was a bit pissed off and told her what she just did, and right at a time when I was getting much-needed answers.

"Excuse me for trying to help you out. I just thought you would want to sleep in your bed instead of the couch," she stated.

I refrained from saying anything else as I knew she did not like to sleep alone as she easily gets scared.

I followed her upstairs, still a bit upset but trying to not make a bigger deal about it as the damage was done and I could no longer go back to this dream state. I got into bed and began to think about the information that was given to me. This unknown soul or sprit gave me coordinates to a pyramid on Mars. I had been given the same coordinates years ago when I was on the vision quest induced by mushrooms with Samantha and Virginia. But now I come to find out that there is a sister pyramid in China no one knows about and continues to elude discovery. Somehow, the two pyramids are connected, and a portal exists that can transport you between the two locations on two different planets within our solar system. "Oh my god – that is crazy amazing!" I thought. Then I slowly fell asleep for the night.

The following morning I jumped out of bed and yelled to my wife, who was still sound asleep, "Babe, I know what those numbers are that I told you to write down while I was coming out of the effects of the general anesthesia from my surgery a few months ago!"

My wife jumped out of bed.

"What the hell are you yelling about, and why are you yelling at me while I am asleep? You scared the crap out of me!" she said.

"No, darling, listen to me. Remember last night when I got pissed at you because you brought me back from some type of dream state I was in, where I was communicating with something who used to live on Mars? That person or remnant of someone gave me the same numbers as an old man did years ago in a vision quest I had. He actually wrote these numbers and two letters into the Martian soil. Well, last night I was told what those numbers were, and they ended up being the coordinates to the location of the pyramid that is still on Mars and apparently intact. Even crazier is that there is a sister pyramid at the same coordinates on Earth, located in China and underground. But I just had a meaningful thought: what if those numbers I had you write down are coordinates, as well? What if I have to only keep them in the order in which I had you write them down but then add some type of directional heading, such as N, E, S or W? It has to be that, and I am going to go online and try to figure it out."

I quickly went downstairs as the laptop was still on the living room table in front of the couch. While I did that, my wife went back to bed, most likely thinking I was insane and wondering why in the hell she said "I do" to me when the preacher in Las Vegas asked her if she would take me in marriage.

While the laptop was booting up, I ran back upstairs to get the napkin where my wife wrote the numbers. Then I headed back downstairs, all the time looking at what she had written: 16, 10, 18, 69, 32 and 28. I then placed the numbers in a common form for coordinates found on grid references. I put 16, 10 and 18 together and 69, 32 and 28. I knew the first numbers had to be the degree. I then started randomly adding N, S, E and W behind the first three numbers and then the second set of three numbers. First I tried N, then E, but this yielded nothing that struck me as important. I continued trying combinations of N and W, S and E, but it was when I typed in 16 degrees 10 18 S, 69 degrees 32 28 W that I almost fell over because of what that combination showed in my Web search. I was now getting matches for a Peruvian Stargate, Hayu Marca, portal to the gods, doorway to the gods and other findings. Not only had I just found out about portals and doorways between pyramids on Mars and Earth, but it looked like I identified another portal that had enough importance for me to have been given its coordinates while I was among the Adamians. I started through the data for this solid rock wall in Peru that was carved to look like a door, twenty-three feet high, with an additional door in the middle that stood just over six feet. It looked like one size was for giants or gods and the smaller-sized door for humans.

In addition, I started having visions of how these great portals worked. I also had these crazy memories in my head of watching as some of them were created, but not while I was on Earth and not fourteen thousand or fifteen thousand years ago, but instead hundreds of thousands of years ago while I was still in Paa Talen form. The Paa Talen were indeed one of the species in this galaxy that created these portals that could almost instantly transport someone over great distances. But for some reason, this doorway did not look like those created by the Paa Talen. Instead, they reminded me of a species in this galaxy I somehow recalled and had advanced knowledge of. There were a group of beings called the Nephilidims who had elongated skulls and were highly intelligent. They created portal doors that could accommodate large and small species, and they always made the entry out of the strongest rock available, even if that meant bringing the rocks a great distance. If I am correct, this would mean that the Nephilidims were on Earth even before the Adamians came to the planet some one hundred and fifty thousand years ago. This would coincide with all the elongated skulls that have been found in South America and at depths of archaeological digs that would have put the skull finds in the three hundred thousand years-plus range. It would also figure into the occasional sighting of a Nephilidim who survived, where the rest of the species did not. As a matter of fact, there are stories told and even documentation of a ruling class in Egypt that fits the description of the Nephilidim. Since I did not live among the Egyptians during this period, I do not have firsthand knowledge of this and can go by only what was written of these rulers. The height of the portal also made me wonder if the Adamians used it as the larger of the two doors would have easily accommodated their greater height as compared with the Nephilidims and humans, and if so, where did this portal lead to?

As I began to pour over the many photos of the Hayu Marca mountain region Stargate in southern Peru, I noticed several other things. First of all, I never went to this location when I was in Peru but remember being there and having lived near Lake Titicaca, which meant I lived there in a previous life. This was after one of the great catastrophes that so heavily damaged the massive historic structures in the area. I also noticed that the area was in a location that was bombarded with thunderstorms and experienced some strange electrical and lightning storms on a regular basis. The last thing I noticed was the small circular indention in the middle of the smaller doorway. It seemed to be a spot where a disc or disc-shaped object would be inserted to activate the doorway to the gods. But I had no clue as to what needed to be inserted. Again, I was just guessing that this hole in the small door served some purpose, and more than likely, that of a keyhole of sorts. So with all this information and questions filling my thoughts, I filled it with one more and again wondered why it was so important in the first place that I pulled the coordinates for this doorway out of whatever realm of existence I was in during my surgery?

A couple of more weeks went by and the year 2012 was drawing to a close. The public was in a tizzy about the Mayan calendar and the prediction of the end of the world on Dec. 21. This date was right around the corner, and my wife and I paid no attention to it as we were now fully aware that the end was on Oct. 22, 2036, and even the Maya knew this. I had been calling around and getting final quotes on land just outside of Tucson and outside of Carlsbad, New Mexico. Both sites had underground cave systems that ran deep. Land around both places was at a reasonable price, and water constantly flowed underground. So it was on a Sunday night at the end of November when my wife and I decided we would purchase the land at both locations and begin working on plans to create underground facilities at each spot. I remember that I went to bed that night feeling pretty good that things were beginning to fall into place and that having twenty-four years to prepare was a record for me compared to prior preparations for catastrophes. I immediately fell asleep, which was rare for me as I always seemed to be thinking about the responsibility that was placed before me and the hurdles I had to overcome this time around, just because of how advanced civilization had become in the last three thousand six hundred and eight years.

While I slept, I began having a dream where I now was on the outskirts of Roswell, New Mexico. My dream started at the side of a road, and the sign said, "Welcome to Roswell, Dairy Capital of the Southwest." As a Watcher, the dream state seemed to be just another form of communication between myself and many other types of sprits and beings, some from the past and others from the present. This dream, however, began to feel like none I had in the past. I had been walking just outside of Roswell in the dirt and brush for a lengthy period when someone or something began to speak from behind me.

"Watcher, Watcher, turn and look upon me," the voice said.

I turned around, and there before me was an extraterrestrial being who looked very similar to humans. Its height was also similar. I recognized my own kind; before me stood the Paa-Talen council leader, Xi Nox Zule.

"I come to you, Patrick, as this planet and its inhabitants are on the brink of a great devastation like none that has been experienced by any human or human-like species. The last time anything like this has happened to Earth was well over one hundred million years ago," Xi Nox Zule explained.

"Council leader, what makes this time different than the others the humans and I lived through?"

"Things have changed, Watcher, and there are other celestial bodies at play in the dark regions of space around this planet and its sister planet Venus. The council has seen the possible future of this planet, and the council has run simulation tests. The tests continue to show that most inhabitants of Earth are going to be wiped out. There is also going to be massive damage to the sky, the atmosphere and the Earth's magnetic field. It is such great damage that no gauss units can be measured in the magnetic field, and the Earth becomes vulnerable to absolutely everything that comes its way for thousands upon thousands of years."

"But Xi Nox Zule, if the atmosphere of Earth is destroyed and there is no magnetic field to protect the planet, will even attempting to live underground be a futile effort by those who survive the initial assault by the planet Venus?"

"This is a valid question, and we, too, are under the impression that survival below ground this time around will be impossible."

I then asked Xi Nox Zule another question: "My Lord, what is different this time that causes even greater destruction than what has been experienced in the past?"

Sullenly, Xi Nox Zule explained, "There are two new satellites that orbit this planet, and they have yet to be discovered by the human scientists. In the very near future, they will discover one, but the second will elude them until that dark year, 2036, when it is too late. The first is an asteroid that will be located soon, and many on this planet will joke that it will be the Earth's second moon. This rock's size in understandable human measurements is 120 feet across by 300 feet wide. The second asteroid is of even greater size, 330 feet across by 520 feet wide. The first orbits Earth in differing distances, with the closest being nine million miles. The second asteroid is at a distance of fifteen million to twenty million miles away. This time, when Venus is disturbed by the hidden anomaly in dark space, its change in distance to the Earth will cause the two asteroids to follow it. After Venus and Earth battle as they have done so many times in the past, Venus will again move away from Earth, but this time will thrust both asteroids directly into this planet, and both will strike solid ground, causing destruction never before seen by the eyes of man. We on the council are saddened to say that nothing can be done, and even if mankind's scientists knew of these asteroids and what was to happen twenty-four years from now, there is nothing they could do to stop it as their technology is still in its infancy. I am sorry, Watcher, to be the one to tell you of this tragic news. But there is something else that the council wants to place before you and something else that can be done to keep some of Earth's humans alive."

This had me guessing. The only alternative I could think of was for man to head elsewhere into the cosmos. Sure enough, this is what the Paa Talen council was going to suggest.

"Watcher, the only other way to save the human race from this global extinction event is to leave this planet and move humanity elsewhere. Earth will not be able to sustain most of the species now living within her for a very long time after this catastrophe takes place. The Adamians saved their species and later created humans on this planet by escaping a similar event on their home planet. Now, it is the time for humans to do the same, and you must be the one to lead them," explained Xi Nox Zule.

"But my Lord, man does not have the starship capability to transport humans to another planet, yet alone another solar system."

But no sooner had I said this that I understood the significance of the pyramid on Mars and in China and the Peruvian Stargate, the timing of my learning about both and the capability of each.

"Yes, Watcher, I can see that you have figured it out already. You can move the humans through one of the two portals you know about. The choice as to which one you use will be entirely up to you. However, you must remember that if you decide to transport the humans through the underground pyramid portal in China, you will all end up on Mars, a planet that has been abandoned for over one hundred and fifty thousand years. The pyramid itself on Mars is a power supply structure and can generate enormous amounts of power for a small amount of humans. The pyramid can also help terraform Mars back to a livable and breathable place for humans as it can also generate the necessary chemical reactions to put oxygen back into the air and to form atmosphere once again. The crystal you have in your possession is not just a crystal that carries enormous amounts of lost knowledge, but it also has a place in the pyramid that when placed correctly, will bring the generators and computer systems back to life and awaken the dormant technology of Mars. There are also vast amounts of water under the surface of Mars."

Just listening to this suggestion by the Paa Talen caused me high anxiety, and I could sense the panic building inside me just like the days of old when I had been trapped underground after a great catastrophe without being able to see the sky, the sun or the stars for lengthy periods of time. It also caused me to realize that I most likely suffered high anxiety levels during this lifetime as Patrick because certain situations made me feel like I was again trapped underground. It is crazy how certain things come gushing to the surface, causing a person to have so much understanding of who they are and how they came to be the way they are. I had no other choice, and I was going to have to figure things out – not just for me, but for the human race.

Xi Nox Zule then continued on with options for saving a small portion of the human population of Earth.

"The other option is the Peruvian gateway in the Hayu Marca mountain region. This gate is a much more stable portal and can allow greater numbers of humans to cross through it to the other side. The biggest concern for the Paa Talen council on your using this gate is the fact that we do not know where it leads as the Adamians were the last to use it and the dial connect system that is used to attach one doorway to another no longer exists. This means that the only option the gateway has is to connect to its last known location. What I can tell you is that the Adamians needed the same levels of breathable oxygen as humans. As a matter of fact, since the humans were made in the image of their creators, everything that a human needs to survive would have been the same for the Adamians, so the other side is most likely a planet that can sustain human life – or at least was able to do so the last time the gateway was used."

I asked another question that I had wanted to ask for some time: "Xi Nox Zule, even if I were to choose one of the portals over the other, how do I activate the doorway?"

Xi Nox Zule then grinned.

"This indeed is the greatest issue of all at hand. Both of the gateways require a portal key. The keys can be used on either gate, but a portal key is needed, and we know of none to provide you with as the Paa Talen did not make either of these gateways. Accordingly, this technology, including its keys, has been lost to us for a long period of time. What I can say is that one or two keys have to be on Earth or at least were on this planet at some period in the past."

Now I knew the Paa Talen had to be able to assist more or they would have never started me down this path to begin with.

"My Lord, there has to be more that you know to assist me with finding these keys to open the portals."

Xi Nox Zule answered, "I will indeed help you more, and this is the reason why we stand where we do now, in the middle of what you perceive to be a place on Earth known as Roswell. See, Watcher, the Paa Talen keep a watchful eye out on what takes place on Earth. Back in your Earth year 1947, an alien species came to Earth and procured one of the portal keys. They did this because it would allow for them to quickly travel the galaxy with no need for starships. They had found one of the keys left on this planet and were about to head home when they had some sort of ship failure and crashed in this desert area known as Roswell. The key was lost here, and to our knowledge, was not taken into custody by Earth's authorities after they took possession of the wreckage and the aliens and covered up the crash. That key remained."

This was finally a piece of somewhat good news, and at this point, I figured I would take anything.

I had continued to ask Xi Nox Zule questions. One of my most important ones was that I needed to know what I was looking for. What did a stargate key look like, and once you had one, how did you use it to activate the gateway?

The Paa Talen explained, "At the Peruvian portal in approximately the center of the small doorway is an indention into the hardened rock. This indention is somewhat circular but still with what looks to be three partial edges. This is where the key must be placed to activate the portal. At the same time, musical tones must be played toward the gate at four hundred and thirty-two hertz to activate the proper vibration frequency of the portal and to unify the aether that occupies the dark matter space. This frequency will also assist the key in forming the correct hold onto the portal doorway as the key has very unique magnetic properties known only to a few species within the galaxy. At this point, with four hundred and thirty-two Hz frequency vibrating the rock doorway, the key will begin to twist and spin. This motion will increase until it matches the motion and speed at which the planets are traveling around the sun. Suddenly, the hard matter of the rock will disappear. The speed of the key will rip open dark space and produce a portal from this gateway to another where you and the humans can then pass. Once you are all to the other side, someone who has stayed behind on Earth must turn off the musical tones and stop the matter from vibrating so it can return to a solid and close the portal. Otherwise, an open portal can cause great destruction to the entire solar system."

This further complicated matters as it meant I now had to worry about destroying the entire solar system, and it also meant that someone would have to stay behind and sacrifice themselves for the rest to survive. Xi Nox Zule also explained that the portal in the China pyramid would look identical to what the Peruvian Stargate looked like – at least for the large door and the smaller door within the domain of the large door.

As I continued to ponder over everything, Xi Nox Zule then described the key to the stargate.

"Now the key itself will look like a small rock that easily fits into the palm of a human's hand. There will be two sets of an Earth and crescent moon within circles and direct opposites from each other, taking into consideration what humans know as the "golden ratio" of your geometry. The opposites represent the fact that as one walks through a portal, he is twisted and bent through space time and exits through the other side as if he had passed through a mirror image of three-dimensional space. The key will also have unusual magnetic properties that can instantly be picked up by having a human compass nearby to make sure the key is not a faked copy. Remember that the true key will have no holes and no access to the inside, so that you will know it was not faked."

I drifted off a bit thinking how finding something like this was next to impossible, and yet it looked to be the only way to save humanity. The Paa Talen was still speaking when I tuned back.

"Remember, that if you do find the key and do activate one of the portals, it can be done multiple times, just so long you close the portal each time. This will allow for you to devise a plan as to how you will transfer humans from one location to another. Just remember that what is on the other side truly is a mystery for the Peruvian gateway. We are truly sorry, Watcher, that there is no more we can do for you as interfering directly is forbidden. This is the reason why we have left these things to the Watchers. May you go and find the strength to be successful."

With that, the Paa Talen was gone, and I was again left wandering around the desert of New Mexico.

Soon after, my dream ended, and I was again in bed wondering what the hell I was going to do next. I kept a pad and a pen by my bed because of all the crap that happens while I am asleep, and this was no different. I began writing down a lot of what just happened this way I would not forget, especially with the minimal description I was given on what a gateway key looked like and what properties it had. I also had to write down everything about aether space and vibrations at four hundred and thirty-two Hz, as I was definitely going to have to do a lot of research on this. This preparation for the catastrophe that was soon to come was going to be a full-time ordeal, yet at the same time, I knew I must continue to work to survive for twenty-plus years and have the monetary means to prepare properly.

I continuously thought about the two gates and the decision that would have to be made on which gate to choose. I thought about who I would select to go through the gate with me. Even after I selected them, would they be willing to travel to Peru or China to go through the gate just based on what I was going to tell them? Also, how was I going to get all these people into communist China without red flags being raised and the Chinese government becoming suspicious? I began to feel overwhelmed. I almost wanted to just forget about the entire gate thing, take my chances on surviving underground like I had in the past and ignoring what the Paa Talen had told me. Could they have gotten all this wrong? Could they just be causing me high anxiety for no reason? I thought that going underground like how it had been done in the past really might be best. "No, I can't do that," I thought. What I needed to do was take one piece of the puzzle at a time and work through that. Then I would take the next piece and the next piece and solve each piece of the survival puzzle separately. This way I would not be overwhelmed and there may then be a good chance that I could save a bit of the human race. So I set this plan into motion.

Before I knew it, the date was Dec. 20, 2012, a day before the world was supposed to end according to a lot of people on the news and on the Internet. I wished I could tell them the truth and maybe even request their assistance in preparing for the real date, but I could not as too much could go wrong if others knew about my plans. The crystal I had in my possession was too important to allow for it to get into the wrong hands. I also could not chance others knowing the correct way of working the portals as this could lead to governments shutting me out of being able to continue with my calling as a Watcher. Everything had to proceed in a covert manner and technically, nothing was going to happen if I could not locate a portal key. I really would have to continue with plan B and prepare to take a group of humans underground if I could not get the portals to work.

"Oh shit," I said out loud. "I'd better work on finding this portal key if it truly exists,"

So I busted out the laptop and began to do a Web search on portal keys, Peru, China and Roswell. To my utter amazement, the search returned multiple hits on something I did not expect to find.

There on my computer monitor were multiple photos of a rock found by a man who was hunting outside of Roswell in 2004. I started going through the pictures and began reading the articles on his findings and sure enough, I was staring at a rock that had two Earth-like circles and two crescent moons in circles, and they were mirror opposites of each other. The articles also stated that the rock had unusual magnetic properties and that this had been independently verified. Could this truly be? Could I have just located the individual who holds the key to saving humanity in Roswell? I had to fly there immediately! I had to speak to this man. I had to figure out a way to get the portal key.

I yelled to my wife, "Cassy, I found it, I found the key. I have to get to Roswell as quickly as possible. No, wait, maybe I should think about this for a moment. I need to figure out what I am going to do if this guy will not give me the key."

I began preparations for the next phase of Patrick Kilian's life. I needed to truly embrace who I was, who I had been and who I must become. I am a Watcher over man, a being discussed in the Christian Bible and a soul who has walked this planet for thousands of years. I must summon the light and the darkness inside of me and between today and Oct. 22, 2036, I must do whatever is necessary to carry out my plans so humanity can survive, no matter where that may be in the cosmos. I must get started on acquiring the portal key at whatever cost.

To be continued…

Made in the USA
Middletown, DE
01 September 2019